I0562950

RELENTLESS HAWKE

A SECOND GENERATION HAWKE FAMILY
NOVEL

BILLIONAIRES OF NEW ORLEANS: THE HAWKE
FAMILY SECOND GENERATION
BOOK 3

GWYN MCNAMEE

RELENTLESS HAWKE

© 2023 Gwyn McNamee

All rights reserved. Except as permitted by U.S. Copyright Act of 1976, no part of this publication may be reproduced, distributed, or transmitted in any form or by any means, or stored in a database or retrieval system, without prior permission of the author.

The scanning, uploading, and distribution of this book via the Internet or via other means without the permission of the publisher is illegal and punishable by law. Please purchase only authorized electronic editions and do not participate in or encourage electronic piracy of copyrighted materials.

This book is a work of fiction. Names, characters, establishments, or organizations, and incidents are either products of the author's imagination or are used fictitiously to give a sense of authenticity. Any resemblance to actual persons, living or dead, events, or locales is entirely coincidental.

Cover Model: Diego

Photographer: Wander Aguiar Photography

Cover Design: Michelle Johnson at Bluesky Design

Editing: Stephie Walls at Wallflower Edits

To anyone who has ever danced that thin line between love and hate...

THE HAWKE FAMILY

Antonia and Sam "The Savage" Hawke

SAVAGE COLLISION

Savage Hawke & Danika Eriksson

|

Kennedy Hawke

STONE SOBER

Stone Hawke & Nora Eriksson

/ \

Isaac Hawke   Coen Hawke

TAINTED SAINT

Solomon "Saint" Clarke & Caroline Brooks

/ \

Pope Clarke   Bishop Clarke

TORTURED SKYE

Skye Hawke & Gabe Anderson

/ \

Atlas Anderson   Astrid Anderson

BUILDING STORM

Storm Hawke (Matthews) & Landon McCabe

/ \

Angelina Matthews   Alessandra McCabe

STEELE RESOLVE

Luca "Steele" Abello & Byron Harris

|

Jude Harris-Abello (ad)

1

KENNEDY

My right hook lands on his jaw with a satisfying thud, and he staggers back a step before a sinister grin spreads across his lips, flashing me the bright-blue mouthguard that matches his eyes.

It didn't faze him at all.

He's used to taking shots from other professional boxers. My blows probably feel like a gentle breeze, and he's more than willing to let me know they won't slow him down or affect him in the slightest.

Smug fucker.

If he weren't family, I would probably hate his guts for letting me dance around and wear myself out, trying to actually hurt him. He knows I can't, but I need to train with *someone* who can challenge me and let me unleash all this...whatever it is...that's been so coiled up inside me lately.

I advance on him, aggressively throwing left jabs to back him against the ropes. He retreats, challenge flashing in his typically warm blue eyes, hardening them into cutting ice.

Atlas *loves* this.

It doesn't matter if he's only light sparring with me and his returning punches don't contain even a *fraction* of the power he's capable of as a light-heavyweight in line to fight for the belt soon. His competitive spirit won't let him lose, and landing that blow to his jaw has cranked it up another level beyond the playful session we've had so far.

Good.

I need the competition.

Facing off against Atlas may be a sorry substitute for taking out my aggression on who I really want to—that fucker Cassius Whitaker and his client, Falco Enterprises—but it's better than holding it all inside.

I was practically vibrating with rage this morning after Isaac told me about Falco Enterprises' latest move through their trusted legal counsel, and since rough sex wasn't an option for releasing my frustration, coming here to the gym for an unplanned match with Atlas was a close second choice.

Each time I land a punch, I picture the man who has caused so much turmoil for the entire family over the last few years and, especially, the last several months. Though we've never met in person, I can vividly call up his smug grin shining at me from his website each time I take a swing or throw a jab.

Atlas advances on me, landing a few punches against my headgear that blur my vision slightly and make me stumble back a few steps, but I manage to stay upright. Dazed but definitely not done. If he had used his full power, I'd be out cold—he knocks out men twice my size on a regular basis—but this is just a "friendly" session—at least, for *him.*

For me, it's the only way I'll be able to make it through the rest of my day without blowing up at someone—likely Dad or Uncle Gabe since they're the ones I'll be spending the most time with trying to get our upcoming events finalized.

Over-exerted muscles ache.

My lungs burn.

Sore joints beg for a hot bath or some fucking ibuprofen.

But I won't stop.

Not yet.

I'll just push harder and faster.

All of it will remind me of what I'm fighting for *outside* the ring without me having to *verbally* spar with those who have to work with me.

Atlas waggles his dark-blond brows, offering another flash of a grin. "You had enough yet?"

His words, slightly garbled by the mouthguard, only spur me forward with a blitz of shots at his flank and a strong right hook at his head. He blocks most of them easily, dancing lightly on his feet, almost like he's floating on air. A left jab hits me square in the chest, momentarily knocking the wind out of me, but anyone who knows him as well as I do understands this is nothing compared to the hurricane he truly is in the ring when he fully unleashes his power.

Another quick set of jabs shifts him back a few steps, giving me time to regain my breath, but he would never allow me to trap him against the ropes. He quickly returns the volley, landing two sharp strikes on my left flank against my ribs, hard enough to send bolts of pain lancing through me and making me wince.

He instantly lowers his gloves, his chest barely moving while mine heaves with each gasp. A light sheen of sweat covers his tattooed torso, but otherwise, no one would know he'd just sparred for half an hour with me in this ring. Concern darkens his eyes, and he spits out his mouthguard. "Shit. You okay?"

I glower at him, pressing my right gloved hand over the searing pain in my left ribcage. "Fine."

Even speaking the single word brings another stab of agony to the area, but I fight the wince, unwilling to show weakness to him. It's nothing compared to what he's done to Isaac during their "friendly" sessions, and I'm not about to look like a pussy.

Atlas gives me a reproachful look that tells me he isn't buying my response. "You don't *look* fine. We're done for today."

"No!" I try to stand upright and wince, doubling over again with my hand at my side. "I'm okay, just need to catch my breath."

Despite my mouthguard garbling my words slightly, he rolls his eyes and brings his glove to his mouth to start tearing off the tape. "Nope. You're finished." He shakes his head. "I don't need Uncle Savage or my dad coming down here to ream me out because I broke your ribs or worse. They don't even want me getting in the ring with you."

I spit out my mouthguard since it's clear there won't be any convincing him to keep going. "They can go fuck right off. It isn't their call. It's mine."

Atlas shakes his head, pulling off the first glove. "Wrong. It's *mine*. My gym. My rules."

I scowl at him, which only draws a crooked grin from my arrogant cousin. "You're a real dick sometimes, you know that?"

He barks out a laugh that echoes through the open high ceiling and off the exposed metal beams. "Only sometimes?" Atlas removes his other glove, then steps forward and tugs my hand toward him to start tearing off my tape. "You weren't hitting *me* today, anyway. Who were you picturing this morning? You came in *all* worked up."

Fuck.

I hate that he can read me so well. He tugs off the first glove, and I immediately press my hand against my still-stinging side, gritting my teeth so I won't wince again and give away how badly he really did hurt me with that final shot.

They don't feel broken, but I am definitely going to have a nasty bruise on my ribs and some painful breathing for a while.

What I *don't* need is the added pain of having Atlas digging around in my head on top of the damage he did to my body.

"Don't worry about it..."

Atlas snorts and tears into the tape on my left glove. "You think I'm going to let you come in here and take out your aggression on me without you giving up the goods on who you're so fucking pissed off at?"

I meet his gaze. "Yes."

He chuckles. "Wrong, Cuz. Spill, or I'm going to ban you from the ring."

I gasp. "You can't *do* that!"

One of his brows wings up as he pulls off my other glove. "The aforementioned rule suggests otherwise."

The bastard's head is getting too big.

I smirk at him. "Actually, Hawke Enterprises owns the gym, and I am CFO of the company, so that means, *I* technically control what happens within these four grungy walls, *not* you."

His eyes darken to midnight. "Don't pull that shit with me, Ken. This is *my* place, even if it *is* under the company umbrella."

"Then don't push me for something I'm not willing to talk about. Deal?"

He scowls but backs away and nods, relenting when I know he wants to push more.

It's not that my wrath for Cassius Whitaker is any big family secret.

We *all* hold disdain for the man who represents Falco Enterprises and who—in all likelihood—was involved in the fire that destroyed Hawke's Daily Grind. But what he did *now*, what Isaac is on his way to deal with later this morning in court, isn't anything we want to worry the rest of the Hawkes with until we know more and have a solid plan on how to handle it and retaliate.

So, telling Atlas what's going on will have to wait—hopefully until Isaac comes back with a win under his belt.

I release a heavy breath and climb through the ropes, wincing and clamping my eyes shut against the pain since Atlas is behind me and can't see it, but as soon as I reopen them on the floor, a familiar wise gaze set in a wrinkled face greets me.

Shit.

Jenkins smiles at me, his old eyes darting to where I've pressed my hand to my side. "Atlas worked ya over, did he?"

Atlas chuckles behind me as he climbs from the ring and steps up beside the time-weathered man. He claps his trainer on his shoulder and squeezes it. "I barely touched her. She's a wuss."

A low growl slips from my lips at his intentionally antagonistic comment, but Jenkins releases a heavy laugh and shakes his head.

He points to me with a shaky finger. "I wouldn't keep talking trash about Kennedy if you value your life, kid."

Atlas grins playfully. "She doesn't scare me."

I square my shoulders, ignoring the pain it causes in my ribs. "I should."

Jenkins nods. "I agree with blondie. This girl is relentless when she gets in the ring. You're about the only one here who can actually beat her anymore besides Savage and your dad. *Maybe* Isaac."

I scoff at that one. "Isaac *cannot* out-box me."

Though he sure likes to think he can.

In life and in the ring, he seems to think he's tops.

He may have a law degree, but I'm the one in line to take over complete control of Hawke Enterprises when Dad and Uncle Gabe retire, and I certainly have the upper hand when stepping inside the ropes. His size and muscle mass make him slow. Physical power isn't everything.

Float like a butterfly; sting like a bee...

It's always served me well to be light on my feet and relentless in my attacks—when boxing or when dealing with business situations. And once I leave here, I'll start digging in on this new Falco and Cass Whitaker problem so we can destroy them once and for all—if I can figure out how to breathe without gasping in pain.

Jenkins gets a wistful look and sighs. "Your grandfather would have been so proud of you two..."

Thinking about the man neither of us ever got to meet makes tears pool in my eyes like they do every time Sam "the Savage" Hawke comes up in conversation here at the gym or anywhere else.

Atlas offers a sad smile, crossing his heavily inked arms over his equally colorful chest. "I would have liked to have him see one of my fights."

The old trainer who worked with grandfather, and now grandson, slaps Atlas on the shoulder. "You're even better than he was, kid."

I snort-laugh as Atlas rolls his eyes.

He points at Jenkins. "You're only saying that because he isn't here to beat the ever-loving-snot out of you while I still can..."

Jenkins grins, then turns and wanders away toward the small office at the back of the gym that is his domain.

Atlas watches as I slowly make my way over to my bag. I tug off my headgear, pull out a towel, and swipe the sweat off my face before I gingerly lift my duffel onto my shoulder.

He narrows his gaze on me. "Where are you running off to so fast? I thought we could head over to Novel Idea and grab a post-workout coffee."

Any other day, I'd take him up on that offer. God knows I can't survive without copious amounts of caffeine on a daily basis. But I have bigger plans today.

Mainly, taking down Cassius Whitaker and his troublesome client, Falco Enterprises.

CASS

SOMETHING OVERHEAD CASTS a shadow across the small café table, and I glance up at the clear early morning sky, searching for the source. Squinting against the bright sun, I raise my hand and scan the vast blue above me, going stock still when I finally find what caused the minor spot of darkness on the otherwise flawless day.

A hawk?

A shiver rolls down my spine despite the still-warm fall breeze blowing around me on the café patio. I can't tear my eyes away from the bird, which hovers like an omen directly over me.

What the hell is a hawk doing this far into the city?

It floats above Café Du Monde, doing lazy, almost aimless, circles. But I know better. Hawks are hunters. They're always looking for small, weak prey, something they can easily swoop in on and snag before it knows what's happening. And if this one came all the way into New Orleans, it wouldn't do it just so it could grab a bite of a beignet.

Something drew it here.

Maybe karma drawing it to haunt me...

I swallow against the unease settling over me and drag my eyes away from the animal and to Jackson Square. Tourists wander around, taking in the sights of this city with wide-eyed wonder, snapping photos and pointing excitedly at things I see every day and take for granted.

It's been so long since I moved here that I don't even remember what it was like to look at it with new eyes. Typically,

I avoid places like this—the tourist traps—but today, I had to combine this meeting with fulfilling a special, time-sensitive request.

My eyes drift to the two bags of beignets on the table before returning to the growing crowd of people heading toward the café to make their purchases. But they're not who I'm looking for.

I glance at my watch.

He's late.

Annoyance tightens my chest. I cross my ankle over my knee and recline slightly, taking a sip of my coffee and chicory. The bitter liquid goes down smoothly, and I tear off a piece of a beignet and toss the sweet into my mouth, glancing down to brush the powdered sugar off my fingers before it can get on my dark suit.

Another shadow falls on the table—this one much larger than the last—and I look up and scowl. Dressed in his typical dark jeans, T-shirt, and leather jacket, dark hair tousled like he just rolled out of bed, he appears completely unapologetic for his tardy appearance to our meeting.

"You're late."

Marcel sighs and slides into the metal chair across from me, resting his elbows on the table. "Five minutes late is on time in my book."

I take another sip of coffee and glare at him. "Your book is wrong. My time is very expensive. I suggest you respect it more unless you want to start paying for it."

He stills, prepared for a fight, then a slow grin spreads across his lips, and his gray eyes twinkle with amusement. "You almost had me there for a second."

I chuckle and turn the bag of beignets in his direction. The man is always eating, and if I have any hope of this being a productive discussion, he needs to fill his stomach while we chat.

"If you were *anyone* else, I *would* charge you or at least take it out of your paycheck. And I sure as *shit* wouldn't be buying those for you."

Marcel smirks. "Thank you for your benevolence, oh great one..."

My lingering annoyance slips away with his wisecrack. Even after thirty years of friendship, the man can still get on my nerves, but he just as easily breaks through any bad mood with his constant humor.

Leaning forward, I rest my forearm on the table and glance around us to ensure no one is paying attention to our conversation. "Your text said you have something for me?"

Marcel grabs a donut and takes a bite, white powdered sugar covering his mouth. He swipes his palm over it and chews, nodding, but lifts his hand and rocks it side to side. "Sort of."

Sort of?

Not exactly the words you want to hear from the man you pay to do your digging and find information for you...

When he doesn't continue, I raise a brow at him. "Well..."

He sighs and sits back, taking another bite and chewing slowly. "I've spoken with *literally* everyone who was at the scene of the fire, including anyone from the fire department, police, and even the insurance investigators, and despite your and the Hawkes' belief that it was arson, I haven't been able to find *any* evidence of that, let alone any clues as to who might be behind it."

"Fuck." I down the rest of my coffee and slam the empty mug onto the ceramic saucer, drawing a few curious and annoyed looks from patrons at neighboring tables. Ignoring them, I open my hands to Marcel. "*Nothing?*"

That's impossible.

That place didn't just go up; it *exploded*. And the timing wasn't accidental, or if it was, it was one hell of a coincidence that Falco was putting in a competing café right down the street.

Someone was making a statement.

It was no accident.

Marcel shakes his head. "Nothing. Though, I tend to agree with you. It *looks* suspicious as fuck. If someone *is* covering it up, they've done a *damn* good job erasing their tracks. They've had to clean up physical evidence and pay off a lot of people very well for them to keep their mouths shut about anything that might implicate someone."

Who the hell has that kind of power?

Anyone who does knows better than to fuck with the Hawkes. Rumors about what Gabe used to do in his time in the military alone should be enough to scare anyone away from touching the Hawkes. Not only are the Hawke men brutal, but they have a former mob head and enforcer in their ranks. They will destroy anyone who gets in their way or crosses them, and if that isn't enough, they'll just make you disappear and pay off anyone looking.

The shadow falls on the table again, and I jerk up my head to see the hawk soar above us, swooping in an ominous glide, eyes locked on something—or someone—below.

That same chill climbs my spine, and I shudder despite my best efforts not to react to it.

I drum my fingers against the table. "Which means the Hawkes are going to keep thinking it was Falco and me."

He shrugs. "Probably."

My frustration boils over, and I release a heavy sigh. "Well, if you didn't find anything, then why are we meeting?"

Marcel leans forward slightly as he examines the people milling around us, enjoying their sweet treats and coffee and the beautiful early fall weather. "The *other* thing you asked me to look into..."

Shit.

I slide forward on my chair, too, angling myself to ensure no one else can hear. "On that issue?"

His face hardens, and he shifts slightly, clearly uneasy about discussing it out in the open. "Someone is *definitely* moving on Roselli. There have been several attacks on his warehouses, shipping lanes, and even one of his personal homes."

"Fuck."

Roselli has done an excellent job of keeping these attacks out of the media—likely to protect his image and ensure it still looks like he's firmly in control of NOLA—but people talk. His *men* talk. And Marcel is an excellent conversationalist.

"Do they know who it is?"

Who the fuck would be dumb enough to try to move in on Roselli?

He shakes his head. "Not a fucking clue, which makes it even more dangerous for everyone tied to his organization."

His statement sparks something in the back of my mind. "Any chance the fire at the Daily Grind was related to Roselli?"

Marcel's brow furrows. "Why would it be?"

I shrug. "Roselli and the Hawkes have reached a strange... *détente*. From what I can tell, they tolerate each other enough to keep the apparent peace, but there's tension there. Maybe someone hit the Hawkes, so they'd retaliate against Roselli and start a war."

Marcel nods slowly, shoving the last of his beignet into his mouth. "It's definitely possible, though I'm not sure how anyone would benefit from that." He dusts off his hands and wipes some stray sugar from his leather jacket. "You want me to dig into that angle?"

"As deep as you can. If someone is trying to start a war, I want to know who it is and why."

One of his dark eyebrows rises. "Why does it matter to you? I thought you loved pissing off the Hawkes on behalf of Falco.

Aren't you happy someone took out the competition for the Falco coffee shop?"

I scowl at him. "There's a huge difference between representing Falco's legal and business interests and blowing up the competition. I don't need the Hawkes thinking I was in *any* way involved. If they retaliate and something were to happen to me..."

He watches me carefully as I swallow through the rock suddenly lodged in my throat. His eyes dart to the second bag of beignets sitting on the table, and he offers me a tight smile.

Marcel is one of the only people in the world who understands what it would cost me if I got caught in the middle of something. "If you're that worried, should you really be poking the bear?"

A good point...

This might not have been the right time to make my most recent legal maneuver, when their eyes are already trained on me with accusation in them, but it was the right move for Falco Enterprises.

"I'll find out soon enough." I glance at my watch. "I'm dropping by my house quickly, then heading to court with Isaac Hawke."

Marcel chuckles low. "What did you do this time?"

I smirk. "Filed an injunction to try to stop Hawke's Daily Grind from reopening because I trademarked the name Daily Grounds for Falco and argued there would be brand confusion."

He barks out a laugh, shaking his head. "You're a real asshole, you know that? First, your client steals their name, then you have the balls to try to prevent them from using it?"

A grin pulls at my lips as I push to my feet and grab the bag of beignets. "I know. And I'll lose. The judge is fed up with the constant lawsuits between Falco and the Hawkes, but"—I offer a nonchalant shrug—"I do what's in the best interests of my clients."

Marcel's humor slips away as he falls back into the role of oldest friend and not just a business associate. "And what about what's best for *you?* You're making a powerful enemy."

His warning tightens my grip on the bag, the implication clear. But it isn't anything I didn't already know. After the confrontation I had with the members of the Hawke clan at the Grind after the fire, it became crystal clear it was too late to play nice with any of them.

"I'm not *making* anything, Marcel. They already see me that way—as the enemy—and they should."

Even if I'm not the one they need to be focusing on...

2

KENNEDY

Downing a third glass of champagne hasn't done anything to help ease my annoyance or frustration from the last two days, nor does the beautiful surroundings of the Marigny Opera House or the pleasant music filling the air coming from the live band.

Given the shitty mood I'm in, I doubt anything can pull me from this funk brought on by the beating from Atlas and the dark cloud hanging over Hawke Enterprises.

I turn back to the bartender and lift my empty flute, wincing slightly at the pain the movement brings to my ribs despite them being wrapped tightly with an ACE bandage. "Another."

He gives me a wry smile, clearly just as perturbed about having to be at this event as I am. At least he's getting paid to be here.

While my healthy salary for my role as CFO of Hawke Enterprises keeps me flush in Louboutins and the rest of the finer things in life, these events make me question whether it's at all worth it.

It's the least fun part of the job—schmoozing with the elite of New Orleans. Begging for donations. Kissing asses of...well, asses...to get the Hawke Family Charity Fund's coffers filled. But it's a necessary evil. One I knew I was signing on for when I decided to work for Dad and Uncle Gabe rather than go off on my own after graduate school.

Not that it was much of a choice.

No one walks away from the Hawkes—at least, not fully.

Atlas may have his boxing career against pretty much everyone's wishes, but the gym is still owned by Hawke Enterprises. Even Coen, who seems least interested in committing himself to *any* one thing in particular, can't break free from the pull the family business and the money it brings has on everyone.

Me included.

It's even drawn all these people here—at our request. They dress in their finest, with masquerade masks that probably cost more than most people make in a week, covering their faces and obscuring their sins.

The bartender refills my drink, and I bring the glass to my lips, enjoying the crisp, bubbly, cool liquid as it slides down my throat.

"How many of those have you had?"

I jerk toward the sound of Isaac's voice, fighting another wince, and he sidles up next to me at the bar, eyeing my glass through his mask with a half-grin.

Rolling my eyes, I take another sip. "Not enough."

He chuckles and motions to the bartender. "Lagavulin 16, neat." Leaning his back against the bar, he scans the massive crowd— New Orleans' richest and most influential citizens, all here because *we* asked them to come and open their wallets. "I don't blame you. If I have to force one more smile tonight, I might lose it."

I chuckle, pressing my free hand against the twinge in my ribs, and mirror his stance, releasing a sigh. "Where's that beautiful woman of yours?"

Isaac inclines his head to the left. "At the table with Astrid and Coen. She couldn't be on her feet anymore."

"Can't blame her." I watch her for a moment, her hand resting on her belly. "Being pregnant seems awful."

He barks out a laugh. "So, does that mean you don't ever plan to have a family?"

I shake my head and snort. "Who has time for that?"

His shoulders rise and fall. "I do."

Sipping at my drink, I turn to face him. "You have your dad helping you manage the family's legal needs. It isn't as if you're doing it alone."

Nodding, he glances toward where Jack sits, laughing and chatting with Astrid and Coen, who looks just as immensely annoyed at having to attend this shindig as I am. "True, but he won't be here forever, and I've taken over most of the court appearances and day-to-day operational things."

"Which is exactly what *I'll* be doing when my dad and Uncle Gabe retire."

Isaac barks out a laugh so loud that it draws the attention of several people mingling around us who cast strange looks our way. "You think Uncle Savage and Gabe will *ever* retire? You're going to have to drag their corpses out of their offices at the Hawkeye Club when they finally keel over."

I scowl at him and turn back to the party, finishing off my fourth glass.

These pours seem awfully small...

"Did you only come over here to remind me I'm stuck in a job that requires a ton of work and no advancement opportunities short of the deaths of those we love?"

He gives me a lopsided smile. "No. I wanted to make sure

you weren't in this shit mood because of what happened yesterday."

I scowl and cross my arms over my chest, cringing at the sharp bite in my bruised ribs. "What, Atlas kicking my ass, or Whitaker walking all over us?"

Isaac's blue eyes sharpen with his annoyance. "He *didn't* walk all over us. Judge Cramer was *not* amused with his injunction request and tore him a new one on the record after I did in my argument against the bullshit filing. The judge denied it because he *knew* it was just a stall tactic on Falco's part and completely frivolous, without any legal basis. We *won*, Ken. So, relax and enjoy the soiree as much as you can, since we *have* to be here."

"You think we won?"

He takes a sip of his drink and nods. "We *did*."

I shake my head, tightening my hand around the empty stemware. "No, we didn't. Falco may have lost the injunction, but they succeeded in exactly what they set out to do."

"And what's that?"

"Get to us." I lock my gaze with his. "Get under our skin. Rattle us by delaying the opening, even if only for a few days. It's bad enough everything *else* they've done, but this crossed a line. They're trying to keep us from rebuilding what *they* stole from us, what they stole from Angelina."

Isaac scowls. "We still don't have proof that it *was* Falco who set the fire."

"We don't need it." My words come out a little more aggressive than I intended, making him recoil slightly. "We both know they're the only ones who had anything to gain from it. That's proof enough for me. And their attack dog, Cassius Whitaker, is going to *keep* coming at us as long as we let him."

"What do you suggest we do?" He takes a long sip of his drink, smirking under the mask. "Drag him out into the bayou, let Saint, Gabe, and Luca work their magic, and leave him for the gators?"

I shrug. "Sounds like an excellent resolution to me."

He chuckles low and leans in slightly. "I agree, but it won't solve the problem. Falco Enterprises will just find another attorney to do their bidding. Removing Cass doesn't resolve the ultimate issue—which is that we don't know *who* we're fighting against. Until we do, we have to dodge each swing he takes at us and hope we don't sustain any damage."

Like the damage Atlas did to my damn ribs yesterday morning.

They burn and ache each time I move, despite the wrapping and this tight dress. Just getting it on felt like someone was drop-kicking me. But I have to look and act the part. That's what being a Hawke requires, especially when we're begging people for money.

The mayor approaches through the crowd, and I stand up straighter, fighting a wince, and force a smile. "Mayor Lavine, how are you this evening?"

He grins at me and holds out his hand for mine, bringing it to his lips to press a kiss to the back of it.

Revolting man...

Every time I'm forced to play nice with him at events and he insists on this form of greeting, I can never wash my hands enough to get the slimy feeling off it.

"I'm lovely, Ms. Hawke. Always a pleasure to see you." He releases my hand after holding it a second too long, then turns to Isaac. "And Isaac"—he takes his hand and shakes it vigorously—"I hear congratulations are in order. Your girlfriend is expecting?"

Isaac nods, offering him a genuine smile but only because the man mentioned his impending fatherhood. "I am. My daughter is very happy to become a big sister."

The mayor chuckles. "Excellent." His eyes shift around us carefully for a moment before he steps in closer to Isaac. "I do have a...*private* matter to discuss with you, if you have a moment."

I fight a grin.

Isaac has dirt on just about every politician in the city and uses it to ensure the family doesn't hit any roadblocks with any of our endeavors. What he has on the mayor could ruin the man if it ever got out, and given how nervous he looks now, we may be getting more ammunition to load the gun pointed squarely at him.

Downing the rest of his drink, Isaac nods. "Of course." He sweeps an arm out, indicating the older man should lead him somewhere private. "I'll catch you later, Ken. Try not to spend the whole night with that sourpuss look on your face."

Easier said than done.

I collect another refill, then move away from the bar before anyone else can corner me for a conversation I don't want to have. For a second, I consider joining Jack, Astrid, and Coen or seeking out another member of the family to commiserate with before it's time to give the speech, but I don't have the stomach for that tonight.

For the briefest moment, I almost slip out the back door and head to the nearest bar to try to find someone to make my night a little more bearable. Only the ever-present guilt of leaving an event designed to raise money for the city we all love stops me from doing just that.

I beeline for the old staircase to the choir balcony that over-looks what used to be a church that housed penitent patrons not so long ago. The sign warning that the balcony is closed doesn't dissuade me from slipping around it and heading up the old stone spiral stairs.

The sounds of the party hit me the moment I reach the lofted area, and I wander over to the waist-high solid-wood banister to watch the revelry. It's a much better position than being smack dab in the middle of it. Up here, I can finally take a deep breath and feel like I'm actually getting some air in my lungs, despite the restriction around my chest.

I take a sip of my champagne, scanning the crowd, enjoying their evening for a good cause.

It is a good cause, Ken.

Get out of your foul mood.

I've been trying to for days, but after that injunction filing, nothing has seemed to be able to drag me from the well of anger—and the rib injury didn't help, either.

It's been one hit after another against us, but I shouldn't let it get in the way of doing my job and doing it well. Maybe a few moments alone will help me get my head back on straight, then I can rejoin the party and do my duty on stage.

Footsteps sound on the staircase behind me, and I tense as they approach across the old, polished floor.

Who came up after me?

I prepare myself for whoever it might be—one of my cousins, an aunt or uncle, or—God forbid—one of the other invitees come to interrupt my much-needed moment of solitude.

Leave me the fuck alone.

A man in an immaculate black tux and matching black mask with silver accents around the edges steps up next to me, a tumbler of amber liquid in his hand. Pale, mossy-green, almost-translucent eyes assess me from behind that mask, slowly snaking down from my face, pausing for a moment on my exposed neck and cleavage, then dipping over the skin-tight silver-sequin gown that stops mid-thigh, to the four-inch stilettos on my feet.

The corner of his perfect lips tips up. "I hope you don't intend on doing any dancing in those tonight. I'd hate for you to break that beautiful neck of yours."

I thought I knew everyone in New Orleans—or, at the very

least, everyone who would be invited to one of our charity fundraiser events.

His gravelly yet somehow velvet voice.

His lips.

The chiseled jaw.

What I can see of him beneath that mask...

None of it sparks even a hint of recognition.

But his comment has certainly ignited something deep inside me.

~

CASS

ANGER FLARES in Kennedy's Caribbean-blue eyes, heating them before it switches to a defiance that freezes them over instantly. My stomach knots, the warm bourbon I've been sipping on since I made a stop at the bar downstairs souring as she shoots icy daggers at me with her hard gaze.

Fuck.

Not a great start, Cass...

I may have just ruined my chance at actually getting anywhere with her tonight.

Show up at the fundraiser.

Try to get Kennedy Hawke alone for a private conversation.

Hopefully, convince the eldest of the Hawke kids, the one closest to the helm of the ship, to trust me when I tell them Falco wasn't behind the fire and that there's another enemy out there.

It was a simple plan...

...that I may have just blown up with one ill-placed flirtation I wasn't able to bite back.

She assesses me for a moment, mulling over my comment before turning to face me fully, an ornate silver mask covering the top half of her face. The corner of her bright-red lips curls slightly, like she's gearing up to jab the spiked heel she wears right into my balls for making such a remark. Given what I know about Kennedy Hawke, it's more than likely to happen. "You underestimate what I can do in heels."

There's that feisty spirit I've heard so much about...

And it appears my balls are safe—at least for the moment—from her stilettos. But if I don't watch my step, I could get crushed under her all the same.

I take a sip of my bourbon, keeping my gaze firmly locked on hers, searching for signs of weakness in the wall of attitude she surrounds herself with.

It would be wise to ignore the opening she gave me, to move the conversation away from the sexual innuendo she's invited in and steer it toward my purpose for coming tonight.

But I can't help myself.

Fighting a grin, I let my gaze drift down to the heels again, then flick it back up to meet hers. "*Do* I?"

Her eyes widen slightly, apparently not expecting me to play her game, and her icy glare melts slightly, replaced with a sudden heat. She swallows thickly, her elegant neck revealing just how difficult it is for her to hold herself back from saying or doing whatever it is she wants to. "You *do*."

Against my better judgment—not learning my lesson after what happened the *last* time I got this close to a Hawke—I lean in slightly until her light, flowery scent fills my lungs and unexpectedly stirs my cock. "*Prove* it."

Most women would recoil from a blatant sexual challenge thrown down the gauntlet, but not Kennedy Hawke. She squares her shoulders, bringing her champagne flute to her bright-red lips, taking a long sip, eyes still on me without a flicker of reaction to my words.

Stone cold and scorching hot all at the same time.

It's no wonder Savage put her in charge. Some would say it's pure nepotism—his only child named CFO of Hawke Enterprises at such a young age—but staring her down for the first time in person, I can see *precisely* why he did it.

Kennedy Hawke must unnerve men *and* women in the boardroom if the way she's sizing me up over her glass is any indication.

This woman is looking for a fight—and she thinks she's going to *win*.

She swallows her champagne, darting her pink tongue across her lips to catch a lingering drop, then offers me a sultry grin. "I *could*, but I'm not in the habit of proving my talents in heels to men just because they demand it."

A challenge lies in her gaze—to *make* further demands and do something that would have those heels digging into my lower back.

Fucking hell.

My cock stirs again, more than willing to rise to the occasion, even though it's the last thing I should be thinking about.

This is stupid, Cass.

Yet my feet move me a half-step closer to her until the heat radiating off her body seeps into mine. "What does a man need to do in order to have you prove your talents?"

It's as direct as I can be without flat-out asking how to get into her pants—or under her dress, as it may be.

Absolutely not what I intended tonight.

But when I saw her standing here, her sleek blond curls cascading over her slender, exposed shoulders, her dress hugging her curves and accentuating her hourglass shape, looking absolutely fuckable as hell in those heels, the shoe remark just slipped out. The same way compliments and flirty comments seem to find their way out of my mouth whenever I'm around a beautiful woman. And Kennedy Hawke is *far* beyond beautiful. Even with the mask partially covering her face, she's absolutely *stunning*.

And she knows it.

The photos I've seen over the years don't do this woman justice. Kennedy wears her sexuality like a badge of honor, not something to be ashamed of or to hide behind a wall of propriety, as most of the people in this world do. It shouldn't surprise me, given some of the businesses the Hawkes own—they peddle flesh in their strip clubs and appeal to the basest of human desires.

She's grown up around it. Her damn office is in the first club they ever opened. Kennedy won't back down now that we're in an unbreakable eye-fuck competition.

It opens up a whole new world of possibilities.

And a new avenue of approach to my problem.

Playing *nice* with Kennedy when she doesn't recognize me may open more doors, and it's clear she has no idea who the hell I am. If she did, we never would have gotten this far in our conversation.

Despite all the active campaigns the Hawkes and Falco Enterprises have waged against each other over the last few years, I've somehow never been in the same room as this woman, instead spending my time staring down Stone and Isaac in the courtroom most of the time.

Tonight, that's definitely played in my favor. But as soon as she knows who I am, she will *undoubtedly* end this flirtation harshly—perhaps with that heel in my balls as I imagined earlier. If I want to get anywhere with her, if I want her to *listen* to my warning, she can't know who I am.

She stares up at me through thick, black, impossibly long lashes, and her free hand comes up to my chest, her sharp, manicured nails digging in through the crisp fabric of my tux shirt. "That depends."

"On what?"

Mischief twinkles in her now-heated gaze that I could swim in all fucking night. "What that man would offer in return..."

Holy hell.

My cock strains against the front of my pants, pushing painfully against the zipper. This may not have been the plan, but I've always been excellent at thinking on my feet, rolling with the punches, and switching tactics, whether it be in the courtroom, cross-examining a witness, or in bed with a woman.

No reason I can't do the same now.

I take another sip of my bourbon, then lower my head slowly until my lips brush against her ear. "I'm not in the habit of picking up beautiful women at parties and fucking them senseless, but if that interests you, I wouldn't be opposed to you proving just what you can do in those fuck-me heels."

A shiver rolls through her, goosebumps pebbling across her exposed skin.

The idea of a quickie with a stranger at one of her family's fundraisers excites her far more than I expected. Most women would slap me for even suggesting it, but the flare of interest in her eyes that I catch when I pull my head back makes my cock twitch with anticipation.

She drags her gaze away from me to scan the party raging on below us. No one casts a second glance at us up on the balcony, too engrossed in drinking, dancing, schmoozing, and reviewing the silent auction items set up along one wall.

I shift closer to her, stepping slightly behind her so I can use my free hand to brush the blond hair off her neck and feather my lips to her ear again. "The only problem is...this balcony leaves us very exposed. All it would take is one glance up for someone to see me behind you, slamming my cock into your cunt." Her body shudders against mine. "Plus, the acoustics in here were designed to carry any noise from up here out across the entire space. And I guarantee that when I'm inside of you, you won't be able to contain your screams."

Kennedy slowly turns her head toward me, catching my gaze out of the corner of her eye. "That's unfortunate. I really could have used the release tonight."

I grin and down the rest of my bourbon. "I didn't say I wasn't going to get you off."

Her eyes widen slightly, and her gaze cuts down to the party again. I set my empty glass on a small table on the balcony to our side and grab hers from her hand to do the same—we certainly don't need her dropping it onto a partygoer because she loses her grip while I work her over.

She watches me do it with interest, not a hint of trepidation despite me being a complete stranger.

Stepping up directly behind her, I press my lips on the center of her neck, sliding my hands to the waist of her sequin gown. "Just make sure you stay quiet, or we'll have some unwanted attention." I tighten my grip on her hips. "And I don't want to get interrupted while I'm making you come."

Kennedy sucks in a harsh breath, her body tensing.

"Unless you'd prefer that I go back down those stairs and return to the party..."

Her hands curl around the banister, and she shakes her head. "The party is quite boring. You aren't missing anything."

I smirk as I glide my hands to the dress hem and work it up over her hips, exposing her beautiful bare ass to me.

Full.

Lush.

My hand itches to smack it, but the very real fear of the sound reverberating through the building keeps me from doing just that. Instead, I slide my palm over the soft, peachy flesh, my cock straining against its confines. Getting Kennedy off will be sheer torture, but I never anticipated this spark between us, this desire to see what she looks like when she completely lets go of all the tension she carries in her body and the weight that rests on her slender shoulders.

Gripping her hip with my left hand, I slip my right down between her thighs. My fingertips brush against her wet heat, eliciting a low groan from deep in my chest.

"No panties? And you're already wet for me. *Pauvre bête*, you really need this, don't you, *Cherie*?"

Her entire body trembles with my feather of a touch, and she shifts her hips, trying to force me to move my hand to where she wants it.

Cupping it up between her legs, I hold her firmly in place, relishing the way she vibrates, trying to grind her pussy against my palm while I prevent her from moving. "I hope you're ready for this, *Cherie,* because I don't plan on taking things easy on you just because we have a potentially captive audience." I slip a single finger up inside her, earning a gasp as she clutches at it. "You better bite your tongue and hold on tight to that banister."

3

CASS

Kennedy's pussy clenches around my finger, and the fantasy of her doing that to my cock makes me shiver this time.

I guess we're really doing this.

The party continues below us, and I shift slightly to adjust my hold on her and to make it appear to anyone looking up that I'm simply leaning in to talk to her over the din rising from the revelry. No one will know I have my hand shoved between her thighs or a finger up her cunt.

I slide another finger into her and slip my thumb over her clit. Her entire body twitches, and I tighten my hold on her hip, keeping her steady. "Remember, we may have an audience..."

Her eyes dart over to mine for a second. She presses her lips together in a firm line, like she's trying to bite back something that threatens to slip out. This woman *wants* to argue, wants to say something back—perhaps chastise me for thinking I need to warn her again—but she swallows it and holds my gaze with hers.

After all I've heard about Kennedy Hawke over the years, I never expected her to be this submissive, so willing to give in when I'm a complete stranger to her.

She must *really* need this.

Good.

It makes me want to be the one to give it to her even more. Giving Kennedy something she wants might get me what *I* want—a cease-fire.

I roll the pad of my thumb over her sensitive nub, and she bucks on my hand, gritting her teeth. I've barely touched her, and she's already dangling on the edge of losing control. Slowly, I thrust my fingers in and out of her, curling them slightly to drag against her G-spot. Her mouth falls open on a silent gasp, and I squeeze her hip to remind her where we are.

She swallows thickly, closing her eyes for a moment as I continue to work her drenched core. Her arousal coats my fingers and slides down onto my hand, making it easier and easier to move inside of her and play with her clit. Her legs start to tremble.

I glance down at the mile-high heels she wears. "You told me I underestimated what you can do in heels, but you're about to collapse in them."

Kennedy scowls and fires icy daggers at me with her eyes. "I'm *fine*."

The sheer determination in her unwavering voice and the fierce glare she gives me only makes me more determined to break her.

I insert a third finger, stretching her cunt wider. "Are you?"

She keeps her gaze locked on mine, her desire lowering her lids partially while she adamantly refuses to look away.

Feisty.

This isn't a woman who concedes weakness often—if at all. Her relentless pursuits in securing the financial success of her family businesses are only the tip of the iceberg. The fire that burns inside her could scald a man with one look, and right now, all that intensity is directed squarely at me as she tries to prove her strength to someone she doesn't even know.

Fucking hell.

I keep pumping into her. Her entire body shakes against mine. Each curl of my fingers, every roll of my thumb, it only brings out more of her fervent desire to show she meant what she said to me. And it only makes me want to see her unravel for me more.

Leaning in again, I check the crowd for any potential curious gazes, then nip at her ear. "You may be standing in them now, but let's see you keep it together while I eat your cunt."

Ocean-blue eyes flare wide, and her red lips fall open. I jerk my hand free from between her legs and quickly scan the party again to ensure no one's watching. With a grin at my shocked companion, I step behind her and drop to my knees onto the choir loft floor.

This was once a place for the residents of New Orleans to worship God, but now, I'll be worshipping Kennedy Hawke's pussy while she tries to bite her tongue and avoid detection. Considering the miracle I was hoping for tonight, it's somehow fitting.

With her beautiful, bare ass now at eye level, my mouth waters.

Fuck.

I thought there was a chance I was going to have to kiss her ass tonight in order to get her to listen to me about why it would be stupid for Falco to have been behind the fire. But instead, I'm *actually* doing it.

And I can't bring myself to regret this change in circumstances.

I lean forward and press my lips against the warm globe of flesh. Kennedy jerks forward, her hands tightening on the railing, but she manages to keep her mouth clamped shut. I softly flutter my lips over the little divots in her lower back, then kiss the other ass cheek before I nudge her thighs open.

"Spread them."

My words seem loud despite the sounds of the party floating up from the main floor, and she freezes for a moment, her body stiffening before she finally tears her gaze away from me and refocuses forward.

She shifts her stiletto-covered feet out wider, and I grin as I turn and slide up under her with my back to the solid wood banister, placing myself in exactly the right position to see Kennedy Hawke in all her glory.

Her glistening pink pussy sits directly in front of my mouth, and while I don't want to waste any time diving in to have a taste, the mask currently covering the top half of my face is going to get in the way of truly enjoying this.

Down here between her legs, Kennedy won't be able to see me anyway. I tear off the mask, drop it on my lap, and waste no time angling forward to drag my tongue across her core.

Kennedy jerks at the contact, and she issues a low moan that has me digging my left hand into her thigh to silence her. Her body tenses, but she makes no move to push me away, doesn't try to stop me, instead spreading her legs even wider in those damn heels, leaving the invitation wide open.

Sweet mother of God...

Kennedy Hawke came to her family's event tonight looking like this with no panties on, and given how easily she fell into the flirtation with me, she had every intention of going home with someone or bringing them back to her place.

But even she couldn't have imagined this...letting someone go down on her while her family parties just below her and anyone could come up and find us. The wrongness of it all only seems to make her want it more.

I glide my tongue through her arousal, her taste coating it and making my cock scream for the same attention.

Jesus Christ.

I'd give anything to bury myself inside her right now, to feel her cunt clasping my cock and drawing out my orgasm, but even I know how stupid that would be.

Even stupider than what we're doing right now.

Anyone can ignore the sign indicating the balcony is closed the same way she and I did. Any one of her cousins, or her aunts and uncles, any one of New Orleans' elite could come up here and interrupt us. The damn mayor I saw flirting with her earlier could waltz up here and try to strike back up that conversation, only to find me with my face buried between her legs.

But I can't bring myself to give a shit about any of the potential negative consequences.

Not when this woman is putty in my hands.

Not when I have her exactly where I want her.

Not when one of the Hawkes is completely at my mercy.

I probe my tongue into her cunt and hear the wood creak as her hands tighten on it directly above me. Somehow, she manages to remain silent, but as I slip two fingers up into her while my tongue laves and flicks at her clit, a gasp of pleasure followed by a low groan fills the space around us.

She better hope the acoustics aren't as good as I think they are, or we will have a very captive audience. There won't be any hiding what we're up to, despite the wooden railing blocking me and her lower half from view.

No matter how much I may want to toy with her and drag this out, we don't have the time. Every moment we're up here, the closer we come to detection.

I start a relentless pursuit of her orgasm, licking and sucking on her flesh while I thrust up into her in a slow, determined rhythm. Her legs start to shake, the warm flesh against my cheeks, and her hips begin to move, rolling against my face as she seeks the thing I'm determined to give her.

Her pussy clenches and ripples around my fingers, searching for something that isn't there. Something she wants as much as I do.

Christ, I should have just dragged her onto the floor and fucked her.

It would have released the tension between us—that she doesn't even know the half of. But I couldn't risk it. Not with so much at stake.

I was terrified that as soon as she figured out who I was, she would throw me off the balcony and down onto the partygoers. Now I have my opening, my chance to prove to her that Falco Enterprises and I had nothing to do with that fire. The Hawkes need to understand there's another danger out there, while the only danger right now is that I'm going to blow my load in my fucking tux pants.

My cock aches and twitches so badly that it feels like having Kennedy Hawke's pussy against my mouth must be some sort of cosmic torture divined to punish me for what I've been helping Falco do to her family.

Her entire body goes rigid.

She's close. So close. Barely clinging to her self-control.

Her thrusts against my face grow more aggressive, demanding.

I continue to probe my tongue inside her and suck her clit between my lips. Her pelvis bucks, and I graze my teeth along her flesh gently.

It's all it takes for her to detonate.

Her hips slam against me, and I wrap my free hand around her thighs to hold her up as her body twitches and undulates.

Head dropped, she bites her bottom lip, keeping herself from crying out. Her fingers tighten on the banister, and her cunt ripples along my fingers.

Fuck.

I barely hold back, my steely self-control the only thing keeping me from coming myself as she comes down my throat.

Wave after wave ripples through her until she finally stills and sags slightly, but I don't relent. I lap at her release, licking away every drop from her thighs and cunt while she twitches with each gentle caress.

She reaches down and pushes the top of my head, trying to move me away, and I glance up at her, keeping my face buried between her legs.

Lust-soaked, hooded blue eyes stare down at me, her lips parted slightly, cheeks pink, and a flush rising up her neck. A challenge lies in her gaze, as if she's asking me *what now.*

As if I fucking know.

I slide down under her, replacing the mask to maintain my anonymity as I climb back to my feet behind her. My hand twitches to smack her still-exposed ass, but I force myself to grasp the fabric pooled around her hips and adjust it back into place, covering her like nothing happened.

Squeezing one of the globes firmly, I lean into her, licking my lips to savor her taste still lingering there. "There's so much more I want to do to you, *Cherie,* but I hope that helped take the edge off whatever has you so tense tonight."

KENNEDY

EVERY CELL in my body still tingles, and that hazy post-orgasm afterglow blurs my vision slightly. The ache in my ribs from the way I jerked so violently with my release barely breaks through the heady, weightless feeling consuming me.

The party continues below—people dancing and laughing, completely oblivious to the debauchery taking place above them.

What the hell just happened?

I glance over my shoulder at the man who shattered me without even giving me his name, blinking rapidly to try to clear my head. Those mossy-green eyes of his dance with humor, and he licks his lips like a wild cat who just enjoyed a delicious meal.

The smug bastard loves this.

Utterly destroying me...

Publicly...

With my entire family below us...

He's reveling in what he did to me—far more than sexually. This man got me all riled up in defending myself and then brought me down by obliterating me with a mind-numbing orgasm.

He didn't simply get me off.

He *won.*

And he knows it.

The gloating tilt of his lips that were just pressed against my pussy screams, *I own you.*

And here I thought I was ruthless.

I clear my throat and try to shake off the lingering fuzziness in my brain, made harder by the fact that the sexy stranger has his hard cock pressed against my ass, and the heat of his body aligned behind mine radiates to my exposed skin.

Did he release some of that tension?

Fuck yes!

I haven't had a man work me over that well in a *long* fucking time, but his arrogance will only grow if I let him know it. "A bit."

Christ, I hate how needy that sounded.

He issues a low chuckle that vibrates his chest against my back. His hand comes to my hip, and he squeezes it. "You don't need to play coy, Kennedy. You can *admit* how much you enjoyed that."

What the fuck?

I spin to face him, narrowing my eyes on the masked face as I brace my ass against the banister and press my hand to my ribs. Somehow, I keep forgetting that sudden movements—or really *any* movements—aren't wise right now with the damage Atlas inadvertently did. "How did you know my name?"

The corner of his mouth quirks up, and he darts his tongue across his lips, lowering his gaze to mine like he's hungry for them. "I know a lot of things, Ms. Hawke. Your name is just one of them, and now, I know what your cunt tastes like, too."

Any loose, pleasant feelings lingering from the orgasm dissipate in an instant at his words. They don't *sound* like a threat, but something about this entire interaction suddenly seems *off.*

Approaching me alone...

The mask to hide his identity...

Goosebumps pebble over my skin, and I shiver. "Who *are* you?"

"*Hey, Ken!*" Dad's voice carries over the din of the party and up to the choir loft, jerking me away from the mystery man to whirl back to face the banister.

I peer over the side and down to the main floor where Dad waits, the soirée continuing around him. "What?"

He motions for me to come down and points toward the stage where the band now plays. "Speech!"

Shit.

I've let myself get so caught up in this stunning stranger that I completely forgot about the speech I'm supposed to give with Dad and Uncle Gabe about the foundation. The entire purpose for this fundraiser, to gather funds to clean up parks, improve schools, and otherwise help parish residents should another natural disaster necessitate it, has so easily been pushed aside in my head so I could wallow in my shitty mood and then search out a quick fix for it.

Nice work, Ken.

It's possibly the *least* CFO-esque thing I've ever done. Though, I doubt it will be the last mistake I make in this role. They expect perfection, and there's no way *anyone* can live up to that—especially not me.

I give a nod to Dad, then twist back toward the man who has my knees still weak. Whoever he is, he didn't take the opportunity to run while I had my back turned.

He watches me cautiously, eyes raking over me with appreciation as he slowly backs his way toward the door leading to the stairs. "Sounds like you have to go perform your duties." His humor-filled gaze drops to my feet. "Be careful in those things on the stairs."

"Wait!" I push off the banister and take a step toward him, but my unsteady legs make me wobble slightly until I come to a stop. "Do I *know* you?"

There's something vaguely familiar now that I look at him more. Something about the jawline. The eyes. But whatever the memory is, it won't come forward.

That smug grin returns as he reaches the top of the stairs, and he inclines his head toward me. "Undoubtedly."

He disappears without another word, his heavy footsteps descending far more rapidly than I could ever keep up with in these heels. The very thing that brought on his comment and our little sexcapade now prevents me from chasing after him to reveal his identity the way I want to.

Fuck.

I hustle as fast as my heels and damaged ribs will allow to the top of the stairs and make my way down, hand braced against the stone wall to ensure I don't end up on my ass—or worse.

It may be too late to run down that smug bastard with the talented tongue, but I still need to arrive on stage without my face smashed up by these old steps. That would be an embarrassment I would never live down—as will letting a stranger eat me out at one of our events if anyone ever finds out what just happened.

Who the hell was he?

The question rattles around my head as I approach the final turn in the stairs and the party spreads out in front of me.

Dad waits near the bottom, blocking my way. He pulls off his mask and raises a dark brow, concern making the lines in his face appear even deeper tonight. "Are you all right?"

I screech to a halt on the last step, my heel slipping on the marble and almost making me go ass over end. "Uh, yeah, why?"

He narrows his shrewd blue gaze at me. "Because you've been in a foul mood all night, and now, you're flushed and seem out of breath from a single flight of stairs."

Damn his laser-sharp perception.

Of anyone in the family, Dad seems to see through everyone with a single glance, and when he really focuses on you, he can read you like an open book.

It's always been annoying.

A bit invasive at times.

But he's the most loving, devoted, thoughtful person in my life, and he only pokes and prods at us all because he cares—probably too much. The man will make himself sick to get to the bottom of what's bothering someone, and he won't let this go until he's satisfied I'm all right.

"I'm fine." I force a smile that I hope he buys as genuine. "Just flush from all the champagne."

A plausible excuse.

Dad's face softens slightly. "Drinking away your problems now?"

The comment immediately raises my hackles. I throw up an annoyed hand and sidestep him onto the main floor. "It's a party, Dad. Shouldn't I enjoy it?"

He follows me through the throngs of partygoers who part like the Red Sea when they see Savage Hawke coming. "Don't be mad that I'm worried about you, Ken. You've been working hard lately, and all this stuff with Falco and the fire at the Grind seems to have you on an edge that could be dangerous to fall off."

The veiled reference to Uncle Stone's fall from grace needs no further explanation, but the fact that he's comparing me to *that* makes me fist my hands at my sides and walk a little faster.

Uncle Gabe waits near the stage, scanning around the large room until his gaze lands on us. He points to his watch as if to say, "We're running late," as we hurriedly approach.

Which we are.

Because of my shenanigans in the choir loft.

The mere memory of it is enough to send heat rushing between my legs again and make my clit throb. But that same unease creeps up my spine, thinking about the man who unraveled me so easily and then fled into the night.

If I weren't staring at Dad and trying to hide that anything is wrong, I might actually tell him about my interaction—leaving out certain details—so he and Gabe could help me determine who he was and what his angle for approaching me might have been. But this isn't the time to throw another complication into the Hawke world.

I place my hand on Dad's shoulder and squeeze it gently. "I'm fine, Dad. Really. Everything *has* put me on edge, but I have outlets."

He raises a brow again. "Like letting Atlas beat the snot out of you?"

That and letting strangers eat me out in public...

"Atlas did *not* beat the snot out of me. He got in *one* good shot."

Dad smirks. "That's all he needs."

No shit.

And I'll be paying for it for weeks with this damn rib injury.

Leaning in to press a kiss on his cheek, I fight my wince, so he won't see the evidence of just what a number Atlas *did* do to me in a single punch. "Really, Dad. I'm good. Let's go make this speech and finish this so I can go home and sleep off the champagne."

He offers me a half-smile that doesn't quite reach his eyes. The man who heads the Hawke family and is always so worried about everyone else and their happiness knows me too well.

Well enough to understand I'm holding something back.

But he's also used to that from me and knows pushing will only lead him down a dead-end road.

The other members of the family may wither under the piercing gaze of Savage Hawke, but he knows I'm more Mom than even *she* is sometimes. And he learned long ago not to push her too far.

Uncle Gabe approaches, his blond brows raised. "What the hell is going on? We were supposed to take the stage ten minutes ago."

I give him a tight smile. "We're ready. Sorry, I was...delayed slightly."

He gives me the penetrating look he typically reserves for someone he's considering shooting, but Dad moves past him with a sigh, drawing his attention away before he can question me further.

The last thing I want to do is climb onto that stage and spend twenty minutes kissing the asses of all these people who are only here to show off their money, but that's ultimately what we're after—deep pockets that can fill the charity's coffers and benefit the entire city.

I'll have to consider the mystery man and his intent at another time.

Maybe once my body has fully stopped singing his praises. Though, something tells me that won't be for a while...

4

KENNEDY

Pinching the bridge of my nose, I release a heavy sigh filled with all the frustration filling my body, not caring if the man on the other end of the line hears it. These calls are part of the job, what Dad and Gabe and the rest of the family rely on me to handle because they know I won't back down—no matter who I'm dealing with.

It doesn't mean I always have to like it, though.

On days like this, I wish I were more like Astrid—sweet, quiet, and focused on helping others because she genuinely *wants* to, not out of a feeling of obligation. It would certainly make life easier than always having to be the relentless, unyielding one.

Always having to be *on*. Always having to wear my CFO cape—and heels. Always having to be the *bad* guy, even when dealing with people I don't want to be *that* person with. But I know the role I'm supposed to play, and I do it well.

Everyone is relying on me now, which means ignoring the fact that this man has worked for Landon at Matthews and

McCabe for decades, and in that time, he's built and renovated dozens of properties for the Hawkes that have only helped us expand our empire.

I suck in a sharp breath and push away any reservations over what I'm about to say to someone who has been so loyal to us for so long. "If you tell me there's one more delay, I swear to God, Jordan, you're fired."

It isn't the first time I've had to take a hard line with someone who has been with us since before I was born—and it sure as hell won't be the last—but I've reached the limits of my patience when it comes to the things that keep popping up to stall every project we have lately.

Hawke Enterprises can't continue advancing and expanding when we hit roadblocks at every turn.

Jordan's indignant gasp echoes through the line. "You wouldn't fire me."

His confidence rankles my already frayed nerves. "I *wouldn't*?"

"I've been working for the Hawkes for almost four decades, and you're going to fire me over something that's beyond my control?"

I slam my fist down on my desk. "It *isn't* beyond your control. We've already had delays with the groundbreaking on The Hawke Hotel that were *beyond our control*, like Falco trying to fuck with our zoning. You've had plenty of time to line up the necessary workforce and subcontractors to get started as soon as those cleared."

Jordan releases a sigh. "You're right, I have, but—"

"No buts."

We can't afford any *buts* or excuses. Not when we have so much money dumped into the hotel launch. Not when so much has gone wrong and we need something to go *right*.

"This time there is one, Kennedy. There's a worldwide shortage. What am I supposed to do?"

I drop my head back against my chair and squeeze my eyes closed, rubbing my free hand on my temple to combat the migraine starting to form. "You find a different source, or you find a different product to use."

"Oh, so you're going to approve me using an inferior product in order to get it quicker?"

Asshole.

He's trying to bait me, but it isn't going to work. After so many years of doing business with Dad and Uncle Gabe, he would never try to pull this shit if he were talking to one of them. He knows where that would get him—nowhere. But he seems to think that since it's *me* making the call this time that he can walk all over me.

Good fucking luck with that, buddy.

"Here's the deal, Jordan." I kick off my heels under my desk and turn my chair to the window overlooking the street outside The Hawkeye Club. "I'll give you until the end of the week to get this sorted out. Groundbreaking is set for the first. We already have the media alerted. We already have a thousand invitations sent out to important contacts and friends in the area."

Literally, anyone who is *anyone* will be at the groundbreaking and party afterward.

We need this to prove Hawke Enterprises is still on top despite the delays and fire at the Daily Grind. That we're still firmly in control of our empire. That it is only going to grow and not wither under whatever enemies may have their sights set on us.

"This is going to be a big event, Jordan. It isn't just a couple of assholes standing around, cutting a ribbon, and tossing a little dirt with a shovel. We want the work to actually start that day. We want the footings in place ASAP and the building going up so fast that people have to crane their necks to follow the progress. We need to make back the time we've lost. I don't care what you need to do to accomplish that, as long as it's safe and maintains the level of quality and integrity the Hawke name stands for. Do you understand me?"

A moment of silence makes me stiffen, waiting for his response.

He could argue. He could point out that *technically,* he works for Landon and Storm and Matthews and McCabe, and they would have to approve canning him, but he hopefully isn't stupid enough to try that with me.

Finally, he clears his throat awkwardly. "I do, but...what about your dad?"

I sit up straighter. "What about him?"

"Well"—he clears his throat again—"I, uh, usually deal with him on these matters. I'm wondering if he would approve of the changes we may need."

And I will forever live in the shadow of Savage Hawke.

Anger tightens my grip on the phone. "Well, you need to get used to dealing with *me.* My father and Gabe are not going to be around forever."

As Isaac so poignantly pointed out to me on Saturday night.

At the time, his comment felt like an inappropriate joke, but he wasn't wrong. The men who have built the Hawke Enterprises multi-billion-dollar empire can't live forever, and they've spent our entire lives training us to take the reins—with me at the tippy top of the Hawke pyramid.

I turn back toward my desk. "If you want to continue working for Hawke Enterprises, then you need to start dealing with me."

He mutters something indistinguishable under his breath. "I'll see what I can do."

"You do that."

I end the call with a frustrated groan, spin back to my desk, drop my office phone back into the cradle, and lower my face into my palms, releasing a heavy sigh.

"That doesn't look good." Aunt Caroline's voice draws my head back up. She leans against the doorjamb to my office, inclining her head toward the phone. "Who was that?"

"Jordan."

One of her brunette brows rises. "Jordan Black?"

I nod.

She laughs, humor dancing in her green eyes. "I don't think I've ever heard Savage talk to him like that."

I snort and shake my head, offering her a grin. "I'm sure he has, over the years. Many times. My dad isn't exactly known for going easy on people."

"No, no, he isn't." Caroline chuckles lightly. "Well, I just wanted to update you on the RSVPs for the groundbreaking."

I groan, sitting back in my chair. "How many people are we going to disappoint if Jordan can't get his shit together?"

She shrugs and wanders into my office, slowly lowering herself into one of the high-backs facing my desk. "Out of the thousand invitations we've sent, I've had five hundred confirmed, two hundred maybes, and a bunch we still need to follow up with."

My gut tightens. "That's a fuck-load of people if we can't actually do the groundbreaking."

She offers a slight shrug. "We could always do the ceremonial thing and then—"

"No." I shake my head. "We are not doing the stupid ribbon cutting, fake smiles, then sending everyone on their way only to have the lot sit empty for months or years before any actual *work* gets done. We need all the machinery there, and we want that ground to *break.*"

She gives me a *you-need-to-back-off-a-tad* look, though she should be just as used to my fiery responses as Dad is, considering she's Mom's best friend.

"You know how important this is to us, Aunt Care. With everything Falco's been trying to do to interfere with us, we need to get the Daily Grind open, and then we need to get the groundbreaking done. Those two things are going to make all the difference and be the ultimate fuck you to the fuckers running Falco."

She nods slowly. "I don't disagree, Ken."

Saint's massive frame fills the door. "Oh, there you are, Bambi." He wanders in and bends over to drop a kiss on Caroline's lips before he steps behind her chair and wraps his hands on the back. "What are you two discussing?"

I give our head of security a tight smile. "The groundbreaking and the Daily Grind reopening. There can't be any delays on either. We can't let Falco keep fucking with us like this. Judge Cramer put the kibosh on his injunction so we can move forward with The Grind. I say we do it Monday."

Saint stiffens. "Monday?"

Caroline's eyes widened. "I mean, I know it's ready, but don't you think we should put a little more fanfare into it? Have time to—"

I shake my head. "No, I don't. I think we need to show Falco that we're not going to accept any more delays at their hands."

It's already taken almost three months to rebuild it and deal with the injunction temporarily blocking reopening. Any further delays are unacceptable.

A slow smirk pulls at Saint's lips. "I heard Isaac and Judge Cramer really tore into that asshole, Cass Whitaker, in court last week."

I chuckle, remembering the smug grin Isaac sported when he told me all about the court hearing. "That's what I hear, too. I just wish I could have been there to witness it myself." I twirl my pen between my fingers, considering the Falco problem for the hundredth time since they appeared in New Orleans several years ago with their sights set on us. "Fighting them would be a hell of a lot easier if we knew who was behind all of it."

Saint nods, his annoyance evident in the tensing of his wide shoulders. "Believe me, sugar, we've been doing everything we can to try to find these fuckers, but whoever is behind Falco Enterprises has covered their tracks well. Holding company, after holding company, after holding company, going back decades in several countries that are tax havens and don't allow access to records that would show us any names."

It's the same non-answer we've had since Falco first appeared here, stirring up shit for us. And it still gets under my skin almost as bad as the mysterious stranger from Saturday night did. "This company has existed for a long fucking time, so what the hell were they doing before they came here to fuck with us?"

He issues a shrug. "I have all my people on it. Gabe has even sent some of his *other* resources to try to delve into it."

"Then why can't we fucking find anything?"

The hard set of his jaw mirrors my own frustration. "Because whoever this is doesn't want to be found." He smiles, his typically positive demeanor breaking through the stress we're all feeling. "I know you're not used to losing, Kennedy, but sometimes, it takes a longer effort to secure the win."

I shake my head. "That's just it, Saint, we don't have time. The longer we let Falco attack us, the harder it's going to be to keep fighting them. I made a suggestion to Isaac in jest the other night..."

Caroline chuckles. "He told me you want to go dump Cass in the bayou?"

Shrugging, I hold out my hands. "It might make them show themselves when they come looking for a new attorney."

Saint's eyes harden and lock with mine. "It might, or it could bring a lot of attention we don't need."

He's right, of course.

"So..." I look between the two people who helped raise me and have become family, despite not sharing blood with any of the Hawkes. They're as much a part of the success of Hawke Enterprises as anyone. Saint keeps everyone and everything safe, and Caroline's role as head of PR for the company has been invaluable over the years. If anyone knows what's at stake, it's them. "What do we do?"

Caroline offers a tight smile. "We keep doing what we're doing. We move forward on both these projects and don't allow any distractions."

Easier said than done when I'm the one who's been sitting here, fantasizing about what happened on Saturday night, alternating between reliving those moments of sheer bliss with a stranger and the ultimate unease that came with the aftermath.

Who the hell was he?

I've reviewed the guest list from the masquerade a thousand times and gone online and eliminated everyone I didn't know personally by comparing the photos of them I could find to my memory of what the man looked like, even with the mask on...

And nothing.

Whoever the enigmatic, sexy Romeo was in the loft, he intended to stay a mystery, and that's what makes me really fucking nervous.

CASS

EVEN AFTER HALF A DAY IN court and working on two motions that took more brainpower than I had to give, I still can't keep my mind from drifting back to Kennedy Hawke.

Days later, her taste still lingers on my tongue. The tiny noises she tried to contain still echo in my ears. And the feel of her thighs clenching against my face and her pussy squeezing my fingers makes my cock stir at the most inconvenient times.

How the FUCK did I end up between Kennedy Hawke's legs when all I wanted was to talk to her?

I scrub a hand over my cheek, churning over all the things I had intended to say that never got a chance to come out because I got so distracted by that woman.

Shit.

Letting my dick get in the way of my goal had never been a problem until the moment I laid eyes on her, and now, I'm going to have to figure out another way to get to Kennedy to have the conversation that was cut off by my tongue in her cunt.

My gaze drifts to the clock...

3:30.

It's late enough that I can head out without feeling guilty about only working a half-day. Besides, it's Taco Monday, and I still have to stop at the store to get the rest of the ingredients, or there will be hell to pay when I walk through the door at home.

I toss down my pen and push to my feet, shaking my head to clear away the cobwebs and the erotic memories. They'll undoubtedly return, just like they have relentlessly over the last few days, but I can't fantasize about Kennedy *all* the time. I still have clients and work to do.

The outer door to my office opens into the reception area, the sound of the squeaky hinge reaching all the way back to me in my office. I pause, waiting for Teresa to handle whoever it is.

"Can I help you?"

"I'm here to see Attorney Whitaker."

"I don't have any appointments down on his calendar."

"I'm a walk-in. But, trust me, he'll want to see me."

For some reason, the words send a little shiver up my spine even though I don't recognize the man's voice.

When was the last time I had a walk-in?

Never.

But this one sounds determined to discuss whatever brought him to me today. It won't kill me to hear him out, and I wouldn't be able to slip out of the office past him to my car without being seen anyway.

I lower myself back into my chair and wait, trying to push away the sudden unease settling over me.

Teresa hustles in, her amber eyes wide, and closes my door behind her. "Cass, there's a gentleman here."

"I heard. Any idea who he is?"

She shakes her head, her dark hair streaked with gray settling right back into place. "None. Do you want me to tell him you're not available?"

Want to—yes.

Should I—no.

People don't just "walk in" to my office, demanding to see me. My piqued interest won't be appeased until I know whatever it is that brought that man in today.

So much for going home early.

Releasing a little sigh, I lean back in my chair. "I'll hear him out."

Teresa nods and pulls open the door. She takes a step out, then swings her arm toward me, inviting in the unscheduled appointment. "You can come right this way, sir."

The older man steps through the door, his silver hair almost shimmering in the late afternoon light streaming in the windows, and my body instantly stiffens.

Something tickles in the back of my mind, a faint memory that won't come.

Where do I know him from?

He offers me a wide smile filled with perfect white teeth and turns to Teresa. "Thank you for your assistance."

She blushes under his assessment, then gives me a questioning look as she closes the door behind him, leaving me alone in the room with the man who already has me on edge for some reason I can't pinpoint.

I climb to my feet and extend a hand over the desk. "Cassius

Whitaker..." I raise a brow when he doesn't immediately introduce himself. "And you are?"

He chuckles lightly and approaches, sliding his hand into mine to shake it firmly. "My apologies for dropping in unannounced. My name is Damon."

I pause, expecting more. "Just Damon?" Still no move to offer a last name. "Like Cher or Madonna?"

He laughs and pulls his hand from mine, shoving both of his into the pockets of his dress pants. While he tries to appear casual with the move, the set of his shoulders and the cut of his suit say anything but.

At least ten-grand.

Italian silk.

Tailored to perfection.

It isn't unusual for one of my clients, but it *is* for someone who just walks in off the street to see me. Which only makes me more confident this isn't a random appearance at my office on his part. He was seeking *me* out specifically for some unknown reason.

Where the FUCK do I know this guy from?

I lower myself into my chair and motion to one of the chairs facing my desk. "Please, take a seat. Why have you stopped in today? Looking to hire an attorney?"

Damon slowly takes a seat and nods, crossing one ankle over his knee. "You could say that. I'm always in need of excellent legal counsel. But what I'm here to talk to you about today is one of your clients."

A chill instantly slides up my spine.

One of my clients?

The only thing rarer than someone walking in off the street to meet with me is someone doing it to discuss a client. Most of the businesses and interests I represent don't make waves in any way, shape, or form. Not enough to draw the notice of anyone else. But this man definitely seems interested in someone. And there's only one client who might draw that kind of attention.

I do my best not to shift nervously in my leather chair. "Which one?"

He gives me a wan smile. "Falco Enterprises."

Trying to school my reaction, I rest my elbows on the armrests and steeple my hands in front of my mouth. "Well, you know I can't discuss anything having to do with any of my clients. Attorney-client privilege."

Damon nods and leans forward slightly, dropping his foot back onto the carpet and waving me off. "Of course. Of course. I'm well aware, and I've availed myself of that privilege many times, so I would never ask you to violate it. But I am here to make your client an offer, and since"—he shrugs slightly—"I haven't had any luck tracking down the actual owner, as Falco's legal counsel, I assume you can get them my offer and the message that accompanies it."

Better to hear what he has to say than guess and be wrong.

"I could probably arrange that."

With all the shit Falco has stirred up in town, there are bound to be a lot of unhappy people—the Hawkes at the top of that list. And the Hawkes are powerful. They have friends in high places. Damon may be one of them...

I lower my hands and smile tightly. "Why don't you tell me whatever it is you'd like me to relay to my client?"

He grins, but it's cold and doesn't reach his soft, brown eyes. "Well, Mr. Whitaker"—he reclines slightly in the chair, now actually looking somewhat relaxed—"I can't help but notice that Falco Enterprises has been popping up around town with a flurry of new businesses, legal filings, now a massive hotel going in."

"Yes, that's all part of the public record, so I can confirm it."

His eyes lock with mine, stony and piercing. "And I've also noticed that all of these legal maneuvers, new businesses, and the giant step in building a hotel all seem to be directly targeted to compete with one particular family's businesses."

I still in my chair. It's one thing for the Hawkes to accuse Falco of it, quite another for a man to walk in off the street and do it. "I don't have any idea what you're talking about."

He chuckles, a low, dark sound that makes the hair on the back of my neck stand on end. "Oh, come now. As their legal counsel, you know as well as I do that Falco Enterprises seems to have set its sights on Hawke Enterprises. I don't know what they did to piss off your client, but it must've been pretty big."

I don't react to his statement. I just wait for him to continue, but he remains silent as well, staring me down. This man is used to people crumbling under his hard glares and pene-trating assessments, but I am not one of those people.

A minute passes without either of us looking away—an old-fashioned showdown. Typically, these happen in the court-room, between opposing counsel and me or with someone on the stand I have to break. Having it happen in my office gives it an entirely different feel. Cracking in front of a man like this would be *very* bad for me.

One more minute slips away before Damon finally allows a wide smile. "I like you, Attorney Whitaker. I can see why Falco trusts you so implicitly to handle their affairs."

"And what's the message you wish for me to pass along?" There are only so many possibilities when it comes to Falco. "To back off? Who are you? A friend of the Hawkes? An old business acquaintance of Luca Abello?"

It would certainly explain the vibe he emits.

Damon barks out a laugh that reverberates through the room. "Certainly not. I'm not here to threaten Falco or you. I'm here because I want to partner with them."

A few seconds pass as I process his words.

He wants to partner with Falco?

I shift forward slightly. "What do you mean by 'partner' with them?"

He shrugs nonchalantly, the expensive silk moving effortlessly with him. "It means that I would like to partner in whatever businesses they're operating or plan to in the future."

"They don't need a partner."

One of his shoulders rises and falls. "How can you be so sure if you haven't consulted with them about my offer?"

"I can speak for Falco Enterprises because I know their financials inside and out, and believe me, they're not looking for a partner, nor do they *need* one. They trust me implicitly to handle their affairs so they don't need to be bothered with pesky interruptions to their operations."

That draws a smug grin across Damon's face. "I believe you on that front, but I want you to pass this along all the same." He leans forward enough to drum his fingers on the desk. "I have a personal interest in seeing that the Hawkes' businesses fail, and it seems as though Falco and I share that. They can't possibly have unlimited resources, and mine are vast. I could sign paperwork today, turning over one hundred million dollars in cash to go toward the hotel. I know they've purchased the land and have initial plans approved, but they're working on lining up everything else, like permits. That money could definitely move things faster, couldn't it?"

Holy shit.

"One hundred million dollars" rings in my ears as my brain tries to process the sum. Falco works with huge sums and operates in the billions annually, but *that* kind of money, so casually dropped, is enough to steal your breath.

Who is fuck this guy?

I narrow my eyes on him, examining his olive skin, silvery hair, and intense, dark eyes, trying to figure out where I've seen him. "Do I know you from somewhere? I feel like we've met before."

He shakes his head and flashes me a grin. "I just have one of those faces. You'll pass my offer along to your clients?"

I nod slowly. "I will."

Pushing to his feet, he pulls a card out from his inside coat pocket and slides it across the desk to me. A local phone number is printed on one side. Nothing else.

I flip it over.

Blank on the back.

Damon inclines his head toward the card. "Call this number when you have an answer. I wish to move quickly, and I think Falco does, too. We would make a fine partnership. I hear the Hawkes are reopening their coffee shop right down the road from Falco's soon, and the groundbreaking on their hotel will be in a matter of weeks. Things are ramping up, and it's time Falco brought on a partner who can help them take the final steps they need to eliminate Hawke Enterprises from New Orleans."

I swallow thickly as I stare at the number, then look back up at the man. "You really think they can be eliminated?"

He flashes me another cold grin. "Anyone can be eliminated. You just have to make the right moves at the right time. I'll expect to hear from you soon."

Flipping the card between my fingers, I watch Damon stalk to the door, pull it open, and disappear into the waiting area.

What the fuck was that?

Besides the strangest meeting I've ever had.

It hits me like a freight train, the sudden image of *that* man in my memory bank.

I know where I saw him...

Drinking coffee at one of the bistro tables outside Hawke's Daily Grind. But it still doesn't explain who he really is or what he's up to.

Marcel's words from the other day trickle back into my head. "*Someone is definitely moving on Roselli.*"

Could it be Damon?

Even if he *is* somehow connected to the attacks on Roselli, there isn't any obvious reason he would care about the Hawkes. I can't make sense of it, but maybe there's someone who can.

I toss the card onto my desk and pull out my cell phone, entering the number I easily found today, and send off a text message.

5

KENNEDY

Staring at the text message on my phone, my stomach twists the same way it did when I received it yesterday afternoon.

UNKNOWN NUMBER:

> We need to meet. I have information you'll want to know. I meant to have the discussion with you the other night, but I was distracted by the taste of your cunt.

A shiver rolls through me reading it, as it has every time I've looked at it in the twenty-four hours since it popped up on my phone. I scan over our brief conversation, even though I know exactly what it says by heart after rereading it a hundred times.

> Who are you? How did you get this number?

UNKNOWN NUMBER:

> Meet me at The Shanty in Cut Off at 7:00 PM tomorrow and find out.

The rickety old building set out on stilts over the bayou housing The Shanty stands in front of me...and it *screams* at me to turn around and *RUN* back to my car.

You're fucking crazy for coming here alone to meet with that man...

You have no idea who he is or what he wants...

Yet, I still came running to the man who knew exactly who I was but who intentionally kept his identity a secret while he seduced me only feet away from my entire family.

Because of the mystery or because I can't stop thinking about what he did to me?

Saying it's the former would be a lie. With the way I haven't been able to stop thinking about his mouth on my core, his tongue flicking my clit expertly, I don't stand a *chance* of getting the man out of my head without knowing who he is and finding out *why* that happened. Besides me making shitty decisions while I'm hopelessly horny and full of champagne.

Hence, walking into this *place.*

Where I very well might get murdered and dumped into the bayou without anyone being the wiser.

I slip my phone back into my purse and slowly make my way toward the restaurant, feeling overdressed in my skin-tight dark-gray dress and matching suit coat and four-inch heels that sink into the dirt and gravel parking lot with each step.

My footing falters, and I almost break my ankle before I manage to right myself and finally reach the front door. Sucking in a steady breath, I tug it open and step inside the dingy establishment.

The smell of fresh fried seafood hits me immediately, and my stomach grumbles, reminding me all I've had today is four cups of coffee. Between all the stress and endless caffeine fuel, it's a wonder I don't have ulcers.

Maybe I can at least get something to eat before he murders me and dumps me into the water for the gators.

I shouldn't laugh at my own dark thoughts, but I do as I make my way farther inside. It draws a strange look from the hostess who stands straight ahead, talking with one of the waitstaff behind a handmade podium that looks ready to topple over with a slight breeze, just like the entire restaurant does.

Shit.

The dim lighting makes it difficult to see too far into the establishment, but I scan the bar stools and tables that are visible for anyone who looks even slightly like the man from Saturday night.

Sandy-blond hair.

Piercing green eyes.

Those sinful lips.

I try to picture everyone I see with a mask covering the upper half of their face, and someone sidles up next to me. An arm brushes against mine, sending a little jolt of electricity through me, and I start to jerk away, but a large, warm hand settles around my hip and squeezes.

"Running off somewhere? We haven't even had a chance to talk, *Cherie*."

That same voice—velvet and gravel all rolled into one—directly in my ear makes my pussy clench and brings the same rush of memories that's been drowning me since I stumbled out of that choir loft.

I whirl to face the man who's had me at such odds for the last few days, trying to figure out what the hell happened and how I ended up with a stranger's face between my legs.

Holy shit!

We may never have met in person before, but I know the face well from viewing it on his law firm's website a hundred times and seeing it spread across the papers every time he made a grandstand opposing the Hawkes.

"*You!*"

Cassius fucking Whitaker.

I shove his hand off my waist. "It was *you?*"

The corners of his mouth twitch like he can't fight his smile at my reaction. He holds up a hand to stop me from saying anything else. "Before you delve into whatever tirade you have sitting between those pretty lips of yours, let's sit down and get something to eat. We have a lot to discuss."

"We have *nothing* to discuss."

His face hardens for a moment, and he takes a step toward me, leaning down so the hostess won't hear us. "Don't walk out of here in those sexy heels without hearing what I have to say first, Kennedy. Please, you owe me at least that after what I did for you the other night."

Fuck, what he did to me the other night...

As if I could forget.

Now that I know who it was, all I *want* to do is forget it and pretend it was all some nightmarish erotic dream, but my stomach rumbles again.

Cass glances down at it. "Have you eaten today?"

I shake my head. "No."

His lips curl slightly. "Then, let's go eat." He dips his head close to my ear again. "I promise if you still want to, you can spear me with one of those stilettos on the way out."

I scowl at him. "Oh, I *will* want to. No doubt about that."

He grins and presses his hand against my lower back as he leads me through the restaurant, following the hostess. The heat of his palm seeps through my dress, warmth spreading from that simple point of contact.

It *should* be the searing fire of hate burning through me.

Should be...but definitely isn't.

The hostess unceremoniously dumps two menus on a rickety table in the corner next to grimy windows overlooking the bayou. I settle into a chair that rattles underneath me on the uneven, heavily distressed, hand-hewn floor.

"This place is certainly"—I scan the tight restaurant, from

its mismatched tables and chairs to random graffiti drawn on the wood panel walls—"quaint."

Cassius removes his suit jacket and hangs it on the back of his chair, then removes his cufflinks, drops them into his pocket, and rolls up the sleeves of his crisp button-down white shirt, exposing thick, muscled forearms.

Christ, why is it so hot when a man does that?

He slides into his chair casually, like he isn't taking a seat across from someone he's spent *years* trying to destroy financially. "Oh, come on now, Kennedy, don't be such a snob." Settling back, he crosses his arms over his chest. "First, this place has the best catfish in all of Louisiana. And second, I knew you wouldn't want to be seen anywhere with me, and out here, we won't run into a soul either of us knows."

I keep scowling at him, unconvinced by his argument about the fish or not being caught here with the enemy. But as I scan the restaurant, the few mostly local-looking people don't seem to be paying us any attention.

"Like I said"—he hands me a menu—"I suggest the catfish. But the jambalaya is excellent, too."

"You come here often?" I sneer at him. "It looks like just the type of place someone as low as you would hang out."

He barks out a laugh, drops his menu to the worn tabletop, and leans back in his chair, absently fiddling with his napkin with the same fingers that brought me to release. "You really think that little of me, don't you?"

The edge in his voice *almost* gives me pause, but then everything he's done on behalf of his client, Falco Enterprises. comes rushing to the forefront of my mind. "Why wouldn't I?"

"All the Hawkes feel the same way?"

"Of course."

One of his sandy-blond brows rises. "Even Angelina and Allie? What about Astrid? My interactions with them at the Daily Grind have always been quite pleasant."

I scoff. "Bullshit. If they were pleasant, it was only *forced* pleasantry because you were a paying customer. My cousins would've kicked you out with their foot up your ass if they could have."

He grins at me. "This is precisely why we needed to talk."

The waitress heads over before he can say anything else. "What can I get for you?"

Cass offers her a panty-melting grin that brings a blush to her cheeks. "I'll have the catfish and whatever beer you have on tap."

I scan the menu and cringe. "I'll have crab legs and a beer, too."

It's going to kill my diet, but I'm on my feet enough running around all day that I'll burn it off tomorrow, hopefully. Too bad my ribs can't put up with another session with Atlas in the morning. Just thinking about it makes them ache, and I absent-mindedly press a hand into my side.

Whatever it is Cass wants, I can't stay here with him any longer than necessary to find the answer. "So, what did you want to talk about? You have until I'm done cracking these suckers open and sucking down the crab meat for me to hear you out. Because if anyone gets wind that I had dinner with the enemy, I'll never hear the fucking end of it. They might crucify me—literally—or dump me in the bayou out here to be eaten by the gators. Which, incidentally, is what I'll suggest we do to *you* when I talk with Isaac on Saturday."

Those mossy-green eyes spark with amusement. "Ah, come on, *Cherie*. You don't mean that."

"I *do*. You think I want to be sitting here across from you?"

A grin plays at his lips again. "You seemed to enjoy my company on Saturday."

That same hot rush floods my body, just as it has *every* time I've relived our little run-in, and I squirm in my seat against a throb between my legs. "That was a mistake."

He arches a brow at me. "Was it now? And if I'd been anyone else, would it still be a mistake?"

I press my lips together, answering his question with a cool look rather than words.

Chuckling, he holds up his hands in surrender. "Okay, fair enough. But you're forgetting one thing."

"Oh, yeah?" I raise a brow at him. "What's that?"

He leans forward halfway across the table until the scent of his crisp aftershave or cologne, or whatever the hell it is, envelops me so completely that it annihilates the seafood smell in the air around us. "That I now know what your cunt tastes like, and that's something I can never forget, no matter how much you might want to pretend the night never happened."

Fucking hell.

Grinding my teeth together, I square my shoulders. "Whitaker, just tell me what it is you want."

"Here are your beers." The waitress drops them at the table and hustles away without a second look.

I grab mine and guzzle down a few gulps of the ice-cold, hoppy liquid to try to cool my body's simmering rage and that same attraction toward the man I absolutely *cannot* be attracted to.

Cassius grins at me and shifts back into his chair, taking an absent sip from his glass. "I want you to listen because I'm trying to stop a war."

∼

CASS

"Prevent a war?" Kennedy's pale brows rise, and then her shrewd, icy-blue gaze narrows on me. If looks could kill, this one would freeze my heart instantly. "What the hell do you mean, prevent a war?"

This is where things get tricky.

Even if I had managed to broach the subject on Saturday night, it probably wouldn't have gone very well then, either. She would have realized who I was and had me thrown out of the event I wasn't invited to in the first place before I could reveal the real reason I wanted a discussion. And now, after what I did to her, she's on the defensive, and maybe she has every right to be. I took advantage of the opening she gave me, clearly at a moment of weakness for her. It put her in a *very* compromising position, and she probably thinks that was all intentional when it truly wasn't.

Touching Kennedy.

Getting her off.

It was a primal need to take care of a woman who was so desperate.

Even if she wasn't mine.

She has all the reasons in the world not to believe a word that comes out of my mouth, no matter how sincere I am, but all I can do is try.

I take another sip of my beer and rub my thumb through the condensation on the glass. "My run-in with your cousins after the fire led me to believe that everyone in your family thinks Falco Enterprises was behind it."

She snorts and crosses her arms over her chest, pushing her ample breasts up farther in the low V-neck dress she wears beneath her suit coat. Professional and sexy. Exactly what Kennedy Hawke is at all times. "Why *wouldn't* we believe it's your clients? They've given us every reason to suspect them."

I nod slowly. "Suspect them, yes, but can you prove it's them?"

When she doesn't answer, I raise a brow at her.

She scowls and shakes her head. "Of course not, because they're too smart for that. But it doesn't mean they're not behind it."

"Or it means they weren't behind it, and that's why you can't find any evidence of it. Have you even once stopped to consider that?"

She reaches forward, grabs her beer, and takes a long pull from it, drumming her nails against the glass. "Of course, we considered it and pretty easily dismissed it since there's no one else who would want to do us any harm."

"No one else, huh?"

My mysterious meeting with Damon yesterday resurfaces in my head. I haven't been able to get it out of my mind since he walked out, which makes this conversation even more important. "I'm not so sure that's true."

"What do you mean?"

I lean forward slightly. "As you know, I'm bound by attorney-client privilege, so there are a lot of things I can't tell you."

"How convenient for you."

Her animosity only stirs my cock under the table. She has a lot of fight in her. This woman is used to getting in the ring—literally and figuratively—and she sees me as an adversary to beat into submission.

Fuck is that hot.

I run my finger around the rim of my glass. "I'm telling you right now, Falco wasn't behind it."

She starts to interrupt, but I hold up a hand.

"Let's just say, for argument's sake, that you believe that."

She scowls but lets me continue.

"That means there is someone else in New Orleans who wants the Hawkes to fail, if not worse. It means there's another danger out there. Another enemy."

And now, I might finally get to tell her what I intended to the other night.

Locking my eyes with her so I can gauge her reaction, I reveal what I've been doing behind the scenes for the last several months since the fire—besides filing bullshit injunctions against the Hawkes. "I've had one of my guys looking into the situation."

Her blue eyes flare wide. "You *what*?"

"I've had a PI friend of mine looking into the fire and into what's been going on around town to see if he can get any sort of leads on who might be after the Hawkes."

"Why would you do that?"

I flash her a half-grin. "Because I'm a sucker for a pretty blonde with a magnificent cunt, I guess."

Her cheeks blaze red. "You did all this in the last three days?"

I shake my head and lean back. "No. I've been looking into it since the day of the fire. When Angelina, Jude, and Luca Abello almost slit my throat for showing up to protest Falco's innocence."

A scowl twists her lips. "They would've been warranted."

"Would they have?" Leaning forward, I rest my forearms on the table. "Why would I go to all the trouble, time, money, and effort of doing this if I knew my clients were behind it?"

"Maybe your clients are keeping that fact from you, keeping you out of the loop?"

"I doubt that."

"So, *if*"—her glares makes it clear she doesn't believe it for a second—"this PI of yours does exist, what has he found?"

I sigh and run a hand back through my hair. "Not much. Just that there's somebody in town who's been going after Roselli."

"Roselli?" She moves forward, scanning the tables around us to make sure there aren't any eavesdroppers who might hear us discussing him. "What does any of this have to do with Roselli?"

"I don't know."

It doesn't make any sense that the head of the mob here in New Orleans would have the same enemy as the Hawkes, but it's the only thing that Marcel or I have been able to come up with after so many weeks of digging into places we shouldn't.

Kennedy chews on the inside of her cheek, brow furrowed in contemplation. "We've heard the same. He actually talked to Angelina after the fire and tried to warn her there was somebody moving in on his territory, but—"

"But what?"

Her slender shoulders rise and fall. "Everyone thinks it's bullshit and that he was just trying to cover his involvement in the fire or force us into the partnership we've been declining for decades. We haven't been able to nail down anything on it despite our resources."

"Neither has my guy, but there's someone else out there, and for some reason, it seems they're gunning for Roselli and the Hawkes."

"How do you know it's the same people or the same person?"

I shrug. "I don't."

It would be so much easier if I did.

Not being able to identify an enemy you can *sense* is worse than staring one down. The longer this drags on, the harder the Hawkes will look at Falco and, inevitably, me. And I can't risk their ire being directed at me.

The waitress reappears with our food, interrupting the conversation, and we both sit back to allow her to drop the plates on the table. "Anything else I can get for you?"

"Two more beers."

She nods and disappears again, and Kennedy watches me for a second before her eyes dart down to the king crab legs on her plate. A mountain of food enough to feed two people. Her eyes widen, and her tongue darts out across her lips.

Shaking out her napkin and laying it across her lap, she gives me an annoyed look. "Let's just say I believe you, and that's a tremendous *if*. Why would anybody be after both

Roselli and us? It doesn't make any sense. We're not his allies.
We're not his friends. We're not tangled up with him."

"No, but you have a sort of truce, don't you? Haven't you
operated in New Orleans side by side with him for the last
thirty years, since Luca Abello stepped aside, without any real
tension or confrontations?"

She chews on a chunk of crab. "Well, yeah."

"So, doesn't that make you guilty by association if someone's coming after him, or him guilty by association if they're
coming after you?"

It's a loose connection, but it's the only one we can make
right now.

She shakes her head. "That's a big stretch. There must be
something else, or maybe it's two separate things altogether."

"It might be, but I don't want the Hawkes to waste their time
focusing their attention and fury on Falco Enterprises. I'm
telling you, it's the wrong direction."

"And I'm just supposed to trust you?"

I chew my food and swallow. "You trusted me Saturday, and
you had no idea who I was. You would really rather trust a
stranger than me when I'm sitting here, telling you this face to
face to try to help you?"

Her eyes rake over me, centering on my lips for one second
too long before she glances away. "It's your face I have the
problem with."

I chuckle. "I have the mask in my car if you want me to put
it back on."

"Ha ha"—she rolls her eyes—"very funny."

"I'm serious, Kennedy. I don't want to see anything happen
to you..."

The admission takes even *me* by surprise, and I trail off,
realizing how insane that sounds.

Her eyes soften slightly for a second. She takes several more bites before she finally pauses, another piece of crab halfway to her mouth. "Why do you care?"

Locking my gaze with hers, I hope to convey the turmoil that's been raging inside me since Saturday—since my entire view of her shifted. The woman I had hoped could be a conduit to Hawke Enterprises, to get them to back off the accusations against Falco so I don't have to be looking over my shoulder or worrying about safety, became something else the moment I touched her.

"Why do you think?"

She shakes her head and digs into her food. "I'm not going to let you try to convince me that this is anything other than what it is."

Here it comes.

Kennedy is gearing up to unload on me now, to unleash all the things she's been thinking since we sat down, to put me in my place—which, according to her, might as well be that murky water outside the window.

"And what's that?"

Her eyes dart up to mine. "A ploy to take the heat off your client. You're a really good fucking lawyer, Cass. Even Isaac says so, despite hating your guts. So, I know you'd do anything to protect your clients. Though, going down on me at my own fucking charity event was a little beyond the call of duty, don't you think?"

I smirk as I lean over the table toward her. "That wasn't for Falco Enterprises. That was for you...and me."

6

CASS

Kennedy's head snaps up, and she finishes chewing the bite in her mouth, keeping her eyes locked with mine. She takes a sip of her beer, watching me over the glass rim, and clears her throat, leaning forward slightly across the table. "And just how, pray tell, was that for *you*, other than maybe having some blackmail material now?"

Ouch.

It shouldn't shock me that she suspects that, given everything I've done on behalf of Falco. Threatening to reveal what we did together to her family would make for pretty ripe blackmail fruit...if that was at all what I wanted or intended.

"That's what you really think of me, *Cherie*, that I went down on you just so I would somehow be able to blackmail you with it?"

She stabs the tiny fork into one of the crab legs and rips out a piece of meat, shoving it into her mouth angrily. Her jaw works violently, her aggression toward me channeled into attacking her meal. "I don't understand how else it could have been for *you*."

Wow.

Given how brutal and brilliant this woman is in business, I can't believe she's so dense when it comes to sex.

Or maybe she really does think so little of me that she believes it's true.

I lean across the table toward her, lowering my voice slightly. "You really don't get it, do you, Kennedy?"

She chews as she watches me. "Get what?"

Ensuring her gaze is locked with mine, I point to my chest. "That was for *me* because I fucking love getting a beautiful woman like you off. I don't like seeing anyone in distress, and you clearly were that night. Getting you off and giving you that release was the best part of my week. You know what I did when I went home?"

She swallows thickly. "I don't think I want to."

I smirk at her. "You *do*." Smirking at her, I raise my beer and take a sip. "I jerked off in the shower, thinking about how incredible you tasted and fantasizing about what that tight cunt of yours would feel like on my cock."

"Fuck." It slips out of her mouth before she can stop it, and that same lust I saw burning in her gaze on Saturday night returns. She quickly averts her eyes back to her dinner and starts shoveling food into her mouth as fast as she can, avoiding looking up. "Well, I'm glad I gave you some spank bank material." Her hand tightens on her knife, and she finally glances up. "But if you ever try to use it against me, so help me, God, you will rue the day we met."

Even with all the wrath oozing from her pores, I only have one response to her statement. "I highly doubt that."

The day we met changed everything.

My entire plan to approach her about Falco went to shit the moment I saw the desire swimming in her Caribbean-blue eyes. I could never regret what I did to this woman, even if I tried.

Returning to my dinner, I wait for her to offer any more comment on what we've been discussing—either the potential threat out there or the fact that I had my face between her legs. But instead, she remains focused on her food, somehow ignoring the sexual tension that still vibrates between us while she works on cleaning her plate.

I push my half-eaten dinner away, suddenly hungry for something else entirely. "How was it?"

She crumples up her paper napkin and tosses it on her plate. "Adequate."

"Adequate, huh?" I chuckle lightly. "You cleaned your plate. It's okay to admit that I was right about this place. Just like it's okay for you to admit that you enjoyed what I did to you the other night."

Her eyes go icy. "Never."

Not bothering to hide my grin, I let my gaze dip to her pink lips. "We'll see about that."

She shoves away from the table with a huff, then grabs her purse from the back of her chair, pulling it onto her shoulder.

I raise a brow at her. "Where are you going?"

"Home."

"We're not done."

Kennedy huffs. "Yes, we *are*." She releases a heavy sigh. "I don't know what you hoped to accomplish here tonight, Cass, whether this was all some giant scheme to try to frighten me into getting Isaac and Stone to back off you in court by threatening to tell them about what happened at the fundraiser, but what I do know is that I don't trust you and I never will. So, thanks for the dinner, but I'm going home."

She stalks away in her stilettos before I can get in another word, and I scramble to tug out my wallet and throw down a hundred-dollar bill, leaving our waitress a massive tip as I grab my suit coat and hustle out after Kennedy.

I tug open the door, and she's only made it two steps onto the gravel parking lot before her ankle turns sideways on the uneven ground.

Those fucking heels.

Somehow, I manage to lunge and catch her upper arm, keeping her upright. It takes her a moment to fully regain her footing, and then she tries to shake off my hold on her.

I tighten my grip on her bicep, leaning in. "Those heels are trying to kill you."

She scowls at me. "Wrong. Falco Enterprises is."

The fire she shoots at me in her glare makes me release my hold, but I keep pace with her as she beelines toward a black Mercedes on the far side of the lot directly under the lamp. At least she was smart enough to park where there was light, even if it meant a longer walk on the uneven ground in her Louboutins.

"I can't believe you still really think that, Kennedy."

Her steps falter slightly.

Maybe I have hit a nerve. Maybe I've somehow gotten through to her, despite how she's acting right now. Maybe she can see that her jabs at me aren't warranted at all.

Or maybe that's just wishful thinking...

We reach her car, and she beeps it unlocked, then throws her purse in before turning to face me, standing in the open driver's side door.

"I don't know what to think, Cass. You have every reason to lie to us, and I have every reason not to believe anything that comes out of your mouth. You've done nothing but make my life and the lives of everyone I love difficult since the day your client started stirring up shit. If you really want me to believe that Falco wasn't behind what happened to the Daily Grind, you're going to have to find proof of who *was*. Until then, I'll remain skeptical and continue to hate your guts."

I stare at her, searching her face for a crack in the hard armor she's put up around herself, but she's built it solidly. It's been in place for so long that she doesn't even know *how* to let it down when she wants to.

"I know what you do for your family, Kennedy. I know how much your father expects from you, and the reason I came to you at that party instead of to him or to one of your uncles or cousins is that I thought you might actually listen to me. I thought you might have some common sense and be more concerned about protecting your family than about your vendetta against Falco."

Her jaw drops incredulously. "It isn't *our* vendetta. All we're doing is responding to what *your* client does to *us*."

"Maybe, but you need to look past that hatred if you want to see what's really happening. I don't want to see you get hurt because you've ignored another potential threat and only focused on Falco."

Something flashes in her heated gaze, a hint at something she doesn't want to voice. Her lips finally open. "Why the hell do you care if I get hurt?"

The slight waver in her words creates a sharp pain in my chest, and I move in closer to her, pinning her against the car. I cage her in with my arms until we're sharing the same breath.

"I *care*, Kennedy, because I haven't been able to get you out of my head since Saturday. I had absolutely no intention of touching you that night, and I certainly never thought I'd have my face in your pussy. But now that it's happened, the thought of anyone else touching you makes me downright violent."

Her breath hitches, and that same lust flares in her gaze again as she stares me down. Those blazing blue eyes dip to my lips, then back up. "I wish I could believe a single word that comes out of your mouth, but we all know what a silver tongue you have."

I can't fight my grin. "I do have a silver tongue. You're right about that. And people pay me to make juries and judges believe every word I say, but you're smart and savvy, and I have every belief that you would be able to see through me if I were lying."

"What about my cousins?"

"What about them?"

Something hard sparks in her eyes I never would have expected from Kennedy Hawke—pure green jealousy. "From what I hear, you flirt with anything and everything that moves."

I shift in even closer, my chest pressing to hers. "Is that a hint of jealousy I detect in your voice?"

She gasps. "What? *No.* Why the hell would I be jealous if you flirt with somebody else?"

I dip my head until my mouth is next to her ear. She shudders as my warm breath hits her neck.

"Because even though you don't want to admit it, and you probably never will, you loved what I did to you the other night, and you want me to do it again."

KENNEDY

THE FULL-BODY SHUDDER that he can undoubtedly feel with his body aligned so tightly against mine is embarrassing as fuck, yet I can't stop it from rolling through me.

He knows he's right, and there's no way to deny it when he just felt the very real evidence of it.

Like this man needs his ego stroked any more?

He's good. He knows it. It's a wonder his head hasn't

exploded with that knowledge, with knowing I haven't stopped thinking about it since Saturday, either.

And this arrogant, pompous, bullheaded man pressing his hard, lean body to mine relishes the fact that he can do this to me, like he did with all those people standing only a few feet from us.

Just like he sets out to win in court, he intends to come out on top where I'm concerned, too. I can't allow that. Can't let myself succumb to his wicked mouth and talented hands.

His lips feather against my ear. "Would you like that, Kennedy? Would you like me to tug up this dress and drop to my knees in the gravel here to shove my face between your legs and lick that pretty cunt of yours?"

Sweet mother of God.

I shudder against him again and squeeze my thighs together, clinging to his shirt to keep my legs from going out from under me. Somehow, I manage to find my voice despite my suddenly dry throat and summon enough brain power to utter the single word I have to. "No."

His deep chuckle vibrates his chest against mine, and the feeling goes straight to my clit, making it throb for his touch. "You're such a bad liar, Kennedy. I do hope you're better at it in a business setting. Otherwise, Hawke Enterprises could be in trouble when you take over the reins."

The jab at my ability to do my job hurts more than it should. He's only saying it to get further under my skin, but it works. "The only one in trouble here is you."

He raises a brow at me. "Oh, I'm in trouble? I would love to hear why, Ms. Hawke."

I press my hands against his chest, the warmth of his body radiating into my palms. "Because you want something you're never going to have again."

The corner of his lips twitches, and one of his hands leaves the roof of the car and drifts down to the hem of my dress. His fingers tickle along it, making me twitch. "Is that a fact?"

Straightening my shoulders, I do my best not to be fazed by his proximity and touch. "It is."

"I'm never going to have this again, huh?"

His fingers inch over to my inner thigh, and my entire body starts to tremble, heat and moisture pooling between my legs, even though he hasn't gotten to where I so desperately want him yet.

This is a dangerous game of chicken. Staring each other down. Neither wanting to look away. Neither of us willing to give the other anything that might be seen as a sign of weakness.

I shake my head. "Nope. And you *wouldn't* have had it if I had known who you were."

He grins, leaning in until his lips are a mere hairsbreadth from mine. "Really?"

That same scent of something crisp and clean clings to him and invades my breaths, making it hard to concentrate on my words or how I *should* be responding to him.

This is Cass fucking Whitaker...

Remember that.

"Yes"—I nod—"really. You think I would've let that happen if I had known who you were?"

He shrugs almost nonchalantly as his fingers drift up between my legs even higher. I clench my jaw to try to will my body to stop shaking as he ascends agonizingly slowly.

Higher and higher.

I can feel the shift of the air against my bare pussy with each minuscule centimeter he advances.

Cass shakes his head gently. "I don't think that's true, Kennedy. I think you feel the same attraction now as you did then. I think you want me to keep moving my hand up, and I think that you are not the type of woman who would've even let me get this far if you didn't want that."

Fuck, he's right.

And I have no response that's going to make any sense when my throat is so dry and my body is so desperate for his touch.

The smart thing would be to scream *no* in his face and shove him away, but this carnal craving consumes me in a way that makes that damn near impossible.

Get it together, Ken.

Swallowing thickly, I steel myself against the fire in his green eyes. "Just because my body wants you doesn't mean it's going to happen."

"You still haven't told me *no.* You haven't asked me to stop."

Fuck.

Because I can't get those words out. My brain wars with my body. I want it so badly. I crave his touch, his mouth, his words. I crave *all* of him.

He presses his hard cock against my thigh, and his hand stops just short of brushing against my now-wet core. "I am not going to go any farther, Kennedy. Not until you admit this is what you want me to do."

I shake my head. "I'll never admit that."

One of his eyebrows rises slowly. "Why not? Because you don't like conceding weakness, or you don't like conceding weakness for *me*?"

"I'm not weak."

My insistence comes out far too defensive, like when I was a little girl and Isaac, Pope, and Atlas could beat me at everything, even though they were younger. It always stoked my rage and pushed me to work harder, to get stronger, to become someone *no one* could walk all over.

And I would have said I had succeeded.

Until Cass Whitaker stepped into the picture.

"I didn't say you were. I think you're incredibly strong to do what you do for Hawke Enterprises, to work as hard as you do. But when you work hard, you need to play hard. And we could play *very* hard together, Kennedy. Very hard."

Each one of his words is like an electric bolt straight to my clit, and I jerk against him. That grin that would've melted off my panties, were I wearing any, makes an appearance as his hand slowly slips out from between my legs and returns to its spot on the car at the side of my head.

"I am glad we had this chat tonight, Kennedy. Thank you for hearing me out."

I release a heavy, shaky breath. "Even if it was all bullshit?"

Cass shakes his head. "None of it was bullshit. I understand why you don't trust me. I've probably given you a very good reason not to. But I'll also tell you this—Falco may want Hawke Enterprises to fail, but it isn't their style to blow things up or physically hurt people. This wasn't them, of that I can assure you. And the longer you go on with the misconception that it was, the more open you become to other dangers. You may not believe it, but I don't want to see you hurt, and neither does my client. I suggest you watch your back very carefully, all of you."

He leans in again and presses a kiss to my cheek. My body returns to the tremble I'd only just managed to contain a few seconds ago.

A slow grin tilts his lips. "If you change your mind about my offer, you know how to get ahold of me."

His offer to play hard.

Cassius Whitaker doesn't seem like the type of man who does life any way *but* hard.

He pushes off the car, leaving me wet, wanting, and angry as fuck. The sound of his thousand-dollar loafers crunching across the gravel fills the night air, joining the croaking of a few frogs in the bayou.

The arrogant son of a bitch walks over to his Bentley and slides in without another look back at me.

Damn.

I thought things were bad before, but now Cassius Whitaker not only has blackmail material on me, but he also has some sort of strange hold over my body that needs to be remedied quickly.

Pressing my hand against my ribs so I can bend, I slowly slide into the car, gritting my teeth. Certain movements still really aggravate my injury, an unwelcome reminder of my weakness in the ring.

I lock the doors and start it up, taking a moment to try to regain my composure.

What I wouldn't give to be able to head to Atlas' for a late-night sparring session to work out some of what Cass just coiled up inside me. But that's out of the question while I heal. Instead, I'll have to go home and do exactly what I've been doing every night since Saturday—getting myself off to the memory of that man, only now I can add my searing hatred of him to the mix.

_____

7

KENNEDY

S taring out at the vast, empty lot, it's hard to imagine what will be here in only six months, despite having memorized the plans and stared at the scale model Storm created for years.

After we've spent years planning, altering, making adjustments, getting everything just right, the fact that it's *finally* time to break ground on The Hawke Hotel should feel like winning, but I can't shake the anxiety coiling inside me.

Could Cass be right about someone else targeting us, or is he just trying to divert suspicion from his biggest client?

That *should* be what I'm obsessing over—figuring out who is behind the violent attack on us. Instead, I've spent days reliving the feel of Cass' warm breath, talented fingers, and the press of his hard body and cock against me outside that dive.

Aunt Storm steps up next to me and nudges me with her arm, her sharp blue eyes assessing me. "Why are you so distracted today?"

I shake my head to try to clear away the images that have

been assaulting my brain since my dinner with Cass. "Sorry, just making a mental list of everything we need to get done for the groundbreaking." I force a tight smile. "I'm fine. Really."

She narrows her always shrewd gaze. "Don't bullshit me."

"I'm not. I swear."

"Uh-huh." She crosses her arms over her chest and watches Dad, Uncle Gabe, and Uncle Landon, where they review the plans spread out across the makeshift table that Landon erected between two sawhorses he pulled from the back of his pickup. "You really think we're going to be able to get this done on time?"

Considering the countless hours Storm spent designing the hotel as the project's architect and Landon has put in leading the construction, they both put a lot of blood, sweat, and tears into it succeeding—even if this wasn't a family project.

I release a heavy sigh. "I sure as hell hope so. Jordan finally got back to me and said he found a way around our supply problem."

One of her dark brows rises slowly as she fights a grin. "I am still shocked you tore into him like that and that he didn't turn around and call Savage immediately when he hung up with you."

Me fucking, too.

I snort and shake my head. "I made it crystal clear to him that he needs to get used to dealing with me."

She nods slowly. "He said as much when he talked to Landon about it."

My stomach churns slightly with the fear that I might have overstepped. "Is Landon pissed that I called Jordan directly instead of letting him do it?"

Storm shakes her head and brushes a strand of dark hair from her face. "Nah, it saved him the time and effort. Jordan's been with him for decades and acts as site manager for all our major projects at Matthews and McCabe, but sometimes, he forgets that he truly isn't the one in charge, that Landon is, and it's nice for him to get that reminder, even if it isn't from your uncle."

"Good." I release a relieved breath. "I never want to step on his toes."

She bumps her shoulder into mine again. "Yeah, right. You love stepping on people's toes." Her eyes drift down to my heels. "But only when you're wearing *those*."

"Ha, ha, *very* funny."

The guys finish whatever they're looking at, and Landon rolls up the plans. They all join us at the edge of the property nearest the main road, staring out at the massive lot that is soon going to become the home of The Hawke Hotel.

Dad narrows his gaze on me. "Is something wrong?"

I throw up my hands. "Why does everybody keep asking that?"

He sighs. "Because you've had a strange look on your face all morning, and you've been distracted the last few days. If you have any reservations about us being able to get this sorted in time for the planned groundbreaking, we need to know *now*."

Shaking my head, I run my hands through my hair. "No, it's not that."

Landon chuckles lightly, tucking the rolled-up plans under his arm. "I thought Jordan assured you that he got things sorted out. He made it pretty clear to me that he understood it wasn't an option *not* to."

"That's not the problem."

He raises a blond brow at me. If there were any hangups on the construction side of things, Landon would know about them. "Then what is?"

Cass' words from the other night echo in my head, and my gaze automatically drifts across the street to the empty lot that's been purchased by Falco Enterprises to build their competing hotel.

"I'm worried about that." I point across the street, and everyone looks in that direction. "And what it means."

Gabe's eyes harden as they return to mine. "We all are, but the only thing we can do is keep our heads down and keep moving forward on our own shit. Let Stone and Isaac deal with the legal end."

I shake my head. "It isn't the legal end I'm worried about."

One of Gabe's blond brows rises. "Then what is?"

"What if..." Worrying my lip between my teeth, I let my gaze drift over Storm, Landon, and Dad before returning to Gabe. "What if...we're *wrong*?"

Storm rubs my arm gently. "About what, Ken?"

Everything.

Cass was right. We *have* been focused on combating Falco Enterprises' moves for so long that we may not be watching for any other potential threats—against our businesses or otherwise.

I look at her. "About Falco being behind the fire at the Daily Grind."

Landon's brows wing up. "Why the sudden doubts?"

Hell.

I certainly can't tell them it's because I met with Cassius Whitaker and almost let him fingerbang me in the parking lot of a seafood shanty in the bayou while he tried to convince me it wasn't his client. "I don't know, just a feeling, I guess. It seems too easy, right? To blame it on them?"

Gabe crosses his arms over his chest. Even in his sixties, the man is a force to be reckoned with and takes ensuring the safety of every member of this family as his top priority. Along with Saint and his crew, the two of them practically oversee their own military force that handles security for all of us and the businesses. "Sometimes the answer appears simple because it's the right one."

I nod slowly. "True, but...Roselli tried to warn us."

It feels like ages ago that he pulled Angelina from the street to issue the ominous warning, though it's only been a few months. At the time, it seemed too far-fetched and self-serving. He wanted an alliance against an "unknown" threat to him and claimed they could be responsible for the fire at the Daily Grind. None of it made sense, and it felt like he'd just invented some enemy to force us into the relationship we never wanted with him.

Until Cass told me almost the same thing and suggested it's true.

Dad nods slowly. "He *did*, but nothing else has happened, and we have no evidence to support his claims."

Gabe's eyes darken slightly. "Except the fact that there *have* been attacks on some of his properties." He looks at Dad, then at me. "But even if it's true and somebody's making moves on Roselli, it doesn't mean they're also making moves on us. There isn't any correlation between the two. None that I can see, anyway."

I chew on my bottom lip. "You're probably right. I just can't shake the feeling that something more is going on."

Landon walks over and wraps an arm around me, squeezing me to him. "Don't look so worried, Ken. You really think Gabe and Saint are going to let anything happen?"

Gabe gives him a tight smile. "We've tripled security at all of our properties, locked down all the warehouses, put extra bodies at the clubs and the bars, additional cameras. We've done everything we can to cover our bases and watch our backs."

I glance at him, a shiver rolling through me. "Then why do I still feel so exposed?"

Maybe because we're standing out here, in front of this massive open lot that's going to be our future, with a giant question mark on it.

Dad finally grabs my hand and squeezes it. "I know you

only worry because you feel like it's your job to ensure that everything goes smoothly, but this isn't a one-woman show. You're too stressed out. You need to find a way to release it—that isn't letting Atlas wail on you."

I glower at him for the Atlas remark, but his words also bring up what Cass said the other night.

"When you work hard, you need to play hard. And we could play very hard together, Kennedy. Very hard."

Another shiver goes down my spine but for another reason entirely this time.

I force myself to brush off the memory. "But it's my job, Dad. You and Gabe built this company, and now, it's my responsibility to ensure things only go up from here."

He cracks a grin. "You say that like we're going somewhere soon."

I smirk at him and squeeze his hand back. "Of course not, but I wouldn't be very good at my job if I wasn't worried."

A car turns down the street and approaches, slowing slightly as it passes us. Familiar pale-green eyes meet mine for a split second before the Bentley continues on, does a U-turn, and pulls in front of the empty Falco lot.

What the hell is Cass doing here?

My stomach tightens, and I clear my throat and turn back to everyone. "Let's just make sure everything's ready to go. This and getting the Grind back open are my top priorities."

Along with forgetting the way Cass left me trembling.

I scowl and glance at the street in time to see the infuriating man climb from the car. Even from here, his broad shoulders and lean frame spark a fire low in my belly.

Dad squeezes my hand again. "Don't give him the time of day. A man like Cassius Whitaker isn't worth your worry."

A week ago, I would've thought the same, but now he has occupied my thoughts on almost an endless loop. I don't necessarily believe anything he told me, but it makes sense in some weird, twisted way.

And that has me more worried than anything...

Except maybe my attraction to that man.

CASS

THE BLACK SUV pulls up behind me and idles at the curb, but I don't pay any attention to my appointment's arrival. Not when there's something much more interesting across the street.

More than once since I arrived, I've felt Kennedy's heated gaze, but it's just as likely her ire as it is the lust I've seen causing it. It warms my skin and stirs my cock all the same. Either way, she's *looking*, and that's a step in the right direction.

I lean against my car, crossing my ankles as the Hawkes all pile into their vehicles and pull away from the lot that will hold their competing boutique hotel. Kennedy drives past me without glancing in my direction, eyes hidden behind her sunglasses but focused forward, her shoulders tense, and I fight a smirk.

If she didn't care, she would've looked.

The fact that she's trying so hard not to acknowledge my presence tells me she hasn't been able to stop thinking about what I said to her the other night, the same way I haven't been able to forget how her body trembled against mine.

Hopefully, I got through to her on the danger front...and the more personal one.

God knows I'm unlikely to get another chance alone with her.

She's on the defensive now and won't let down her guard again. The chances of me getting within ten feet of her again are slim to none. She won't make the same mistake again and get blindsided by me.

That woman is too damn smart for that.

When the final Hawke disappears around the corner, the back door of the dark SUV with heavily tinted windows swings open onto the sidewalk that runs along the front of the lot that will hold Falco's hotel.

I push myself off my car and approach the reason I'm out here today.

Damon climbs out slowly, buttoning his suit coat and running his hands across it to work out any wrinkles sitting in the backseat has caused. He steps toward me, extending his hand. "Mr. Whitaker, I was so pleased to receive your call. Does this mean you've spoken with your client?"

I nod slowly, once again examining the man who came out of nowhere to propose the partnership with Falco Enterprises. Just like the last time we met, his impeccable suit, perfectly styled silver hair, and magnanimous attitude give him an air of respectability, yet something about him doesn't sit right. "I have."

He hasn't given me any reason to doubt him, but his unwillingness to reveal his reason for wanting to go after the Hawkes means I don't know everything, and that isn't a position I like being in.

The only way to win in court is to be prepared for any and all possibilities. I have to know my opponent's case as well as they do and anticipate any potential hiccups that could occur so I can get in front of them.

That's impossible when the field of play isn't even defined.

Damon motions toward the empty lot that will hold Falco Enterprise's future. "Does the choice of meeting location mean that your client is interested in partnering?"

I follow his gaze out across the 100 acres of land. This is the future of Falco Enterprises...and it means millions in my pockets, too, as legal counsel for the entire project.

This dusty, empty space will change everything so soon.

Turning back toward Damon, I narrow my eyes on the man. "There are a few requirements my client has indicated are necessary before they can go any further in discussions of a potential partnership."

One of his silver brows rises slowly. "Such as?"

"Falco Enterprises will enter into a partnership with you only under the following conditions." I square my shoulders and lock gazes with him, ensuring he understands there is no room to waver on these. "Number one, Falco Enterprises always maintains veto power and ultimate control on any and all decisions relating to any projects partnered on. Number two, each project is assessed on a case-by-case basis. You want to be involved in the hotel project, and they've agreed to that, but on anything else, they'll have to consider the offer."

The corner of his mouth twitches. "Is there more?"

The smug tone makes me internally cringe, but the kind of money this man is offering is too good for Falco to pass up, especially when the Hawkes are already poised to break ground in only weeks.

"And *third*, a written clause indicating that Falco can terminate the relationship for *any* cause or none at all, at *any* time."

It's the ultimate *out*. Something I insisted on. The only true way to ensure Damon doesn't try to overstep or seize control. Falco needs his money, not his input.

Damon smirks. "And if they choose to execute that provision, I'm out everything I've invested."

I shake my head. "There would be a stipulation for repayment to ensure no unjust enrichment."

They're tough terms—I ensured that was the case. It essentially makes Damon a partner with no power. Anyone in their right mind would refuse.

Damon tucks his arms behind his back and considers me for a moment, tapping his foot, his Italian leather shoes shining in the sun. Releasing a little sigh, he wanders out onto the empty lot, scanning almost absently before he turns back to face me. "I can live with these conditions, but I have a few of my own."

Acid churns in my stomach, and I swallow thickly. "Such as?"

His lazy grin only further aggravates my unease. "I insist on being personally involved in the building of this hotel. I would like to be present for all meetings with any contractors, subcontractors, designers, or anyone else who plays a role in the building and running of the facilities. I don't just want to drop my money in and run." He gives a smooth smile, clearly understanding the intent of the requirements I've outlined for my client. "I want to monitor things and ensure they're going smoothly, not simply rely on *you* telling me they are. I think that's only fair."

Smarter than I imagined.

If Falco didn't need his money to ensure they get one step ahead of the Hawkes, I would reject his requirements outright. But as it stands, the only way of beating the Hawkes to opening is by paying off a lot of people behind the scenes and making things happen in half the time they normally would.

I nod slowly, wishing I could tell him to fuck off instead. "I'm sure that can be arranged. Anything else?"

He looks across the street over to the now-empty Hawke 150-acre lot that will soon be buzzing with activity. "And I want to ensure our hotel opens before theirs."

I almost choke on my breath. "Well, that's a tall order considering they've been planning this for half a decade and Falco only just bought this land earlier this year. We're in the beginning stages, only initial plans drafted, while they're already prepared for groundbreaking and have all their permits."

That same smooth grin that holds something darker under it appears on Damon's face. "I have no doubt that Falco has the connections to streamline the process of obtaining anything necessary to get our groundbreaking underway. Even if it means doubling my investment to make it happen to pad the right pockets, I want us open before The Hawke Hotel does."

Doubling his investment?

"You have $200 million to give to this project?"

Something dark twinkles in his eyes as he approaches me. "I have as much as we need."

Fucking hell.

The first time we met, I suspected he might have been a friend of the Hawkes, somehow connected to Luca Abello and his former life as head of the Italian mob here in New Orleans. He certainly exudes the same type of energy other mafia dons have, yet this man still hasn't given me his last name, which makes it damn near impossible for Marcel or me to run down any information on him.

"If Falco's going to partner with you, I'm going to need a last name. We need to put it on the paperwork."

He grins at me now and takes a step closer. "All in due time, counselor. I'll be partnering under one of my business identities, so that won't be necessary right now. Just know that Falco and I are on the same page and share an ultimate goal. This partnership will be good for both of us."

I glance over at the Hawkes' lot.

And bad for the Hawkes.

When I return my focus to him, he narrows his intense gaze on me. "You're going to make an awful lot of money off this deal, given your hourly rate, Mr. Whitaker. Why do you look so concerned?"

I lean back against my car and cross my arms over my chest, gazing out at the property. "Because I don't like surprises, and you are one. Falco Enterprises is doing what they believe is best as a business decision. It doesn't mean that it doesn't raise the hairs on the back of my neck as their counsel."

Damon chuckles and wanders back toward me, making me immediately aware of just how close he is. "If you weren't worried, I'd be concerned. A good lawyer always advances the best interest of their client, and that's what you're doing here. You don't have to like me, Mr. Whitaker, but you do have to work with me since Falco Enterprises likes to maintain their anonymity. That can only go so far, though. Eventually, they'll have to show themselves, and when they do"—he grins at me—"then maybe you'll get my last name."

He walks casually back to the SUV and opens the rear door, but before he climbs in, he pauses. "Draft up an agreement with the terms we discussed. My attorneys will make any adjustments as necessary and return it to you as quickly as possible." His gaze darts to the empty lot. "As I said, I want us open and operating at full capacity before The Hawke Hotel does. I don't care what sort of bribes we need to pay or what we need to do behind the scenes to make that happen. You're going to ensure that it does."

It shouldn't, but for some reason, that sounds like a threat.

That man shouldn't be crossed, and I know better than to ever give him my back. He climbs into the SUV, slams shut his door, and pulls away, leaving me alone at the property.

I've been here at least a hundred times in the last few months, but today, it looks different. Maybe because things are finally set in motion.

Or maybe it's because of the blond woman who was standing just across the street when I got here.

I've tried to issue her a warning—one she doesn't seem to want to heed. But she needs to. And fast.

I can't afford to have the Hawkes targeting me. I don't want to be caught in the middle of a war. I have too much to lose. Things that I'm not willing to sacrifice.

If the bullets start flying, they better not be in my direction.

8

KENNEDY

The elevator car doors slide open, releasing me onto the main floor of The Hawkeye Club that is as much my home as the offices above it or my own condo.

Deep, sensual bass thumps through the room, vibrating the floor. The melodic beat moves through me, making my entire body hum and my ribs ache slightly.

I don't need to look at the stage to know who's wrapped around the pole. After working here every day for so many years, I've memorized each girl's routines and songs and could probably replicate them if I ever attempted to take the spotlight myself, but I'll leave that to Maxine for now.

She's the expert, and though I may be able to do a *lot* in heels, dancing on a pole naked isn't one of them.

Casting a glance at her lithe body wrapped around the metal tube in front of a row of patrons tossing bills at her, I push through a crowd that appears to be a bachelor party and make my way toward the bar. Normally, the last thing I'd want to do after finishing an exhaustingly long day of work is hang out here any longer than I need to, but my desire to get the hell away from the office is hindered by the idea of being at home, alone with my thoughts.

And I could *really* use a drink.

Coen's familiar mop of dark hair appears bent over behind the bar, where he's busy mixing a drink. He lifts his head, his eyes widening slightly as I sidle up to the long, polished slab of wood that has been the center of the Club since it opened so long ago. He leans forward so I can hear him over the music and chatter of patrons around us. "You just stop to say hi, or do you want to drink?"

I release a heavy sigh and slide onto one of the stools, giving him a *do you really need to ask* look. "I need a drink. I didn't know you were working tonight."

He gives a little half-shrug. "Wasn't supposed to. Byron called me and said there's some sort of stomach thing going around, and a bunch of people on the schedule today called in sick, so here I come to the rescue like Superman or Captain America or whatever."

I snort as he pushes away from the bar to go make me a drink without having to ask what I want. He doesn't need to after the number he's mixed for me over the years.

With as much time as Coen spends filling in various roles at our varied businesses, he could do any number of jobs almost by rote, yet he still refuses to commit to anything. He's happy to be whatever we need him to be at any given time and seems to excel at any job we ask him to do.

Today, apparently, that means bartender. He slides a pomegranate martini across the bar to me, and I lift it to my lips and enjoy the crisp liquid and the alcohol immediately hitting my bloodstream.

His sharp Hawke-blue eyes scan the club. "You don't normally hang around here any longer than you need to, especially on a Thursday night. What's going on?"

I gulp down some of the drink I should be sipping at slowly to avoid answering his question, but when I set down the glass, he just keeps staring at me, waiting for me to respond. "Nothing."

Shit. That was a terrible lie.

Coen stiffens slightly, instantly sensing my dishonesty. "Did something happen at the site today?"

Of course, he would know we were there.

He probably should have been there with us, given all the time he's spent traveling with Dad to scope out the other boutique hotels along the Gulf Coast that will soon be our competition.

If he had an interest in actually doing it, he could help run the damn project and might end up managing the hotel once it opens, but he's shown no interest in stepping up to do anything other than what he has been for years—moving around the Hawke empire restlessly, never really settling down.

I have no intention of mentioning to him that he could have such a major role. Whenever anyone brings it up, Coen only gets testy and says he doesn't want to discuss his future plans, likely because he has none.

And I sure as hell won't tell him that Cass showed up at the Falco property or how completely thrown off I was after seeing him this morning.

Hedging, I move my hand from side to side. "Sort of."

Perhaps Coen might have some insight I don't or can talk me out of these crazy ideas I haven't been able to get out of my head.

Coen leans his elbows on the bar, scanning up and down to see if anyone needs a drink. "Do tell while I have a minute."

I run my finger around the rim of the martini glass. "I don't know. Do you think things have just felt...*off* lately?"

He narrows his eyes on me. "Off how?"

A heavy sigh falls from my lips, and I suddenly feel stupid

for bringing it up. Everyone else has already told me I'm over-thinking things and worrying too much. "I don't know; that's the problem. I can't put my finger on it. But ever since"—I hold up a hand—"and please do not take this the wrong way and tell your brother."

He sucks in a sharp breath, grinning. "Oh, Lord, here we go."

"Ever since Jack and Viviana showed up here, everything's been kind of a clusterfuck."

Snorting a laugh, he bobs his head. "I mean, you're not wrong about that."

"Aren't you worried?"

He lifts a dark brow at me. "About what?"

"About something worse than what happened to the Grind going down?"

Someone raises their hand down the bar to get his attention, and he smacks his palm against it next to my drink. "I'll be right back."

Coen wanders down to the other end and pours a few tap beers while I sip my martini and spin to face the stage. Maxine ends her set and glances toward the bar. Her eyes meet mine, and she tosses a wink.

I lift my glass to her and nod, giving her a smile.

Of all the girls who work at our various clubs, she's one of my favorites. Sweet. Down to Earth. A hard worker who spends her days studying with Astrid to get her bachelor's degree while she shakes her ass on the pole at night. Someone I might actually spend time with outside of work if she weren't an employee, but I have to keep things professional.

You weren't very professional when you let a stranger go down on you at the charity function you were hosting.

I wince and turn back to the bar with my drink, taking another sip.

Coen returns, leaning his elbows on the bar again. "You think Falco's going to do something else?"

I scan the club, watching everyone enjoying themselves so carefree. "Everyone seems pretty convinced it is Falco."

Coen recoils slightly. "Who the fuck else would it be?"

They *are* the most obvious suspects after years' worth of attacks on the business and legal fronts, but we still don't have any actual *proof.*

"What about what Roselli said?"

He rubs at the back of his neck. "I don't know, Ken. I feel like Gabe and Saint and all the people we pay to keep everybody safe have a better handle on this than we do."

"You're right, of course."

I'm just letting Cass get under my skin—in more ways than one.

It never would have crossed my mind that anyone else might be responsible, but as easily as I let him stick his tongue in me, I also let his crazy suggestion occupy far too much of my time. And after seeing him this morning, I haven't been able to shake what he said.

He knew more than he was letting on, definitely holding things back. Whether it was due to attorney-client privilege or simply because he doesn't *actually* want to help the Hawkes and this whole thing with me was just some game to try to get inside information, I need to find out what he knows.

It's the only way I'll be able to move forward and focus on what I should be spending my time on.

I drum my fingers on the bar top and finish off my drink.

Coen motions to my empty glass. "You want another?"

Shaking my head, I climb to my feet. "No. I should probably head home."

I definitely *should.*

It would be the wise decision—one I would have made before I met Cassius Whitaker.

I hate lying to Coen by telling him I'm going back to my condo, but it's a lie I need to tell. If I let him in on what's really bothering me and why, it isn't something he's going to be able to keep to himself. Despite his reluctance to commit to anything in his life, he is loyal to a fault to the Hawkes—especially Dad and Uncle Stone. He wouldn't keep my dalliance with our enemy secret for me, even with as close as we are.

No one can ever know about what happened with Cass.

Coen watches me with a keen eye. "You sure there isn't anything else?"

He's far too insightful and can see too much. If I don't get out of here, he's liable to crack me wide open and get me to spill all.

I squirm under his assessment and offer him a tight smile. "I'm good."

He drums his fingers on the bar top. "Really?"

"Yep!" I grab my purse and fumble around in it for my phone. "I should go."

A customer approaches Coen, saving me from any further questioning, and I push my way through the bachelor party again and step out onto the parking lot, the chilly fall air settling over me.

I pull up the text chain with Cass, still labeled "unknown number," and fire off the text I know I need to send.

> We need to talk.

If I have any chance of finding out what he really knows, it's going to take some time and effort. Convincing him to trust me enough to open up and potentially violate attorney-client privilege won't be an overnight effort, but I'll do anything to protect my family.

Anything.

Even meet with its enemy—who also happens to be the one

man who seems to be able to unravel me with one heated look or whisper of a touch.

But I can do this. I can get to whatever Cass is hiding. At this point, there isn't any option *not* to.

The future of Hawke Enterprises and the entire family is at stake and now rests on my ability to resist Cassius Whitaker.

~

CASS

KENNEDY PULLS UP to the curb and leans over the passenger seat to stare up at the house. I watch on the doorbell camera screen installed right next to the front door. She slowly climbs from her car, her eyes wide, and looks down at her phone.

Probably checking the address again.

"This can't be right." Her voice floats through the speaker embedded in the display. "No fucking way."

I tug open the door and lean against the jamb. "It's right."

Her entire body jerks, my voice startling her, and she fumbles her phone, only barely managing to catch it before it falls onto the street. She narrows her gaze on me, and she looks back up at the house. "*This* is your house?"

Offering a shrug, I grin. "Business is good."

She mutters something under her breath I can't quite make out, slides her phone into her purse, closes her car door, and makes her way around the back of it slowly, approaching the waist-high iron fence that runs along the front of my property and looking at me as if I might bite.

Which I might.

The woman *is* delectable in a way I never anticipated, and what this *thing* is between us is complicating things—professionally and personally.

She unlatches the gate and approaches down the walk,

moving effortless in her sky-high heels down the stone pathway to the bottom of the steps that lead up to the front porch of one of the most beautiful houses in New Orleans—and one of the most expensive. "When I saw the address in the Garden District, I assumed you were at a party or something and were having me meet you out."

I glance down at my simple white T-shirt and gray sweatpants, bare feet, and then raise a brow at her. "Do I look like I'm dressed for a party?"

Her eyes zero in on my crotch, and a flush spreads across her cheeks before she quickly jerks her head up, clearing her throat. "No."

Could have fooled me with that response.

I push off the jamb and step back, sweeping my arm. "Come in, unless you want to stand out in this chilly breeze all night?"

As if on cue, it kicks up, and she shudders slightly. Fall has definitely hit New Orleans, and while I welcome this change every year, it can sometimes bite.

She takes a tentative step up, then another, until she finally reaches me, pausing slightly too close. Her light floral fragrance wafts over me. "Don't get the wrong idea, Cass."

I hold up my hands in surrender, fighting the twitch of my lips. "I don't have *any* ideas."

At least, not any I'll readily admit at the moment.

She snorts. "Yeah, right."

Kennedy steps past me, her heels clicking on the foyer's marble floor. She moves into the center of it and stares up at the massive chandelier that hangs above and between the twin curving staircases that lead up to the second floor.

I close the door behind me and lock it, watching her assess my house with a discerning eye.

She turns to face me. "This is really your place?"

"No." I smirk. "I broke in and stole some guy's sweatpants

and T-shirt so I could hang out all night and hope you might message me."

A scowl twists her lips. "How do you—" She stops and shakes her head. "Never mind. I forgot you sold your soul to the fucking devil. Apparently, evil pays well."

I bark out a laugh that echoes a little too loudly off the marble, then motion for her to step to the left and into the parlor. "You said you wanted to talk."

She purses her lips and stares at me for a moment, almost like she can't decide whether she wants to accept the invitation farther into my domain or try to run. Finally, she turns toward the parlor and steps over through the sliding recessed doors I've already pushed open. "Jesus..."

Her eyes eat up the room, from the floor-to-ceiling fireplace taking up the far wall, to the Chesterfield couch and leather smoking chairs, to the bar in the corner, and every other piece of furniture, painting, and throw pillow.

I pull the sliding doors closed behind me.

A little appreciative sigh slips from her lips. "I have to say, as much as I hate to admit it, you have beautiful taste."

I certainly do.

While she enjoys examining every minute detail of the true-to-period furnishings, I spend *my* time memorizing every detail about her.

The cascade of blond hair.

The swell of her hips and ass in the black dress that hugs her curves.

The slope of her elegant neck leading to her heart-shaped face.

I grin at her. "I like to think so. But I'm surprised that you're surprised." I offer a shrug as I make my way to the bar. "Isn't your parents' house a lot like this?"

She snorts. "I mean, they spent a couple million dollars building it, but it pales in comparison to the beauty of this place." She runs a finger over the old marble mantle. "Their house is beautiful but more modern. I've always had a soft spot for these old houses. I love the architecture, the history."

"That must run in the family."

Kennedy freezes, looking away from the fireplace at me. "What do you mean?"

"Well, doesn't Stone have an old Victorian?"

She nods slowly. "Yes…"

"And I've seen Storm and Landon checking out my house from the street."

Stilling, she inhales deeply, then turns fully toward me, her confusion furrowing her brow. "What?"

I pour myself a drink and lift the decanter. "You want one?"

She shakes her head. "I'd rather keep a clear head."

I fight my chuckle as I recap the bourbon and take the drink in my hand. "Did you not know your aunt and uncle go on walks through the Garden District twice a week?"

Stiffening again, she narrows her eyes on me. "Really?"

I nod and take a sip of my drink. "Really."

"And how the hell do you know that?"

Shrugging, I lean against the other side of the mantle, giving her ample space since I'm still not sure what the hell she's doing here. "I'm observant."

Kennedy gives me a look that tells me she doesn't believe it for a second and moves away from the fireplace to scope out every other inch of the room, but whatever brought her here tonight, she doesn't seem too interested in jumping into it.

"So, Kennedy, what did you want to talk about? Have you reconsidered my offer from the other night?"

Her steps falter slightly, but she regains her balance and keeps walking around until she's put the couch between us. She drops her purse into the corner, then rests her hands on the top of the tufted leather. "What you said about there maybe being another danger in town…"

Not the reason I had hoped she stopped by...

I smirk and take a sip of my bourbon, knowing full well she's thought about the other offer I made just as much as I have. "What about it?"

"I know you're holding something back."

I chuckle low. "Of course, I am. I told you as much. Attorney-client privilege. There are a lot of things I can never say, even if I might want to."

She scowls at me. "Even if it might cost somebody their life?" Her worry creases her forehead. "We're about to reopen Hawke's Daily Grind, and I can't help but think..." She swallows thickly, shaking her head slightly. "I can't help but think what would've happened if Allie or Angelina or Astrid or one of their employees had been there."

"Why do you think I've been so concerned about making sure you are focused in the right direction instead of the wrong one?" I shove off the mantle and approach her slowly, keeping myself on the other side of the couch so that we're facing each other with it between us. "I don't want to see anyone get hurt."

"You don't think what you're doing in court hurts us?"

I grin over the edge of my glass and take another sip. "Business is business, Kennedy. It doesn't mean it's personal."

"It is for us." She straightens her shoulders. "It is for *me*."

"Yet you still quivered under my touch the other night." Her cheeks redden again at my words, only encouraging me to keep going. "You still *wanted* me to keep going."

She stares me down for a few moments as silence fills the room. "Maybe I'm a glutton for punishment, a masochist, or maybe I'm just fucking stupid."

I shake my head. "You are a lot of things, *Cherie*, but stupid is not one of them. It's okay to want things, you know."

"Not things I shouldn't have."

Her response comes so quickly that it's clear she's been

thinking about me just as much as I have her since the first time we met.

"Who says you shouldn't have it?" I raise a brow at her. "I meant what I said. When you work as hard as we do, you have to play hard, or you'll drive yourself insane. There has to be a break from it, some sort of release of the tension. And I can give you that release, Kennedy. I promise you won't even remember your own name when we're done, let alone any of the problems that are plaguing you now."

She sucks in a sharp breath at my words, that blush spreading across her cleavage, up her neck, and over her cheeks. Her manicured nails dig into the leather couch back, the slight creak of the material filling the air. "Just because you sold your soul to the devil doesn't mean I'm going to."

I bark out a laugh and shake my head as I slowly make my way around the couch to her side, giving her all the time in the world to move. She maintains her position, watching me with her head turned to the side like she's a helpless deer and I'm a bobcat about to strike.

Her body visibly trembles the closer I move, and I down the rest of my drink and set the tumbler on the end table before I reach her. I brush a chunk of her blond locks behind her ear, my fingers lightly feathering over her cheek, making her shudder at the contact.

"Why fight what you know you want, Kennedy? Devil or not, I can make you see Heaven..."

9

CASS

Standing this close to her allows me to witness, up close and personal, the way her pupils dilate with my words and feel the subtle shift of her body closer to mine, even if her words push me away.

That's it, Cherie.

Kennedy may not want to admit how much she wants this. She may fight it tooth and nail. Her years of anger at me for what I do for Falco may rule her head, but it can't stop what her body wants. When it comes down to it, she's going to end up in my bed tonight, and she knows it.

It's what's making her so uneasy right now.

She doesn't fear me; she fears what we could be together.

I didn't know what she wanted when she texted me tonight. It could very well have been to *talk* about what we discussed at dinner. She likely does have questions about Falco and the other potential dangers out there. But that isn't why she reached out.

Not really.

This was about wanting *this*.

To be close to me again.

To feel this same tension and desire permeating the air around us.

To see where it might lead.

Twisting a strand of her flaxen hair around my finger, I tug gently. "We don't have to keep fighting, Kennedy. It would be so much more fun if we didn't."

For days, I've imagined taking Kennedy in any and every way possible, lived in those fantasies every night while I lay alone in bed or when I took my cock in my hand.

Now she's here, so close, yet trying so hard to push me away and keep up her walls.

I lean into her and feather my lips across hers. Not really a kiss, a tease meant for her, yet my cock, already stirred awake by the woman simply being in my home, hardens fully against her thigh.

Something about the way she so thoroughly refuses to admit the attraction makes me crave to get her to give into it even more. To see her cave. To watch her crumble. To be the one who shatters her. All of it calls me to her, despite all the reasons touching this woman is a horrible idea.

Weaving my fingers through her hair, I hold her face steady. "Let me bring you upstairs and show you what you could have had after the fundraiser if we had been able to be alone."

Kennedy trembles against me, her sharp mind warring with what her lush body wants. With her scorching gaze locked with mine, I get to witness first-hand the struggle she tries hard to win. "You know I can't."

"Yes, you *can*, *Cherie*."

Frustration flashes in her eyes, the same one I saw there at dinner the other night. She isn't used to having her decisions questioned, and it makes her vibrate with barely contained rage. "You know what it would mean if I did."

I brush my lips against hers again. "I know what you *think* it would mean, but it doesn't *have* to mean anything. It can simply be taking what you want and allowing me to do the same."

She clenches her eyes closed and shakes her head. "I-I can't."

The slight hesitation in her voice only spurs me forward toward what I know we both want, what she's *so close* to reaching out and grasping.

"You can't?" I glide my thumb across her lips. "Or you *won't?*"

Her eyes snap back open to meet mine.

"And here I thought Kennedy Hawke would never be afraid of anything."

Those perfect lips of hers twist into a scowl, and she straightens her shoulders, as if trying to ready herself for a physical fight. "I'm *not* afraid."

I grasp her waist with my other hand and tug her fully to me, my chest pressing into hers. "The way your body's trembling suggests otherwise."

I tighten my arm around her, and she winces slightly, closing her eyes again.

Almost instantly, my body stiffens, and I narrow my eyes at her, concerned about her reaction. "What was that?"

Her eyes snap back open widely, as if I just caught onto something I shouldn't have, something she was trying to hide.

"Are you...in pain, *Cherie?*"

She presses her lips together in a hard line and tries to pull out of my hold, but I keep her firmly aligned against me.

"Kennedy?" I raise an eyebrow. "What happened?"

"Boxing injury to my ribs. I'm fine."

I loosen my hold on her slightly and lean forward until we're sharing one breath. "Then I'll just have to be a little more gentle with you tonight. But have no doubt"—I let my gaze dip to her lips then back up to meet the fire burning across her blue eyes—"the time *will* come when I will destroy you, Kennedy."

She brings her lips even closer to mine. "That's what I'm afraid of."

Me fucking too.

Things with Kennedy have spiraled out of control so fast that I'm not sure which way is up anymore, and the line between wrong and right has worn so thin that it's almost invisible.

That imperceptible barrier shatters the moment I crash my mouth to hers in a searing kiss that draws a long groan from deep in her chest. Despite all her protests against this ever happening, Kennedy wraps her arms around my neck and crushes herself to me even tighter, seemingly unworried about whatever damage happened in her boxing match.

This woman was born to fight. She thrives on the challenge —whether it be in the boardroom or the ring. And something tells me it won't be any different once I get her in my bed.

Which is at the *top* of my to-do list tonight.

I glide my tongue along the seam of her lips, and she opens for me, tangling hers with my own in a desperate pull, a war for supremacy that I have no intention of letting her win.

Giving Kennedy an inch means she'll take a mile—likely more—and I can't afford that kind of risk, that kind of *threat*.

I reach down and scoop her up into my arms easily.

She releases a little yelp of surprise into my mouth, pulling her face back slightly, panting heavily. "What are you doing?"

"I'm taking you upstairs."

"I can walk."

I issue a low chuckle. "If you think I'm taking my fucking hands off you for a second so that you can try to run away from this, you're insane."

Instead of answering, she slams her lips to mine again with a hunger that matches my own. I manage to pull open the sliding recessed door and make it to the stairwell before I push her against the wall to devour her mouth even more thoroughly.

My cock aches where it's pinned between, desperate for what I've been fantasizing about all damn week. All this time I've been watching the Hawkes, been battling with them in court on behalf of Falco Enterprises, I never imagined it would end up here with this woman in my arms, driving me absolutely mad with the need to sink into her, to possess her, to have and own every single inch of her.

She scores her nails along the back of my neck, and that sharp little bite of pain is what spurs me to pull her away from the wall and make my way up the steps as quickly as my feet will move.

I carry her down the hall and into my bedroom, kicking the door closed with my foot and bee-lining straight for my bed. As soon as her back hits the mattress, I sink on top of her, allowing her to feel the press of my entire body and my hard length.

Kennedy's throaty moan fills my ears, and she wraps her legs around my waist, digging her heels into my lower back.

I tear my mouth away from hers and take her face in my palm, tilting her chin up to me. "You're keeping those fucking heels on."

Flames dance in her already-heated gaze, and I take her mouth again as I reach down for the hem of her dress and tug it up to the top of her thighs. My fingers find her pussy bare again, moisture already pooling at the apex of her legs.

"Sweet fuck, *Cherie.* Just like the other night, you're dripping for me."

Her little groan makes me fight a grin, and I glide my fingers through her arousal but avoid hitting the spot where I know she wants the contact. "Tell me what it is you want, Kennedy? I want to hear it from these beautiful lips of yours."

She lies underneath me, her chest heaving, breaths slipping

from her already kiss-swollen lips, and my hand shoved between her legs, but the defiance still glimmers there in her gaze. Her need to fight me at every turn hasn't dissipated with her desire. The anger and the hatred she's had for me for so long, mixed with the lust she can't deny, all still swim in her Caribbean-blue eyes. "I want you to drop dead."

I bark out a laugh and lower my head to run a trail of kisses from behind her ear, down her neck, onto her partially exposed collarbone while I cup her pussy tightly. "That isn't what you want, Kennedy. Not really. Or maybe it is, but there's something you want *more*."

It would be a huge win to actually force her to vocalize it, to *admit* what we're both feeling. But getting it out of her won't be easy.

Good thing I'm not above playing dirty.

I roll my hips, pressing my length against her thigh while I shift my hand between her legs ever so slightly, just enough to give her a ghost of contact where she wants it.

She groans again, tossing her head back and closing her eyes. "I fucking *hate* you, Cass."

I kiss lower to where her cleavage is slightly exposed in the low *V* of her dress. "That may be true." I tug on the stretchy fabric until I find the black lacy bra underneath. "You may hate me; you may even wish me dead, but you also want my cock inside you right now, and I want to hear you say it."

Kennedy shakes her head, pressing her lips together so she doesn't accidentally admit it's true, but her lids flutter open.

I tug the bra cup back to find her dusky nipple hard as a fucking rock. Grinning, I lock eyes with her to ensure she'll see everything as I suck it between my lips. Her body jerks under mine, her hips twisting against my weight. I flick my tongue over the taut peak.

"Fuck." The word tumbles from her lips. "Jesus..."

While she bucks under me, I pull her nipple between my

lips and suck, my hand still wedged between her thighs, unmoving, keeping control. She rolls her hips, trying to find the friction she needs, but I keep her prone, refusing to bend until she *speaks*.

"Just say it, *Cherie*. Just say the words. Tell me how you like it, and I'll let you have it."

She tilts her head down, and I lift mine so I can stare at her and watch her when she says it. I move my other hand to twist her wet nipple, and her mouth falls open on a gasp, her hips bowing into my hold between her legs again.

"I fucking hate you, Cass. I hate everything you've done to the Hawkes. I hate the way you look at me and the way you touch me."

"And?" I wait for her to say the words, enjoying the way she fights it so fucking hard, but it's a battle I know she's going to lose. "You can say it, *Cherie*. I won't think any less of you."

Finally, she levels her gaze on me, determination and anger filling it. "And I want your fucking cock."

∿

KENNEDY

EVEN WITH THE mask over his face the other night, I've always been able to see the hunger in Cass' gaze, but the way he looks at me now is downright feral. Like whatever he sees pulls at every primal urge buried deep in his DNA to take and satiate his need.

Before I can open my mouth to tell him how much I hate him again, he slams his lips to mine. He shifts his hands from between my legs to shove his sweatpants down, freeing his cock, and I immediately drop my hand to it, wrapping around the thick base.

He groans against my mouth, rolling and thrusting his huge

cock into my firm grip. His fingers finally move back between my thighs, and he slips one into me easily, then a second, his thumb finding my clit.

My entire body bucks with the contact, a spark of pleasure rippling through me and tightening every muscle.

The man is winding me up so damn tight, and he's barely done anything.

Every move. Every touch. Every kiss.

Each designed to lead me down a path I won't be able to stray from.

He kisses me with the same wild abandon I feel when I look at him, when I know what we're doing and that we shouldn't be. He kisses me like he doesn't give a flying fuck how much his client hates the Hawkes, like he doesn't care who I am or the complication this creates for both of us.

It isn't going to stop what's happening now.

Nothing could.

He pulls back, and a little groan of frustration slips from my lips as he slides off the bed, but he quickly tugs off his shirt, tosses it to the floor, and steps out of his sweatpants, giving me the first glimpse of Cassius Whitaker in all of his natural glory.

Jesus Christ, he's a beautiful man.

The light streaming in from the window casts a slight shadow over every perfectly honed muscle, making it appear as if he were chiseled out of marble. His broad shoulders and wide chest taper down to perfectly ribbed abs that lead to a cock that will undoubtedly make it difficult for me to walk tomorrow.

Good God...

He's the kind of man who can make a woman lose control in a split second, and I clearly lost it a *long* time ago. There isn't any way to go back, and Cass promised to make me forget all my worries and show me Heaven.

Fuck if I'm going to let him renege on the deal.

His eyes roam over me where I'm spread on the bed, my dress hiked up around my hips, like I'm a feast laid out just for him, and his tongue snakes out over his lips as he takes his cock in his hand and strokes it. "Take off your dress, or I'm going to rip it off you."

Fuck.

I press my thighs together at the ache his words create deep inside me. "I like this dress."

A low growl slips from his lips. "Then take it the *fuck* off."

I reach for the hem and pull it up and over my head, tossing it absently to the side, and his eyes go not at all where I anticipate.

Not between my legs.

Not to my breasts pushed up by my bra.

Not even to meet my gaze.

They immediately drop to the bruises along my rib cage.

His hand stills on his length. "Jesus. That happened in the ring?"

I glance down at them and nod. "Atlas hits hard."

He stares far too long at the damage Atlas unintentionally inflicted, then shifts forward and kneels on the bed between my legs, bracing one hand beside my head and lowering the other to my purple and yellowed skin. His feather-light touches over the area make me suck in a sharp breath, and goosebumps break out all over my body. "I don't like seeing your beautiful skin marred like this. It makes me want to fuck him up."

My laugh echoes around the room. "Atlas would *kill* you."

One of his brows rises. "I thought that's what you wanted—me dead?"

I wrap my arms around the back of his neck and drag him down to me, pressing my mouth against his aggressively. "Not until you're finished fucking me."

"Jesus, Kennedy." He mutters the words against my lips, his

hand pressed against my injury delicately. "I don't want to hurt you."

"I may bruise, but I don't break."

He issues another low growl, this one full of hunger. "Good, because I've been dreaming about this all fucking week, and I'm not going to go easy on you."

Hell.

More moisture pools between my legs, even though I should probably be scared by what he might have planned, and he reaches between us and drags the head of his cock through my arousal and over my clit.

My entire body twitches with the contact, and I dig my nails into his nape. "Are you going to toy with me, Counselor?"

He shakes his head. "Not right now. Definitely later. I need to taste your cunt again and swallow you down. But I'm going to make sure you come on my cock at least a half dozen times tonight, too."

I raise a brow in challenge. "That's a mighty tall order, Attorney Whitaker. Don't make promises you can't keep."

Anger flashes in his eyes. "You still don't trust me, Kennedy?"

He sounds so hopeful, and I don't want him to end this before it starts. I almost tell him I do, but I can't forget who and *what* he is. This man has made the Hawkes bend over backward to protect our businesses and good name, and his client may have been involved in even worse.

That's who Cassius Whitaker is under all this muscle and sex appeal.

I shake my head. "I don't trust you, Cass, and I *never* will."

He leans closer, almost kissing me again, aligning his body perfectly to mine so his cock brushes against my clit while he tugs the cups of my bra down to expose both of my breasts. "Yet you're about to let me stick my cock in you."

"Because we both know neither of us is stupid enough to do

it if it wasn't safe for both of us." I dig my heels into his lower back, shifting his hips slightly and giving me that delicious friction my body craves. "I never said you weren't smart, just that I hate you."

"Good"—he growls low again—"then hate me while my cock splits you in two."

He aligns the head at my opening and thrusts into me in one hard motion that sends me rocking back on the mattress.

Holy fuck.

I drop my head back as my body struggles to adjust to his size. My lungs can't seem to take in air, heaving but dragging nothing in, and my pussy burns, trying to stretch enough to take him easily. I inhale sharply, attempting to force myself to breathe, but I fail miserably, losing my ability to perform basic functions while he's filling me.

He brushes his lips over mine, stilling inside me. "Fuck, you're tight, *Cherie.*"

Fuck. Fuck. Fuck.

I nod sharply and squeeze around him, trying to loosen the muscles enough that my body doesn't resist him. He kisses across my cheek and down my neck as he drags his hips back slowly, then slams into me again.

My head falls back. "Jesus..."

Cass reaches up and grasps my hands, pulling them above me on the bed, one large palm wrapped around my wrists, holding me in place, and his hips start to drive against mine in a hard, languid rhythm.

Not fast.

Almost agonizingly slow.

My body trembles with every brush of his pelvis against my clit.

"Faster." The world falls from my lips like a plea, like a prayer. "I *need*—"

He shakes his head, hovering his lips just above my rock-hard nipple, his hot breath pebbling it even more. "Trust me, Kennedy, when I tell you I know what the fuck I'm doing."

To prove his point, he rolls his hips in a way that makes the head of his cock drag along that perfect spot inside me, and I choke on the air in my throat, my pelvis rolling up to meet his. His free hand grips my hip and pins me in place so he can grind down against me exactly how he wants to.

My brain fogs, a white haze starting to descend over me as he sets my body aflame with his slow, sensual movements. "Wh-what are you d-d-doing?"

His lips move to my ear, and he pulls the lobe between his teeth and bites down gently. My body twitches at the sharp bite of pain, my clit throbbing painfully, too.

"I'm giving you what you need, Kennedy. A long, slow, drawn-out orgasm will always beat a quick, rushed one."

I shake my head from side to side, trying to move in his grip, but he holds my wrists so tightly and has me pinned so well that I can barely budge an inch. "No. I need it *hard* and *fast*."

"You don't know what you need, *Cherie*."

I open my mouth to try to argue with him, but he slows even more, ensuring I feel every single inch of him with each retreat and thrust. My body heats, all the nerves tingling with an intensity I've never felt before.

Instead of the quick, harsh orgasms I'm used to having with partners and alone, this feels like he's priming me. Building up to the point where he'll rip something from deep inside me that I'm not prepared to give him. But I can't fight, either.

Every roll and grind of his hips, each glide of his cock, makes my body tremble harder until I can't take it anymore. "Christ, for the love of God, please...just..."

He keeps going, capturing my words in his mouth, silencing me with his lips and the continued thrusting of his magnificent cock.

The man knows what he's doing.

Good God, does he...

It would be so much better if he sucked at this, if he didn't make my whole body sing and feel alive for the first time in thirty years. It would be so much easier to keep hating him.

He tears his mouth from mine, still holding my hip down and cuffing my wrists in his hand. "Look at me, Kennedy."

I squeeze my eyes closed tighter, gritting my teeth to stop myself from full-on begging while he slowly decimates me.

"Look. At. Me. *Cherie.*"

His fingers dig into my wrists and hip sharply, and I wince and open my eyes.

He stares me down and slowly picks up the pace, not sufficiently to give me what I need, but *just* enough to slowly raise me up another notch. "Keep your eyes on mine."

"I-I can't."

The green is too green.

The desire too fucking real.

I close them, and his hips still instantly.

"Open your *fucking* eyes, Kennedy."

God knows I don't want to listen to this man. I want to pretend he's anyone else, that I'm *with* anyone else, but his scent invades every sharp breath I take, and his sweat-slicked body gliding against mine while his cock fills me so completely finally makes me open them.

His lips twitch into *almost* a grin. "Good, *Cherie.* I want you to see that it's *me* that's doing this to you. That *I'm* the one who knows what you need and can give it to you."

He's too smart.

He knew *exactly* what I was doing.

Why I was avoiding having to stare into his mossy-green eyes filled with so much hunger.

He plunges into me again, his rhythm faster this time, pushing me toward something I'm not sure I can handle. The longer he pumps into me, the harder it becomes to control the trembling of my body, the shaking of my limbs, the desire to thrash and steal what hangs on the horizon.

His grip on me is so hard, I'll undoubtedly have bruises to rival the one along my ribs, but I can't even care. Not when I'm so close, when I'm right there.

"Tell me what you want, Kennedy, at this exact fucking second. Tell me."

I try to look away, try to bite back the words, but I'm too far gone. He wants to hear it, and it's the only way he'll give me what I need.

"I want to come on your cock."

His low growl of approval makes my pussy clench around him. "Good, *Cherie*. I want you to."

And suddenly, it's like a flipped switch, and he's plowing into me fast and hard, driving up with a little twist of his hips. The only thing keeping me from shifting on the bed is his firm grip.

The sound of our bodies slapping together fills the room, soft groans and muttered curses mixing with it.

It creeps up along the edges of my vision.

A soft white light.

A murky feeling of something heavenly encroaching.

I cry out as my orgasm finally reaches me. The blast that detonates is stronger than anything I've ever felt, obliterating my ability to breathe or think or see or hear.

My entire world becomes a piercing brightness that blocks it all out while cataclysmic waves of pleasure course through my body.

He keeps pumping into me, rolling his hips and grinding down to drag it out until he finally comes, roaring like the silver-tongued beast he is and collapsing on top of me.

10

KENNEDY

I wake slowly, my head still fuzzy and not wanting to come fully online yet. A little groan slips from my lips as I roll onto my side and bury my head under the pillow. Cass' scent permeates everything. So does the smell of the raunchy sex we had all night...and into the early morning.

The ache between my legs and the unfamiliar bed finally fully rouses me.

Jesus Christ, Kennedy, what the fuck did you do?

Reluctantly, I peel open my eyes and peek at his side of the bed.

Empty.

I release a heavy breath, but my relief doesn't last very long.

How the hell do I get out of here without having the awkward morning-after interaction?

All I want is to tuck my tail between my legs and bolt so I can get home, shower, and wash away any signs or memories of what I just did with Cassius Whitaker, before I have to head into the office and pretend I didn't fuck the enemy.

I roll over toward the side of the bed and press my hands across my naked breasts. Even though there's no one else in the room and Cass took me ten ways from Sunday, somehow, *now* I feel exposed.

Probably because whatever insanity overtook me last night has faded and what I've done has settled into the pit of my stomach like a boulder of guilt.

You fucked Cass Whitaker.

What the hell is wrong with you?

Apparently, a lot since I just slept with the man whose client is trying to destroy everything we've worked so hard for...

Get close to him to get the information we need on Falco and determine their role in the fire...it seemed simple. But I forgot to add, *don't fuck Cass* to the list of my own instructions.

I climb to my bare feet and scan the room I didn't have any time to see last night. Ornate moldings adorn each door, ceiling, and baseboard, and my eyes drift over the antique furniture until I spot my dress, carefully laid over a chair in the corner, like he picked it up off the floor so it wouldn't get any more wrinkled than it already was by the time he did it. My purse, which I left on the couch downstairs, and my bra lie next to it, bringing memories of his lips and skilled hands on my breasts.

A little zing of something I hate far too much shoots through me at the simple gesture, and feelings rush through my body again.

The man is sexy as fuck, is a generous-as-hell lover, has a beautiful house, has manners, *and* seems to actually care about little shit like this.

Don't let it distract you from why you came.

Cass didn't offer up anything helpful last night, and I don't have the energy to try to pry something out of him this morning—nor do I want to face him after how he destroyed me so easily and made me toss away all my resolve to withstand his charms.

I slip on my dress as fast as I can, the evidence of what we did last night still very much between my legs. My heels sit next to the chair, stood upright by the same talented hands that worked me over.

Shit, shit, shit.

With these hardwood floors, I don't dare slip back on my shoes so he can hear me coming. If I have any chance of getting out of here without running into him, I need to be fast and silent.

Float like a butterfly...

Not exactly what my training in the ring was designed for, but it could do me some good all the same this morning.

I tiptoe to the door and ease it open slowly, listening for any signs of movement, but the house remains silent. If I didn't already know Cass is awake, I'd think he was sound asleep somewhere, leaving me to make an easy escape. But I'm not stupid enough to believe anything with Cass will ever be easy.

My best hope of getting out of here unscathed by his scorching gaze is to find a back stairway and less conspicuous door that doesn't make me walk right down the front stairs, through the gate, and to my car parked on the street.

Instead of heading down the way he carried me up last night, I make my way to the other end of the hallway, past row after row of closed doors, until I find what I'm looking for—a back set of stairs.

Thank God.

I hustle down them quickly, trying to stay light on my toes so I don't make a sound, but halfway down, the step releases a giant creak. Cringing, I freeze, listening for any sound or movement from above or below.

Only silence greets me, and I release a relieved breath and continue until my feet hit the marble floor of a kitchen at the bottom. The back door stands only five feet away, and I take a step toward it, my hand itching to turn the knob and make my getaway.

"Going somewhere?" Cass' gravelly morning voice floats over me.

I freeze and squeeze my eyes closed, as if that simple action can make him disappear as easily as I'd like him to.

SHIIIIT!

Even with my back to him, the heat of his gaze sears my skin, warmth crawling up my neck and over my cheeks. I can't ignore him forever, so I finally glance in the direction his voice came from to find him leaning against one of the marble coun-tertops in those damn gray sweatpants, bare-chested, a coffee mug in his hand, looking smug as fuck.

"Um, I have to go."

He raises a dark-blond brow at me and motions toward a massive, professional-looking espresso machine next to him. "Not going to stay for a latte or cappuccino?"

I narrow my eyes. "If you have *that* at home, why were you always coming to the Daily Grind?"

Cass smirks. "Why do you think? To scope out the competition."

"And get under our skin?"

His shoulder rises and falls nonchalantly, but I know I've hit the nail on the head. Cass enjoys rattling us, and what I've just let him do to me is the ultimate win for him.

He knocks back the rest of his cup and pushes off the counter.

That's my cue to leave.

I slip on my heels and hustle the few remaining steps toward the door. "Well, I've got to go."

"If you run, I'm only going to chase you, *Cherie.*"

Looking over my shoulder, I flash him a grin. "Sprinting in these is one of my many talents."

The corner of his lips twitches, and his eyes dip to my shoes before returning to my face. "It might be, but they're going to sink into the grass if you try to walk around the house to your car. You're better off staying to enjoy a cup of coffee with me and walking out the front when we're done."

I shake my head. "I can't."

He assesses me for a moment, moving closer. "Can't or *won't*?"

"Does it matter?"

Cass stops directly in front of me and tilts my chin up until I'm staring him directly in the face. His eyes heat with something other than the lust we both feel. "Of course it does. I want you to trust me, *Cherie*."

"That's impossible."

For a split second, what looks a lot like pain flashes through his gaze, but it vanishes just as quickly. "Stay. I promise to make you the best espresso you've ever had."

I pull out of his hold and laugh. "You better hope I don't tell Angelina or Allie that you just said that."

Cass smirks and nods toward the machine, slipping his hand into mine and tugging me to the island.

It would be in my best interest to pull my hand out of his, open that door, and rush out of here as fast as possible, but it may not be the best *play*. If I have any hope of him ever telling me what he's been holding back, I can't be running all the time. Getting even the tiniest shred of information from him this morning might make all this worth it.

"Sit." He points to a tufted stool, then grasps my hips as I slide onto it and set my purse on the counter. His lips find my ear. "How do you like it?"

Heat spreads through my body, remembering similar words he said last night—and how he gave me *exactly* that and then some.

He's asking about the espresso, Ken.

How do you DRINK it?

I shake my head to clear it. If we're going to do this, I need to be firing on all cylinders, and a few shots of the good stuff he undoubtedly has will help with that greatly. "Strong and black."

No matter how smug he is or how expensive a machine he owns, he won't win in that regard.

He smirks again as he sets to work putting the espresso bean grounds into the portafilter. "That doesn't surprise me at all."

While he works the fancy machine, I force myself to avert my gaze from the bunching and flexing of his muscled back, shoulders, and arms and to the stunning kitchen around us. Though renovated, the antique-styled appliances and details still make it *feel* old, even though I have no doubt everything is top-of-the-line.

I hate how much I love this damn house...

The sound of the machine brewing my drink fills the air, and he turns to face me, leaning against the counter and crossing those damn arms over his chest, which only draws my attention back to them. "Kennedy?"

I jerk my gaze back up to meet his, and he smirks at having caught me ogling him. We stare each other down, but he doesn't say a word. He just uses his pale-green eyes to devour me the same way he used his mouth last night.

People always talk about being eye-fucked, and I never really understood what they meant until this moment. The man could make me come just from this alone.

Heat spreads out from my core, my pussy clenching for something that was there only a few hours ago and that I could undoubtedly have again if I only asked right now.

Each moment that passes, the harder I have to fight the desire to squirm. I won't give him the satisfaction, not as long as I can help it. But the need to look away or move almost wins.

Only the sound of the machine finishing the brew finally forces *him* to stop eye-fucking me and give me his back again.

I release a heavy breath, fanning my face while he can't see me, but he turns back toward me quickly, catching the motion. Another lazy grin tugs on his lips as he approaches the other side of the island and slides the espresso mug across to me.

"Enjoy."

"You didn't poison it, did you?"

He shakes his head slowly, leaning an elbow on the counter and propping his face in his palm. "No trust at *all*...even after last night and this morning?"

Are we really going to talk about what we did?

The sound of approaching footsteps on the back staircase makes him freeze and stand upright, and I turn toward the sound just as a little blond girl appears at the bottom of the stairs in pink pajamas, holding a gray bunny to her chest.

She yawns, then her pale-green eyes land on me. "Daddy, who's that?"

∼

CASS

Fucking hell.

Of all the days...

Kennedy's wide eyes meet mine in question.

Shit.

Running my hand through my hair, I make my way over to Charlotte and scoop her up as she stares at Kennedy, her little brow furrowing. I press a kiss to the side of her head, hoping to distract her from the stranger sitting at the counter. "Charlotte, baby, what are you doing up so early?"

She shrugs. "I don't know." Her eyes narrow on Kennedy. "Daddy, who *is* that?"

There's no way to avoid responding. Four-year-olds are worse than the Spanish Inquisition when trying to get to the bottom of something, and a woman sitting in our kitchen, especially this early, isn't something I can smooth over with a non-answer.

"Charlotte, this is my friend, Kennedy." I look to where she sits, dumbstruck at the counter. "Kennedy, this is Charlotte."

Kennedy's wide eyes dart between our faces, and she swallows slowly. "Um, hi."

Charlotte gives her a once-over, then turns back to me. "Will you make pancakes?"

I glance at the clock. "I have court this morning and have to stop by the office first, so I need to leave early, but I bet you Abby would make them for you later before you go to school. Are you hungry now?"

She shakes her head. "Not really."

I set her back on her feet. "Then why don't you go back to your room and play until Abby gets here and it's time for breakfast?"

"Okay." But she doesn't leave right away. She turns and looks at Kennedy, her interest renewed. "What's your friend doing here?"

I rub my nape.

This is why I've never brought a woman home, but when I invited Kennedy over last night, I had no idea where it would lead. And once things started, I certainly wasn't thinking about what I would say if Charlotte saw her here.

"Kennedy and I are just talking about some things for work."

Charlotte gives me a disbelieving look. "Is she a lawyer, too?"

Kennedy laughs. "No, sweetie. I'm not."

Her brow furrows again. "Then what work are you talking about?"

I pat the top of her head and nudge her toward the stairs to go back up. "Don't worry about it, *Bebelle*." Even now, I still see her as that little baby doll she was when she came home from the hospital and earned the nickname. "I'll send Abby up when she gets here."

Charlotte casts one last concerned look at Kennedy, then traipses up the stairs, her little feet pounding.

There will be a lot of questions later—ones I'm not at all prepared to answer, and as soon as I turn to face Kennedy again, I'll have to face hers as well.

I find her wide blue eyes on me. "You have a daughter?"

The guilt of knowing what I've done to hide Charlotte from the Hawkes and everyone else for so long, only to expose her because I couldn't say no to Kennedy, claws at my chest.

I walk over to the espresso machine and turn away from her, pouring the grounds in and packing them to buy myself a moment to consider what I'm going to say. "Yes, she's four, almost five."

Silence lingers in the air as I tamp down the grounds and prepare them for the machine, but it's heavy with the question I know is coming. Even though I brace myself for it, I still flinch all the same when it comes.

"And where's her mother?"

Hell.

I throw the grounds into the machine and press the button to brew the espresso before I turn to face Kennedy and lean back against the counter, shoving my hands through my hair. She watches me carefully, waiting for me to respond.

No matter how badly I don't want to have this discussion, there's no avoiding it now.

Sighing, I cross my arms over my chest. "Her mother is my ex-wife, and she's not here, nor is she in any way involved in Charlotte's life."

Kennedy's brows wing up. "What do you mean, she's not involved in her life?"

Gripping the edges of the counter, I stare at my feet rather than at Kennedy. "When I met her mother..." I trail off slightly, wishing I didn't have to tell this story, especially to her. "We were both at places in our lives where we didn't want kids and didn't think we ever would. We were happy, just the two of us, or so I thought." I release a heavy sigh, glancing up at Kennedy. "She unexpectedly got pregnant even though she was on birth control. We're not really sure what happened, but she didn't want to have the baby."

Kennedy swallows thickly. "But you did?"

The memories come flooding back—of the arguments, the tears, the pain I didn't think I would ever feel when she said she didn't want it. I close my eyes and nod slowly. "I never thought I wanted kids and didn't want to be a dad. I never had that urge or desire, but as soon as I knew she was pregnant, it was like something shifted and I couldn't imagine *not* having that baby."

"So, what happened?"

My life changed completely...

"She was adamant she didn't want to have kids, and I was adamant I did. It ended up tearing apart our relationship very quickly because even if she didn't go through with the pregnancy, we knew we wanted different things in the long run. I knew I would want a family at some point. We ultimately came to a deal. She would carry the pregnancy to term, and I would raise our child completely by myself. I filed divorce papers the same day we reached that agreement."

"Shit." Kennedy's single uttered word hangs in the air between us, mingling with the sounds of the machine brewing me another shot of espresso. "So, you've been raising her by yourself this whole time?"

"Not totally by myself."

"Do your parents help?"

I do my best to school my expression at the question I should have seen coming. "They're both dead."

Kennedy drops her face in her palms. "Oh, God, I'm sorry. I'm an idiot."

"No, it's okay." It's an obvious question, one I would have asked, too, if I were in her position right now. "I have a great nanny named Abby who came to me from one of my clients, whose kids outgrew her. She comes every day and gets Charlotte ready for preschool, picks her up after, and then stays until I get home at night. But otherwise, yeah, it's just me and Charlotte."

She lowers her hands and locks her gaze with mine. "And that's why you were so worried."

It's finally clicked for her, what I've been trying to prevent this entire time, getting caught in the crossfire of some war, something that might take me away from that little girl who is my entire world.

I turn back to the machine and pour my drink into a mug before I face her again. My hand trembles holding it, and I lock the other one around it to try to conceal how badly talking about this really fucks with me. "I'm all she has. If something happens to me..." I suck in a shaky breath, the weight of what we're discussing weighing heavily on my chest. "I don't know what would happen to her."

Kennedy stares down into her coffee cup, curling her hands around it tightly, and she's silent for a few minutes while I sip at my espresso. "I'm not really sure what I'm supposed to say. I'm a little surprised that you're a dad."

The true shock in her voice makes me chuckle. "Why is that so surprising?"

She offers a slight shrug and finally lifts her eyes to meet mine. "I don't know, you're just so..."

"Sexy?"

The corner of her mouth twitches into a smile. "No."

"Oh, I'm not?"

She shakes her head. "Definitely not."

"Yeah, okay." I take another sip to fight my grin. "Definitely not."

"You're just so..." She considers her words for a moment. "Serious, I guess? And aggressive, and, I don't know, not the things I think of when I think of a father."

I bark out a laugh. "Right, and the men in your family aren't serious and aggressive? Your own father? Your Uncle Stone?" I tighten my grip on my mug. "They do what they do for you and your family. I do what I have to do to protect her—*my* family. My entire focus is ensuring she has everything I never did and is always safe."

Kennedy's gaze hardens. "At whose cost? The Hawkes?"

Shit.

This is definitely *not* how I wanted this morning to go.

I thought we may have opened a door, or at least a window, that would allow me to figure out what the Hawkes are thinking, doing, and planning. But instead, all I've done is piss her off more.

She slides off the stool at the counter, grabs her purse off it, and hustles to the door. Her hand hits the knob, but before she can turn it, I finish my approach and press my chest against her back, aligning my body to hers.

My breath flutters her hair, and I reach up and brush it all over her left shoulder so I can dip my head in and put my mouth against her ear. "Why are you trying to create a reason to run?"

"I'm not *creating* anything, and I'm *not running*..."

"Hmmm." The word rumbles my ribcage. "Aren't you?"

She shakes her head and stiffens her body, like she's gearing up for a battle. This fiery, relentless woman never backs down, yet she's fleeing when she really wants to stay and argue with me. "I have to leave, Cass. I have meetings today."

I run my fingers down her arm, and goosebumps pebble in their wake. My hand settles over hers on the doorknob. "Go, if you have to, but I want you to remember something..."

"Oh, yeah?" She turns her head slightly toward mine. "What's that?"

"Remember that you came to *me,* and that I gave you everything I promised. Remember that you're leaving with my cum still inside you and that I'm the reason you can barely walk this morning." I brush my lips against the sensitive skin behind her ear. "I want you to be thinking about that while you're sitting in your meetings. I want you to be thinking about the fact that I *own* your body."

Her head snaps toward me, fire burning in her gaze. *"No one owns me."*

"That's not what you said last night."

Those perfect pink lips I want to kiss so badly twitch. "Anything said during sex is moot."

"Is that a legal defense?"

She scowls at me as I rub my growing cock against her ass. "You tell me, counselor."

"Definitely." I press a kiss to her neck. "Not."

A shudder rolls through her, and she slightly sags into me, making me grin against her warm skin. "You seem to enjoy getting me off my game."

I chuckle. "I do enjoy getting you off, *Cherie,* but there is absolutely nothing wrong with your game. While you're thinking about me being inside you, I'm going to spend my day thinking about what your cunt felt like wrapped around my cock."

She drops her forehead against the door in front of her and releases a shaky breath. "Please stop talking like that."

I grind my erection against her, caging her in with my hand against the door and squeezing the other over hers on the knob. "Why the hell would I want to do that, Kennedy?"

"Because..." She shakes her head. "I can't *think* when you do."

Pressing my lips in her hair, I inhale the heavenly scent I've come to associate with her. "What's there to think about?"

"Jesus, you can't be serious." She finally turns, forcing me to take a step back and pull my hands from the door, as she searches my gaze for something. "About the fact that I just fucked my family's biggest enemy."

And we're back to this...

"I'm only an enemy if you want me to be."

She doesn't respond, just turns back to the door and opens it. For a brief moment, I think she's going to spin toward me and unleash one of her famous verbal assaults, but instead, she walks out without another word, pulling it closed behind her.

11

CASS

"Daaaaddyyyyy!" Charlotte releases an exasperated sigh filled with all the angst her tiny body can hold, motioning wildly toward me. "You're doing it all *wrong.*"

I still my hands, then hold them up in surrender as she leans across the table and snatches the half-made bracelet from in front of me.

"You have to do the right patter-en."

"Pattern."

She scowls at me. "That's what I *said!* Patter-en!"

"It's *pat-ern* not *patter-en.*"

Trying to teach a four-year-old to speak properly is a lesson in futility. No matter how many times we've had this discussion, she refuses to say it correctly. Almost as if she's testing the limits of both my patience and what I'll let her get away with— which she seems to enjoy greatly.

Charlotte rolls her eyes, dropping the argument and

turning her focus to the bracelet she just rescued from my help-less clutches.

I point to the beads. "I *was* doing a pattern."

She issues another huff, as if I can't *possibly* understand. "Not the *right* one."

Serenity now...

Four-year-olds are so demanding. Every day I spend with her, I feel like she's grown five years and become a little adult overnight. But I can't help feeling like it's moving too fast, and I'm losing my baby to all this attitude.

I have learned, though—some things are not worth arguing over. Bracelets certainly being one of them. She wants it done a certain way, and there will be no talking her out of it or how she pronounces *pattern.*

"Sorry, kiddo." I reach for the bracelet in front of her. "Why don't you tell me how you want it done—"

Before I can snag it, she dumps all the beads off the string into the small bowl and sets to work correcting my mistake. Her little fingers easily pick up the tiny hollow, shimmering beads and slide them on when my thick ones fumbled them help-lessly, making it take me twice as long to—improperly—complete one.

She shakes her head as she does it, like she can't believe the mistake I made. Already perturbed at four...

"I'll help you, *Bebelle*, if you tell me how."

Shaking her head, she maintains her laser focus. "I'll just do it myself."

I can't fight the smile at her response. Sometimes, she's so much like me that it's terrifying.

God...what will she be like as a teenager?

I shudder at that thought. "Why don't I just cut the string, then, and get it ready for you to do the rest of these?"

She glances up at me, her green eyes assessing me for a moment, as if wondering whether I can really handle that assignment or if it is above my skill level. "Okay." A tiny smile curls her lips as she works on her creation. "They're going to love these."

"I'm sure they will, sweetheart. And it's very nice of you to make bracelets for all your friends at school."

She nods. "Becca is my best friend."

"I know, *Bebelle*."

It would be impossible not to with the way she chatters on about her endlessly every day after school. I was so worried that everything I've done to try to keep her hidden from the world would make it difficult for her when it came to socialization, but she's an outgoing, busy bee, flitting around, making friends with everyone.

"Is *your* friend coming back?"

I freeze with the scissors poised to snip the stretchy bracelet material and swallow thickly. By the grace of God, I managed to avoid her inquisition last night when she got home from school by distracting her with dinner out, but I should have known she wasn't going to let Kennedy's appearance in our kitchen go so easily.

"I'm not sure, *Bebelle*."

She keeps slipping beads onto the string, not even bothering to look up at me. "You've never brought a friend home before other than Uncle Marcel."

I nod slowly as I cut the string, weighing the best route to take this topic. "I know. Did it bother you that she was here?"

Charlotte's hand stills for a minute, and she stares at it, thinking about her response, then she shrugs. "Not really."

I release a relieved breath. "Good..."

"When will she be back?"

My spine stiffens, and I cut another string. "Um, I don't think she will be back."

She finally looks over at me, her brow furrowed, eyes soft and confused. "Why wouldn't she come again?"

Her choice of words makes me wince. "Believe me, sweetie. I want her to. But sometimes, it isn't that simple for adults."

Returning to her project, she slips on the final bead and examines her handiwork. "What, being friends?"

"Any of it."

She glances up at me, then hands me the bracelet to tie it off. "How come? If you like someone, you're friends." Her tiny shoulders rise and fall. "If you don't, you're not."

I can't fight the smile at the simplicity of the four-year-old mind, at how innocent they are at this age, so sheltered from the realities of the world around them.

"You're right." No point in crushing her soul by explaining that it isn't that simple once you get older. I tie off the bracelet and hand it back to her. "This one looks great."

She nods, her blond bob swinging around her face. "I know."

My phone buzzes on the table beside me, and I glance down and tense instantly at the name on the screen. "You keep working on these. I need to take this phone call, okay?"

She doesn't even acknowledge me, too engrossed in her craft project to care if I step away. In reality, she's probably happy I'm leaving her to do it alone so I don't mess it up. *Again.*

Shoving back my chair, I slide my finger across the screen to answer it. "Hey, Nancy, thanks for the callback."

"You never just call to chat...if you left a message, it must mean you need something from me."

As much as I hate how bad that sounds, it's true. Time is *not* on my side with this—not when the Hawkes are poised to break ground in only a matter of weeks.

While my friendship with Nancy has helped me advance Falco's plans for the hotel far quicker than I ever imagined, Damon's demands that we beat the Hawkes to the punch necessitates moving things along even faster. And she's the one who might be able to make that possible in her role managing all the building inspectors.

"Don't we all want something, Nancy?" I make my way back into my office and settle into my chair. "I don't think anyone does anything that's one hundred percent altruistic anymore."

Still, my eyes drift to the photos on my desk, the reason *I* do what I do.

She offers a light laugh. "I can agree with that. So, tell me what you need."

Kennedy Hawke in my bed again.

It's the first thing that pops into my mind, and it's the last thing I should be thinking about *or* doing. Yet here I am, literally sleeping with the enemy while trying to figure out a way to help Falco and Damon fuck over her entire family.

"I need to get the Falco hotel open before the Hawkes get theirs completed."

Nancy's tinkle of laughter floats through the line, making me cringe. "You're kidding, right?"

I shake my head and rub at my nape and the tension growing there. "No. It needs to happen." Not only is it a contingent of all the money Damon is bringing with him, but it would also be the ultimate slap in the face to the Hawkes, something Falco has been trying to do for *years*. "Is it possible?"

She releases a little sigh. "I don't know, Cass. That's a pretty tall order. You know I can move things along quickly, cut through some of the bureaucratic red tape for you on zoning, permitting, and getting inspections completed, but if I play favorites too much, it's going to raise questions I don't want to have to answer."

Nancy doesn't want anyone to know the amount of cash that's been fed to her by Falco over the last few years, and I can't blame her. She's worked hard to get where she is in her career, and a scandal like this could ruin her future—which might include the mayor's or governor's office not too far down the road.

The Hawkes have their people, and they protect them well. Falco does the same for theirs.

"I would never ask you to do anything that would jeopardize your position. Falco needs you there as much as you need to be there, but tell me who else might be able to grease the wheels. Falco is happy to pay. You know that."

She considers my words for a moment before she gives a conceding sigh. "Send me the full list of dates and what you want done by when, and I'll see what I can do. I have someone in mind who could potentially assist us so nothing gets tied to me."

"And you think they'd be amenable?"

"This particular person has a mistress who is very pregnant. I have a feeling he's going to have a lot of expenses coming his way soon, one way or another."

Just the kind of new friend I'm always looking for—one with skeletons in his closet who is going to need an influx of cash. Whether he's paying to support that baby and keep the mom quiet or for a good divorce lawyer when his wife finds out, he's going to need money. And that's something we have plenty of to go around on this project.

"You make sure he gets to me before the Hawkes get to him."

I'm not the only one who understands how to utilize people's bad behavior for their own benefit. He's exactly the type of person the Hawkes would leverage when they need "favors" just as quickly as I would.

"You know"—Nancy offers a little sigh—"they're reopening Hawke's Daily Grind on Monday."

It should be a good thing, but my gut tightens. "That's what I hear."

"Falco planning anything in response?"

Acid crawls up my throat. "Have to wait and see."

She offers a light laugh. "You know I have a soft spot for Angie and Allie. They make a mean latte."

"I know." I laugh. "You're in bed with the enemy."

The irony of my words isn't lost on me—considering that it's exactly what Kennedy and I did the other night.

And I want to do it again...

"I just like good coffee." Nancy laughs again. "I'll send you the information. Unless you'll be at the mayor's fundraiser tonight for me to give it to you in person?"

Shit.

The fundraiser—I had almost forgotten since it I wouldn't be seen at *anything* held in support of a man who is in so deep with the Hawkes.

"Send it to me."

"Will do."

She ends the call, and my mind immediately starts racing, thinking about Kennedy. The Hawkes have the mayor in their pocket, which means at least one of them will make an appearance tonight at the fundraiser, likely to hand over a big check.

It might well be the blonde I can't get out of my mind. But I have to deal with another one first.

I return to the kitchen to see what kind of disaster Charlotte undoubtedly created while I was gone and slide back into my chair.

Charlotte looks up at me from another bracelet in a row of ones she completed while I was in my office. "Was that your friend?"

I examine her handiwork. "A different one."

Her little brow furrows again. "I didn't know you had so many friends."

Ouch.

I give her a tight smile. "I don't."

In this business, I have a lot of people I rely on for favors and people I pay to be loyal. People who do things for me because they like money or because they have things to hide that I am willing to reveal if need be. I wouldn't call any of them friends, and Kennedy Hawke certainly isn't one of them.

But it doesn't need to be that way.

"Hey, Char, I know we were going to do a movie and pizza tonight, but I have to go out."

Her lips start to droop, but I quickly recover.

"So, we'll do it early, and then Abby's going to come hang out with you tonight."

Hopefully.

I hadn't planned on going to the fundraiser, but it's likely the only place I can get Kennedy alone again since she'll undoubtedly go out of her way to avoid me after the other night.

Her brow furrows. "Where are you going?"

"Somewhere for work."

Her little lips pout in that way she knows always works on me. It almost does me in and makes me cancel my plans, but then her eyes light up.

"Can Abby bring ice cream?"

I nod. "I'm sure that can be arranged."

She bounces in her chair and claps her hands, releasing the bracelet she was working on and sending beads flying all over the floor.

I cringe at the sound of them bouncing and spreading out across the marble. "And you and Abby may spend some of the night searching the floor for beads."

KENNEDY

THIRTY MINUTES TOPS, then I'm out of here.

It's just enough time to see and be seen so that everyone knows the Hawkes were here and that we own Mayor Lavine. I can't possibly handle any longer than that, not with the way my mind has wandered endlessly since I left Cass' place yesterday morning.

His words became my reality.

All day at the office, despite having stopped home to clean up—I couldn't stop thinking about his touch, his kiss, him coming inside me. Over and over and over again. Everything he said and did to me replayed like a movie in my head. One I couldn't turn off. And the same rang true today, like the most torturous *Groundhog's Day* of all time.

I need to concentrate on the reopening and the groundbreaking, but instead, all I can think about is that arrogant bastard and the fact that he was right when he said he would show me Heaven.

Only now, I'm in a Hell of my own making—drowning in guilt and decidedly unsaintly images and wants—and having to be here as the Hawke family representative only makes it worse.

The same people I saw only a week ago at our own event smile, nod, and wave. A few approach to say hello. My eyes drift over one shoulder after another to the bar. If I'm going to make it through tonight, I'm going to need something strong. But before I can make my way over there, Mayor Lavine spots me.

Shit.

He approaches with his hand extended, and I slide mine into it, knowing the dirty old perv is going to bring it to his gross lips and kiss it like he always does. "It's so nice to see you, Ms. Hawke."

I fight my gag response as he lets his mouth linger a second too long against my skin.

"You too, Mr. Mayor." I jerk my hand from his to motion around the event. "It looks like you have an excellent turnout."

Lavine nods. "Yes. Yes." He gives me a wink. "Not quite what you managed."

I share a forced laugh with him. "Well, we have a good cause. That makes it easier."

His brows rise. "Supporting my campaign isn't a good cause?"

Smooth...

With a saccharine-sweet smile, I dig into my purse and pull out a check. "Of course, sir. I just meant the Hawke Foundation as a charity is a much bigger draw than a political campaign. Everyone wants to help the city by donating to us so we can step in when disaster strikes."

He presses a hand against his chest and chuckles. "Yes, yes, I know." His eyes drop to the check. "I was making a joke. It was nice of you to come. I know how busy you are right now."

God, I hate these things.

I hold out the small piece of paper with a very large number written on it to him. "Unfortunately, I won't be able to stay long, but this is from Hawke Enterprises. A donation for the campaign."

Mayor Lavine grins and accepts my proffered check in his fingers. "Greatly appreciated."

Before he can pull it from my hand, I lean in, ensuring no one mingling around us can hear a word I'm about to say to the man. "A reminder that we'll expect the same continued cooperation during your next term, or the information we hold will become very public, very quickly."

He stiffens, then pulls back slowly, narrowing his eyes on me. "I don't respond to threats, Ms. Hawke."

I smile at him. "You *should*, Mayor Lavine, because we don't make them idly."

Someone calls his name, and when he glances in that direction, I use it as an opportunity to dart away and head to the bar

—the one place I might find a single moment of peace this evening and hide out before I can finally bail.

The young bartender steps up, his eyes raking over me with appreciation. "What can I get for you, ma'am?"

I scan the booze behind him. "Double Blantons, neat."

"That's a strong drink..." Cass' gravelly voice floats over me.

Fucking hell...

Goosebumps immediately break out across my skin, and my pussy clenches, remembering that voice in my ear while he railed me.

I don't look in his direction, just keep staring straight ahead at the booze, like that will somehow make him disappear when even drinking all *that* couldn't get him out of my head. "You weren't surprised by me taking my coffee strong and black, but the fact that I like strong bourbon does shock you?"

Cass leans against the bar next to me, keeping an appropriate distance, which is unusual for him. Likely intended to ensure we aren't seen commiserating—for his sake, as much as my own.

He takes a sip of his own drink, and I finally turn my head to look at him fully.

A lopsided grin tilts his lips. "Nothing about you really surprises me, Kennedy. I was just wondering why you're hitting the hard stuff right away."

I scowl at him.

The man knows damn well why I'm hitting the hard stuff— because I hit the sheets with him when he's the last man on the planet that I should have let touch me.

Clearing his throat as he approaches, the bartender slides my drink across the bar, and I open my purse to pull out my cash to pay him.

Cass is too fast, whipping out and throwing a hundred-dollar bill at the man. "Keep the change."

"Thanks."

He hustles away to the register to make his change and pocket his tip while Cass slides slightly closer to me and dips his head until his lips are almost at my ear. "I had hoped I'd see you here tonight."

I shift a half-step away and turn to fully face him. "I'm surprised they even let you in the door."

He chuckles, and the sound goes straight between my legs. That low rumble vibrated through my entire body more than once during our night together.

Fuck, I'm in so much trouble with this man.

Cass scans the event before refocusing his attention on me, his eyes heating instantly. "I don't think Mayor Lavine knows I'm here."

"Come to think of it, I still don't know how you got into our event last week."

He grins. "I have friends, Kennedy. Unlike you, a lot of people *actually* like me."

I bark out a laugh and take a sip of the spicy bourbon. "Only because they don't *know* you. They *pretend* to be your friends. They *pretend* to like you so they can get something from you. That's the way the world works, especially where *you* are concerned."

"Ouch!" He presses his free hand against his chest, feigning injury. "So, you still insist that you hate me, huh?"

"Even more now."

My answer comes too fast to be the truth—and he knows it.

The way the green in his eyes darkens and his body shifts toward mine makes my core heat. He leans closer. "Why? Because I gave you something no one else ever did or ever will in the future?"

Yes, exactly that.

But I sure as fuck am not going to admit that to this man.

I grab my drink, take a sip of it, then leave the bar without another word to him. My heels click against the wood floor as

I weave my way through the throngs of people here to support Mayor Lavine's re-election campaign, the sound somehow sharp and clear over the din of voices surrounding me.

A few familiar faces say hello and try to engage me in conversation, but I keep pressing forward until I hit the hallway to the set of double glass doors leading out onto the balcony that overlooks the water.

I may hate these events, but at least this one's in a beautiful building that offers an incredible view, somewhere I can get some fresh air and a break from all the ass-kissing and schmoozing in there.

And away from Cass Whitaker.

I've made my appearance and handed over the check, along with the personal message. It's good enough for what I was sent for. I've done my CFO duties for the evening, and once I finish this drink, I can head home.

I take a sip, allowing the fiery heat to roll around in my mouth for a moment before I swallow it to warm my belly. A chilly breeze kicks up off the water, the familiar smell invading my lungs for a brief moment before I feel Cass approaching.

Every nerve in my body hums, and goosebumps break out across my skin. Then *his* scent hits me, that crisp, almost ocean-like aftershave he wears. The heat of his body comes next as he slides behind me, not touching me but close enough that the warmth radiates through my dress.

He doesn't say a word, just stands there, waiting for me to say or do something.

Normally, I might make him wait forever, but I don't want him here, and the only way to get rid of him is to ask the obvious question. "What the hell are you doing here, Cass?"

"Here, where?" His breath flutters the hair at my nape. "The balcony? The fundraiser? New Orleans? Earth?"

"Don't be a smart ass."

"Oh"—he issues a low chuckle—"but you love that I'm smart and an ass."

"I absolutely do *not*." I refuse to turn around and acknowledge him further. "I think we have established that I hate you."

His lips brush my ear, and I fight the shiver that wants to roll through me at the simple contact. Warm breath flutters over me, the scent of the smokey scotch he's drinking hitting me. "You don't hate me, Kennedy. You hate that I gave you something no one else can or will. I think we just established that with the way you ran away from me."

"You're right. I don't hate you. I *despise* you even more for it."

He doesn't even flinch at my words, just nuzzles the back of my neck. "You know, they say it's a thin line between love and hate."

I turn my head until my eyes meet his. "It's pretty fucking thick from where I stand. And I'm firmly on one side."

Instead of being offended or in any way fazed by my comment, Cass grins.

Keeping my eyes locked with his, I take a sip of my bourbon, letting my favorite drink glide down my throat and flow into my belly, warming it as the chilly wind kicks up.

This time, I do shiver, and he moves even closer, pushing his body to mine.

And fuck if it doesn't feel incredible having this man pressed against me again.

His lips find my ear, and his free hand glides over my chilled, exposed skin. "You should have worn a coat or a wrap over this dress. It's chilly tonight."

I shake my head. "I'm not staying long."

"Where are you going?"

Not where I want to.

As much as I don't want to admit it, if Cass asked me to go back to his house with him tonight, I don't know that I could say no. But I force myself to look back at him. "Home."

One of his brows rises. "Alone?"

"Why do you care?"

He grins. "I don't. I was just thinking that if you brought anyone back with you, you're going to be sorely disappointed. Because no one is going to be able to live up to what you had with me."

I snort-laugh, bumping him with my ass to get him to give me a little bit of much-needed space between us so I can think, which is so fucking hard to do when his body's pressed to mine. "I'm not worried about it."

"You should be, and I think you are. Because you can't deny that whatever's happening between us isn't going away."

Straightening my shoulders, I clench my hand tightly around my glass, anger heating my blood now. "I can do whatever I want."

He reaches up and grips my chin between his fingers, squeezing it roughly as he drags my face up until my eyes meet his. "I have no doubt you can, Kennedy. You've proven that in business and in your life. But I'm telling you right now, this is not going away. *I'm* not going away."

"Yes, you are." I press my free hand against his chest. "I already suggested we kill you and throw you into the bayou."

Instead of being angry, a slow grin spreads across his lips, and he leans in, almost pressing them to mine. I fight the urge to close that tiny bit of space.

"Like I said, *Cherie,* the line between love and hate is thin, and you just proved it. You can't hate that strongly without there being something more there, too."

"Watch me."

12

KENNEDY

I spin on my heel and sidestep him in a desperate attempt to get back to the open doors that will lead me inside and away from his overwhelming presence, but Cass moves too fast and grasps my shoulder, twirling me to face him. Before I have a chance to object, he advances, backing me up against the brick wall—a tight, dark corner where no one will see us unless they check behind the door.

His jaw tenses. "Oh no, you don't…"

"What the hell are you doing, Cass?"

He downs his drink and then smashes the glass against the concrete next to us. I flinch at the sound, but he grabs my drink and does the same with it, scattering sharp shards around our feet.

"I warned you that if you ran, I would chase you." He grips my chin. "I let you flee from me before only because my daughter was awake and in the goddamn house and she would've asked a lot of questions I didn't have answers for. But we're *not* done, Kennedy. We're *far* from done. You don't get to decide that."

I raise a brow at him, anger flooding my veins, mixing with the pure lust that always seems to consume me when I'm near this man. "Don't I?"

"Tell me that if she hadn't woken up and come downstairs, you wouldn't have let me bend you over that counter and fuck you before you left."

Hell.

A shudder rolls through my body, and I press my palms against his firm chest, trying to force him back, but with his hands braced on either side of the wall, he's not budging.

This man seems intent on pushing me tonight, and I'm not about to be bulldozed by the person responsible for ensuring his client can do just that to everything the Hawkes have built.

I made that mistake once, and I won't do it again. Even though he's right—I would have let him take me any and every which way in that damn kitchen. But that weakness isn't anything I'll concede to him. "That never would've happened, Cass. I came to my senses..."

He issues another one of those low, deep chuckles that goes straight to my core, then leans in, pinning my hands between us and rubbing his growing cock against my stomach. "Bullshit, *Cherie.* You may be great at your job. You may be able to convince people to do all sorts of things for the Hawkes. You may intimidate the hell out of them, but you don't scare me, nor can you lie to me because I can see the truth."

Fear tightens my gut. Terror at the idea that he might *actually* know what I try so hard to hide from everyone all the time, that he truly can see my weakness and intends to use it against me and the rest of the Hawkes when it's my responsibility to protect them.

"What truth is that?"

His eyes soften slightly, and he pulls his hand from the wall to feather his fingertips across my cheek. "That you're burning yourself out. That this empire your family has built is too much for you to manage, and your father and your uncle are relying on you more and more to handle everything..."

His words seep into my blood like some sort of drug, and I drop my gaze from his, suddenly unable to bear looking into the mossy-green eyes that see far too much.

Christ, am I that transparent?

If this man I barely know can see through me so easily, then I'm doing a really shitty job hiding what's really weighing down on me so heavily.

Cass grips my chin and tilts it up. "I could see you didn't want to be at the Hawke fundraiser the other night, and you sure as fuck don't want to be here now." His thumb brushes across my bottom lip. "I only came because I wanted to see you, and I knew it was the one place I could get to you where you couldn't run."

"I told you...I can run in heels."

The corner of his lips twitches. "I'm sure you can, but you won't make a scene, not in front of all these people, not when they're so important to the Hawkes and appearances are everything. You're very good at your job, Kennedy, but it's costing you personally. More than you have to give."

His statement tugs so hard at the things I've forced down that they start to come up before I somehow manage to swallow them.

"You don't know anything, Cass."

"I do know because I do things I don't want to, either. Everything I do for my clients, I do for Charlotte so she can have the life I never did."

"You *justify* it that way, but I don't know how you sleep at night."

He grins and feathers his lips over mine. "Hmmm, well, last night, it was with my hard cock in my hand thinking about you.

And two nights ago, it was with you beside me and my cock buried in your cunt."

Fuck.

I squeeze my eyes closed and press my lips together so that I don't give into the desire to smash them against his and give him a repeat of that night.

"We can be good for each other, Kennedy." He sounds so genuine. "So good."

He says the right things, but it's all an act, a ploy to get far enough under my skin that he'll know all the Hawkes' secrets. And if I ever got caught sleeping with Cass Whitaker, I wouldn't want to know the consequences I'd face.

I shake my head. "No, we can't. I don't trust you, and even if I did, if anyone ever found out—"

"No one has to."

"I don't keep things from my family, Cass. I don't lie to them."

"Bullshit." His eyes flash with anger. "Everyone lies to someone at some point. You're lying to me right now, saying you don't want this. If I reached between your legs, I'd find you just as wet as you've been every other time my fingers have been there."

Fucking hell.

I hate how right he is.

Shifting slightly on my heels, I press my thighs together, trying to conceal the evidence of just how accurate his words really were.

"It doesn't matter what my body wants, Cass. Not when my head keeps telling me this shouldn't happen."

Not again.

Not ever.

His head dips closer, bringing him close enough to smell the smoky scotch on his breath. "Shut your head *off* and just feel. Let me do to you what I did the other night."

I clench my eyes closed and shake my head, but he tightens his grip on my chin.

"Look at me, Kennedy."

Those words again, the same ones he said to me as I came that first time, the first of so many.

The mossy-green I stared into when he made me come over and over again appears darker out here with only the faint lights from the surrounding buildings illuminating them, or maybe it's his arousal changing their color. But they still burn into me like I'm his oxygen and he's a fire trying to consume me.

I'll never admit it—that I want this as much as he says.

I can't.

He nips at my lips, then kisses me with that same barely restrained hunger as the other night.

I moan into his mouth despite doing everything I can to keep it in, my fingers curling against his crisp white shirt under his suit coat. It's everything dark and forbidden—and fucking perfect. He steals my breath and my resistance away with the move of his lips over mine, the slow sweep of his tongue, the taste of his drink and *him* filling my senses.

My head spins. My knees weaken. My hands cling to him far too tightly.

I tear my mouth from his, my chest heaving, breaths heavy. "I still hate you, Cass."

He kisses his way across my cheek to my ear. "And I still know you're lying."

"I'm not." I shake my head, trying to get away from his sinful lips. "You'll never get me in your bed again."

"I don't need you in my bed to get you off, *Cherie*." He pulls back and grins. "We both know I've already proven that."

CASS

THAT FIERY ANGER I love to see so much flashes in her gaze when she realizes I'm right, and hidden underneath it is the same inferno of lust that always seems to mingle with her pure hatred of me.

"I may never get you in my bed again, *Cherie*, but I can fuck you right here and make sure you never forget everything I can do for you."

Her eyes dart to the open door to our left, barely covering us in the dark corner of the balcony. "You wouldn't."

I raise a brow and grind my hard cock against her thigh. "Wouldn't I?"

"Shit." She shakes her head and clamps her eyes closed. "You *would*."

I lower one hand to her bare thigh and skim it up toward the hem of her dress. "You remember what my touch felt like. How good it can be between us. Stop fighting it."

Kennedy opens her eyes. "I'm not fighting *it*. I'm fighting *you*."

"Same thing."

"No, it isn't. You are the one who made us enemies, Cass. You are the one who continues to keep that unsurmountable impediment between us by representing a piece of shit company like Falco."

My chest tightens, the need to defend myself outweighing my desire for her for a moment. "You *know* why I do it."

"You use your daughter as an excuse for your behavior. That's all it is, an excuse. She doesn't need that big house. She doesn't need you to have a fancy car. She doesn't need you to have the kind of money you flaunt, the kind of money you make from working for soulless fuckers like Falco Enterprises. All she needs is a father who loves her."

I recoil slightly at her words, my jaw hardening. "It's more complicated than that."

She shakes her head. "No, it isn't."

My anger at her accusation should give me pause. It should make me take a step back. I should turn and walk back in that door, leaving her furious and wanting out here with only her hatred to keep her warm and satisfied.

I should do all those things.

But I don't.

I *can't* walk away from this woman.

Leaning in, I hover my lips over hers, gliding my hand up between her legs. "You go ahead and think you know me, think you understand everything about my life, but you don't have a fucking clue, Kennedy. I came here tonight because I haven't been able to stop thinking about you since you stormed out of my house the other day with completely the wrong idea about who and what I am. I came because I *need* to feel your cunt wrapped around my cock again. I *need* to hear you moaning in my ear. I *need* all of it again. I need it like I need my next breath."

Even when I shouldn't.

She trembles against me, still pinned between my chest and the wall, and her hands snake up around my neck. For a split second, the thought that it might be to strangle me crosses my mind, but she loops them around it and releases a heavy, full-body sigh.

The same war that raged inside of her at my house the other night resurges. I can see her fighting it, debating which side she should let win. That sigh wasn't of resignation; it was the frustration of wanting something she thinks she shouldn't have.

"Take what you want, Kennedy." I kiss the corner of her mouth, molding my body firmly to hers. "Let me give it to you."

Instead of answering, her nails dig into my skin, and she

tips her head so she can crush her lips against mine. Her hips grind against my cock where it pulses between us, and a tiny whimper falls from her mouth.

Fucking hell.

Doing this with Kennedy Hawke is playing with fire. A conflagration that will undoubtedly burn both of us. But whenever we're like this, neither of us seems to give a flying fuck about the consequences.

I pull my other hand from the wall long enough to fumble with my pants and get them lowered down my thighs, freeing my cock between us, then grip her legs and lift her up to wrap them around my waist.

With my dick pinned between our bodies, she rolls her hips, gliding it along her already bare and soaked core. "Fucking hell, Cass. The goddamn mayor's just inside that door."

I grin against her warm skin and kiss down her neck. She tilts her head to the side, giving me better access despite her worry about the very public nature of our current situation.

Anyone on the street below could look up and see us tucked behind the door. Any of the campaign fundraiser attendees could come out for a breath of fresh air and stumble upon us going at it like teenagers.

We both have a lot to lose if we get caught—my reputation, my clients, my law license. But it doesn't stop me. When I'm with Kennedy, it seems nothing can, not even the reason I work so hard for Falco.

What's right and reasonable flies out the window the moment I get my hands on this woman. Plus, knowing we *could* get caught somehow makes this all the hotter.

Reaching between us, I pull my hips back slightly to align my cock with her slick core. "I know, Kennedy. That's what makes this so much fucking fun." I plunge into her in one hard thrust. "Fuck..."

She gasps, her head slamming back against the brick behind her. But she doesn't even seem to notice, just squeezes around me, her hot cunt cocooning me and rippling along my length.

Fucking hell, this woman.

I roll my hips back and slam into her again, pushing her against the wall and capturing her little cry with my lips.

Everything about this situation only makes me drive deeper and push her harder. She groans, and I roll my hips to allow the head of my cock to drag against her G-spot with every retreat.

"Fuck." She mutters the words against my lips.

I kiss her deeply again, tangling my tongue with her own. Her grip on my neck tightens as she starts to move with my rhythm, thrusting her hips against mine, grinding down against the base of my cock to give herself the friction she needs.

Muffled conversation comes from the open door, and she freezes, but I keep going, pumping into her as I slide my hand up and over her mouth to silence her. Her eyes widen and lock with mine, and she clenches down around me, trying to keep me still inside her while whoever is right on the other side of the door passes.

But it doesn't deter me.

Kennedy Hawke may hate every fiber of my being, but when we're like this, all that hatred turns into something else, into a desire neither of us can deny. Now that I've had a taste of her, I don't know how I'm going to inevitably walk away.

I can't get enough of this.

Of *her.*

I keep pistoning my hips, ignoring the voices just inside from the balcony. She moans against my palm, thrashing her head from side to side and continuing to bow her hips to meet mine as I pummel her, the sharp brick abrading her bare shoulders.

The voices in the hallway move closer, and her eyes warn me that we're going to get caught.

"Shhh..." I whisper against her lips as I take her mouth again, ensuring that I capture any cries or groans that might slip out as we keep going, racing toward that fast, hard orgasm I know she wants.

It wasn't what she needed the other night. Not at first. But tonight, it's the only thing either of us is capable of.

Finally, her body stiffens, and her pussy clenches around mine as she gasps into my mouth. Her cunt grips my cock so tightly that it drags my own orgasm from me.

I come inside her on a groan that I barely manage to bite back.

Someone steps out onto the balcony as the last hot spurt of cum fills her, and she sags against the wall. I press my hand back over her mouth and wait as the couple moves to the railing to look out at the water, my still-hard cock buried inside her with her pinned against the wall.

We wait silently. The couple chats about what a beautiful night it is until the woman shivers at the cool breeze, and the man guides her back inside.

I slowly pull my hand away from her mouth, staring down at the woman who just made me throw everything I thought I knew out the window.

Public sex, with the woman who *should* be my enemy—for the second damn time.

She looks up at me with hooded, lust-soaked eyes through thick, dark lashes. "I really fucking hate you, Cass."

I pull my cock out of her, and she winces slightly at the loss, releasing the death grip her thighs have on my hips so I can help ease her feet down to the balcony.

Leaning in, I pin her to the wall again, knowing my cum is dripping between her legs. "You can hate me all you want,

Kennedy, but you'll never forget what I do to you, and you'll keep coming back for more. I promise you that."

Her kiss-swollen lips open and close, like she's trying to formulate her response, but I tuck my cock back into my pants, button them, then press a kiss to her cheek before she can utter a word.

A strange pain hits my chest, and I back away from our dark corner, walk out the door, down the hallway, and away from the woman who drives me absolutely fucking mad.

And who will do so much worse.

Especially when she learns the truth.

13

KENNEDY

The cool breeze whips around me, and I pull my jacket tighter and scan the crowd gathered outside the Daily Grind to celebrate its reopening. Familiar scents I always associate with this place fill the air—coffee and fresh baked goods—and I inhale deeply.

It feels so good to be back here. The last few months since the fire, a dark cloud has hung over all of us, but now, the sun is shining down again, and things almost feel like they're getting back to normal.

With so many patrons crammed inside, the party has spilled out onto the front patio. People sit around the small bistro tables and stand chatting with drinks in their hands.

It's a massive success by anyone's standards, and Angie seems absolutely thrilled with the response and to see her former customers flocking back. Nothing should be able to crush the good vibes, but I can't help turning to look down the street to where Falco's Daily Grounds sits, their patio filled with just as many customers as ours.

Their huge buy one, get one free sale today has certainly drawn quite a crowd on *our* big day.

Greedy fucking bastards.

Intentional...and we all know it.

They'll do anything to draw business away from ours, especially on a day like this that means so much to everyone. It's our time to literally rise from the ashes, and they're throwing a giant bucket of ice water on us.

Uncle Stone steps up next to me, arms crossed over his chest, jaw clenched tightly. He stares down the street toward The Daily Grounds. "Does that piss you off as much as it does me?"

Far more after fucking the man who makes that possible for them.

But no one can ever know about that. My ire will have to continue to appear to come from the same place it did before—solely because of what Cass does for his clients, not what he does to *me*.

"I would imagine it probably pisses you off more, considering you and Isaac are the ones who have to fight those assholes in court constantly. At least I never have to see them..."

Except for when Cass is driving his cock into me.

I cringe as the memories of what we've done flood my brain. It's all I've been able to think about since he walked away from me Saturday night when I should have been concentrating on going over all the plans for *this* event again and again to ensure everything was perfect.

Instead, I was reliving every single thing that man did and said to me. And wondering why his having a daughter bothers me so much.

Maybe because it makes him more...human.

Watching Isaac with Viviana at family dinner last night, it was impossible not to picture Cass and Charlotte. See that genuine love he has for her, and feel the force of his words when he said everything he does is for her.

Cassius Whitaker has always been like some kind of boogeyman I had built up in my head after so long fighting Falco on so many fronts. He was dark and mysterious and evil. It was easy to hate him when those were the *only* things he was, but when I know he's going home every night to that little girl and tucking her in, raising her all on his own, he suddenly starts morphing into something other than a complete monster.

That can't happen.

I'm already far too weak when it comes to that man. If I started thinking of him as anything other than the enemy, the results would be catastrophic.

For both of us...

Isaac slips out the door of the Grind, cup in hand, the music from inside seeping out, and approaches us on the sidewalk, his gaze following his father's. "You two bitching about Falco again?"

I snort and finally force myself to look away from the competition and to Isaac. "What else do we have to bitch about?"

He smirks and takes a sip of his coffee. "True."

It's part of why Falco Enterprises is such a painful thorn in our side—because without them constantly interfering, things would be smooth sailing. Before they showed up in NOLA with Cass as their legal viper, everything was on track. We were prepared to open The Hawke Hotel and take the next step in securing our future. Now, everything has changed—and not just on the business front.

Trying to keep myself from dwelling on what's happening down the street, I scan the large windows at the front of the Grind, trying to see what's going on inside.

Angie works the counter with Astrid while the rest of the

Hawkes sit around various tables, chatting with other patrons and enjoying the music provided by one of their usual acts— Dan Ro. Even Jude shut down Novel Idea long enough to come across the street and join the celebration, though his stiff posture, bouncing knee, and the way he watches Angie like a hawk demonstrate how uneasy he is being here.

The same way I feel.

I can't shake this undercurrent of tension that hangs in the air, but I plaster on a smile and do my best to get in the right state of mind for a party. My guilt and my sour mood shouldn't affect everyone around me. Especially when we have the groundbreaking to prepare for next.

We may have smoothed over the supply-chain issues, but it doesn't mean another problem won't pop up when we least expect it.

I turn back to Isaac and Uncle Stone. "One down, one to go, right?"

"We're good for the groundbreaking, Ken." Isaac offers a look he intends to be reassuring, but I can't miss the worry lingering there. "We're ready for it."

Rubbing my arms against the chill seeping in, I nod, running through the mental checklist I've memorized of everything we have done and need to do before the shovel hits the ground. "I hope you're right."

Isaac offers a smirk. "I usually am."

I glower at him. "Don't get started with that bullshit today. My ribs still hurt, and I don't think I could handle another round in the ring right now."

He takes a sip of his drink and chuckles. "Just admit you can't beat me."

I poke him in the chest. "I *have* beaten you."

"*Allegedly.*" He offers a shrug. "I don't see any proof because no one else was there."

Lucky for him...

If there *had* been any witnesses to me knocking him out cold that day, I'd be having them sign affidavits to that effect for posterity purposes.

I poke him again. "You know as well as I do that I kicked your ass."

He smirks. "*Allegedly.*"

Stone scowls at us, releasing an annoyed sigh. "Will you two *stop* bickering? We're supposed to be celebrating."

Isaac grins at his father. "We're not bickering."

I shrug. "It's friendly banter."

The same way we've always gone at each other our entire lives.

Stone chuckles. "Yeah, sure it is. You two sound like how I was with your aunts and uncles growing up."

I release a little sigh. "Sometimes I wish Mom and Dad had another kid so I would know what it's like to have a brother or sister." I motion to Isaac. "But then I remember I'm stuck with all you assholes as cousins, and you're basically like having siblings, anyway."

Isaac rolls his eyes. "Ha, ha. *Very* funny."

Grinning, I elbow him in the ribs as Jack steps out from the café, her hands settled over her growing stomach.

She leans against the open glass door, Dan's smooth voice floating out to us as she scans the crowd gathered outside. Her gaze lands on Isaac, and a smile curls her lips. "Vivi's asking for you."

Isaac's humor slips away instantly as he goes into worried dad mode. "Is she okay?"

Jack rolls her eyes. "She's fine. She wants you to play some board game with her."

He relaxes instantly. "Okay, I'll be right in."

She reenters and lets the door close behind her, and Isaac turns back to say something to me, but his eyes dart to the road, hardening, along with his jaw.

"Isaac, what is it?"

I turn and follow his line of sight as a black sedan pulls to a stop at the curb.

Even without recognizing the car, my stomach knots immediately. Something about this just doesn't feel right. The front passenger door opens, and one of Roselli's goons steps out, scanning the street.

The back door of the vehicle swings wide, and Roselli climbs onto the sidewalk, straightening his suit coat. His gaze sweeps over everyone else on the patio and lands on us. He approaches, and a slow grin spreads across his face.

Several of the patrons hanging around take note of the newest arrival, a few of them grabbing their drinks and hustling away while others sit transfixed, unsure what to do now that the head of the mob in New Orleans has just arrived uninvited to the party.

Roselli stops in front of us. "Stone, Isaac, Kennedy, congratulations on the reopening." He holds out his hands and steps back to stare up at the new front of the Daily Grind, as well as the buildings on either side of them that were all rebuilt after the fire. "It looks as though nothing ever happened."

Stone takes a step toward him. "But we all know what *did* happen. And you weren't invited, so get the fuck out of here."

Roselli raises an eyebrow slowly. "Or *what*? You'll call the police?" He issues an ominous low chuckle. "I *own* the police, or have you not figured that out yet?"

Shit.

He isn't wrong about that.

Roselli has people everywhere. It's one of the reasons we've done our best not to fight with him. Luca turned over his business to Roselli thirty years ago with the intent to keep the Hawkes neutral, to keep us out of any sort of mob entanglement by playing nice. But now, it seems as though life wants to drag us back into the spider's web.

Between Isaac having a child with the heir apparent to the Marconi crime family in Chicago and the Hawkes taking out Satriano in order to save her, we've ended up in the middle of it again.

The *last* place we want to be.

Roselli grins as we all stare him down. The door to the Grind opens again, and Jack starts to step out, but her eyes land on Roselli and she goes stock still.

Isaac rushes over to her, ushering her back through the door with a hand on her lower back. "Go back. Keep *everyone* else inside."

Stone has finally had enough, and he practically growls at the man. "What do you want, Roselli?"

"I just wanted to offer my congratulations and to see if you've given any more consideration to the conversation I had with Angelina back when this unfortunate incident happened. I've given you time to look into the information I provided, and to consider my offer. I'd hate to think not hearing from you means you've rejected it because that would be..."—he gives a hard grin—"unwise."

Isaac steps up to him, his chest almost brushing the other man's. "If you're threatening me or anyone else in my family, so help me, God, I will kill you with my bare fucking hands. I might've needed a gun with Satriano, but I definitely don't when you're this close."

Instead of cowering, Roselli just grins, his eyes darting over to Stone. "Your son has the same fire you do, or at least, that you used to all those years ago when you worked for Dom."

Stone's entire demeanor shifts, his shoulders tensing even more at the mention of his former life as a lawyer for the mob. Working for Dom Abello almost ruined his life, and it isn't anything he wants reminders of. "Get back in your car and drive away."

Roselli raises a brow. "So, is that a no to my offer?"

Before anyone else can respond, an engine revs, tires squeal on the street, and the sharp crack of gunfire fills the air as pain slices through me.

~

CASS

THE MOMENT I step out of the courtroom and into the hallway, people rush by me, wide-eyed and talking frantically with each other in hushed tones. Hair on the back of my neck stands on end, and my throat goes dry, watching the panic and confusion in their gazes and the urgency in their steps.

Something's wrong.

Judge Masterson's clerk slips from his courtroom to my left and starts to rush by, her eyes on her phone, fingers flying across the screen, typing something.

Maybe she knows what's happening?

I step in front of her, cutting off her direct path down the corridor. "Diana..."

She jerks to a stop, almost colliding with me, her head snapping up. "Attorney Whitaker?"

I motion around us, toward the other courthouse personnel bustling around and chattering excitedly. "What's going on?"

Her eyes widen. "You didn't hear?"

I shake my head, scanning the busy hallway for any signs of what might be causing the apparent uproar. "No, I just got out of a hearing."

She releases a heavy sigh and steps closer, lowering her voice as if she shouldn't be telling me. "There was a shooting. Apparently, Isaac and Stone Hawke were somehow involved."

My blood instantly freezes in my veins, my entire body tingling and going numb as I struggle to process her words.

"What?" I swallow past the lump in my throat. "What happened?"

Diana shakes her head, glancing at her phone again. "I'm not totally sure. Something at that coffee shop, the one the Hawkes own. Rumor is, Cristiano Roselli was there, too. I don't know all the details. It happened a few minutes ago." She holds up her phone. "Some social media postings about it mostly. Not a lot of information."

"Oh, my God." Acid burns my throat, and I fight to stay upright as the hallway seems to spin around me. "W-was anyone hurt?"

Diana shrugs. "I don't know."

Fuck.

Today was the grand opening.

All the Hawkes would have been there.

Everyone.

I suck in a sharp breath, forcing myself to smile at Diana when it feels like the walls are closing in on me. "Thank you."

She rushes off, head dipped to her phone again, and I immediately pull out mine and dial Kennedy's number while I run toward the main courthouse exit.

Come on, come on, come on.

ANSWER!

Each ring that goes unanswered tightens my chest more, and I throw open the door and rush out into the late morning sunlight as her voicemail finally clicks over.

"Hi, you've reached the voicemail for Kennedy Hawke—"

Fuck, fuck, fuck.

I shouldn't risk leaving her a message. If I do and anyone else listens to it, it could make things worse, but I have to know she's all right. "It's me. Call me the moment you get this."

Bolting down the courthouse steps, I shove my phone into my pocket and grab my keys to unlock my car from across the parking lot. My hand shakes as I tug open the door, toss my briefcase onto the passenger seat, and push the start button.

Blood rushes in my ears as I tug on my seatbelt and tear out of the lot with squealing tires, cutting off several cars that lay on their horns. The sound barely registers over the thundering of my heart.

A shooting...

This is exactly what I was trying to warn Kennedy about, what I was trying to prevent, and now, it might be too late.

I weave through traffic, laying on my own horn to avoid collisions and make my way toward the street that holds Hawke's Daily Grind, as well as Falco's Daily Grounds.

A police roadblock stops me only a few blocks away, and I pull right up to it and start to get out.

The uniformed officer standing near the cruisers blocking the street holds up a hand. "Sir, you can't park here. The road's closed."

"I'm an attorney. One of my client's businesses is on the same street as the shooting. I'm trying to get over there to see what happened."

He shakes his head. "No one's allowed within the locked-down area."

"Shit." I shove my hands through my hair, scanning the corner and the faces of the confused and anxious people milling around on the sidewalks. "Can you tell me if anyone's hurt?"

"I don't have that information, sir."

Fuck.

The weight of utter helplessness crushes my chest, making it hard to breathe. If I try to make it past the roadblock, I'm going to end up arrested—and without answers.

I climb back into my car, reverse it out of the intersection, and head toward University Medical Center. If anyone was hurt, they'd be taken there—a level one trauma facility, where

Stone Hawke's wife happens to be the chief of the emergency department. If anyone knows what happened, they'll be there.

My hands tremble, gripping the wheel, and I barrel through the streets, barely seeing what's in front of me.

She's probably fine.

She probably wasn't even there.

I know it's a lie, even though I tell it to myself.

Of course, she was there. It was the grand reopening. They were all there. *All* of them.

"Shit, shit, shit." I slam my palm against the steering wheel and try to fight the rising panic threatening to consume me. "*Shit!*"

Somehow, through the haze of panic, I manage to pull into the hospital parking lot without getting into an accident and ending up as a patient myself. I throw the car into park, climb out, and race inside the emergency room entrance, quickly scanning the faces for anyone familiar as I make my way toward the nurses' station for admissions.

Several people stand in line ahead of me, but there's no way in hell I'm waiting here. Keeping my eyes peeled for any of the Hawkes, I head past the desk and toward the rows of curtains that line the ER.

Nurses and other staff bustle around, darting in and out of the makeshift rooms, and I do my best to try to look like I belong here while peeking over shoulders, searching for any sign of Kennedy.

The agonized faces of the patients match how I feel not knowing what the hell is happening. Screams of pain and sobbing fill the air, twisting the knife in my gut.

Could that be Kennedy?

A woman in blue scrubs steps in my path, narrowing a dark-brown gaze on me. "Sir? Sir, you can't be back here."

"I'm looking for someone."

She scowls. "Go back to the registration desk—"

"Please..." I swallow thickly, shoving a hand through my hair. "I-I just need to know if she's okay."

The woman's eyes soften slightly. "Family?"

Fuck.

As soon as I say *no*, they'll definitely kick me out and send me back to the waiting room. But I've made a career out of lying, of convincing people by choosing my words carefully and telling them what they need to or want to hear.

"I need to see Kennedy Hawke..."

The woman eyes me suspiciously for not answering her question, but she must sense my panic, see something that makes her point to the next curtain on the left. "She's been stabilized, but she's about to be taken up for surgery."

Surgery?

I rush past the woman and tug back the curtain. All the air in my lungs rushes out. Kennedy lies on the bed, her skin deathly pale, eyes closed. Spots of dried blood sprinkle her neck and cheek, evidence of the violence that almost makes me heave. "Kennedy?"

She stirs slightly, her eyelids fluttering, and she winces, blinking against the fluorescent lights above her.

I tug the curtain closed behind me and move to the bed. "Kennedy?"

Unfocused eyes search until they finally find mine. "Cass?"

Just hearing her say my name makes hope bloom in my chest, but the bloodied bandage wrapped around her arm stops it immediately. Rage replaces it, heating my blood and tightening my fists.

She shifts uncomfortably, gritting her teeth together. "Wh-what are you doing here?"

"I heard about the shooting. Are you okay?"

Stupid fucking question, Cass.

The woman is *clearly* not okay.

And seeing her like this...neither am I.

Kennedy swallows thickly, her eyes barely cracked. "I guess that depends on your definition of okay."

"You were shot?"

She nods, her gaze, glassy from whatever medicine they've given her for the pain, finally meeting mine fully. "My arm. But you shouldn't be here." A tear slips from the corner of her eye and trickles down to the pillow. "You *can't* be here."

The FUCK I can't.

I shift forward until my thighs hit the mattress and lean over her slightly. "I'm *not* leaving."

Her eyes plead with me, and the tears flow freely now. "You need to get out of here, Cass, before someone from my family sees you and wonders why the fuck you're here or kills you before you can even answer."

I cup her blood-streaked cheek in my palm. "I'm *not* leaving. They said they're taking you for surgery."

"Yes, you are, unless you want to make this whole situation even worse." Tears streak down her face, and she sucks in a sharp breath. "They need to take out some bullet fragments and check for any major damage to my arm. But Isaac and my uncle"—she squeezes her eyes closed—"it's bad. You don't want to be here. You don't want my family to see you. I don't know what they might do, what they might think..."

It's there in her gaze, along with her panic and concern— the accusation she hasn't voiced.

She thinks this was Falco.

She thinks I knew.

I brush my thumb over her cheek, across one of the dried spots of blood that makes my stomach turn. "I'll go, for *now*. But—"

The curtain pulls open, and the same nurse who directed me in here gives me a stern look. "You need to leave. We're taking her to the OR."

"You're going to be okay, *Cherie*."

She shakes her head, her lips trembling, and all I want to do is pull her into my arms and comfort her the same way I do Charlotte every time she gives me that look. "I don't know. I don't know if anything's ever going to be okay again."

The nurse pushes me away from the bed with a firm arm, and I back away, letting her set to work on the machines hooked up to Kennedy.

Each step I take feels like an ocean opening up between us, and she closes her eyes and turns her head away, as if she can't bear to look at me. "Don't come back. I don't ever want to see you again..."

She thinks I knew.

That realization keeps echoing in my head. She thinks Falco was behind this and that I knew and said nothing. She thinks I'm *responsible*, yet she still warned me to leave. She was still worried about what the Hawkes would do to me.

I turn and stumble out of the ER toward the waiting room, my head spinning with a thousand questions.

Who the hell did this?

Why?

I pull out my phone and dial Marcel, waiting for the call to connect as I move toward the sliding ER doors. There's no way in *hell* I'm leaving with Kennedy like that, but she was right about what might happen if any of the Hawkes find me here.

The line rings a few times before he finally answers. "Cass?"

"Who did it?"

"*What?*" His voice sounds like he's in a metal box. "*I can barely hear you...*"

"Who *did* it?" I grit out the words through clenched teeth. "Who shot at the Hawkes?"

Static makes me pull my phone from my ear for a moment before I can finally bring it back.

"*I don't know, Cass. But I don't think it had anything to do with them. Roselli was there.*"

That halts me in my tracks before I'm halfway to the doors. I've been so worried about Kennedy that I almost forgot Diane said Roselli might have been at The Grind. "What the fuck was Roselli doing there?"

Kennedy made it sound like the Hawkes wanted nothing to do with the guy. They sure as hell wouldn't invite him to the reopening.

Marcel slams a car door. *"I don't know."*

"Well, find the fuck out!"

14

CASS

Someone steps in front of me, blocking my path to the exit and the parking lot. At this point, my entire body vibrates with barely contained rage at what's been done to Kennedy. Anyone who gets in my way to fresh air where I might be able to breathe again and try to tamp down this anger will likely regret it.

I end the call with Marcel and glance up, stiffening immediately.

After all these years, I'm finally face to face with Gabe Anderson, and he's just as volatile and intimidating as evidence would suggest. He stands only feet away, arms crossed over his broad chest, shrewd green gaze locked on me with sheer wrath filling it. "What the *fuck* are you doing here, Whitaker?"

The fury in his voice sends a chill through me.

Of all the Hawkes, he's the last one I'd ever want to mess with. A well-trained killer who doesn't think twice about pulling the trigger, no matter who is in his crosshairs, and he has his sights set on me with the same accusation Kennedy just made.

They *all* believe this was Falco and that I knew.

"I heard about the shooting, and—"

He sneers. "And you came to see the results of Falco's attack so you can relay it back to them and gloat?"

"What?" I stagger back a step at the allegation, even though I knew he was thinking it. Hearing it out loud, the words strike me like the bullets I'm sure Gabe wishes he could shoot right now. They think I would *gloat*. "Fuck, no. Falco had *nothing* to do with this. I heard what happened from one of the clerks at the courthouse and wanted to come see if everyone was okay."

"You don't belong here, Cass." He takes a menacing step forward, the bulge of the weapon at his hip obvious. The ex-Army Ranger doesn't even need it. He could probably still kill me with his bare hands, and he'd likely do it right here in front of the entire hospital staff if I let him. "We don't need your fake sympathy. Get the fuck out and stay the fuck away. We'll deal with you later."

I shake my head, holding out my hands again. "You don't understand. I'm just trying to find out what happened, so I can help—"

"Help?" He lurches forward, making me retreat another step, but Savage appears and moves between us, preventing Gabe from advancing. Gabe glares at his best friend, then points an accusatory finger at me. "Isaac and Kennedy were hurt, and Stone might not make it..."

Emotion seems to steal his words, and he glances away for a moment, his hands fisted at his sides. The man I always assumed felt nothing, to be able to do what he has done, almost breaks right in front of me, but he somehow regains control and releases a long, slow breath.

"You can *help* by getting out of here because if I kill you now and get arrested, it's only going to make things worse for us, and I don't know how long I'm going to be able to hold back."

From anyone else, it might seem like an empty threat being made by a man on the edge because of the trauma his family just suffered, but Gabe doesn't make idle threats. He does whatever it takes to protect those he loves—and three of those people are lying in hospital beds because of a shooting they think I'm somehow tied to.

If we had met anywhere private, this would have ended very differently.

Only the ER waiting room full of people and the various hospital staffers hustling around are preventing Gabe from unleashing on me, and the longer I stay, the more tense it's going to become.

It would be wise to leave, to get out while I can, but this might be the only chance I get to try to talk to any of the Hawkes somewhere they can't attack me without consequences.

Savage settles his steely blue gaze on me, eyes red-rimmed, cheeks streaked from his tears, his entire face bearing the evidence of his turmoil. The patriarch of the Hawke Family seems eerily calm, but it's an act. His anger burns as hot as Gabe's; he's just doing a better job of controlling it at the moment. "You need to *go*."

I take a deep breath, trying to calm my racing heart long enough to say what I need to in a way that might actually make them listen. "I will. But I need to say something first—this wasn't Falco Enterprises."

One of Gabe's brows wings up. "And we're just supposed to believe you?"

It's my own fault they don't.

I've been pushing Falco's agenda so hard that I've given them every reason to suspect the worst.

"This is why I came to you after the fire. I tried to warn you.

I've had a feeling that things weren't right in town for a while. I've had my private investigator looking into it. I think whoever was behind the fire at The Grind was behind this, too."

Savage shakes his head. "I think it's pretty clear who the target was. They were standing right next to Roselli—and he's dead. Falco tried to kill two birds with one stone, so to speak. Remove Roselli for whatever grander purposes and hurt us in the process."

"No!" I scrub my hands over my face, my frustration building as people mingling around us near the entrance start to watch our confrontation. "Falco has no reason to attack Roselli, and—"

Gabe scowls. "But Falco has done everything in their power to try to fuck with our businesses. What's lighting one of them on fire or showering it with bullets? If Falco has their sights set on taking over Roselli's territory, it all makes sense."

I take a step forward, then try to contain myself. Lashing out at them isn't going to make it any easier to get them to believe me. "Filing injunctions is a whole lot different than fire-bombing a business or punching it full of holes. You really think that's Falco's MO?"

Gabe moves to stand next to Savage, removing the only barrier keeping him back. "How the fuck would we know when we don't even know who Falco is or what they're trying to achieve besides our destruction? Who's running it?"

"You know I can't give you that information."

"No...yet, here you are again. You show up immediately after The Grind goes up in flames. And now, you're here after three of our family members were shot. You're either stupid, or you have a death wish."

"I don't." I shake my head. "I want to avoid getting tangled up in a war that has nothing to do with me."

I have to protect Charlotte.

If I'm gone, she'll be on hers, and I would never do that to her. I could never. I know what it's like to lose everything as a child. She's never had a mother, and I'm not about to let them take away her father because the Hawkes have the wrong idea.

"I'm truly sorry that this happened, that Stone and Isaac and Kennedy got hurt." Just saying those words is like a knife slashing through my chest, the image of her so pale, so weak, seared in my memory like a brand. "I hope they're all okay, but I'm telling you—"

"Yeah, yeah, yeah." Gabe throws out a dismissive hand. "It wasn't Falco."

Savage advances slightly. "Get the hell out of here. I don't want to have to take out another restraining order against you."

Shit.

They would, too.

I already can't get within a hundred yards of Hawke's Daily Grind due to the bullshit restraining order Isaac had rubber-stamped by a judge they own post-fire.

After this, it's only going to get worse—for everyone.

I take one last lingering look back down the hallway where Kennedy lay only minutes ago, hurt and terrified. They were taking her into surgery, and even if I stayed to await the outcome, with Gabe and Savage standing watch, I'll never get near her again.

"I'm going, but please...watch your backs."

It sounded more like a threat than I intended it, but there's nothing else I can do if they won't listen. Reluctantly, I brush past them and make my way out of the hospital and to my car.

When I get to it, I finally stop and let the adrenaline crash happen. I rest my palms on the roof and drop my head, taking several deep breaths.

Kennedy was shot.

A few more inches to the right and she would've taken it right in the heart.

Bile climbs up my throat, and I swallow it back, shaking my head. This wasn't supposed to happen, none of this.

I tried to warn them, but if they won't listen, what the fuck else can I do?

Maybe nothing.

But if I sit back and watch, more people are going to get hurt. I have to figure something out, and fast.

～

KENNEDY

THE CLICK of the door opening and light from the hallway streaming in and hitting my face wakes me from a restless, drug-induced sleep. My mind still heavy and foggy with the pain meds, I try to force my eyes open, blinking against the brightness until whoever came in closes the door behind them, leaving only the glow from the various machines I'm hooked up to around the room.

Footsteps approach the bed, and I tense, immediately recoiling slightly.

"It's okay, baby. It's just me."

Mom...

I relax instantly, and she sits on the chair next to the bed and pulls my right hand into hers, squeezing it gently. The familiar feel of her palm against mine, of the soothing brush of her thumb against my skin, instantly relieves some of my unease.

She leans in and presses a kiss to my cheek. "I didn't wake you, did I?"

"Sort of."

For hours, this cloud of narcotics has kept me lingering between sleep and wake, unable to fully grasp anything that's happening around me beyond a few words from nurses and familiar voices. But despite still being heavily drugged, and even in the dimly lit room, it's impossible to miss the swelling and redness around Mom's eyes. Her puffy, stained cheeks, either. Getting Danika Eriksson Hawke to cry is a pretty tough endeavor, and my stomach twists.

The events of this morning all come rushing back. Roselli. Gunfire. Pain. Blood. Screams. "Are Isaac and Uncle Stone okay?"

Her bottom lip trembles, and she tightens her grip on my good hand. "Isaac will be okay. Two bullets hit him, but like with you, they missed anything vital. Pope confirmed he made it through surgery okay and should be fine." She swallows thickly and clenches her eyes closed. When she reopens them, I already know what she's going to say. "But Uncle Stone is in bad shape..."

She fights back a sob, and my own tears burn my eyes.

"They've had him in surgery for hours. They're still working on him." She sucks in a sharp breath. "He coded once."

"Oh, God—"

"They got him back."

"Oh, God. Oh, God—"

She squeezes my hand again and presses a kiss against the back of it. "Calm down, baby. You don't need to be getting upset right now."

How can I calm down?

The panic welling up inside me threatens to drown me, and I release a sob.

"Oh, baby." Mom runs her fingers through my hair. "He's in good hands. Nora is watching the surgery from the Observation Gallery. They wouldn't let her in the room, which really pissed her the fuck off." She gives me a tight smile. "You know your Uncle Stone and I have had our issues in the past, things that came between us, things I held against him."

I squeeze her hand. "You had every right to feel the way you did."

She drops her forehead against the mattress, her still-blond hair spilling around her. "It seems petty now that I held something against him for so long that happened when he was just a child, that things were never the same between us as they were with everyone else because I didn't let them be."

"He understood, Mom. He *understands*." I shake my head, fighting the desire to fall apart completely. But there's a very real chance that Stone might *not* be okay. "This is all my fault..."

Her eyes widen. "What? No."

I nod as tears flow down my cheeks onto the pillow under my head. "It is. I rushed everyone to get the Daily Grind reopened quickly. Once Isaac settled the injunction issue with Falco, I pushed. Maybe if I hadn't, if Saint and Gabe and Bishop and everyone had more time, they could have figured out security better. They could have—"

"No." She shakes her head. "Stop right there. You're not going to blame yourself for this. This was about Roselli. You couldn't have anticipated him showing up or somebody trying to shoot him while you guys were there. This had absolutely nothing to do with the opening. Somebody was looking for an opportunity for him to be out and unprotected somewhere, and they found it. It just happened to be on our day, that's it. You *can't* blame yourself for this."

Nothing she says can change anything.

This *is* my fault.

If I wasn't literally sleeping with the enemy, if I wasn't so damn distracted, I might have anticipated this. We could have locked it down tighter, done more to protect everyone.

It's a miracle no one else was hit with all the bullets flying.

It was so well targeted...

Only the four of us standing together...

"But, Mom, what if it wasn't about Roselli?"

She narrows her eyes at me. "Your father told me what you said about questioning if someone else is involved with everything that's been going on." Her fingers brush through my hair. "But I'm telling you, I've used all my resources with the media and my less scrupulous contacts, plus anyone else the family can think of, and we can't find *anything* to suggest that."

Only the word of the man who probably betrayed me and is covering for those who are really behind it...

Mom squeezes my hand again. "I'm not going to let you blame yourself for this. No one else does."

I suck in a shaky breath.

They would if they knew I had slept with Cass, if they knew that only a few days ago, I spent hours and hours in his bed— under him, above him, letting him do things to me that are more intimate than anything I've ever done with any man.

I bite my lip to keep from confessing everything to her. Only the door opening stops me from word-vomiting my sins.

Caroline enters, closes the door behind her, and walks over behind Mom. She squeezes Mom's shoulders and offers me a tight smile. "How are you feeling?"

Like shit.

The pain in my arm is dulled by the drugs, but it's still there on the periphery, the constant throbbing with the occasional little jolt if I move even an inch.

"I'm okay." I'm not going to complain when Stone's life hangs in the balance. "Do you have an update on Uncle Stone?"

She shakes her head. "He's still in surgery. Everyone's here waiting."

"Where's Isaac?"

Caroline tips her head sideways. "Next room over with Jack."

"Where's Vivi?"

Mom offers a tight smile. "Bishop has her at their place. Isaac didn't want her to see him like this."

I fight the tears again, trying to blink them away, then reach up my good arm and swipe at them.

Caroline sighs, glancing between Mom and me. "We have to postpone the groundbreaking."

That stills my hand. "What?"

She shakes her head. "We can't do it, not after this. We can't have—"

I nod. "Yes, we can. We have to." This makes me even more determined to ensure it happens on time. "I don't care if Gabe and Saint need to hire every former Marine and Ranger and Delta Force operator they know to get down here and form a fucking line around the property...we're *having* that ground-breaking."

Mom gives me a concerned look. "I don't think it's a good idea."

"What did Dad say?"

She releases a sigh and pulls her hand out of mine to run it back through her hair. "The same thing you just did." Shaking her head, she gives me a smile. "You're so much like him."

I laugh and wince at the pain it causes. "And he always tells me I'm a carbon copy of you."

Caroline chuckles. "I'd say you're a pretty even fifty-fifty mix, if I really thought about it."

I smile at the compliment, but Mom's lips twist, and she looks up at her best friend.

"Those are the things that always got me in trouble, though."

Caroline nods. "That's true, too."

Mom runs her hand over mine. "I am worried about you, baby."

"I'll be all right. When can I get out of here?"

Caroline motions behind her to the hallway. "One of Aunt Nora's friends is your treating physician. He said another few days, but I really think that's only because Nora and Pope want to keep you here, not because you actually need to be. They just need to get your pain levels manageable. There isn't really anything else to do."

The door opens again, and Pope slips in, wearing his white lab coat, and approaches the foot of the bed, offering a tight smile.

Mom stiffens and looks at him. "Do you have an update on Stone?"

He nods slowly. "I just went in there to check. They're still working on him, but they have him stabilized." He pauses for a moment. "They won't know the true extent of his injuries or if he suffered any brain damage from when he coded until they finish and he wakes up."

Brain damage?

"But..." I fight back a sob. "He's going to be okay?"

Pope inhales a sharp breath and tightens his hands around the end railing of the bed. He's always been so serious and brutally honest, and now that he's a doctor, he's had to work on his bedside manner. But we aren't strangers, and we need the truth. "I could lie to you guys as a member of the family and tell you he'll be fine, but as a doctor, I need everyone to be prepared that he might not be."

A cold boulder of dread settles into my stomach as I stare at him and see the truth in his words.

It's bad.

Really bad.

We could lose him.

And that's not something the Hawkes would survive.

15

KENNEDY

Allie opens the door to my condo and holds it for me, allowing me to shuffle through. The ache in my arm ratchets up to a sharp stab every time I inadvertently shift it slightly with each step. "You should have just taken the wheelchair Aunt Nora and Pope offered to help get you home and into bed."

I glower at her as I finally make it all the way in. "I was shot in the arm, not the leg or ass. I can walk."

She allows the door to shut behind us. "Uh-huh." Giving me a reproachful look, she lifts the plastic bag in her hand containing my meds and inclines her head toward the kitchen. "Come take your pain medication before you go lie down."

My eyes drift toward the hallway leading back to my bedroom, and I'm tempted to forgo the narcotics and collapse into a familiar bed and hide forever, but the increasing pain in my arm forces me to follow her instead.

Pope lectured me on how important it was to stay on top of pain, especially the first few days after surgery like this, and I can't handle arguing with Allie about it right now. She's likely to call him over, or even worse, Bishop, to get me to take them if I protest.

Allie sets the bag on the counter, along with her purse. "I really wish you would've just gone to stay with your mom and dad like they wanted."

I shake my head. "I haven't been able to live under their roof since I was eighteen without them driving me crazy. I'm definitely not doing it now." I lean my hip against the counter, needing the support after barely being on my feet at all for days on end. "I'll be fine."

She gives me that look again. "You're not fine, which is why I'm here and I'm going to stay." Her hand shoots up to stop me before I can argue. "Whether you want me to or not. You and I are going to have a little slumber party for the next couple of days until you feel better and can defend yourself if...if anything else might happen..."

The pain and fear in her voice make my chest tighten, the same guilt that's been weighing down on me for the last few days since the shooting returning so quickly that it practically suffocates me. "I think you should go stay with Jude and Angie. I need some time alone."

She starts pulling my prescriptions from the bag. "You know that won't happen. Or have you forgotten what family you're a part of?"

"How could I ever forget that?"

It's the thing I love the most and hate the most about the Hawkes. No one is ever truly alone. We watch each other's backs and defend every last member of the family to our dying breaths.

That also means little to no time alone, especially when there still isn't any answer about the shooter—nothing but a burned-out car found miles away, with any evidence destroyed by the fire they started to do just that.

Allie watches me carefully, like she's expecting me to break down, even though I have somehow managed *not* to since I first woke and spoke with Mom and Caroline. "Just because you're out of the hospital doesn't mean you're okay, Kennedy, and it's all right to admit that."

No, it isn't.

Everyone needs to be focused on Uncle Stone right now, not on me. It's why I've held myself together through the doctors' visits, talking with Dad, Gabe, Aunt Nora, and everyone else. Even visiting Isaac in the room next door and seeing the extent of his injuries, I managed to hold it together.

I'm not about to break now, not in front of Allie.

"Al, I wish you would go back to the hospital and sit with Aunt Nora and Coen."

She sighs and turns back to face me, pill bottle in hand. "I have to be honest with you." Her free hand drops to her growing stomach. "The hospital just makes me..."—she shakes her head like she doesn't want to say what she's really thinking —"it's the last place I want to be right now."

"Because you have to see Pope?"

Allie stiffens slightly, then twists off the cap and dumps a pill into her palm. "I don't know what you're talking about."

I snort. "Oh, please. The two of you clearly had it out over something recently because you can't stand to be in the same room with each other and haven't been able to have a conversation in a *long* time. Things have been a little cold between you for years, but lately, it's been downright arctic."

Instead of answering me, she shoves the pill toward me, then grabs a bottle of water from the fridge and removes the cap. "Take it."

I stare at the pill for a moment, debating throwing it right back into the bottle, but the dull ache that is quickly growing as my last dose wears off ultimately makes me grab it and swallow it down.

A knock on the door draws both of our attention toward it, and Allie sets the bottle on the counter. "I'll get the door. You go lie down."

I glower at her. "I can answer my own fucking door. You figure out dinner."

No one besides family can get into the building without passing security and having them call up to us, anyway. It's likely just Bishop, Astrid, or Angie stopping by to further fuss over me with Allie.

I shuffle back over to the door and pull it open, but it isn't the gaze of one of the Hawkes that falls on me. Pale-green eyes lock with mine and scan from my head down to the slides on my feet.

Cass' chiseled jaw, now covered with several days' worth of stubble, tightens, and a muscle there tics violently under the whiskers. "What the hell are you doing out of the hospital?"

I glance behind me, but Allie's still busy with something in the kitchen and hasn't noticed our uninvited visitor. "How did you know I was home? How the fuck do you know where I live?" I lean out and scan the hallway. "And how did you get past security?"

He snorts like any of that's hard. "Can I come in?"

"No." I peek at Allie again. "This isn't a good time, and I don't have anything to say anyway. I told you I never want to see you again."

His jaw tightens again. "If it were up to you, it would never be a good time." With one quick step, he brushes past me. In my condition, I definitely can't stop him. He makes his way a few steps into the living room, then turns to face me. "And you don't really mean it when you say you don't want to see me."

Allie steps out of the kitchen, her eyes wide. "Cass?" Her gaze darts between the two of us. "What are you doing here?"

He stiffens, glancing from her to me. "Hello, Alessandra. I came to talk to Kennedy."

Allie immediately tenses. "I don't think that's a good idea."

It definitely *isn't*.

I made it clear to him that I never wanted to see his smug face again, that I never wanted him anywhere *near* me, yet the bastard still shows up, gets past security, and forces his way into my home.

He's determined; I'll give him that. But that determination to help his client destroy the Hawkes is what led to all of this in the first place. All I want is to shove him out the door, but if I don't allow him to say whatever it is he came to say, he'll just keep coming, and next time, there may be more witnesses.

"Allie, go make up the spare bedroom for yourself while I talk to Cass." I force a half-smile at her. "It's fine."

Her dark brows rise. "Really?"

I nod, trying to convey with my gaze that she shouldn't ask any more questions in present company. She gives me a look that says we'll be having a major *talk* later and disappears back down the hallway.

"Say whatever you have to say and get the hell out."

It's as direct as I can be, and I move past him into the kitchen to lean back against the counter. The fast-acting pain meds have already started making me dizzy, and it won't be long before I will drop.

Cass follows me slowly, never taking his eyes off me. "I'm serious, Kennedy. Should you be out of the hospital?"

I glower at him. "The doctors released me, didn't they?"

"That doesn't mean anything. Look at you. You can barely stand up."

"Did you just come here to tell me I look like shit?"

He closes the distance between us and takes my cheek in his palm, tilting my face up until my eyes meet his. I try to pull out of his touch, but he forces me to keep looking at him.

"No, *Cherie,* I came because I was fucking worried about you. I've been going out of my mind the last few days. But with all the Hawkes circling around the waiting room, there was no way I was getting back to see you again."

I tense at his mention of the family. "Did you talk to any of them when you were there?"

No one mentioned anything about seeing Cass at the hospital, but they haven't exactly been filling me in on everything, either. They've walked on eggshells since the moment I woke, no one wanting to say anything that might distress me.

All they've ended up doing is pissing me off by keeping me in the dark.

His back stiffens. "I told your father and your uncle Gabe the same thing I've been telling you, that this is what I was trying to stop." Cass lets his gaze drop to my arm in the sling. "They can't keep you safe because they won't listen. They've just proven that by letting *this* happen to you."

The more he talks, the more outraged I become until my body trembles. "How the fuck can anybody keep me safe when I let the one responsible get this close?"

He growls, fury sparking in his gaze. "This *wasn't* Falco!" His sharp words carry around the condo, filled with far more than simply anger. He has the nerve to actually look *hurt*. "You think I would let one of my clients do this to you?"

I jerk out of his hold, retreating a few steps until my shoulders hit the refrigerator behind me, and I wince at the contact with my bad arm, the pain rushing through me despite the meds I just took starting to settle in.

Cass is on me so fast that I barely have time to swallow my sob. "Are you all right?" His hand cradles my neck, and he softly brushes his thumb along the skin there. "You look like you're in pain."

I glance down at my arm in the sling. "Just bumped my arm, that's all."

He keeps stroking the side of my neck, the contact sending shivers through my body, ones I don't want to acknowledge, not when his client might be responsible for what happened. "Do you really think I could ever allow something like *this*?"

The agony in his words, the true emotion, almost undoes me.

I look deep into his eyes, but all I see there confuses a mind already overrun with narcotics, guilt, and pain. "I don't know. You've done everything else your clients have asked to try to put us out of business. Then we reopen, and at the goddamn grand opening party, someone shoots up the place while Falco has a damn sale down the street."

Cass issues a low growl, stepping closer, pressing his body to mine while making sure to keep from touching my arm. He brings his lips a hairsbreadth from my own, the scent of his crisp aftershave filling my breaths. His hand slips up around my throat. "If I wanted to hurt you, Kennedy, I had every chance to a thousand different ways the other night. But did I?"

My body heats at the memory of just what he did to me, how generous and giving he was as a lover. How completely he destroyed me with his hands, his mouth, his cock, in the most delicious of ways.

But I can't respond.

I can't admit it.

Tears burn in my eyes, but I fight them falling.

He's already broken me in so many ways; I can't let him do it again.

His grip tightens slightly, not restricting my airflow but enough to prove he could. "I could have wrapped my hand around your throat like this and squeezed until you stopped breathing. I could have done worse...but I didn't because I don't want to see you hurt. Seeing you like this..." He strokes his thumb across my thundering pulse. "It hurts me more than I want to admit. You might be looking for someone to blame, for an enemy, but it isn't me, no matter how easy it would be for you to pretend that it is. You know deep down that it isn't, that I didn't do this, that I never would or *could*."

With his body aligned to mine so tightly, the feel of his hard cock wedged between us makes my clit throb. Even now, after everything that's happened the last few days, this man's touch, his words, completely unravel me.

Dropping his head, he feathers his lips against my ear. "I will *never* hurt you, Kennedy. Not like this. Never."

The sound of a round being chambered jerks him back from me, and we both whip our heads in the direction of it.

Allie stands at the entrance to the kitchen, the pistol in her hand pointed squarely at Cass. "Take your fucking hands off her before I blow a hole through you."

~

CASS

I WOULDN'T THINK there's anything worse than having a gun trained on you. It's one of the scenarios I've lived in fear over, one of the things I've dreaded. Yet seeing Kennedy like this, hurt and terrified, is a thousand times more agonizing than her cousin pointing that thing at me.

Still, Charlotte's face flashes before my eyes, and no matter how badly I don't want to leave Kennedy when she's like this, I don't stand a chance of walking out of here unscathed if I don't release my hold on her.

"This isn't what it looks like." I slowly take my hand off her throat and back away with both of them raised. "Really..."

Allie squares her shoulders, shifting nervously on her feet, the gun still pointed squarely at me. "It sure as hell looks like your hand was around her fucking throat."

"Okay"—I glance at Kennedy—"it *is* what it looks like, but—"

"Was it you?" Allie's lips tremble, her voice wavering slightly, though she maintains a steady grip on the deadly weapon. "Was it your client? Was it Falco?"

Shaking my head, I look between them—from Kennedy's glassy gaze to Allie's harsh one.

I half expect Kennedy to tell her to go ahead and fire, but instead, she releases a heavy breath and shakes her head.

"No, Allie. It wasn't him. It wasn't *them*." Kennedy offers me a sad look, like admitting that has completely deflated her. "And this isn't what it looks like."

Allie's eyes move from her cousin back to me, then drift down to the very obvious erection pressing against the front of my pants. "Holy shit. Are you two—"

Kennedy gives her a glare that silences her. "Put the gun away."

Allie starts to object, but Kennedy points a finger at her.

"Put the fucking gun away."

Storm's youngest daughter considers me for a moment, probably imagining the story she could create to justify actually shooting me. But after what feels like a damn eternity, she slowly lowers it.

I do the same with my hands and release a heavy breath, trying to control the thundering of my heart against my ribs.

Kennedy sags slightly against the fridge. "I need you to go, Allie."

"What?" Allie's eyes widen. "No, I'm not leaving you. I'm especially not leaving you here with *him*."

Allie always was feisty whenever I spoke with her at the café. Just like *most* of the Hawke kids, she doesn't back down, not even from a member of her family. There's no reason she would now, not when Kennedy is so obviously struggling and asking her to leave her in the hands of the man the whole family thinks knew of the attack and did nothing to stop it.

Kennedy closes her eyes, clearly suffering from being on her feet for so long. "I need to talk to Cass alone."

The tiny pregnant woman stands her ground, not willing to budge. "No. You know what would happen if anyone found out I left you here alone with this asshole?"

Slowly, Kennedy opens her eyes, and they drift down to Allie's growing belly, then back up. "I haven't questioned you about the father of that baby, and I expect you to give me the same courtesy of not inserting yourself into my personal life. Unless you want the entire family to know what I suspect?"

Allie swallows thickly, shaking her head. "You wouldn't."

"Just go, Al. I'll be fine." The words aren't very convincing, but Kennedy does her best to hide the waver in her voice. "Go home. Take the gun with you. Lock your door, and don't open it for anyone. Come back tomorrow, and no one will ever know you left..." Kennedy forces a smile that doesn't reach her partially hooded eyes. "I'm just going to sleep, anyway. So go."

It's an order Allie doesn't seem inclined to accept. She tightens her grip on the gun at her side and opens her mouth to argue. Kennedy lets her gaze drift to Allie's stomach.

Apparently, Kennedy's un-repeated threat is sufficient because Allie turns to walk away, stopping to set the gun on the edge of the counter. "I'll go, but I'm leaving this here in case you need it."

The corner of Kennedy's lips twitches into an almost smile. "I might, but you know I can handle myself."

Under any other circumstances, I would agree with her, but she looks like she's about ready to collapse right here in the kitchen. The turmoil of the last few days, coupled with the physical strain on her body, is enough to crush the woman who usually stands so strong and unmovable.

Her cousin sees it, too, making her even more reluctant to leave. Allie offers her one last lingering look, snags her purse from the counter, then shakes her head and moves toward the door, muttering something under her breath.

Releasing a heavy sigh, I run my shaking hand through my hair and turn back to Kennedy, who's trembling against the fridge, barely able to stay up on her own two feet. I move back over to her and take her face in my palms. "You should be in bed."

She squeezes her eyes closed. "I would argue with you...I got rid of Allie so I could..."—a sigh slips from her lips—"but I'm too tired to right now. This is the longest I've been on my feet in days."

"They released you too soon."

Kennedy opens her eyes, and the pain she's feeling physically and emotionally shifts the normal warm blue to a darker shade that carves at my chest. "I took my pain meds before you got here. I just..." Her words slur slightly, and her eyes drift closed again. "...need to lie down..."

"You're not staying here."

Her lids flutter until that hazy blue gaze meets mine. "What?"

"I'm taking you home with me."

She laughs lightly and cringes, tugging her arm tighter against her in the sling. "No, you're not."

Like fucking hell I'm not...

"Yes, I *am*."

The tiniest annoyed sigh slips from her lips. "I have a thousand people in my family who have made it their mission to take care of me, Isaac, and my uncle. You don't need to do it."

It shouldn't surprise me that she would push me away, given everything that's happened and what she believed up until only a few moments ago, but it still hurts all the same in a way I don't want to acknowledge. If I did, it would change everything, and I'm not ready to face that yet.

"Yes, I *do, Cherie*."

She locks her gaze with mine. "No, you *don't*." Fighting against the narcotics flooding her system and the sheer exhaustion, she tries to square her shoulders but can't manage it. "You don't have any reason to..."

"I have *every* reason to, Kennedy, because whether you believe it or not, *this*"—I motion between us—"this *whatever* it is we feel besides the hatred is real, and I can't see you like this. I can't know you are in pain and suffering without doing whatever I can to make it better."

Her bottom lip trembles, her eyes glassy and now filling with unshed tears. "It isn't your job."

"It *is*." I don't leave any room for further argument with the statement. "I'm going to go pack you a bag, then you're coming home with me."

She opens her mouth to argue again, but I press my lips to hers, silencing her protest that wouldn't have meant anything, anyway. I expect her to shove at my chest and push me away, to fight the way I've become so accustomed to with her, but instead, she sags against me, pushing her weight off the fridge and onto my body.

I wrap my arms around her gently, careful not to squeeze her injured arm between us, and kiss her softly. "Don't fight with me, Kennedy. As much as I love it, I don't want you to waste the energy on anything other than getting better."

Her legs waver under her, and I adjust my hold on her to support her weight.

"Come on, let's go to your bedroom and get whatever you need."

Kennedy nods reluctantly, and when she tries to take a step, she almost collapses, her legs giving out, my arm around her waist the only thing keeping her upright.

"Shit." I scoop her up into my arms, making her wince. "What?" I must have jostled her arm too much, her pinched face showing how uncomfortable she really is. "I'm sorry."

She shakes her head and rests it against my shoulder. "No, this is better."

Fuck. She must really be out of it to admit that.

I carry her through the unfamiliar living room and down the only hallway until I find the master bedroom. Her scent slams into me, my cock stirring back to life again at the thought of taking her here on this bed. Her utter defiance. Her unwillingness to give me an inch but to take a mile. Her smart mouth. All of it makes me want to crawl under these sheets with her and hold her until it's all better, then make her come so many times she forgets any of this ever happened.

As carefully as I can, I lower her onto the mattress. "I would stay here with you, but..."

She opens her eyes and stares up at me from under hooded lids. "Charlotte."

I nod.

"And you have to work. You can't—"

"Fuck work." I scan the room, from the dresser along the far wall with the mirror above it to the two doors that must be an ensuite and closet. "What do you need me to pack for you?"

Kennedy mutters off a list I can barely hear, her eyes drifting closed again, and she motions toward one of the doors. I hustle over to it, enter the closet, and grab a gym bag from the floor beneath the hanging clothes.

Staring at the shirts, suits, and dresses hanging on the racks and the drawers built in next to them, I wrack my brain for what to grab. It's been a long fucking time since I've lived with a woman, and trying to remember what she might need on a daily basis is like dredging in an abyss I never thought I'd be back in.

I dig through her drawers, throwing in sweatpants and yoga pants, then snag a few button-down shirts and anything else that looks easy to get in and out of.

She still hates my guts.

Probably always *will*.

I'm the *last* person who *should* be looking after her, but I can't stop this primal need to make sure she's all right and comfortable. No one else can do this. No one else *should* do this.

Stepping back out in the room, I beeline for the dresser and toss in underwear and bras, trying not to linger on the beautiful lace and colorful negligées I'd love to see her in, rather grabbing the things she will be most comfortable in.

I make my way over to the bed and set the bag at the foot. Kennedy's eyelids droop as she stares up at me, barely managing to stay awake.

Reaching down, I brush hair back from her face. "Where's your medication?"

She swallows. "Kitchen counter."

By the gun...

"I'm going to go grab it, then we're out of here."

Her head bobs in what I think is supposed to be a nod.

The thought of leaving her even for the minute it's going to take to grab the bottles from the kitchen twists my gut, and I lean down and rest my forehead against hers. "I'm so sorry."

She doesn't respond, maybe because she doesn't know what I'm apologizing for any more than I do.

For everything I've done for Falco Enterprises.

For everything that's happened to her and her family.

For the fact that she might lose her uncle.

All of it.

I rush out of her room as quickly as I can to snag the bottles from the counter, then make my way back to her. Her eyes are closed. Her lips part slightly as she releases soft, even breaths.

Asleep already.

I toss the bottles into the bag and pull it onto my shoulder, watching her for a second, hating the feelings building up inside me. They're too dangerous. They're the kind that will fuck up everything I've worked for. But they're there all the same.

And the longer I watch her, the worse the vise around my chest tightens.

I scoop her up into my arms. She mutters something and snuggles against my neck.

Shit.

All I wanted to do was talk to her that night at the masquerade, to give her the information I had and get as much as I could from her. None of this was ever supposed to happen, but now I have Kennedy Hawke in my arms.

It feels so fucking right.

And that's a big fucking problem.

16

KENNEDY

I wake to the familiar scent of the man I want to hate so badly filling my lungs, and I inhale deeply, sucking it down, letting it relax me even more into the comfortable bed that is definitely not mine.

Shit.

My eyes snap open, and I immediately regret it, groaning and blinking against the harsh morning light. I try to turn away from it, and the pain hits me, making me cringe and mutter a curse.

"Fuck!"

Yesterday comes rushing back—at least, bits and pieces of it that managed to break through the drugs that apparently kept me sleeping all night.

That man actually took me from my goddamn condo.

I must've been dead on my feet to allow him to scoop me up and carry me out of there like that.

What the hell was he thinking?

A fuzzy memory of him bringing me into the elevator and

stopping to say something to the security guards in the lobby comes back. Then he secured my seatbelt and pressed a chaste kiss to my lips before we sped away.

After that, all I remember is this soft bed and warm, comforting touches all night each time I started to wake that allowed me to fall back asleep. It's the first time since the shooting I've gotten any real sleep, not plagued by nightmares that make me relive that day over and over again.

I blamed that on sleeping in a hospital bed, with all the machines and noises and lights, but apparently, all I needed was the bed and embrace of Cass Whitaker.

I use my good arm to push myself up slightly, and a feeling like I'm being watched settles over me. Slowly, I turn my head to check the right side of the bed and find Charlotte, her face propped in her hands, blond bob hanging around her cherub cheeks, intense green eyes locked right on me.

Fucking hell.

I jerk away slightly, surprised to find her sitting here, watching me the moment I wake.

She lies flat on her stomach in her pink jammies, where her dad slept all night, kicking her legs aimlessly up and behind her. "Hi."

"Um..." I try to brush the hair from my face, but it falls right back over my eye, partially because of how I'm propped up on my right arm and looking over my shoulder at her. "Hi, Charlotte."

Swinging her legs idly, she continues to stare me down. "What are you doing here in Daddy's bed?"

Shit.

I scan the room quickly, looking for Cass to jump in and save me because this is not a question I'm about to answer for his daughter. But there isn't any sign of him.

Shit. Shit. Shit.

Shifting myself more upright, the covers fall down, exposing my arm in the sling.

Her eyes dart down to my injury and widen slightly. "What happened to your arm?"

"Oh, I..." I use my free hand to push the hair out of my face again, tucking it behind my ear to try to get it to stay there. "I hurt it."

She tilts her head slightly. "How?"

Some psychopath shot up my cousin's cafe.

My eyes start to burn, tears threatening with the memory, but I push it aside, searching for a way to answer her that won't terrify her. This type of violence shouldn't touch a child. They should remain blissfully unaware of how vicious and hateful people can really be.

What the hell are Isaac and Jack telling Viviana?

She was there, in the café. She witnessed all of it and saw her father hit the sidewalk, riddled with bullet holes. That's the kind of trauma you don't overcome, and I will not subject this sweet little girl to that ugly truth.

"It was an accident."

About as far from an accident as it could be, but it seems like the right response for a four-year-old.

She continues swinging her legs, tilting her head from side to side while she examines me. "What are you doing *here*?"

Oh, we're back to that, are we?

Shit.

I'm not remotely prepared to handle this conversation at this moment—or maybe ever.

"Your dad is a brute who literally kidnapped me and brought me here mostly against my will" probably isn't the right response.

I open and close my mouth a few times, trying to think of what to say, anything that might get her off the topic or appease her curiosity even slightly. My recent "aunt experience" with Viviana hasn't prepared me for this—not at *all*.

Cass appears in the doorway, his brow furrowing, looking sexy as fuck in a pale-gray T-shirt that hugs his muscled chest and stretches at his biceps and a pair of black jogging pants. "There you are." His gaze narrows on Charlotte before darting over to me and back to her. "You need to get ready for school. Abby's going to be here in a few minutes to pick you up. I just laid out your clothes for you."

Charlotte looks between him and me, still swinging her legs. "Why is your friend in your bed?"

Her father stiffens at her question and approaches, running a hand along the back of his neck and tilting his head to the side. "She got hurt and needed someone to take care of her."

The precocious blonde considers his answer while staring me down, then looks back at him again. "But you told me you didn't think she'd be coming back."

His jaw hardens, and a muscle there tics as he locks his hard green gaze with mine. "I didn't think she would be."

An uncomfortable tension filled with a million unsaid things builds between us before he shakes his head to clear it and marches over to the right side of the bed to scoop her up.

"Now stop harassing her and go get ready for school."

"But...Daddy!"

Charlotte tries to wiggle out of his hold, but he stalks to the door and sets her on her feet, swatting her playfully on the butt. "Go. Abby will be here in five minutes."

She takes a lingering look back at me, then disappears down the hallway. His shoulders slump slightly before he turns back to face me, rubbing his hand along his jaw, making his T-shirt tug across his chest.

"Sorry about that. I thought I had her well distracted in the kitchen this morning and could get her off to school before she realized you were here, but she's too inquisitive for her own good sometimes. She snuck away while I was packing her lunch."

I nod slowly as I shift back to sit against the headboard, wincing slightly.

His eyes immediately narrow on me. "Are you in pain?"

Fuck yes.

Anything I took has completely worn off, but I don't want to admit it to him. It only gives him the upper hand again to concede weakness while I'm literally in his bed.

"Did you really let me pass out and then bring me here?"

He approaches the bed and lowers himself next to me. One of his brows rises. "Did you really think I wouldn't?" His hand settles on the comforter over my thigh. "And you didn't answer my question. Are you in pain?"

I try to shift to find a more comfortable position and end up wincing again.

He scowls slightly, then climbs from the bed and disappears into what must be the bathroom, returning with a glass of water and a small white pill in his hand. "Take this."

I shake my head. "I don't want the drugs."

A low growl rumbles in his chest. "You're not fighting me on this, *Cherie*. You were shot, and you're in pain. You're going to take the medicine the doctor prescribed if I have to shove it down your throat myself."

I scowl at him, but he seems undeterred, pushing it toward me.

"If you don't stay on top of pain, it's only going to get worse."

Raising a brow at him, I stand my ground. "Oh, you know because you've been shot before?"

He gives me a wry look. "No, but I've taken care of people who were pretty damn banged up over the years. My best friend, Marcel, has a habit of asking questions of people who sometimes don't appreciate it."

"Does he work for Falco, too?"

Cass stills, then slowly lowers himself to the bed and hands me the pill, holding out the glass of water. I reluctantly pop it into my mouth and take a swallow, handing the glass back to him so he can set it on the nightstand beside the bed.

"You should feel better soon."

Completely ignoring my question, of course.

"How am I supposed to feel better when you kidnapped me?"

He leans in closer, all amusement gone from his gaze. "Stop saying I kidnapped you. You were dead on your fucking feet, and you think your pregnant cousin was going to be able to help you to bed and bathe you and do everything else you can't do for yourself?"

I recoil slightly. "I'm not an invalid. I can take care of myself. I've lived alone for fifteen years."

His jaw tightens again. "And were you shot during those fifteen years?"

Smartass.

I scowl at him and cross my good arm over my chest, gritting my teeth when I bump the bad one. "I mean, no, but—"

"That's what I thought."

He leans forward and presses a kiss on my mouth so quickly I don't have time to react. When he pulls back, the corner of his lips twitches like he's fighting a smile. "God, you love to fucking fight about everything, don't you?"

It's how it's always been. *Fighting.* It's what Hawkes are always taught to do from the day we're born. For most of us, it became about coming out on top in school, business, and life, and for Atlas, it *literally* means beating the shit out of people in a ring, but fighting is just part of our DNA.

Even when we're all together, the friendly banter and—as Uncle Stone would call it, *bickering*—is just part of the deal. Everyone has an opinion, and no one wants to waver on it. It makes for interesting family dinners. But I wouldn't change who I am at my core, even if I tried. Even if I wanted to, which I don't.

And if I stay here, it's going to make things so much worse —for the Hawkes and for Cass and Charlotte.

"You need to take me home."

Anger darkens his gaze. "Like fucking hell."

"You do realize who my family are, right? Somebody, likely Gabe and Saint, will show up here armed to the fucking teeth to bring me back home if you don't do it."

He releases a sigh and pulls out a cell phone from his pocket and hands it to me. "Not if you call them and tell them you're somewhere with a friend recuperating and that you think it's better no one knows where you are, safer."

I release a laugh and shake my head. "You really think that's going to fucking work?"

"It will if you do it convincingly."

"How am I supposed to do it convincingly when I don't want to be here?" The words feel all wrong coming from my lips, but I don't know why. I shouldn't want to be here. It's too complicated. Too risky. Too...much. "What I should do is call them and tell them to come pick me up."

His lips press into a firm line. "But you won't."

I raise a brow at him. "Oh, yeah? Why is that?"

"Because this is the safest place you can possibly be right now. No one knows where you are except your cousin, Charlotte, and me, and no one's going to expect you to be holed up at the house of the attorney for Falco Enterprises, especially no one in your family. If I'm right and whoever took those shots wasn't just aiming at Roselli, then I don't want you anywhere anyone can find you."

His words sound so genuine, and he does have a point about no one expecting me to be here. But I have a lot of faith in the Hawkes, and making that call to say I don't feel safe with them will be a slap in the face to the people who have protected me my entire life. "Gabe and Saint are pretty damn good at protecting us."

He gets deathly still, and all humor drains from his face. "Really? Because from what I hear, Satriano's man waltzed right into Isaac's condo building and snatched his daughter."

Shit.

"How the hell do you know about that?"

Cass gives me that look that says *the same way the Hawkes seem to know everything about everyone else, too.* "I have my sources." He shoves the phone into my good hand. "This is a burner phone. Can't be traced to me or tracked by them. Now make the call, and make it convincing."

CASS

ABBY PULLS AWAY from the carriage house, and I wave to Charlotte until they disappear out onto the street, then close the back door and lean against it, releasing a heavy sigh.

What a fucking morning

Jesus...

I rub my hands over my face and roll my neck, trying to work out the kinks there. After barely sleeping last night, trying to keep an eye on Kennedy to make sure she was all right, I can hardly keep my eyes open.

I'm definitely not in any shape to be fielding the questions Charlotte was rapid-firing at me as I tried to get her out the door to school.

You're fucking up left and right.

And if Kennedy does a shitty job convincing her family that she's somewhere safe and all right, I'm going to have very well-armed, very volatile people showing up here soon.

What are you exposing your daughter to?

"Shit."

I push off the door and make my way to the espresso

machine because copious amounts of caffeine are the only thing that will get me through this day.

And even that might not be enough, especially if the Hawkes find out she's here.

Barely having to think about it, I grind the beans and load the machine. It starts brewing, and my phone buzzes on the counter. I wince at the name that flashes across the screen.

Fucking hell...

I completely forgot where I was *supposed* to be this morning. *This isn't going to go well.*

But it isn't a call I can avoid, no matter how badly I may want to. I accept it and pull the phone to my ear, stepping away from the noise of the machine. "Damon..."

"Good morning, Cassius." The icy timbre of his voice doesn't make the morning sound very good. "I'm wondering why I'm at your office for our appointment and you are not."

His even tone doesn't fool me.

The man is *pissed*. And rightfully so. Missing meetings isn't my usual MO, and certainly not with someone who has invested millions into a project that's so important to Falco Enterprises. It's a slap in the face to Damon, and he isn't the type of person to take that lightly; I've learned that much in the short time since we met.

"I'm so sorry I didn't get a chance to call you. Something came up, and we're going to have to reschedule."

A small silence hangs through the line before he finally responds. "What came up that was more important than our meeting?"

I bite back the truth and pour some milk into the steaming canister so I can make Kennedy a latte. "Just some personal things."

Damon issues a little grunt. "I think it goes without saying, Cass, that this project is of the utmost importance. I thought I made that abundantly clear at our last meeting. You indicated that we had something to discuss, and now personal issues are interfering with that. That's unacceptable. If we can't get things on track, then I'm going to pull my funding."

I wince.

That could be devastating for Falco. Even though the hotel project was originally going to be fully financed by Falco alone, the money that Damon brings with him offers a way to not only open faster but also to go bigger and better.

A real way to stick it to the Hawkes.

Failing here would mean failing Falco, and that's not something I'm prepared to do.

Sucking up my pride, I try my best to sound convincing. "Don't worry. Nothing's going to interfere with the project."

Except maybe the beautiful blonde in my bed.

"So, you have good news, then?"

I sigh. "Potentially. I've located a contact who might be able to speed along some of the permits we need to get ready early. And I already have the architects working on the changes you requested to some of the plans so we can rush through those approvals."

Damon claps, the sound so abrupt and loud I have to pull the phone away from my ear for a moment. "Excellent. I only wish I could have heard this update in person."

When I don't respond to his clear cut at me, he continues.

"I expect another update tomorrow and daily, from there on out."

His order raises my hackles, and I tighten my grip on the phone. "I don't like being told what to do, Damon. You're not my client."

A cold silence falls across the line.

"You're right, Cass. I'm not your client, but I am your client's partner, and if you want to do what's best for Falco, you are going to make sure I'm happy."

It feels like a threat and is likely meant as one. I almost start to argue back, but I don't have it in me this morning. Not when I'm worried about Kennedy upstairs and what the Hawkes might do if they find out she's here.

I have to temper my response so it's clear but doesn't insult the man. "Look, Damon, I'm doing my best to work on behalf of Falco and this partnership you've created, but I don't answer to you, and I never will."

"Be careful, Cassius. That almost sounded like a threat."

Maybe not the best job concealing my anger on that one.

"You should know one when you hear it since you're so fond of making them—thinly veiled or not."

He issues a low, deep chuckle. "I expect more good news tomorrow. Perhaps an update on this acquired contact. Don't stand me up again."

He ends the call.

"Fuck."

I stick the milk canister under the steamer wand and throw it on. The high-pitched sound fills the kitchen and drowns out the blood rushing in my ears from my heart pumping so hard during the conversation.

That man is dangerous, far more than I realized when we first met. The longer Falco works with him, the clearer it becomes that he won't settle for anything but full involvement in every single step of this process.

Which makes my job ten times harder.

I finish making the drinks before I make my next call. If I'm going to be stuck dealing with Damon, I need more information.

All of it.

Marcel answers on the third ring. "I was just about to call you."

I sigh, squeeze my eyes closed, and pinch the bridge of my nose against the headache forming there. "I hope it's good news."

"Well, it's news."

"Shit."

"I've been following the contact, the one Nancy put you onto."

The man I need to help push things through and appease Falco's new partner. While I've spent the last several days worrying about Kennedy and what this shooting means, Marcel has been busy on that avenue. "And?"

"She's right." He chuckles. "He definitely has a few skeletons in his closet that we can utilize."

Yet there's a hesitation in Marcel's voice, concern lingering beneath the words that *should* be good news for us.

My gut tightens slightly. After being friends for thirty years, I can read him like an open book, and he's worried about something. "So, then, what's the problem?"

"The problem is...I just saw Bishop Clarke."

"What?" I stand up straighter. "Are you sure it was her?"

"She's a hard woman to miss, so I think the Hawkes are following him, too. Probably doing the same thing we are and scoping him out as a potential source and contact inside the permitting department."

"Shit. We need to move on him now, then. We need to secure his assistance and make him an asset before they can."

"Agreed." He hesitates slightly. "But what are you going to do when they approach him? He can't tell them he's working for us."

I grind my jaw. "No, he can't. And they're not likely to back down or accept any sort of explanation for him saying no. I will come up with something. In the meantime, make your usual approach."

"How much do you want me to offer him?"

"Falco is willing to pay whatever it takes to secure what we need to get rolling on the hotel. Start with $50,000 and work your way up if you have to, but remind him we have his balls in a vise. I assume you have photographs."

Marcel barks out a laugh. "I have photos, *video*, and then some."

"Good. Play it for him if you have to. Make it clear that he can either make an enemy out of Falco or a friend."

"Will do."

And now, it's time to get into the more important question. "Have you been able to dig up anything on Damon?"

Marcel releases a frustrated sigh. "I wish I had a better answer for you there, Cass, but you're right—the guy's a fucking ghost. The corporation he used to sign the contract with Falco is just a holding company and there are two dozen other ones behind it. The deeper I dig, the less clear it becomes. I even tried running prints I took off the door handle of his car when I managed to track him down."

"And?"

"Nothing."

How the fuck is that possible?

Marcel's contacts can typically get him *anything* and find anyone. No one is *this* good. Which means Damon is even more powerful and dangerous than I thought.

"Even internationally? I swear I detect a hint of an Italian accent every once in a while."

"Even internationally. I tried Interpol, my connections there. Whoever this guy is, he doesn't want to be identified."

"And I got Falco in bed with him."

Marcel releases a humorless laugh at that. "I'll keep digging. You know I always will. Same on the Roselli and Hawke fronts, but there's been very little chatter since the shooting. Roselli's men are all scrambling for control, but no one's claiming responsibility for taking him out."

"Motherfuckers. Why would you take out the head of such

a huge organization and not accept responsibility, not make it public so that you can take over?"

"I wish I knew."

Me, too.

Because if we knew who was behind it, I would know how to protect Kennedy and ensure she doesn't get hurt again. The longer I watched her sleep last night, the clearer it became that I'm in way too deep with her.

"You just keep digging on all fronts and see what you can come up with."

"I will."

I end the call and slip my phone into my pocket before I grab the drinks and head up the back staircase.

Walking in to Kennedy Hawke in my bed should feel like a massive win, like a victory to celebrate after she insisted she would never be here again. But seeing her so weak and hurt, I can't find any joy in this moment.

She still leans back against the headboard, her eyes half-closed now, phone on the nightstand beside her. I enter the room, and she lifts her head slightly as I approach, her eyes on the mug.

"What'd you slip in there? Something to knock me out completely?"

I smirk despite the real accusation in her question. "A whole lot of caffeine, if you want it. But if you'd rather just let that pain medication work and go back to sleep, you don't have to drink it. I made lattes rather than straight espresso. Easier on your stomach while you're taking that stuff."

She yawns and covers her mouth with her good hand, shifting slightly and trying to cover the wince so I won't see it.

I set her mug on the nightstand and take a sip of mine as I settle on the edge of the bed next to her. "Did you make the call?"

She glances toward the phone, toying with the comforter with her good hand. "I spoke with my dad."

I raise an eyebrow. "And?"

Her gaze shifts to meet mine. "I explained to him that I didn't feel safe at my place and didn't want to be anywhere associated with the Hawkes. That I thought it would be better to be somewhere where *no one* can find me. I think he bought it..."

Kennedy could be lying to me, trying to give me a false sense of security before her entire fucking family shows up here armed to the teeth and blasts through the front door to rescue her from the big, bad boogeyman they all think I am.

I don't want to believe that, but she looks at me with such trepidation that it's hard to know whether that's because she's lying to me or because she feels bad about keeping things from her family.

"Really, *Cherie*? Or did you tell them where you were? Is Gabe going to march in here with Saint and anyone else willing to handle a gun and shoot up the place to get you out?"

The corner of her mouth twitches into a smug grin. "Wouldn't you like to know?"

I tighten my grip on the mug. "My daughter lives here, Kennedy. And she'll be back in a few hours. If you—"

Her free hand lashes out and tightens around my wrist, and she squeezes it. The sudden seriousness of what's happening removes all humor from her instantly. "I would never put your daughter in danger."

The heat of her palm wrapped around my arm spreads up through it and into my body the longer I stare into her Caribbean-blue eyes. Her words sound so sincere, and I want so badly to believe them. But this woman hates me.

She may love what I do to her body, but she hates *me* and everything I stand for. That means I *can't* trust her any more than she can trust me.

Kennedy squeezes my arm gently. "I'm telling you the truth. I talked to my dad, and I think he bought it."

"What about your cousin? What will Allie tell them about why she left you alone and what she might know about where you are?"

The woman held a *gun* on me, so there's no telling what she'll do when the Hawkes confront her.

She releases her hold on my arm. "I called her, too. I told her what I said to my dad and that she should tell everyone I was sleeping when she left to grab something from her house and was gone when she came back so she doesn't know where I went or who I'm with."

I left her cell at her place so the Hawkes couldn't track it, and I already offered security at her building a fortune to let me up to her place and to delete any surveillance video of my arrival and our exit. They know to tell the Hawkes the tech malfunctioned so they won't get waterboarded for letting someone leave with Kennedy. Which means, theoretically, there isn't any way to know she's here.

That should at least buy us a little time.

I release a relieved sigh and loosen my grip on the mug slightly. "Good, because that war I told you I want to avoid being caught in the middle of? I feel like it's already started."

17

KENNEDY

The fog the pain medication creates in my brain dissipates a little easier this time, but it still takes me a second to get my bearings.

Soft sheets.

A pillowy mattress.

That damn ocean-crisp scent I've come to associate with Cass and guilt.

The click of computer keys fills my ears, and I open my eyes and turn my head, peeking over my shoulder toward the other side of the bed. Cass sits against the headboard, laptop across his legs, pen in his mouth with a stack of papers between us, staring intently at something on the screen. I shift slightly, trying to find a comfortable position, and he glances over at me.

His eyes widen slightly, and he pulls the pen from between his teeth. "Hey, I didn't wake you, did I?"

I raise my good arm to stretch and try to pop out some of the tension in my shoulders and back, but it only ends up pulling at the stitches from surgery in my bad arm and making it hurt again. Cringing, I shake my head. "No. How long was I out?"

He looks down at the clock on his computer. "About five hours since I brought you lunch."

"Really?"

His head bobs. "That pain medication really knocks you out."

I nod slowly as I struggle to push myself up into a seated position. He sets down his computer and reaches over to help me, but I hold up my good hand, stopping him.

"No, I can do it."

He gives me a little half smirk. "So damn stubborn."

Scowling, I settle against the plush fabric headboard. "You basically hand fed me a sandwich for lunch like I was a child."

His low chuckle shakes the bed. "Sorry, force of habit. I'm used to having to hover over a toddler to make sure she actually *eats*, but you need something in your stomach, or that medicine's going to make you sick."

"I know." I shove a hand through my oily hair and groan at how disgusting it is. "Gross."

Other than the sponge bath and hair wash the first day in the hospital to remove any blood from me, I've been basically living in my own filth. For someone who usually ends up showering twice a day—once in the morning before work and once in the evening after a good workout or sparring session—I can't ever remember feeling so dirty.

Cass narrows his eyes on me, trying to assess me without poking at me in a way that will make me lash out at him again. I've been on such a razor's edge. It's no wonder he looks at me with such trepidation. "Can I get you anything?"

My eyes drift over his stack of papers and laptop. "Have you been here the whole time?"

His brows wing up. "Of course."

He says it so matter-of-factly, like it should be obvious that he would stay by my side and do his work here. Thinking about him sitting in bed, working for hours, watching me sleep, checking on me, and keeping me company makes me shift and look away.

"You don't need to do that, you know?"

The man who has made me dance along that thin line between love and hate so carefully grasps my chin and turns my face back to his. "Yes, I do." His jaw hardens as his eyes drift to my arm in the sling. He focuses on it for far too long, like he's lost in his own thoughts and isn't even seeing it. "I don't like seeing you like this, Kennedy." He looks up at me, finally meeting my gaze again. "This is what I was trying to avoid— you getting hurt, me getting caught in the middle of it."

The pain in his eyes when I talked to him at the hospital comes racing back.

You accused him of doing this...

A different kind of guilt settles over me, so much worse than what I've felt over what I've done with Cass.

"I know you didn't know about the shooting." I sigh slightly because he won't like the second part of what I need to say. "I don't necessarily believe that Falco wasn't involved in all this, but I do think that if they were, they did it without you knowing about it. You would have warned me, tried to stop it."

His shoulders relax slightly, like a weight he's carrying around since I accused him back in the ER has just lifted, and he leans in and presses a kiss to my forehead, letting his lips linger there for far too long.

The buzz between us only grows the longer his warm breath flutters over my skin, until he finally pulls back and climbs to his feet on the side of the bed, stretching his arms high above his head. The motion pulls up the hem of his T-shirt, exposing his hard abs and that smooth skin my hands still itch to glide over.

Why does he have to be so damn hot?

It almost makes me hate him more. But even with all the animosity between us and my inability to fully trust him because of his loyalty to his client, I do believe he wouldn't have let this happen. If for no other reason than he wants to protect his daughter and knows the Hawkes would come after him for the attack.

"Where's Charlotte?"

He rubs the back of his neck and motions toward the closed bedroom door. "Abby's with her. She got home from school a couple of hours ago and just had dinner. Are you hungry?"

I shake my head. "Not yet."

Even though I need to eat so the meds don't destroy my stomach, my appetite hasn't returned. And maybe it won't.

It's hard to eat and go on like things are okay when Uncle Stone is still unconscious in the hospital, and we still have no idea why any of this happened. The last I heard before Cass kidnapped me, the police had zero clues that weren't destroyed when the car the shooters used was torched. Even using surveillance cameras to try to track it and catch any of them on video failed. Whoever did this knew how to avoid getting caught.

Which is even more terrifying.

Cass watches me intently for a moment, like he's about to argue and force me to eat again. He's slipped right back into "dad mode," taking care of me like he does Charlotte.

Before he can, I motion to his computer and papers. "I don't want you ignoring your daughter to be up here and take care of me."

He barks out a laugh. "Believe me, I'm not. She's just fine with Abby. They're best friends. And she's been waiting for you to wake up."

I stiffen slightly. "Why?"

A slow smirk pulls at his sensuous lips. "Because she made something for you at school today."

Something tightens around my heart, that same thing that hit me the first time I met Viviana and she called me "Aunt Kennedy" even though I'm technically not her aunt.

He raises a brow. "Are you up for a visitor?"

That kid is far too inquisitive and insightful for someone who isn't quite five yet. I can't even imagine what she'll be questioning me about when she comes up here. And her sweet, simple gesture of thinking of me while she was at school makes all sorts of uncomfortable feelings rage inside me.

I want to say no, but the fact that she made something for me is so damn sweet that I couldn't bear to disappoint her. "Okay."

He walks over to the door and tugs it open but pauses and turns back to me before he steps out. "Thank you."

"For what?" I laugh lightly. "I haven't done anything. I should be the one who's thanking you."

Cass shakes his head. "Thank you for believing I didn't know and for trusting me to take care of you."

Tears burn my eyes, and he steps out before I sag back against the headboard, a sudden lump forming in my throat.

For trusting him.

Do I?

My eyes automatically drift to his open computer and the papers scattered across the bed where we slept last night, where he took care of me and ensured I was all right even after I accused him of all sorts of horrible things.

The name Falco appears on the top of a massive spreadsheet filled with a list of dates, names, figures, and other things I can't quite decipher.

I swallow thickly and lean toward it, trying to catch anything I can that might help the Hawkes or point to who is actually behind Falco, but a giggle followed by the pounding of little feet in the hallway makes me jerk back.

Charlotte barrels into the room, something flapping in her

hand with her frenzied speed. She launches herself onto the bed, jostling the mattress as she lands with a bounce.

Cass is hot on her heels and scoops her up before she can climb into my lap, which appears to be her intent. "Nope, you need to stay back. I don't want her to get hurt. No climbing on Kennedy, okay?"

The little girl scowls at him and refocuses her attention on me, holding up something bright red. "I made this for you today."

He lets her go to allow her to climb onto the bed and hold it out to me. I reach out with my good hand and take it from her.

"Get well soon" is scrawled across the middle in almost indecipherable letters with a lopsided rainbow over it.

That same tightness returns to my chest as I stare at it, and my eyes burn again. "Thank you, I love it."

She grins proudly. "Are you feeling better?"

Her question takes me by surprise, though I don't know why. It's the obvious thing for a child to ask, especially after the explanation Cass gave her this morning for me being in their home and in his bed, but answering it is a lot harder.

I take a second to take stock of my body and nod slowly. "Actually, yeah, I am a little bit."

That dull ache still plagues my arm, and if I move it, I instantly regret it, but apparently, a good night's sleep and napping all day was exactly what I needed to start to feel human again.

Charlotte's smile grows. "Do you want to play Monopoly with us?"

I glance up at Cass. "Monopoly?"

He smirks and crosses his arms over his chest. "It's her favorite game."

"Isn't she a little young to be playing?"

Charlotte gasps. "I'm almost *five*."

Cass barks out a laugh and scoops her up. "Charlotte's the

Monopoly queen. She's kicked my ass many times. Are you up for coming downstairs and playing with us? Don't feel obligated."

The tiny, blond girl pleads at me with her soft-green eyes. "Come on, it'll be fuuuuuun."

I've lain in this bed for far too long already, only getting up to use the bathroom when absolutely necessary since I arrived. All my muscles itch to move. "Yeah, okay. I'll come down for a little bit."

It beats sitting here, sleeping, or letting my mind race with the horrible memories of what had happened.

He sets Charlotte down and motions toward the open door. "Go get the game set up while I help Kennedy."

She rushes out, and he turns back to me, suddenly looking serious.

"You sure you're up for this?"

I nod, and he throws back the covers and holds out his hand. A huge part of me wants to slap it away. Accepting help from *anyone* is hard, but from *him*, it's ten times worse. But my body feels so heavy, like it doesn't want to release itself from the grip of the mattress, so I slip my good hand into his and let him tug me up from the bed. I practically collapse into him on shaky legs.

He catches me, his arms wrapping around my waist. "I'm glad you're feeling better, but don't pretend you're okay, Kennedy. It's all right not to be."

Everyone keeps saying that...

I shake my head and fight the tears that want to come again. "No, it's not."

"Yes, it is." He brushes my hair back from my face, and I cringe, thinking about how disgusting I am right now. "Do you want to call anyone before you come down?"

I glance at the phone he gave me to call Dad and Allie. My conversations with them run through my head. Dad wasn't happy about me disappearing, and if he had his way, he would send the damn National Guard out to find me, but I played on the fear we all have to convince him I needed to feel safe. Even if it hurt him.

Right now, I can't handle another one of those conversations. They know I'm safe. That's all they *need* to know for now.

I shake my head. "I'm afraid if I call…someone will give me bad news about Uncle Stone."

He presses a kiss to my forehead. "I think if there were any change, they would call you right away, wouldn't they? You gave them that number to reach you when you called this morning, right?"

That makes me feel a little bit better—but not much.

I nod. "Yeah, I did, and you're right. They would tell me if anything had changed—either way."

The sympathy in Cass' gaze almost breaks me on the spot, and he pulls me against his chest, burying his face in my hair. "He's going to be okay, *Cherie*. I've known your uncle a long time, and he and Isaac are both stubborn as hell and have unbreakable spirits." He pulls back and takes my face between his hands. "He won't let this take him from everyone he loves so much."

He says all the right words, but I can't help the sense of dread that continues to build inside me. That even if Uncle Stone does survive this, nothing will ever be the same again.

CASS

CHARLOTTE HUFFS and sits back in her chair, crossing her little arms over her chest and pouting the way only a preschooler can. "That's not *fair*."

I motion to my hotel on Boardwalk where she just landed.

"I am sorry, *Bebelle*, but you don't have enough money to pay me and have mortgaged all your properties, so you're bankrupt."

Kennedy fights a grin from across the table. "I could loan you some money—"

As sweet as it is for her to try to help Charlotte, I hold up a hand to stop her. "No, we play by the rules of the game, and if she lands on my hotel and she can't pay the rent, then she's out of the game." I waggle my eyebrows playfully. "You know what they say, the person with the best properties and the most hotels usually wins."

The humor drains from her face immediately, replaced by an angry scowl that instantly makes me regret what I said. Between her and Charlotte, I'm batting 0-2.

Shit.

Kennedy scans the board and sighs. "Your dad is right. He has the most expensive properties and has hotels on all of them." She looks at her properties scattered across the boards, including her set of hotels on much cheaper spaces. "Mine just can't compete. I guess it means I'm screwed."

Well, this went careening downhill pretty fucking quickly.

Our playful game of Monopoly has suddenly become a metaphor for the war that rages between Falco Enterprises and Hawke Enterprises, and any goodwill I've built up with Kennedy today has disappeared in an instant by reminding her my client's sole focus is crushing them.

She pushes up from the table and runs her good hand back through her hair, suddenly looking as exhausted as she is mad. "I think I'm going to go back upstairs since the game's over. I'm tired."

Lie.

Well, maybe not a lie, but certainly not the whole truth.

"Are you all right?"

She's pissed. Maybe this wasn't the best game to play, considering all that's going on outside of this house.

Forcing a smile, she nods. "I'm fine."

Shit.

She's definitely *not* fine. And if I don't try to fix it fast, the tension might rip her apart in her weakened state.

I glance at the clock. "It's bedtime for you, anyway, *Bebelle.*"

Charlotte groans. "Aww, really?"

Nodding, I climb to my feet to gather Charlotte from her chair. "Yep. I even let you stay up an extra twenty minutes to finish the game, which means we don't have time for a story tonight."

She pouts but doesn't argue, knowing it's not going to get her anywhere.

I turn back to Kennedy. "I'm going to go get her tucked in. Do you need anything?"

Kennedy shakes her head. "No, I don't need *anything* from you."

I recoil slightly at her emphasis on the words.

And here I thought we had come to a truce of sorts, but it appears her animosity toward me hasn't abated, despite what's happened since I took her from her place. It was always there, just suppressed by her current situation. All it took was one little reminder of our quagmire to bring it to the forefront again.

I follow Kennedy up the staircase to make sure she doesn't fall and lead Charlotte to her room while the woman who seems to be back to despising me disappears into mine.

Charlotte quickly changes into her pajamas and brushes her teeth before she climbs into bed. I tug the covers up over her, and she settles in with her favorite bunny.

I flip off her light and lean down to press a kiss to her forehead. "Goodnight. See you in the morning."

"How long is Kennedy staying?"

I have no fucking clue.

"I'm not sure, sweetie, until she feels better, I guess."

Her brow furrows, her lips drooping. "And then she's leaving?"

Her question hurts me more than I thought it would, far more than I thought it could. So does the way her voice breaks asking it.

"Then she'll go back to her place."

"Oh." The disappointment in her voice matches my own. "Okay..."

But I can't let her see it.

I've already managed to drag her into all this—the uncertainty, the violence—when all I've ever done is try to shield her from anything that might ever hurt her. Now, by helping Kennedy, by being selfish and bringing her here, I've made it even worse.

I give her another kiss. "Goodnight. No messing around. Stay in bed and go to sleep."

She nods, but I know she'll likely spend a few minutes playing with her Barbies or reading with her flashlight or doing something else she shouldn't be.

At this point, I've given up trying to corral her. If she's amped up and can't sleep, the best tactic seems to be letting her wear herself out quietly in her room before she puts herself back to bed.

I close her door behind me, then make my way down the hall toward my room.

The silence of the house is almost deafening.

An ominous feeling settles over me. Maybe because I know I'm going to be walking into another argument with Kennedy when the last thing she needs right now is to be getting all worked up and upset.

I nudge open the slightly ajar door to my room and find her sitting on the windowsill, staring out at the street.

She turns toward me as I enter, giving me a look that says I should probably just go sleep in the guest room tonight rather than face her wrath.

I close the door behind me and lean against it. "You're pissed."

Releasing a bone-weary sigh, she returns to staring out the window. "I'm not pissed."

Barely biting back a full-blown laugh, I chuckle and push off the door, making my way to her. "Yes, you are. I've seen it enough from you that I can recognize it." I stop next to the window, annoyed with her refusal to look at me when she's trying to lie. "I didn't mean anything by the hotel comment."

She waves her good hand dismissively, keeping her attention on the street. "It's just a game. I know that." A sigh slips from her pink lips. "But this isn't. This is my life. All of our lives. What Falco is doing"—she shakes her head and swallows as if trying to stop a sob—"what they're doing is making it really fucking hard. And now Roselli is dead, and my uncle—"

Her sob ends whatever she was about to say, and I close the distance between us and settle next to her on the windowsill, pulling her good hand into mine and squeezing it. "Your uncle will be okay. Everything I know about him has me absolutely convinced of that. That man isn't going down without a fight."

Kennedy opens her eyes to meet mine, a fiery determination burning across the vibrant blue. "Neither are we."

"I would expect nothing less."

The Hawkes have been battling Falco in the courts for years, and they won't allow a few bullet holes to stop them from following through with their plans for The Hawke Hotel and expanding beyond that.

She stares down at our hands for a while, then pulls hers from mine, holding it against her chest. "My cousin called while you were tucking Charlotte in."

A dozen different faces flash through my head. "Which one?"

Her lips twitch slightly at the question. "Allie..."

"What did she say?"

"She just wanted to give me an update. She said Stone is still stable and Aunt Nora and Coen are at the hospital with him pretty much twenty-four-seven. Isaac was released today and is at home with Viviana and Jack, and her dad flew down from Chicago to help ensure they stay protected."

I cringe. "So, Cutter Jackson is in town again."

Kennedy's gaze cuts to me. "You know who he is?"

"It would be hard not to, after what happened with Satriano."

When the head of the Calabrian 'Ndrangheta shows up in New Orleans, chasing the daughter of Cutter Jackson and Valentina Marconi—who control their territory in Chicago with an iron fist—it's impossible not to take notice. And when Satriano ended up dead, and it had the potential to start a mob war, it raised the stakes even higher.

Of course, I've kept my ears and eyes open, and I've had Marcel scouring the streets for anything that might affect Falco's plans.

The mention of Satriano sends a shiver through Kennedy, and she rests her temple against the glass. "Do you really think this shooting had to do with us or Roselli...or both of us?"

"I wish I fucking knew, *Cherie*. I really do, but I don't. It would make it a hell of a lot easier, wouldn't it?"

She nods slowly. "It would."

"But you know you can trust me, Kennedy."

One of her pale brows rises. "Can I?"

I sit upright, my anger straightening my spine. "You really think after all of this that I would do anything to hurt you?"

She chews on her bottom lip. "Maybe not physically, maybe not intentionally..."

Hell.

I don't bother correcting her because she's right.

The things I do for Falco do hurt her and her family, literally everyone she cares about, and I don't have any intention of stopping. But the need to offer an explanation for her earlier accusation about Charlotte slices at my chest. She needs to understand *why* I do this. Why I *have* to.

"You know, it isn't just about the money." I shake my head. "It really isn't about the money at all."

Her brow furrows. "Then what is it about?"

"Before, you told me that I use Charlotte as an excuse for what I do but that she doesn't need all this." I motion around the room. "But it isn't about buying her expensive things. It's about giving her the security I never had."

True confusion fills her gaze. "What do you mean?"

"Shit." I scrub my hand over my face, then stare out the window at the light drizzle starting to fall on the front lawn and street. I hadn't intended to get into this with her, and I'll have to watch my words very carefully. Returning my gaze to Kennedy, I find her waiting patiently for me to continue. "My parents both died when I was very young, and I went to live with my mom's mother when I was about Charlotte's age. It wasn't"—I glance away, out the window again—"very pleasant."

Just mentioning it at all sends a chill through me that has nothing to do with the weather outside.

"I never felt love or safety in her home. I never felt wanted. I never knew that I had somebody I could rely on who would always be there for me. I was a burden. Half the time, I wasn't even sure if we'd have a home because she would get evicted, and we'd have to move in with friends or stay at shitty hotels for a while. Sometimes, we didn't have electricity, or food, or any of the things a child needs to thrive." I peek over to Kennedy, and her mouth hangs open slightly. I give her a sad smile. "I know it's a far cry from *this*." I sweep my hand out to the room again. "That's only because when I got to high school, I realized getting a good education and a good job was the only way I'd ever change my life. So, I studied, and that's all I did. I got a full-ride scholarship to college and then went to law school." I suck in a heavy breath, fighting against the emotions threatening to choke me. "And the moment I found out my ex-wife was pregnant, I made a promise to that baby that she would never feel any of those things that I did growing up. So, when I tell you that what I do is for Charlotte, to give her what I never had, it isn't about this house or my car. It's about what she feels here and when she's with me, that she has a roof over her head, that she'll always know that I'll take care of her."

A tear trickles out of Kennedy's eye, and she swipes it away and clears her throat, looking back out the window. "I'm pretty lucky to have what I do."

"Your family is unshatterable. When they set their sights on something, they get it done, and they protect each other, doing whatever it takes, no matter what."

I try to keep the anger out of my words, but it seeps in slightly all the same. She turns to look at me and opens her mouth to say something, but she swallows the words instead.

We stare at each other for what feels like an eternity, the rain hitting the window harder, coming faster and with more aggression.

I push to my feet, releasing a sigh. "It's probably time for you to take your medication again. You want to go back to bed?"

She shakes her head and glances down at herself. "Honestly, all I want right now is a shower. I feel disgusting."

Holding out a hand to her, I offer a smile. "That can be arranged."

18

CASS

With my hand at her lower back, I usher Kennedy toward the bathroom.

She gives me a dubious look. "How the hell am I supposed to take a shower when I can barely move my arm?"

I stop her in front of the glass enclosure and press a kiss to the side of her neck. "Because I'm going to help you."

She stiffens slightly. "You're not getting in the shower with me. I'm not a child who needs to be bathed."

"No, you're a stunningly beautiful"—I press kiss against her partially exposed collar bone—"intelligent"—another kiss —"capable-of-putting-my-nuts-in-a-vise woman who needs help and hates admitting it, but I'm going to force you to accept it from me."

Her pretty pink lips open like she's about to argue, but I give her a look that silences her immediately and reach around her to crank on the water. Either she desperately wants this shower, or she isn't as mad at me as she's pretending to be. Likely the former. Because she still seems really pissed.

Though there's a hint of something else there, an underlying trepidation I haven't seen from her before.

She watches me carefully as I shuck off my sweatpants and T-shirt, then reach for the waistband of her yoga pants. I nudge them down, along with her underwear, and she uses her good hand to brace herself against the counter and allow me to tug them off her feet. Then I reach for the buttons on her shirt and slowly undo them one by one.

Her breathing picks up slightly the lower I go, and I pull it off her good arm and then help her unhook the sling and ease the shirt from the bad one.

Fuck.

I wince, looking at the surgical wounds where some doctor had to repair the damage the bullets did and dig out fragments of metal that would eventually cause even more problems. Even with the stitches and the derma bond over it, it looks nasty and painful.

She glances at it. "It isn't as bad as it looks."

I feather my fingers over the marred skin, barely touching it, not wanting to hurt her. "Yes, it is. I'm sorry this happened to you."

And I want to *kill* whoever did it to her—wrap my bare hands around their throat and strangle them until they stop breathing and I watch the life drain from their eyes.

But the police have no leads—nothing but an abandoned, burned-out car. Even Marcel hasn't been able to find *anything* that might lead to the shooters. And since no one is taking responsibility for Roselli's death, we're in a bit of a stalemate—waiting for something to happen.

Kennedy doesn't respond. She just holds her ruined arm tightly against her chest and lets me shift her in, past the glass and under the hot spray. She releases a tiny sigh as it hits her back, and I turn her to avoid it running directly over her wound, even though everything I found online said it's okay to get a little bit of soap and water on it while showering as long as she doesn't submerge it.

The water cascades across her shoulders and back, down her high, full breasts, over her stomach, and between her legs, and despite it being the completely wrong time and insanely wrong scenario for it, my cock stirs.

I can't control it when I'm around her.

This pull.

This attraction.

This primal *need* for this woman.

It consumes me.

But I ignore the demands of my body in favor of giving her what she needs because this isn't about me. It never has been. Everything I've ever done has been for others—Charlotte, Kennedy, even the man who died when I was almost too young to remember him.

I grab the bottle of shampoo and squirt some into my hand.

She narrows her eyes on it. "You're going to wash my hair?"

Rubbing my palms together, I glance up at the disheveled blond locks that haven't been washed in days. "Yep."

A little annoyed huff slips past her wet lips, but she tilts her head back to get it fully wet, then turns to give me better access. I dig my fingers into her hair, massaging the shampoo into it, letting my nails scrape along her scalp.

She issues a little groan, her eyes sliding closed as she wobbles on unsteady feet.

I jerk one hand free and wrap it around her waist to hold her steady, back against me, while I use the other one to finish the job. "You all right?"

Her head falls backward to rest against my shoulder, her face turned to my neck. "Just got dizzy for a second."

"You haven't spent much time on your feet the last few days. Your body's still weak."

Her eyes open.

"And before you argue with me, I know *you're* not."

She clamps her mouth closed and lets me rinse her hair, then grab the bar of soap and begin gliding it over her body as well as I can while trying to keep her upright.

Her muscles twitch under my palm, reacting to my touch the same way they always do, and she shifts against me, her ass grinding against my cock. I reach down to get her legs and slide the bar of soap across her taut stomach and up over her breasts, slowly letting my thumbs graze against her nipples.

They pebble under my touch, and she moans and rolls her hips back against mine.

My cock hardens fully, aching against her smooth, wet skin. "Fucking hell, *Cherie.*"

"Cass..." My name comes on a whisper, barely audible over the pounding of the water.

"I'm sorry, I shouldn't be—"

Hard.

Wanting you.

So fucking crazy about you.

She turns her head and opens her eyes to let her gaze meet mine. "Keep touching me."

Shit.

Even after having a goddamn bullet pulled out of her, the woman still wants me as much as I want her, but I'm not about to turn this into some illicit shower sex.

It was never meant to be that.

"No." I drop the soap and push her farther under the water, letting it rinse all off. "I brought you in here to get you clean, not to get you dirty."

She chuckles softly, then turns in my arms to face me, draping her good arm around my neck, her other one held tightly against her chest. Her lips hover over mine for a second, the water beating down on us, and she kisses me before I can object.

I groan against the movement of her mouth, almost frantic, desperate, before I tear myself away. "Kennedy, please."

"Cass, I need..." She whimpers slightly, but she doesn't have to say the word for me to understand.

This woman is controlled by her primal desires, her most base needs, and denying her it, preventing her from finding this release, would hurt her even more. Orgasms are supposed to be excellent pain relief, anyway, a surge of endorphins and hormones coursing through her—if I do it right.

I turn us and back her over to the bench seat, slowly lowering her onto it. The water beats hard against my back, and Kennedy stares up at me, her thick black lashes clinging together, water still trickling over her breasts and body.

Of course, I drop to my knees for this woman.

Fuck the hard tile floor.

Fuck the fact that we have so many things standing between us.

Fuck all the lies and hidden truths.

She *needs* this right now, and I'm the only one who can give it to her.

The tile bites into my knees, and I push her legs open. "You know I'd do anything to help you, to make you feel better. All you have to do is ask."

Her fingers thread through my wet hair, and I drop my head between her legs and run my tongue up her slick slit.

"Fuck." Kennedy's eyes roll back, and she drops her head against the wall, shifting slightly on the bench seat to give me better access to her core.

I grip her thighs and tug them up over my shoulders, angling her so I can probe my tongue into her cunt the way I know drives her insane. The flavor and scent of her arousal fills my senses, and I groan my approval against her wet flesh.

She moans and tightens her grip on my hair, rolling her hips against my face, matching each glide of my tongue. I slip a finger inside her and then a second, and she gasps and clutches around them as I curl them up into her G-spot.

Her body jerks under my ministrations, and I lave my tongue over her clit while I grasp my cock in my left hand and stroke it slowly.

Each buck of her hips makes my dick ache harder, makes me want to be inside her even more, but something more primal tugs at me—the need to *care* for her. To ensure she isn't in pain. That she's happy. That she's content.

All the things I also work so hard to ensure *don't* happen for the rest of the Hawkes.

"Cass!"

My name falls from her lips almost like a prayer, but it's a plea from a woman who needs something *good* right now. She thrusts herself against my face harder, begging me for more. If an orgasm will make this woman feel better, can in any way ease her suffering of the last few days, I will be the one who gives it to her.

I suck her clit between my lips and pull on it in long, hard sucks that have her arching fully off the bench, her legs draped over my shoulders, her upper shoulders pressed to the tile behind her.

It should hurt her.

It should aggravate that wound in her arm.

But it doesn't seem to.

She doesn't tell me to stop.

If anything, her tightening grip and frantic roll of her pelvis only searches for more.

I keep going, thrusting my fingers in and out of her while I devour her cunt until she finally explodes, her body convulsing, her hips bucking against my face, her release shooting down my throat.

Fucking hell.

Watching Kennedy Hawke come is like seeing a glimpse of Heaven every time, and her release is the elixir of life. I swallow it all down and wait until she sags and utters that tiny sigh before I finally release her, slipping my hand out from between her legs and slowly lowering them back to the bench.

She lifts her head, and her eyes flutter open to meet mine. Her chest heaves, her breaths coming in harsh pants. The heat of the water and her orgasm have turned her pale skin pink, and a redder flush covers her chest, neck, and cheeks.

I release my cock and rise to my feet, holding out a hand to her. "Come on, let's get you dried off and into bed."

Kennedy shakes her head. "No."

"What do you mean, *no*?"

She allows me to pull her to her feet, and she presses herself against me, then tugs her hand out of mine to reach down and grasp my cock. "I want this."

God fucking damn.

As incredible as it feels to have her touching me, I shake my head. "No, not when you're like this. I don't want to hurt you, and I don't need—"

Kennedy ends my objection with a searing kiss, stealing my words as she twists the palm of her hand against the head of my cock, making my hips buck against her.

I tear my mouth from hers again. "Fucking hell, Kennedy, what the hell am I going to do with you?"

∼

KENNEDY

HIS QUESTION MAKES ME LAUGH, the sharp noise bouncing off the wet tile around us, mingling with the sound of the water cascading from the shower head. It was meant rhetorically, but many different things rush through my head.

This man could crush me easily.

He could utterly destroy me, mind, body, and soul, in the blink of an eye, especially when I'm already dangling over the edge of completely losing my grip on reality right now.

But he won't.

Despite all the reasons not to, I trust Cass to take care of me, to give me what I need.

"Do whatever the hell you want, Cass." I brush my lips over his. "I won't break. I promise."

He issues a low growl and tangles his hands in my hair. "Says the woman who had bruised ribs the last time and now has a damn bullet hole in her arm."

It's a fair assessment, and his pure rage at my injuries sends a little thrill rushing through my already buzzing body.

"I'm okay, Cass. Please." I grip him tighter and stroke his length, my pussy clenching, my clit still throbbing for what it desperately wants. "Please. I need it to take my mind off the pain, off everything that happened, off all the uncertainty that lies with waking up tomorrow."

Especially in this man's bed.

This can't last forever. Not even if we both want it to. There's still someone potentially targeting the Hawkes, and this man is still the one who makes the actions of one of our enemies possible.

Our situation makes Romeo and Juliet's struggle seem easy.

But they had something to fight for: their love for each other.

This isn't love with Cass. It can't be. It's just some weird, cosmic vibe that pushes us together and messes with our senses.

He groans and takes my mouth in a mind-bending kiss as he turns us so his back is against the shower seat. His green eyes burn with so much more than the usual passion I see there —concern, longing, and something else I don't think either of us want to recognize. He slowly lowers himself onto it, then takes his cock in his hand and strokes it as I watch.

"You can have anything you want from me, Kennedy."

What about the truth?

The question sits on the tip of my tongue, the same one I've wanted to ask him since I first understood who he was. Because I want to know what he's been holding back, what he's been hiding, what all of this is really about. I want to know who Falco is, who has been calling the shots that result in so much pain for the Hawkes. But pushing it would ruin the moment, and I wouldn't get what I really want right now, which is him inside me.

Stepping forward, I use my good hand to brace myself on his shoulder. As I straddle his waist, he aligns the head of his dick at my slick entrance, and I slowly sink down on him.

His thick cock stretches me.

So much bigger, so much tighter this way.

He issues a low growl that shakes his chest, all his muscles tensing under me. "Fuck, Kennedy."

I ignore the ache in my arm pinned between us and finally sink all the way down, fully embedding him inside me.

Fuuucccccckkkkk...

It's everything I wanted and yet not enough.

I drop my face against his neck, pressing a kiss there as I clench around him. He shudders under me, his hands coming to my hips, and I lift myself slowly then sink back down, grinding my clit against the base of his cock. His fingers dig into my skin, and his breath hitches in my ear.

It isn't just me.

He feels it, too.

The connection that seems too real to just be sex.

Pulling my head back, I lock eyes with him. The normally mossy-green has darkened to an almost emerald as he stares up at me, but he might as well be reaching into my soul.

My wet hair falls into my face, and he pushes it back, clutching my cheek and dragging my mouth to his while I start a slow glide up and down his cock.

He doesn't raise his hips to meet mine. He doesn't buck under me. He lets me take control, lets me *take* what I *want*, moving slow and determined, deliberate, until I finally can't anymore.

My body needs more.

Demands it.

I start speeding up, driving down on him with a hard thrust that draws a low groan from deep inside him. He doesn't look away from me, just holds my gaze as I continue to ride him, my movements becoming more frantic and frenzied.

All the pain of the last few days dissipates on the cloud of lust surrounding me, the steam from the shower and the sound of the water falling around us swallowing my gasp each time he bottoms out inside me.

He brushes his thumb across my lips, then slips it between them. I bite down, and he winces, but his hips buck, driving him a fraction of an inch deeper and hitting that spot inside me that draws a low groan and makes me close my eyes.

"No." He tightens his grip on my chin. "Keep your eyes on me."

"Fuck, don't do this to me, Cass." I shake my head and keep them closed. "I can't."

"Open them, *Cherie.*"

"Please don't do this."

He's going to force me to look at him, force me to watch the man who seems intent on taking everything from us also give me what I need in this moment when I'm at my absolute weakest.

What the fuck am I supposed to do?

Just walk away?

This can never work.

Not with my family.

Not with what he does.

None of it.

It's so wrong, but being here with him has felt so right. It felt *safe* for the first time in a long time...in the last place I should.

"Please, Kennedy."

This time, it isn't a command.

It's a request.

And I can't deny him.

I let my eyes flutter open to meet his, and he leans forward and rests his forehead on mine as I move up and down on him. He drops his hand to my hips to help, and my rhythm increases, each grind sending jolts of pleasure through me until the low burn starts in my core.

The orgasm comes slowly, but once it hits me, it's like a cataclysm of every feeling I've ever experienced in my life hitting me all at once. Fear, anger, lust, love, all of it crashes down on me in a wave that steals my breath.

My eyes drift closed, bright lights exploding against my lids. I jerk on him, my pussy clenching and milking his cock until hot spurts of cum shoot inside me.

Sweet mother of God.

When I finally come down, I sag against him, burying my face in his neck. His arms come up to wrap around me, and he trails his finger slowly up and down my spine, sending goosebumps skittering across my skin despite the heat and humidity in the shower.

His body twitches, and I grin against him.

Finally, he nuzzles my neck and kisses behind my ear. "Are you okay? Are you in any pain?"

I slowly push myself back to look at him and shake my head. "Definitely not."

It's a lie.

The dull throb in my shoulder returned the second my orgasm started fading, and I'm sure I'll pay for the movement and disregard for keeping it in the sling later. But it was worth it for this moment with him because it somehow feels like it might be the last one we get.

His eyes suddenly narrow on mine. "What is it? What's that look?"

I shake my head. "No look."

"Don't lie to me, Kennedy."

A tear slips out of my eye, one I hope he can't see while we're surrounded by all this water.

But he reaches up and brushes it away with his thumb. "Why are you crying? Don't lie to me this time."

I bury my face back against his neck, his heart thundering under my palm. I can't look him in the eye while I tell him the truth. "I'm terrified."

His arms tighten around me, careful to avoid jolting my shoulder. "Of what? Me?"

The pain in his words makes me stiffen. "Yes." I'm not going to lie to him about that. "You, your employer, what's going to happen now that Roselli's gone and the city's up for grabs. I'm fucking terrified that we don't know who took those shots at us, and the police don't seem to have any fucking clue."

He's silent for a few moments, just holding me and letting me cry, before he finally nudges me to pull back and takes my face between his palms. "I know it seems like everything's a mess right now, but we'll figure it out. All of it. We'll figure out who's behind this and why. We'll make sure you're safe."

"What about everyone else?"

He stiffens under me, brushing his fingers over my cheek almost reverently. I know why he isn't saying anything. Because he knows as much as I do that we're in a quagmire of our own making.

Cass can't walk away from Falco, and I can't walk away from my family.

They're on a collision course.

And there's someone else out there ready to demolish both of us.

Finally, he swallows thickly and shakes his head. "I don't know, but I can promise you this: I'll do everything in my power to make sure you don't get hurt."

"What if that means choosing between me and Falco?"

It's a question he can't answer, and I know it. If he does, if he voices his response, it'll change everything between us.

Agony darkens his gaze. "I told you, *Cherie*, I have to do it for Charlotte so that she never goes through what I did."

Somehow, I manage to find words through the physical and emotional anguish threatening to drag me into hysteria. "And you're always going to choose her, and you should."

"You're right. I always will." Determination sparks in his gaze. "But it doesn't mean I can't protect you, too."

I glance down at the wound on my arm, the marred skin that will be a constant reminder of what happened that day, a reminder that we aren't ever safe, even in a place that should be. "Evidence would suggest otherwise."

Cass tightens his grip on me and drags me back against me, crushing me to his slick body harder than he probably should, given the state I'm in. Instead of fighting it, I just burrow closer to him as we sit under the hot spray, relishing a moment we might not ever have again.

19

CASS

I turn onto the road where my office sits, scanning ahead of me for any signs of where Marcel is set up because if I can spot them, Damon and his men certainly will. "Are you ready to go?"

"All set, *boss*." Marcel emphasizes the word, and despite how anxious I am, it makes me smile. "As soon as they get here, I'll start snapping pictures of him and his guys. Their prints might not be on file anywhere, but their faces could be. If I get my friends at Interpol to run them through facial recognition, we might be able to figure out who these fuckers are."

That's the hope.

Since my tense call with Damon yesterday morning, I've wracked my brain for any way to figure out who he is or what he wants, since he seems disinclined to reveal it to me.

The idea of running facial recognition came as I stared down at Kennedy, fast asleep next to me this morning, admiring her flawless features and natural beauty.

She has an unforgettable face—and hopefully, Damon does as well.

Someone has to know who this guy is.

"I'll touch base with you after the meeting." I end the call as I pull into my office lot.

I didn't spot Marcel wherever he's camped out to take the pics, so theoretically, neither will Damon. He has to know I'm trying to gather information on him, but he hasn't seemed the least bit worried about it—almost like he knows I'm going to hit brick wall after brick wall.

Smug fucker.

Hopefully, the game ends today with something we can use.

Teresa's car is already parked in her spot, and I park next to her, shutting down the engine. She's always been an early riser, typically getting here even before me, but today, I'm later than usual.

I found it impossible to leave this morning. After waking up with Kennedy in my arms, her warm body pressed against mine, her scent filling every breath I took, all I wanted to do was stay in bed with her all day.

But I can't ditch another meeting with Damon.

Not when I can't shake this feeling that Falco may actually have entered into a deal with the Devil, who might be somehow connected to what happened to the Hawkes.

He's far more than what he lets on, and his desire to see the Hawkes fail could have gone a step further. If it did, I need to know without him suspecting what I'm doing.

Good thing I lie for a living...

I climb from my car and step into the office.

Teresa smiles. "Hey, I thought you weren't coming in for a couple of days."

Returning her smile, I set my briefcase on her desk and lean against it. "Damon's coming in soon."

Her good mood falters instantly, her face falling. "He was

pretty pissed yesterday when he showed up and you weren't here."

I release a heavy sigh. "I know. He called me, and I'm so sorry you had to deal with that. I should have contacted him to cancel the meeting when I knew I wouldn't make it in. I was just...distracted."

Teresa shudders. "I don't like him, Cass. He gives me the fucking creeps."

"I don't blame you, but he's somewhat of a necessary evil for Falco right now, and you know how important their business is to this office staying open."

She nods. "I do."

"So, we'll plaster on smiles. We'll welcome him with open arms, and we'll pretend we love the guy. Deal?"

Ever the professional, she nods. "Deal."

"He'll be here soon. Send him in when he arrives."

The quicker I can get this meeting over with, the quicker Marcel can get those photos to his contacts and I can get back to Kennedy.

I hustle into my office and shut the door, then boot up my desktop computer and pull open the file containing all the information on the hotel project, including the revised timeline.

The Hawkes are groundbreaking in a few weeks. If we have any chance of catching up with them, we need these revised plans approved and the permits issued immediately. And if I can't make it happen, Damon's going to have my throat.

A soft knock sounds on my office door.

"Come in."

Teresa opens it. "Damon's here to see you."

She gives me that tight smile and ushers him in.

He enters with the same smug grin he always wears. "Nice of you to show up for the meeting, Cass."

I stiffen. "I'm sorry."

"You should be." He sneers. "My time is very valuable, or don't you give a shit about my money anymore?"

It's the first time I've seen him break character, the only time he's cursed and lost his professional demeanor in front of me. Missing the meeting really did set him off.

He takes a seat, and Teresa leaves me alone with the man who might be responsible for putting that hole in Kennedy.

One of his silver brows rises. "Any updates since we spoke yesterday morning?"

I guess we're dispensing with pleasantries today.

"We've approached the contact, and he seems receptive to working with us."

"Excellent." Damon's face lights up, his dark eyes curious. "It's just the kind of news I had hoped for."

I nod slowly. "It is good. We made him an offer last night, and he accepted. Now it's only a matter of him actually doing the work." Watching Damon carefully for any reactions, I ease my way into my real purpose of having this meeting—broaching the subject of the attack on the Hawkes. "And the shooting at the Hawkes' café may be beneficial to our endeavor as well."

It's the first time either of us has mentioned it since it happened, and Damon doesn't react; he just continues to stare at me for a long while.

Finally, he offers a little bob of his silver-topped head. "I heard about that. How unfortunate."

The man doesn't give away anything. If he was involved, he's doing a damn good job of covering it. Which isn't surprising the way he's covered his own tracks, making it damn near impossible to identify him or discover his motivations.

Despite the dangerous vibe emanating from him, I push further into the topic, hoping he'll eventually slip. "I hear now that Roselli's dead, the city's underworld is a bit chaotic. No one really knows what's happening or who's in control. People are scrambling, but no one has accepted responsibility for his assassination."

Because that's what it was, a calculated removal.

It's possible the Hawkes were targets, too, or perhaps only bystanders caught in a plot designed to shake up New Orleans. Either way, it seems impossible Roselli being there was just a coincidence.

Someone wanted this destabilization that hasn't been felt in over sixty years. First, Dom Abello controlled the city, then his son, Luca. Each one did so with authority and without remorse for their actions. No one dared move against them. And once Luca retired, he turned things over to Roselli, who maintained aniron grip on The Big Easy. No one thought it would ever weaken, but those bullets shattered it.

Damon chuckles and holds up his hands. "I wouldn't know anything about that."

"Of course, you wouldn't."

It's as close as I've come to actually accusing him of being connected, of being somehow involved in the shooting and in what's been happening, including the attacks on Roselli's businesses over the last few months.

But he just smiles, taking it all in stride and admitting nothing.

I lean back in my chair, trying to appear casual while my heart slams wildly against my ribcage. "I remembered where I know you from."

One of his eyebrows rises. "Really?"

I nod. "You used to get drinks at the Daily Grind, sitting out on the patio."

His lips curl into a slow grin. "You're right. I did. Those girls make a mean espresso."

I smile at him. "They sure do."

He leans forward slightly. "I'm surprised you frequented

The Grind, considering Falco owns the competing business down the street."

"Well, at the time, Falco's Daily Grounds wasn't open yet."

His gaze sharpens. "And as soon as it did, the Hawke's café went up in flames. How convenient for Falco..."

Is this asshole accusing Falco of doing it? Is this the reason he wanted to partner with us in the first place because he thought that's the type of action Falco would take?

"I'm not sure what you're suggesting, Damon. But if you think my client would resort to arson in order to get rid of a competitor, you're very far off base."

He chuckles and holds up his hands. "No, no, of course not. That level of violence would be"—he shrugs—"overkill. I'm just trying to get a better idea of the lay of the land because it seems things are heating up."

"You could definitely say that."

"Given our limited window to get ahead of the Hawkes, I assume there won't be any more personal conflicts for your time."

His words make my back stiffen. Even if Kennedy wasn't lying in my bed at home, Charlotte will always come first, and there will be times when I won't be at his beck and call.

"I'm going to reiterate what I said to you yesterday, Damon. I don't work for you, and while I can appreciate the amount of money you've put into this project with my client, I do have others and other responsibilities. My personal life doesn't interfere with work."

"Except for when it makes you miss a meeting with one of your biggest client's biggest partners."

"And I've apologized for that. I assure you it won't happen again. But you have to understand that I cannot be at your beck and call. I'll keep you abreast of anything important. But unless there's some reason for us to meet in person, a simple phone call will suffice."

If the man is going to lose his temper, it will be now.

I brace myself for whatever he might unleash, but he simply assesses me, a muscle in his jaw ticcing.

Finally, he offers a tight smile. "I appreciate you standing your ground, counsel. I'm the type of man to do the same. As long as your personal life doesn't interfere with what we have happening"—he holds out his hands—"who am I to say anything about it? Just don't let what happened yesterday happen again."

"It won't."

"You mentioned the shooting may help us. Do you anticipate the Hawkes pushing back their hotel opening after what happened?"

I shrug. "I wouldn't have any way of knowing that, but even if they don't move the date, I have several motions ready to file that can potentially force them to postpone the *actual* work. It would make the groundbreaking ceremonial only."

Damon grins. "I heard it's going to be quite the extravaganza."

"That's what I hear, too."

He pushes to his feet, giving me a cold smile that sends a chill through my blood. "I hope it goes better than the last."

~

KENNEDY

Kennedy -

I'm sorry. I had to go into the office for something that couldn't be avoided. I didn't want to wake you. Make yourself at home, and call or text if you need anything.

- Cass

I SET the note back on the nightstand and swing my legs out of bed. Sunlight streams in through the windows that face the street, and I check the clock.

9:00 a.m.

Before everything that happened this week, I hadn't slept past 5:30 since high school. Getting on top of things early, being the first one into the office or the gym, was always necessary to get ahead.

Look where that got you...

I try to roll my shoulder back and lift my bad arm, and the pain isn't nearly as bad as it was yesterday—at least, the physical part of it.

Being awake, moving, stepping toward the window to watch people bustling by on the street only makes me think of Uncle Stone lying in that hospital bed, hooked up to all the machines. Not in court like he should be. Not helping figure out why any of this happened. Not being the strong, demanding, unbendable force he always has been in my life.

Tears blur my vision, and I swipe them away and grab the phone Cass gave me from the nightstand. The pain medication has made me so groggy the last few days that I haven't had much of a chance to see any of the house beside his bedroom, the hallway, and the kitchen, but now that I'm feeling better, I can't stay in that bed any longer, waiting for him to come home.

I need to move.

I need to think.

I need to call and get an update on Stone and check in so they know I'm okay.

My hand shakes, dialing Bishop's number. Of anyone, she's going to be the most pissed that I left my place and won't tell anyone where I am. She takes everyone's safety as her personal job—and it is, I guess. When Saint retires, she'll be the one running the Hawke Enterprises security department.

Which is why I've been dreading talking to her. It was a giant slap in her face, her father's, and Gabe's to tell Dad I didn't feel safe at home or anywhere with the Hawkes. She's going to be hurt, but she's also the one I know will be brutally honest with me about what's happening outside the walls of this stunning home.

I start exploring with the door directly across from Cass' bedroom, opening it just as Bishop answers.

"Hello?"

"Hey, it's me."

Another glamorous suite lies in front of me, decorated beautifully with period-style furniture and accents. It's out of the pages of *Home and Garden* magazine. He must've spent a fucking fortune decorating this place.

And you know where he got the money.

Acid churns in my stomach, and I swallow it back. If I let myself think about his role as Falco's attack dog, I won't be able to stay, and I don't think I'm ready to leave yet. Not when everything still feels so...*off.*

"Where the *hell* are you, Ken? Your dad won't tell anyone anything."

Shit.

I close the door and move to the next one—another bedroom. "I'm at a friend's house. Somewhere *no one* can find me. It's how I want it."

"Let me come get you." She releases a little annoyed breath that I know hides what she's really feeling. Bishop has always been a little badass—excelling at martial arts and with handguns, a little carbon copy of her dad—but she also has a soft spot for those she cares about. It's her one weakness: caring too much. "Your dad said you don't feel safe anywhere, but we can keep you safe, Ken. You should be with the family."

That same guilt claws at my chest as I check the next door. Another bedroom.

"I just can't. It isn't about me not having faith in you and your dad and everyone else. I just…" Have no way to explain this to her without revealing all the things I need to hold close to the chest. "Can't be there right now."

Bishop sighs heavily, and silence hangs on the line as I check the next few doors.

Eight bedrooms.

Who the hell needs eight bedrooms?

"Ken, please be honest with me. Are you *okay*? I know what you told your dad, but I can't help feeling something isn't right."

The final bedroom makes me pause to consider her words, and I smile as I lean against the jamb. A pink princess canopy bed occupies the center, and all the dolls scattered around on the floor immediately bring back memories of my own childhood, of fighting over them with Astrid, Allie, and sometimes Bishop, even though she was much more interested in wrestling with the boys and trying to show them up.

Cass truly has given Charlotte everything, and his words from last night race back to me.

It really isn't about the money at all. It's about giving her the security I never had.

I cringe at the memory of the vacant look in his eyes when he spoke.

Whatever happened to him as a child definitely shaped him into the man he is today. A man who I can't deny has so many sides to him.

He's a pit bull in court, with his jaws set on the jugular of any Hawke he can find. But then, when he's with me, he's an attentive, caring lover, intent on making sure I get everything I need. And when he's with his daughter, he's a really fucking good dad, and he believes he's only doing what's best for her.

Tears start to prick my eyes.

What the hell am I going to do?

"Kennedy? Did you hear me?"

Shit. Bishop...

"Sorry."

"I asked if you're okay because you don't *sound* okay."

I can't stay here forever, even if I wanted to. The family is only going to buy this "I'm staying with a friend" nonsense for so long. I can't remain locked away here and pretend none of this happened.

My concern for Uncle Stone battles with my desire to just pretend the outside world doesn't exist for a few more days, and it offers me a way to divert Bishop's focus away from me.

"I am okay. I promise. But I'm worried about Uncle Stone. Do you have any updates?"

I close Charlotte's bedroom door and make my way down one of the spiral staircases to the foyer.

Bishop jostles her phone slightly, probably moving away from whoever is near her. "He's stable, but there hasn't been much change since he got out of surgery."

My bare feet hit the bottom of the steps, and I freeze with my hand on the banister. "Does that mean he's in a coma?"

No one's mentioned the word since he came out of surgery, but if nothing's changing, it seems like that's what's happening. I don't know a damn thing about this type of stuff and usually rely on Aunt Nora and Pope to explain it to me, but they're both tied up with far more important things than fielding my calls.

"Yes, he's technically in a coma. Aunt Nora said it's not necessarily a bad thing. That his body needs time to heal."

Oh, God.

I slap my hand over my mouth to stop the sob threatening to come out and move away from the stairs toward a set of closed sliding double doors on the opposite side of the room I was in with Cass only a week ago.

"Ken? You still there?"

Swallowing my grief, I clear my throat. "Yeah."

I tug open the doors, and a beautiful, extravagant dining room filled with shining crystal and a table large enough to seat at least twenty greets me.

Holy shit.

The man could hold quite the dinner party here if he wanted to. It might even fit all the Hawkes.

I chuckle at that, then cringe again. The weekend is here. In two nights, it will be time for Sunday night dinner.

What the hell will that be like without me, without Uncle Stone, probably without Isaac or Viviana or Jack?

The tears I've been fighting finally well over and trickle down the side of my face. I don't bother swiping them away. I make my way through the dining room and to a swinging door that leads into the kitchen.

Bishop says something to someone, then returns to the line. "I'm really worried about you, Ken. Can you *please* tell me where you are?"

For a split second, I consider it. Seeing her might make me feel better, but I can never reveal where I am or why. This isn't the type of complication the Hawkes need right now.

I move through the kitchen and down another small hallway toward the back of the house. Even the halls are beautiful, with ornate, period-accurate wallpaper and light fixtures. It's the kind of home everyone who lives in New Orleans dreams about, the kind I dreamed about as a child. Uncle Stone and Aunt Nora's place can't rival this.

"I need to stay here for a bit longer."

To figure out what the fuck I'm going to do.

A closed door on my right draws my attention, and I turn the handle slowly and peek my head into an office. The large wooden desk standing in the center fills most of the space, with floor-to-ceiling bookcases behind it and across from it, filled with everything from fiction to legal books.

I step in, and my eyes zero in on the laptop sitting in the center of the desk. Chewing my lip, I approach it.

He had it open on the bed the other day.

There were files on it about Falco, likely the very information I had hoped to get from him that he's never forked over. Mainly, a *name* of whoever is behind everything Falco has done to us for years—one I can pass on to the rest of the family to get them digging.

I drum my fingers on the top.

Shit.

Why do I feel guilty about betraying him?

He'd do the same to me in a fucking heartbeat if I had information about the Hawkes that he wanted.

"Are you sure, Ken?" Bishop sounds so hopeful and worried. "Because wherever you are, if it's with someone you don't want the family to know about, some guy you're embarrassed by or something, I'll keep that secret for you. I just want you home with us."

Her words tear at my already-flayed heart. Bishop *would* keep that secret, just as I've kept my suspicions about the father of Allie's baby to myself this entire time.

It's what we do for each other, what we've *always done.*

I let my eyes drift over the desk to a photo of Charlotte sitting on Cass' lap on the front porch, smiling for the camera, looking absolutely blissfully unaware of what goes on in her father's world while he isn't here with her.

"I'll be home soon. I promise. A few more days."

Walking away from them will be so much harder than I thought it could be. Though it shouldn't, this house, Cass' home, has come to feel like a sanctuary, somewhere to hide from all the uncertainty raging outside the walls.

Another picture sits behind the one of Cass and Charlotte,

though partially covered by it. The face of a little boy with sandy-blond hair and green eyes sticks out of the edge.

Cass as a child?

Given everything he told me about his grandmother, I'm surprised he would hang onto anything from that time.

"Bishop, hold on a sec."

Only having one working arm means I can't hold the phone and grab the photo at the same time, so I flip it to speaker-phone and set it on the desk. I reach over the picture of Charlotte and Cass and grab the other one, suddenly anxious to see what Cass might have looked like before he grew into this infuriating, handsome man.

My breath stops when I see the whole thing.

The two men in the picture with Cass send a rush of terror through me that makes every hair on my body stand on end and dread coil deep around my spine.

What the hell?

"Kennedy?" Cass' voice carries through the home, and I flinch and turn toward the open door. "Where are you?"

What the hell is going on?

His footsteps echo off the marble as he makes his way back toward the office. "Kennedy?"

I could put it back.

I could try to hide what I've seen.

But I'm frozen in place.

He finally appears in the door, a smile curling his lips. "Hey, what are you doing in here?"

His eyes dart down to my hand and the photo in it, and his smile falters, his face slackening.

I swallow through the lump in my throat and turn the picture toward him. "Why do you have a picture of you with Dom Abello and Matteo Cortesi?"

The men who tried to kill Mom...

The men who would *have if Uncle Gabe hadn't stepped in with some well-placed shots...*

Cass takes a tentative step toward me, and instinctively, I shift back slightly, keeping the desk between us.

His gaze locks with mine, any humor draining away instantly. "Because Matteo was my father."

20

CASS

Kennedy's eyes widen slightly and dip down to the photograph in her hand, then back up at me. "He's your what?"

This isn't how I wanted her to find out.

Not how I imagined any of this going.

I was going to tell her, somehow come up with a way to explain it all to make it sound less...deceptive. But it's too late now to try to salvage anything when she knows the truth—my father tried to kill her mother before Kennedy was even born.

Why the fuck didn't you hide that picture?

Because I never thought I'd have Kennedy Hawke in my house, in my life. I never thought any of this was possible. And now I'm watching it crumble before my eyes while I struggle with a way to respond to her, to search for words that might somehow resolve this without her walking away.

Her hand holding the photo starts to shake, and she drops it, letting it clatter to the desk, the glass in the frame shattering across the gleaming wood beside my computer and the picture of me with Charlotte.

Kennedy shakes her head as she stares down at it, sucking in sharp, quick breaths. "That's what this is all about...why you're helping Falco hurt us. This is why you burned down The Grind and—" She presses her hand over her mouth as she fights back a sob, her eyes flicking up to mine, soaked with tears. "You tried to hurt us; you tried to *kill* me."

"No." I rush forward around the desk toward her. "I couldn't!"

She backs away, stumbling over the chair until she puts the huge piece of furniture between us again, a very real physical barrier to match the wall I see her rebuilding that I've worked so hard to break down. "Don't fucking touch me."

Don't scare her.

EXPLAIN!

"It wasn't like that, *Cherie*. You don't understand—"

She shakes her head, her blond locks flying around her face. "I do. This is all about revenge, you getting back at the Hawkes because of what happened to your father."

I should have known this would happen, should have seen it coming. There was no way I was ever going to be able to explain this to her or make her understand. It was always a losing proposition; I just never wanted to admit it to myself because it meant losing *her.*

In the blink of a fucking eye, I've come to care far too much about Kennedy Hawke, enough that I let it blind me to what was coming, what was inevitable.

I drop my palms to the desk and lower my head, staring down at the photo covered by shards of glass. One large piece distorts Dad's face, and I reach out and brush it off.

Kennedy continues to stare at me, the heat of her accusatory glare warming my chilled body even though I can't look at her. "This is why you work for Falco. You found someone else with a vendetta against us and you latched on to them to further your own plans to make us pay."

If only it were that simple.

I wince and lift my head, meeting her gaze. It's the least I can do when I reveal this, when I say the words I had hoped I'd never have to. "I don't work for Falco. I *am* Falco."

She recoils again, retreating farther from the desk.

"It all started from one of my dad's original shell companies he used to hide his assets from working for Dom Abello. I built on it, added layers and layers of shell corporations to protect my identity and the money he left me, and eventually, I created Falco Enterprises and started acting as its legal counsel."

Her wide eyes remain locked on me, like she's staring at a stranger, not the man who spent the last few days caring for her.

"Everything I told you the other day was true, *Cherie*. He was killed when I was four, almost five. My mom was a waitress from Baton Rouge. He used to drive over on weekends or whenever he had time to spend it with her. They never got married because I'm sure she was just one of many for him. Whitaker is her last name..." I release a sigh, glancing down at the photo again, of how happy I look to be with him and "Uncle Dom," completely oblivious to who and what they were. "I might have only been Charlotte's age, but I remember him, Kennedy. He was a good father. He was—"

"A *monster*." The anguish in her words feels like blades carving into my chest. "He was a *hitman*. He worked for one of the most dangerous men in the country. Don't pretend like he was some angel just to justify what you're doing."

I slam my fist against the desk, jerking my head up to meet her fiery gaze again. "I'm not *doing* any of this, Kennedy. I tried to warn you that Falco wasn't involved, and I *know* because I'm the one making all the fucking decisions." I motion toward her arm. "My revenge never included *hurting* people, not *this* way. I was prepared to dismantle the Hawke empire one piece at a time, to throw up any roadblocks to expansion that I could, to do any underhanded, dirty thing I needed to in order to make sure you all *failed*. But do you really believe I would hurt you, that I could hurt *anyone* after what *I* suffered losing my father to Gabe's fucking bullet?"

Her jaw hardens, and she takes a step forward, that relentless drive returning with her anger, replacing the fear and shock that had her backing away only a moment ago. "*That's* why you're doing it, to make everyone suffer the way you did when Gabe killed your father."

"No." I shake my head, but her words hold a truth I don't want to admit to myself, let alone hear. "Maybe *before*, but not after having Charlotte. You really think I would take Isaac away from his daughter, that I would take you away from your family?" My voice wavers slightly. "How can you possibly think I could hurt you?"

The tears stream down her face, unbidden now, leaving pink streaks on her peachy skin. "That's what all this was." She motions idly between us. "You and me. It was never about warning us about anything. It was about distracting me from what you were up to and trying to use me to get insider information on the Hawkes that you could use against us."

My hands tighten into fists at her accusation. "Are you telling me you didn't do it for the same reason?"

She flinches slightly.

"You think I didn't leave that computer open intentionally on the bed to see what you would do with it? That I didn't leave it here"—I tap it with my hand—"to see what you might take from it and tell your family?"

Her brows fly up. "You were testing me?"

I shake my head. "No, I was hoping you wouldn't. I was hoping I was *wrong* about what you were doing. I was hoping that maybe this was real."

She barks out a mirthless laugh and shakes her head as the tears continue to fall. "*None* of this was real."

I push up to fully standing. "Yes, it is, Kennedy. The warnings I gave you? They were all real. I could tell something was happening, something that wasn't me." I swallow through the emotion clogging my throat and muster up the strength to say the words I know will end things but that can also prove my point. "I wanted to be able to be the one to destroy the Hawkes, not someone else."

The fury filling her right now makes her body vibrate, the shaking so bad that I can see it even from here. "So altruistic of you to warn us."

I grit my teeth.

She has every right to be pissed, but the fact that she was doing the exact same thing to me makes her just as guilty as I am. And what her family does, what they *have* done, not only to me, but to countless other people, can't be brushed aside so easily.

"You judge what my father did for Dom, what I'm doing as Falco. But the Hawkes are no different. You're a bunch of fucking thugs, doing whatever it takes to get ahead, just with fancy pedigrees dressed in nice suits and heels."

She flinches and shakes her head. "No, we're not. We're nothing like your father, nothing like the Abellos."

Now it's my turn to laugh. "Luca Abello is one of *you,* and don't tell me that he and Gabe and Saint and whoever else you have doing your dirty work haven't dropped some bodies in the bayou like you joked about doing to me."

She clenches her jaw. "I wasn't joking, and it's sounding like a better and better idea."

"I can see that." It would be impossible to miss the sheer hatred she has for me now, but I have to get her to see past it to the truth. "But I also see what you don't, that there's something else happening, something bigger, something that has nothing to do with me."

"Bullshit." She takes another step forward until her thighs almost touch the other side of the desk. "I don't believe a fucking word that's coming out of your mouth, and I never will."

I stare her down. The anger radiating off her is stronger than anything I've ever felt during any of our confrontations. This is the kind of fury you don't come back from, the kind that never gets forgiven.

She's lost to me now.

But the least I can do is try to save her. "I might have an idea who's behind this."

Kennedy snorts. "Easy when you're that person."

I shake my head. "Believe that if you want. But I'm telling you, there's someone else in town, someone who—" I swallow thickly, thinking about my meeting with Damon earlier today and all the ominous things he's said since he barreled his way into my life and business. "Someone who wants the Hawkes gone as badly as I do, maybe more. I thought—"

"You thought what?"

"I thought he was like me, that he just wanted to fuck with your businesses, that he wanted to ensure you lost billions and lost your power over New Orleans. But now, I'm not so sure. Maybe..."

"Maybe what?"

I hate to say it because it means I've been blind to his intent all along. That I've been naïve and too trusting of the man I insisted I would never give my back. "Maybe he's the one behind all of this."

Kennedy doesn't look convinced in the least. "Who?"

"His name is Damon."

Her heated gaze narrows. "Who the fuck is Damon?"

I shake my head. "That's just it. I don't know. Marcel hasn't been able to find anything out on him, not even a goddam last name. He has companies set up behind a million different shell corporations around the world. We haven't been able to track anything. All I know is he wanted to partner with Falco on the hotel."

"And you did it."

"Of course, I did. He was bringing billions to the table, the kind of money that could help me get things moving faster, help us grow bigger and better than The Hawke Hotel."

She sneers, anger darkening her eyes to an almost midnight blue. "And you'd do anything to beat us, right?"

"If I'm right and it's him, I didn't know he would resort to any of this. I didn't know he would go this far—"

"Stop." She holds up her good hand, shaking her head and squeezing her eyes closed. "I can't listen to your lies anymore."

"Kennedy, don't."

Her lids fly open. "Don't what?"

"Don't believe that I'm capable of that. You know me better than that."

"All I know is what you wanted me to believe. It was all a fucking act, and I should have seen right through it. But I'm the idiot here and now"—she motions to her arm in the sling —"I'm not the only one paying the price. Isaac—" She swallows down a sob. "My uncle..."

I move around the desk to try to pull her into my arms, but she snags her phone from the desk and bolts away from me, backing toward the door.

"I swear to God, Cass, if you touch me, I'll kill you."

I grind to a stop a few feet from her, holding up my hands. "I would never hurt you, Kennedy."

"You already have."

The vise around my chest tightens until I can barely breathe. "Where are you going?"

She offers a slight shrug, like the answer should be obvious.

"Where I should have been this whole time. Back to my family."

~

KENNEDY

I turn away from the man who has become a total stranger to me and stagger out of the office, transferring the phone into the hand of my slinged arm so I can brace myself against anything I can find to keep from falling over.

My head spins with everything Cass just said and the reality of what I didn't see, making the world around me impossible to navigate properly.

I've been an idiot.

How could I not have seen it?

How could I not have known?

Because you were too busy thinking with what's between your legs instead of what's between your ears.

I stumble down the hallway, hand against the beautiful wallpaper I admired only a few minutes ago, trying to make it to the front door. Every fiber of my being *screams* for me to get away, to put as much distance between myself and that man as possible. But each step gets more difficult, my body going into some sort of shock and refusing to cooperate.

If I know Bishop, as soon as she heard Cass and I talking through the line I left open, she would've alerted Gabe and her father—and anyone else she could.

They'll be coming for me soon.

I make it out into the foyer and glance up at the spiral staircase.

My bag of belongings is still up in Cass's room, but there isn't anything in there I need badly enough to try to go get it before they arrive. He can keep it and anything it holds—

mementos of the time he seduced and fucked the dumb bitch who was too caught up in the moment to know what was going on behind those green eyes of his.

His heavy footsteps follow me down the hall, and I stumble, grabbing the banister to keep myself upright. I turn back to see him approaching, his strong, angular jaw clenched tightly.

"Kennedy, don't leave like this."

The closer he gets, the more acutely aware I become of how vulnerable I am to him—physically and emotionally. "Leave me alone. Don't try to stop me."

He releases a heavy sigh, coming to a stop a few feet from me. "How are you even going to get home?"

I bark out a laugh that has zero humor as the tears continue to stream down my face and take the phone from my other hand to turn it toward him, showing him the connected call. "By now, my entire family knows where I am and what you've done, and they're going to come for me."

Cass goes stock still, and almost as if on cue, tires squeal on the street in front of the house.

I glance that way, then turn back toward him with a sad smile. "Tell Charlotte goodbye for me."

His face falls, and he takes a step forward, his Adam's apple bobbing with his thick swallow. "Kennedy, please, you have to believe me. I was trying to stop this war because I don't want anyone to get hurt."

I shake my head and release the banister so I can move toward the door on unsteady feet, keeping an eye on him over my shoulder.

"If your family comes after me, if they—" He cuts himself off and shakes his head. "Charlotte won't have anything. She won't have *anyone*."

I scan the beautiful foyer and peek into the room where he kissed me the other night, letting my gaze drift to the stunning dining room I explored earlier, and release a sardonic laugh. "She'll have all this. She'll have the memories of playing Monopoly with you and your *friend*, right? And unlike you, she won't have to *pretend* her father was someone to mourn because no one will ever know the truth. You'll just disappear the same way you've accused us of disappearing others."

A single tear slips from one of his mossy-green eyes, and he swipes it away. "You wouldn't do that to her. That isn't you, Kennedy."

"And I would've said you weren't capable of any of this, either, but you've been lying to me from the beginning. All of it."

He shakes his head and takes a step closer. "Not all of it."

"Enough of it." I grab the handle of the front door and tug it open in time to see Saint, Gabe, Luca, and Bishop climb from an SUV parked at the curb, each of them with guns drawn.

They move through the gate and approach the house, the pure fury on each of their faces enough to strike fear into me, even though I know it isn't directed my way.

I make it out the door and onto the porch, then stagger down the front steps and partly down the path to Bishop. She pulls me into her strong arms, and I finally lose all control, sobbing, my legs sagging under me.

Gabe, Saint, and Luca step up next to us, guns trained toward the front door, where Cass stands motionless, still dressed in his dark suit and crisp white shirt, looking like he just stepped off the pages of *GQ*.

I look at Bishop. "Did you hear all of it?"

She nods and inclines her head toward her dad and our uncles. "I filled them in on what they missed."

"Good."

This information will change everything.

I end the call that led them to me, then let her wrap her arms around my waist to help support me. Saint steps in front of us to shield us from Cass with his huge body, offering me a sad smile.

Gabe leans in. "Did he hurt you?"

Reluctantly, I let my gaze move back to Cass, having to peek around Saint's massive frame.

That's such a loaded question.

Almost impossible to answer.

The way he stares at me from the front door, I can still feel the same heat I did that first night at the masquerade. It isn't that of hatred, but maybe I don't know the difference anymore. He once said there's a thin line between love and hate, and now, I'm starting to see what he means.

I look back at Gabe. "He did, but not the way you think."

Gabe's jaw tightens, and a muscle there tics as he stares at me, concern mixing with disappointment and anger.

I'm going to have a lot to answer for, a lot to explain. A lot of people are going to be really fucking pissed at me, and they'll have every right to be.

What did I think was going to happen?

Where did I think this was going to go with him?

How did I ever think I would just walk away from him with no consequences?

Because I never could've stayed.

Luca circles around and pulls me into his arms. He drops his lips near my ear and murmurs into it. "None of this is your fault, *carina*. It's easy to be taken in by someone when you believe their lies."

The words are meant to make me feel better, but all they do is bring another round of sobs. Luca pulls me in closer, rubbing my back with his free hand while keeping his weapon ready in the other.

Gabe steps forward, closer to Cass. "Give me one good reason why I shouldn't shoot you dead right now?"

Cass glances at me, waiting for me to interject, but there

isn't anything I can say in his defense—nor would I even if I could manage to speak. "Because my daughter's going to be home from school in a few hours, and I don't ever want her to have to suffer for the consequences of my actions."

Uncle Gabe seems completely unmoved, his broad shoulders tensing. "Maybe you should have thought of that before you set out to take us down, Cass. You fucked with the wrong people."

The man who has morphed into someone completely different from the one who held me in the shower last night finally steps from the door onto the porch, walking closer to the gun pointed directly at him. "And you killed my father."

Gabe doesn't flinch. "I had to, or he would have killed Danika."

Cass shakes his head. "You didn't have to." His gaze meets mine, as if he's asking for confirmation from me—confirmation I will *never* give him. "That one action destroyed my life."

Yet, if Gabe hadn't stepped in, my mother would have died that day and I wouldn't even *be* here. Something Cass seems incapable of grasping over his desire for revenge.

"Yeah." Gabe looks up at the house. "Looks pretty fucking rough."

Barking out a mirthless laugh, Cass takes another step toward Gabe. "All of this, I worked for it, I fought for it, I earned it. It wasn't handed to me the way it was to all of you."

Gabe snorts incredulously. "Savage and I built our company from the ground up with the help of people who shared the same vision. *Nothing* was handed to anyone."

"You just took out anyone in your way." Cass gives a cold smile. "I guess we share that, don't we?"

His words send a chill down my spine, despite his insistence that he wasn't behind the fire or the shooting. The difference he suggests between his type of revenge and any other is so minute, so damn minuscule, that there really is none.

A distinction *without* difference.

Police sirens sound in the distance, and Saint, Luca, and Bishop all scan the area around us. Several people in neighboring houses stand at their windows, watching, many with phones to their ears.

Someone called the cops, and they'll be here soon.

Saint motions toward the SUV. "We need to get Kennedy out of here before we have unwanted company."

Cass raises a brow at Gabe in challenge. "You're going to shoot me here before you leave? With all these witnesses?" He motions toward one of the neighboring houses. "The Hawkes have been able to buy their way out of a lot of things, including the murder of my father, but you wouldn't buy your way out of this. I have friends, too, you know, in high places."

"And I hear you have a new one." Luca interjects, referencing what Cass said about the mysterious Damon on the call they listened to.

Cass looks at him. "If you take away anything from the conversation I just had with Kennedy, it should be this—I wasn't behind either of the attacks on the Hawkes, and I don't know who was. All I do know is that the man who is my new business partner in the hotel appeared with a very strong grudge against the Hawkes that he won't explain. Neither I nor my investigator have been able to find anything on him, but maybe you'll have better luck figuring out who he is and what he wants."

Gabe offers him a wicked smile. "At least we finally know who's behind Falco."

Those mossy-green eyes meet mine again. "Do you know what Falco means in Italian?"

Luca tightens his grip on me. "It means hawk."

Cass grins. "I thought it was fitting to attack you with your own name, to use it against you. And I'm not about to stop just because you put a gun in my face."

The sirens grow closer, and Gabe starts to retreat, keeping the gun trained on him. Bishop, Luca, and Saint guide me to the SUV. Bishop and Luca help me in, sliding into the backseat on either side of me while Saint gets behind the wheel. Gabe climbs in last, pulling shut the passenger door.

We peel away from the curb as the first squad car turns the corner in front of us, coming toward Cass' house. I bury my face against Bishop's shoulder and sob.

Gabe pulls out his phone. "I'm calling the mayor and then the police chief. I'll explain the issue has been handled, and he will call off his men—if he knows what's good for him."

Friends in high places.

The connections the Hawkes have made over the years have served us well, made things possible that otherwise never would have been. None of us are going down for the little showdown that just happened. But it's too late to stop the damage I've done.

21

CASS

Staring at the shattered remains of the picture frame on my desk, I take another sip of my bourbon—the most potent stuff I have—but it doesn't help stop my hand from trembling.

Having a gun pointed at me isn't an everyday occurrence, nor do I ever want it to be. It's precisely what I've been trying to avoid, yet my actions have brought it down on me.

You knew you were going to have to tell her at some point.

I tighten my hand on the glass and take another drink, then reach out and pull the photo from inside the frame, shaking off the tiny shards of glass remaining on it.

It hasn't faded after more than thirty years—as crisp and vibrant as the day it was taken. I couldn't have been more than three or four in this picture, standing with Dad and "Uncle Dom" in front of Dad's brand-new Camaro.

A hazy memory of that day still lingers in my head. How excited he was when he bought it. How thrilled I was to get my first ride. I couldn't even see over the dashboard, but we flew down a country road so fast that I was pushed back into the seat.

At the time, I didn't realize it, but we must've been going 120, maybe 130.

I shudder now to think about putting Charlotte in that position as a father, but as a child, man, it was fun, and it's one of those times I always remember with Dad.

There weren't many. But I always had this *one*. Now, even *it* is tainted by what just happened with Kennedy.

Fuck...

She called him a monster, but staring into his eyes in the photo, I can't see him that way. Some of the things he did were horrible, but he did them for the same reason I do the things I do for Charlotte.

I chose a legal way to attack the Hawkes and get my revenge with court filings and destroying them in the public eye rather than with guns, but it hurt her all the same, maybe worse than the bullet that actually hit her.

I'm tempted to crumple up the picture and toss it into the trash can with all this glass so I can try to put the past behind me, but I can't bring myself to do it. Not even knowing who and what these two men were. I was so innocent at that age, and Charlotte isn't much older, but her life will always be free from this.

Or so I thought.

I squeeze my eyes closed and down the rest of my drink, trying to steady my hand. If they had come a few hours later, Charlotte would've been here. She would've seen them come and take Kennedy at fucking gunpoint.

"Jesus Christ..." I scour my hands over my face as the sound of the back kitchen door opening makes me jerk my head up.

I glance at my watch.

Fuck, she's home from school already.

"Daddy! Kennedy!"

Her yell echoes through the house, and I hear feet thunder through the kitchen and down the hallway toward the front stairs, probably to check if we are down here before she goes up.

Shit, she's going to go look for Kennedy.

I scramble from my desk chair and out into the foyer, managing to scoop her up and catch her when she's only two steps up the flight.

She flails her arms and legs, struggling against my hold. "Daddy, let me go."

Hugging her to me, probably a little too tightly, I press kisses over her little face.

She shoves at my chest. "Daddy, I want to go say hi to Kennedy."

I set her down on the steps, making her sit next to me. Abby rounds the corner, sees the look on my face, and motions back to the kitchen before she disappears.

There isn't any way to avoid telling Charlotte the truth—or at least *some* version of it. "Kennedy's gone, *Bebelle*."

Charlotte's bottom lip pouts out. "What? Why?"

"She, um…" I rub the back of my neck and stare at the front door, where, only a few hours ago, Kennedy ran from me. "She was feeling better, so she went back to her family."

The little girl, who has changed my life so much, stares up at me with her blond brows drawn low over her green eyes that match mine. "Why couldn't she stay here with us?"

I drag her up onto my lap. She has no idea how badly I would've liked that or how impossible it would have been. "Because Kennedy has her own life and things she needs to do, people she needs to be with."

Her bottom lip quivers, and her eyes start to shimmer.

Oh God, not the tears. I can't handle the waterworks today.

I brush her hair back from her face, wild after spending the day running around with her friends. "I would've liked her to stay, *Bebelle*. I really would have, but sometimes, it's just not possible."

And no four-year-old is ever going to be able to understand that. The complications of the situation we found ourselves in would be impossible for *anyone* to comprehend, let alone a child.

Hell, I barely understand it.

None of this was ever supposed to happen.

I was supposed to approach Kennedy to try to get the Hawkes to listen to me so that Charlotte and I didn't get caught in the crossfire of violence between them and whoever the hell is out there. But now, all I've managed to do is fuck everything up and make it more dangerous for me and Char by being unable to keep my damn hands off Kennedy.

Squeezing Charlotte to me, I try to think of anything that might cheer her up and take her mind off Kennedy leaving, even if nothing will ever erase that image from my own head. "How would you feel about going away for a few days?"

She looks up at me. "What do you mean?"

"You and me? Maybe we go on a trip for a little bit. You don't have school on Monday, so we have a long weekend."

She considers me for a moment, and I hold my breath that the bribe will work. It'll not only improve her mood and draw her attention away from Kennedy's absence, but it'll also get us out of New Orleans. We'll be out of the way of the Hawkes, so they can do whatever they need to do to confirm what I've told them—that I'm not the biggest threat.

Maybe they'll have some luck finding something out about Damon where Marcel and I have failed. I pray they do because I can't shake the feeling that Damon wants more than just to destroy the Hawkes' business empire the way I do. He's out for blood, the kind that's already been spilled.

"Where would we go?"

"That's a good question." One I probably should have

thought of *before* I suggested it. "We could go to Baton Rouge. We could go to Florida—"

Her eyes light up. "Disney?"

I smile at her excitement. "Yep, if that's what you want."

She claps her hands excitedly and leaps from my lap, running down the two steps and back toward the kitchen. "Abby! Abby! We're going to Disney."

Crisis averted.

For the time being.

Undoubtedly, she'll be questioning me more about Kennedy and her abrupt departure, but this at least buys me a little time to breathe and to come up with something to say that might appease a little girl who seems to have become as attached to Kennedy as quickly as I have.

I exhale heavily and push myself up. My phone buzzing in my pocket makes me freeze, and I slowly reach in and tug it out to look at the screen.

Damon is the last person I want to talk to right now after that showdown with the Hawkes, especially when he may be the reason all of this is happening. But if I have any hope of getting out of this unscathed, or not any further damaged, I need to figure out what his end game is, what all of this is about.

I slide my finger across the screen to answer the call and bring it to my ear as I make my way to the front door and tug it open. Staring out at the street, scanning for anything unusual, I'm unable to shake the feeling that something is coming. "Damon, what do you want?"

"What do I always want, Cass? An update. I heard rumors you had a confrontation with the Hawkes today after our meeting."

How the fuck does he know about that?

I glance at the neighbors' houses—the busybodies who called the police.

Seeing armed people storming my lawn isn't exactly an everyday occurrence, so I should probably be thankful they cared enough to try to get help. But by the time the police arrived, the Hawkes were gone, and I had no intention of throwing them under the bus when I know they own the chief of police as completely as they do the mayor.

Being "unable to identify" who was here made it a lot easier to get the cops out of the way, and after a few radio calls back and forth with someone, they seemed willing to let the incident go—likely because of a well-placed call by the Hawkes.

But it seems my neighbors have been talking to someone. Either that or Damon's watching me a lot more closely than I imagined.

I clear my throat. "A misunderstanding, that's all."

"A misunderstanding involving Kennedy Hawke?"

Acid churns in my stomach. "Nothing you need to worry about."

"You keep saying that. You keep making assurances, but I think it's time you and I sit down and have another little chat. One where you lay all your cards on the table."

Again, it isn't an overt threat, but the chill still settles over my skin. "I'm at the airport, about to board a plane to leave town for a few days."

"Then you'll just have to catch a later flight, won't you?"

I cringe. As much as I want to unravel the Damon mystery, getting Charlotte on a plane and away from here as quickly as possible has to be my top priority. "That isn't possible. I'll be back Monday and can meet with you that evening."

An uncomfortable silence falls on the line, one heavily filled with his annoyance at my brushoff. After missing the meeting yesterday, I'm doing it again—putting him second to something else.

"Fine. But, Cass, I expect to have answers to my questions, not just placations."

He ends the call, and I slide my phone back into my pocket and close the front door, leaning back against it and squeezing my eyes closed.

This entire day has gone to shit, and to think I woke up with Kennedy in my arms.

How the hell am I ever going to fix any of this?

KENNEDY

POPE STANDS outside Uncle Stone's room, chatting with Coen and Angelina, their heads dipped together. No one looks particularly happy or well—bags under their red-rimmed eyes, shoulders slumped, utter exhaustion overtaking each of them.

They see Bishop and me approaching, and their spines stiffen.

Everyone knows.

I'm the traitor.

I'm the reason Uncle Stone might die.

A sob threatens to climb up my throat, but I swallow it back, forcing myself to continue moving forward down the hallway toward them, Bishop at my side.

She loops her arm through my good one and leans in. "Don't worry."

Easy for her to say.

Bishop doesn't have to stand the looks of accusation everyone's been giving me since they pulled me out of Cass' house this morning.

All I wanted to do was go home, crawl into bed, and never come out again, and I might still do that. But first, I had to answer a whole lot of questions I didn't want to. Now, I have to see him. I have to see that he's still alive and breathing and fighting. And I have to apologize.

It won't be enough, not *nearly* enough, to make up for what I've done, for the danger I allowed to get so close to us—to me —but I still have to do it.

We make it to Stone's room, and Pope pulls me in for a hug.

His long arms wrap around me, and he squeezes gently, paying careful attention to my arm and trying not to crush it. He should probably be doing his rounds and checking on his own patients right now, not hanging out here with us, but with Aunt Nora's pull around here, I don't think anyone would ever say anything to him. "How are you doing?"

Pulling back, I look up at him, towering over me by at least a foot. "Are you asking as my 'cousin' or a doctor?"

The corner of his lips twitches. "Both."

I shrug and cringe a little bit at the bite of pain in my arm. "Okay, as long as I don't move my arm very much. It's better than it was yesterday, though."

He glances down at it, still in the sling. "You'll feel better in a few days. It probably doesn't seem like it right now, but you will, and so will Isaac."

The mention of his name brings a renewed threat of tears. "I just went and saw him."

And it was truly awful.

Seeing him laid up in bed.

The pain pinching his features when he tried to move.

His anger when I had to come clean to him and Jack about my relationship or whatever the fuck it was with Cass.

I deserved all of it and then some from him and everyone else, but it doesn't mean taking their shots didn't hurt.

Pope raises a dark brow at me. "And how did he seem?"

"Angry."

His lips press into a tight line, and he nods. "I bet."

He doesn't say anything else; he doesn't have to. Everyone has made how they feel about the situation very clear.

Still, Angie wraps her arms around me, and she squeezes my hand. "We can talk later if you want to."

She probably thinks she understands what I'm feeling after she and Jude hid their relationship because they didn't think anyone would understand it, but it's completely different.

Jude isn't likely responsible for putting bullet holes in three of us. Jude hasn't been attacking our family for years because of a personal vendetta over something that happened thirty years ago. Jude's one of us and always will be, and Cass never can be.

I appreciate her offer, her reaching out to me when everyone in the family has every reason to shut me out for what I've brought down on them. She pulls away, and I nod, even though I don't plan on following through with it, then walk to the closed door of Stone's room.

"Is it okay if I go in and talk to him?"

Pope nods. "Nora is in there."

Of course, she is.

Coen looks at the room. "She hasn't left his side all week except to go shower in the staff locker rooms. She even eats in there. I've tried to get her to go home for a while to sleep, but..." He trails off, his concern for his mom evident. "I'm here as much as I can be, but sometimes, she just wants to be alone with Dad."

If anyone has a reason to be livid with me, it's Coen. His *father* lies in that room, riddled with bullet holes, fighting for his life when he should be fighting in a damn courtroom, and his brother is at home trying to heal from his own wounds caused by how stupid I was.

I release a heavy sigh, looking into his eyes that match my own. "I'm so sorry, Coen. I—"

He cuts me off by pulling me against him a little too aggressively. "Please don't. We can talk later." His voice cracks, and he tightens his hold on me. "Just go see him. He'd want you in there."

Would he?

A few weeks ago, if something like this had happened, without a doubt, I would have been sitting by his bedside until he could walk out of here and go home. Cass changed everything, and I honestly don't even know what Uncle Stone would say about this fucked-up situation.

I pull out of Coen's hold, offering him a tight smile and trying not to focus on the unshed tears shimmering in his eyes. Everyone watches me put my hand on the doorknob and pause for a moment. I suck in a deep breath before I push it open and step inside the dimly lit room.

Aunt Nora lifts her head from staring at the book on her lap, her eyes widening slightly when she sees me. "Kennedy."

She closes the book and sets it on the small table to the side of the hospital bed where Stone lies, tubes down his throat, attached to a thousand machines, even more than I was when I was in here.

The sob I've been fighting crawls out of my throat, and I can't bite it back. It slips from my lips just as Nora pulls me into a hug and holds me tightly.

"I'm so sorry, Nora. This is all my f-f-fault."

She squeezes me and shakes her head. "Don't say that."

"But it is. You don't understand."

Pulling her head back, she nods. "I do. They told me what happened with you and Cass. At least, what they figured out from that phone call..."

She knows there's so much more.

She can see it written all over my face.

"It's my fault." I sob, shaking my head. "I wasn't paying attention to what I should have been. I wasn't careful enough."

Her gaze darts over to Stone, and she wraps her arm around me and guides me to the chair she just vacated. She gently pushes me down into it, then pours some water into a glass from the stack of them sitting next to the bed and hands it to me.

"You're going to hyperventilate if you don't calm down."

Always the doctor.

Caring for others.

When I'm the last person she should be taking care of.

I try to control the sobbing, but every time I think I do, my eyes land on Stone again, and it comes right back. "Is h-h-he going to b-b-be okay?"

Her jaw tightens as she runs her hand through his disheveled dark hair, her fingers finding the pieces at his temples that are already graying. "I don't know, sweetie. As a wife, I say yes, of course, but I'm also a surgeon and he's been through a lot. His body has. There are a thousand different things that could go wrong, but it doesn't mean they will. We just have to stay positive and keep praying for him."

"There's nothing else you can do?"

She shakes her head. "No. We just have to wait and see what happens when he wakes up."

When he wakes up, not if.

Her word sends a little flutter of hope through my chest. Nora will never let him go, not without a hell of a fight. None of us will. She knows all the best doctors in the country, and I'm sure she's spoken to every single one of them about Stone's condition.

"Can I talk to him?"

She nods. "I'm going to go out in the hall." She presses a kiss to the top of my head. "Take your time."

I wait for her to slip out of the room, leaving me alone to face the consequences of my betrayal of the family. It looks an awful lot like death.

Pale skin beneath a week's worth of stubble. Sunken cheeks. Tubes down his throat and running out of both sides of him.

Fuck, this is hard.

I reach out with my good hand and pull his into it, squeezing it. "Uncle Stone, it's me. It's Kennedy."

Fighting back another sob, I stare at the hand that lifted me up as a child, that always supported me through everything—sports and mock trial competitions, debate club, anything and everything. Uncle Stone was *always* there, like another father to me.

And now, I've put him here.

"I don't know if you can hear me or if anyone has told you what happened." I release a heavy sigh, thinking about this morning. "I fucked up bad. I got involved with the wrong person. Someone..." I shake my head. "I should have known better. I should have known I couldn't trust him. I didn't want to. I just..."

Charlotte's face flashes before my eyes.

That sweet little girl who relies on him so much, who trusts him so implicitly. The one he claims to do it all for. She's the reason I let down my guard around him, that I allowed him to weasel his way into my heart, but it was all a smokescreen.

Cass Whitaker has been after us his entire life.

He claims this wasn't him, but that doesn't mean a fucking thing.

How can I believe a word out of his mouth when everything's always been a lie?

I squeeze Uncle Stone's hand again. "I'm sorry you're here like this, that I wasn't more careful, that I didn't figure out who he was and what he was doing sooner, so I might have prevented this. But I'll make sure he gets what's coming to him. I won't let him get away with it."

I can't get any more words out between the sobs, and I kiss his hand before I push myself to my feet, stumbling slightly.

There's only one way to make this right.

We have to keep going.

We have to do whatever we can to destroy Falco and Cass,

to do to him what he's been trying to do to us, and it starts with the groundbreaking of the hotel.

I slowly make my way to the door and tug it open. Everyone in the hall turns toward me. Coen, Angie, Pope, and Nora all stare expectantly.

They may not like what I'm about to say, but at this point, there's no swaying me. I step out, swiping at my eyes.

Coen wraps his arm around me. "You okay?"

I shake my head. "No, but I know what we have to do."

It's the same thing I insisted on when I woke up in this hospital, that we keep moving forward, that we don't let anything get in the way of our plans. At the time, people placated me, saying we would make a decision later when we knew more.

But now we do know, and everyone looks at me, waiting for me to continue, to say something that will somehow shed some sort of light on the future that looks so dark and murky right now.

"We're going to go ahead with the groundbreaking, and we're going to destroy Falco."

22

KENNEDY

Silverware clanks against plates, and everyone sips at their wine, but the more I watch, the more I notice no one's really eating anything. They're just pushing around Nana's lasagna, chicken parm, garlic bread, and the rest of our usual Sunday supper spread on their plates to make it look like they actually did.

I don't have to ask why.

The empty chairs where Uncle Stone and Aunt Nora sit might as well be coffins, and the eerie silence when the table is usually filled with so much life and chatter only ratchets up the tension building in the air.

My knee bounces under the table violently, only getting worse the longer this horribly awkward Sunday dinner continues.

Nana clears her throat from the head of the table. "Kennedy, dear, would you like another glass of wine?"

I glance down at my almost-empty glass. "No, I'm all right."

It's the first alcohol I've had in a week since I didn't want to mix it with the pain medication, but now that I've stopped taking that, the wine I usually enjoy so much somehow doesn't taste as good as it once did.

But I'm enjoying the lingering pain.

I deserve it.

Given everything, it's God's way of ensuring I know what I've done and pay for it *somehow*. The constant ache and sharp stabs when I move my arm keep reminding me of what we could still lose and the very real danger still out there—wrapped up in that handsome, sexy, sly package.

I finger the stem of the glass, spinning it and watching the light from the chandelier over the table trickle through the red liquid and onto the tablecloth.

"Ooh, that's pretty." Viviana leans across her plate and points to the crimson shade.

I give her a tight smile, then return to watching it. It's better than having to look anyone in the eye. Until the red of the wine suddenly morphs into flashes of blood splattered across Stone, Isaac, me, and the sidewalk outside The Grind.

Fuck.

Squeezing my eyes closed, I raise a shaky hand to push the glass away then let it drop into my lap to try to hide the trembling, but the images only grow more vivid against my lids.

My eyes snap open, and Isaac gives me a hard, concerned look from across the table. I can't believe he even came today, that less than a week after being shot three times, he would leave his place and sit at this table with me, the one who caused the attack in the first place.

I would've bowed out if I were him, no matter how pissed Nana might have been. And I would've stayed at home tonight myself if I didn't think Nana would come to get me herself, dragging me out, kicking and screaming to ensure I show up.

Maybe that's why he did; he's too afraid to face her and would rather accept the pain it causes him to sit here for several hours, chatting and pretending everything is fine rather than face her wrath.

He presses his hand over where one of his wounds is, and Jack leans over and whispers something to him. His blue eyes flash as he stares at her, and he nods and returns his assessing gaze back to me.

I can't fucking take this anymore.

Shoving my chair back from the table, I climb to my feet. Everyone looks over at me, surprised, their brows furrowed, utensils raised over their plates or halfway to their mouths—for those of them who *actually* are eating anything.

Dad reaches out from next to me and squeezes my hand. "Kennedy, are you all right?"

The tears come before my words do. Warm and salty when they hit my lips. "Are you kidding?" It comes out more like a screech. "Are we really all just going to sit here and pretend like Uncle Stone isn't lying in that hospital right now?"

Anyone who was holding any silverware lets it clatter to their plates. Almost two dozen sets of hard eyes stare back at me as I scan down the table.

From Nana over Gabe and Skye, Atlas and Astrid, to Isaac, Jack, Viviana and Coen, Storm and Landon, Allie, then back up my side to Angelina and Jude, over Saint and Caroline, Pope and Bishop, Byron and Luca, Mom and Dad.

And finally, to our visitor, Jack's dad, Cutter, who refused to accept a seat but stands against the wall, aviator sunglasses covering his eyes, only half concealing the scars on his face, arms crossed over his chest.

"Are we really not going to talk about this?" I tug my hand from Dad's grip. "I know you're all pissed at me."

Though no one has said the words, the tension since they came and rescued me has been so thick that it's been hard to wade through it. "I know you all blame me, and I'm sorry. I thought maybe getting involved with Cass would give me a way to find out who was behind Falco, who was controlling every-thing, who might have set the fire. But instead, all I did was distract myself so I couldn't see the real danger—"

Dad squeezes my forearm. "Honey, is that really what you think? That we all blame you?"

I jerk out of his hold again and stumble back from the table slightly. "Of course, I do. How could I not? It's my fault."

Luca pushes back from the table and walks over to me. I try to move away, but he grabs me and pulls me to him, and even at my best, I know better than to fight the man who has probably killed—or at least ordered the killing of—more people than I've met in my life.

His warm brown gaze locks with mine, the softness there calming me instantly. "I know how you feel because Byron went through the exact same thing when he and I got together. It might've been over thirty years ago, but the pain he felt at thinking he had betrayed all of you was very real."

Byron comes over and rubs my back. "He's right. And it took me a long time to understand that while I may have been lying to all of you and trying to hide my relationship with Luca, that if I had just come clean, it might've changed things and made them so much easier. We could have had a conversation with him and heard him out so much earlier."

It's impossible not to see the parallel they're trying to make, but it isn't true here.

Not at all.

I shake my head. "There isn't anything to hear Cass out on. He's said his piece, and it was all bullshit. Every. Single. Word."

Byron offers me a kind smile. "Where we are right now has nothing to do with you and Cass. What happened would've happened whether you were with him or not."

I release a sob, the tension finally snapping. "That's not true."

Luca tilts my chin up and forces me to look at him. "Do you

really believe he's behind the shooting? In your heart? *Do* you, *carina*?"

I stare into his dark eyes. The man who once controlled one of the most dangerous and violent crime organizations in the country but who has been nothing but kind and gentle and giving to all of us since I was born.

The same way that Cass was with me when we were alone...

The same way he always was with Charlotte...

Finally, I shake my head. "I don't know. I don't want to. He says he's not. He swears it. But he also swore he would never hurt me..."

Luca brushes some of my hair back behind my ear. "I know he hurt you, *carina*, but do you think he's the one who ordered the attack on you, Isaac, and Stone?"

I sniffle and shake my head.

"Neither do I." Cutter's interjection makes everyone freeze, and all heads turn toward him.

The silent, stoic man has mostly stayed out of the conversation tonight, instead watching and listening, keeping his eagle-eyed gaze on his daughter and granddaughter, the entire reason he came down here.

Luca releases me and turns to him. "Do you know something we don't?"

Cutter sighs and rubs at his jaw. With his eyes covered, it's so hard to read the man, but something tells me even if he took them off, it would be difficult.

His focus darts over to Gabe, then to Savage, and back to Luca. "You know I've had my friend, Preacher, digging since the shooting, searching for anything that might suggest there was another player involved. And after what we learned the other day from Kennedy"—he looks to me—"I had him dig into both Cass and the supposed Damon."

Angie looks at Allie. "I just can't believe Damon would be

involved. He's so nice. He came to the café every morning for months and was always so friendly."

Cutter nods slowly. "Likely scoping out the place and planning."

Angie shivers, and Jude pulls her against him, wrapping his arm around her shoulders.

"You think this man was involved?" Gabe's voice carries across the table, hard and full of the hatred he feels toward whoever was behind the shooting. "This *Damon* character?"

Cutter shrugs. "I think it's suspicious as fuck that this guy shows up a few months before the fire at the café, inserts himself into Angie and Allie's life by going there daily, and then once it burns to the fucking ground and you're ready to reopen and do the groundbreaking on the hotel, he all of a sudden partners with Falco. It sounds to me like someone with a vendetta."

Luca nods, his hands fisting at his sides. "Or something completely made up by Cass to cover his own ass after what he did. He would've seen Damon outside The Grind when he went there and when he was down the street at Falco's Daily Grounds. He could have picked anyone to point the finger at to take the heat off himself. We don't have any confirmation that their partnership is even real."

Cutter finally pushes off the wall, stalking around the table to rest his hands on the back of Jack's chair. "And I would agree with you that's possible. Except Preacher's the best hacker in the world, and I'm not just saying that because I'm biased. And right now, he can't find anything on this guy or his company. Cass set up Falco Enterprises so that he would never be discovered, and that's exactly what this Damon guy has done as well with the company listed on his contract with Falco. There are only so many people in this world who have those kinds of connections, who go to those lengths to conceal their identities.

My guess is Cass used some of his father's old ones to do it for Falco."

Luca nods. "His father was my father's right hand. There are a lot of people who would do a lot of things for Matteo's son."

A shudder rolls through me, just like it always does when I think about who Cass really is and what he was doing since that first minute he approached me at the masquerade. He was being his father's son—finishing the job Matteo started so many years ago.

"We're going to keep looking for this Damon guy, trying to figure out what his angle is, but until then"—Cutter scans the room—"everyone needs to lay low. No one ever goes anywhere alone. Everyone is always carrying a weapon, especially the women. We cancel all public appearances—"

"No." I push past Luca and Byron toward Cutter, apparently not valuing my life at all by approaching the volatile man. "We're still doing the groundbreaking."

He shakes his head. "No, you'll be too exposed. It's literally a goddamn open lot. Anyone in the crowd could have a weapon, or a sniper could shoot from any window or roof. He could take all of you out before we would ever have the chance to get you out of harm's way."

"Not if we're prepared for it. Not if we buy every goddamn building around the hotel site and ensure that we control the security of it."

Cutter's lips twitch slightly into something almost resembling a smile. "A good sniper can hit you from a lot farther away than you think, sweetheart."

Gabe snorts.

I glance at the former Ranger sniper who saved Mom from Matteo all those years ago. "What's your distance record?"

He leans back in his chair, casting a quick glance around the table at everyone. "You don't want to know. It would scare you."

Skye smacks him in the chest. "Will you shut up? She just got shot."

And that would be the perfect reason to do what I want, what Cutter wants, to go home and hide away from everyone and the world. It's what I *want* to do more than anything.

But we can't.

I can't.

Staring down Jack's father, I try my best not to look like the pathetic, broken woman I've become. "The last thing we should do right now is back down. We need to prove that we're not afraid, that nothing is going to stop us. We need to fucking crush Falco and Cassius Whitaker, and if Damon is involved, then him, too. We use the groundbreaking to draw him out, and then, we crush them both."

～

CASS

THE SUN DROPS low on the horizon, and darkness creeps over the city, bringing a shiver down my spine. New Orleans can be as deadly as it is beautiful, and tonight, that truth somehow feels more real.

Probably because of where I'm heading and why.

After landing at the airport and getting Charlotte home with Abby, the last thing I want to do is come to the office and meet with Damon. Not after already spending the entire weekend lost in thought about what happened with Kennedy and the fact that my business partner could be the one responsible.

The only saving grace was that I somehow managed to keep Charlotte oblivious to the drama and how much of a cluster-fuck my life has become. Even the update from my new "friend" in the permitting office yesterday couldn't lift my spirits because things are coming to a head, and I can't see a way out.

Especially not when the paths forward are so shaded by lies and deception.

With Marcel's contacts going over our photos of Damon and sending them through facial rec to try to get him identified, all we can do is wait, but in the meantime, I have to play nice and do anything else I can to attempt to force him to show his hand.

Which means meeting with him tonight despite the horrible dread settling over me. I park my car outside my office and pull out my phone to dial Marcel.

He answers on the first ring. "Yep."

"I'm going into the meeting now. I'll leave the phone on and mute you, and I'll do my best to get it somewhere that will allow you to create a good recording. Maybe he'll say something that will give us a lead on who he is, and you can help me listen back to it and find it."

"Got it."

I slide my phone into my suit coat pocket, climb from the car, and make my way inside my building as a dark SUV pulls up in front and parks next to me.

Damon steps out, looking casual in dark linen pants and a button-down shirt. He spreads his hands wide as I hold open the door for him. "Mr. Whitaker, so nice of you to find the time to meet with me."

I force a tight smile at him and usher him into my office as two of his goons take up residence just inside the door by the waiting area.

Interesting.

They've never joined him for meetings before, instead waiting in the car while he did his business with me. If they had, I would have had Marcel photograph *them* to see if he could locate info on Damon through his men.

I close my office door and take off my suit coat, hanging it immediately next to the chair Damon takes a seat in. "Sorry, I wasn't able to meet with you before I left town."

Damon gives me an incredulous look. "Must have been pretty important?"

He leaves it as an open-ended question more than a statement, and I'm not about to fill him in on it. His earlier comments from Friday suggested he was watching me, which means he likely knows far more than he lets on.

As the silence lingers between us, he grins. "So, the update I've been expecting? It's been three days, so I assume a lot has happened in your absence."

I lower myself into my chair, ignoring his jab. "Things are moving along even while I've been out of town. The new contact who can help us with permitting and inspections is completely on board. He'll do what he can within the confines of his job and without raising suspicion, the same way my previous source did, and he was already starting on it today. It's really all we can ask for at this point."

He raises a brow at me. "It's all we can ask for? With the amount of money I'm giving Falco Enterprises, I would think we could have this hotel up tomorrow."

I flash him a grin. "That would be nice. But we also can't draw attention to what anyone's doing for us, or we'll lose them."

He nods and spreads his hands. "Duly noted, and I agree. If this is somebody who can be a long-term asset, we don't want to burn them early."

Don't want to burn them early.

Which suggests he does want to burn them...eventually.

When their usefulness is gone, he will make sure they are, too.

Likely permanently.

Damon doesn't strike me as the type to leave loose ends or

anything that might be tied to him. He's too careful. He's gone through far too much not to cover his tracks.

I lean back in my chair and watch the man, trying to get a better read on him. The idea that he might be behind the fire at the Daily Grind and the shooting hovers in the back of my head, mingling with the other possibilities.

Maybe the fire was just an accident.

Maybe the two events really were unrelated, and the shooting was someone after Roselli, not the Hawkes, making Kennedy, Isaac, and Stone mere bystanders to the violence.

I'd love to believe that was true, that the man I've tied myself to isn't responsible for hurting Kennedy, but his mysterious nature and the lengths he's gone to in order to protect his identity make that highly unlikely.

He's hiding something.

Something that will affect me and the future of Falco Enterprises.

Damon finally cracks a cold smile. "You left town so quickly...are we going to discuss what happened with Kennedy?"

Shit.

I knew it was coming. There was no way he was going to let me go without explaining what happened on my front lawn the other day.

They always say the best lie has a kernel of the truth. It's always worked for me when representing Falco's interests—thinking of Falco as its own entity allows me to try to remain detached. It keeps me from letting my personal feelings—like those for the feisty blond Hawke—from interfering with what is best for the company.

And the company is Charlotte's future.

The *only* thing that matters.

"Ms. Hawke and I had a mutually beneficial sexual relationship. It ended. That's all there is to it."

Damon smirks. "Is it? You were consorting with the enemy."

"I was using her to get information on our competition. I never said the Hawkes were an *enemy*, and I'm surprised you would describe them as such. It's a strong word."

He sits up slightly. "Anyone who gets in my way is an enemy in my eyes, Cass. And I am wildly curious as to what information you were able to get out of her that's beneficial to us?"

Here we go.

I steeple my hands in front of my mouth, assessing him while he waits eagerly for me to reveal something I don't have. "Before we discuss the Hawkes' plans, I have a few questions for you."

He chuckles. "Do you, now?"

"I do." I lower my hands to the armrests. "Falco has gone into business with you because they think that your influx of cash will be beneficial to them. But I have my reservations, especially with your unwillingness to provide any sort of personal information about yourself or why you care what happens to the Hawkes. It makes your motives questionable."

Damon shifts, keeping his gaze locked on me. "I hope you haven't developed a soft spot for them. What would your father think?"

I stiffen in my chair. "I'm not sure what you mean."

He leans forward and rests his elbows on his knees, giving me a sinister grin. "Now, now, Mr. Whitaker, or should I call you Mr. Cortesi?"

Fucking hell.

He knows.

How the FUCK does he know?

Every conversation I've ever had with Damon races through my head, seen in the new context of the man knowing my lineage, and it's abundantly clear that he's had that little tidbit of information the whole time.

Damon raises a brow, his lips twisting into a knowing smile.

"You think I didn't know precisely who you were before I walked in this door the first time? You think I didn't know that you're the one behind Falco Enterprises, that you simply pretend to be their lawyer when you are really the entire company? You think I didn't know *why* you've been targeting the Hawkes?"

How the hell does he know all of this?

He smirks. "I can see it in your eyes. You're wondering how I know. Well, let me tell you, Counselor"—he shifts back casually in his chair, crossing his ankle over his knee—"you did a very good job of hiding things. But I have a lot more power than you do. I have friends in much higher places." He sweeps out his hands. "The Hawkes may have a lot of power in New Orleans. They may have important people in their pockets. They may think they're the ones in control here. But the world is a lot bigger than this one city, and I have friends who are far more powerful than one family on the Gulf Coast. People who can tell me that Cassius Whitaker is Matteo Cortesi's son and that he has a daughter named Charlotte who goes to New Orleans Day School and will turn five next month."

It's as close to an actual threat against me as he's ever made, and my throat goes dry at the mention of Charlotte.

I tighten my grip on the armrests, shifting forward slightly so I'll be ready for my next move if need be. "Who the hell are you?"

"I told you." Another grin. "My name is Damon."

My fingers inch forward, toward the center drawer of my desk where I always keep a gun. "That might be the name you use now, but what's your real one?"

A slow grin curls his lips. "There we are. I haven't used my birth name in quite some time. Even if I gave it, I doubt it would mean anything to you, but it did to your father and Dom Abello."

Shit.

It's just like I thought the first time I met him—he's connected somehow, somewhere, and he's been around long enough that he knew the players in town decades ago.

All I ever knew about Dad's business I learned from Grandmother complaining about him, and then when I was eighteen, the surprise envelope from a lawyer gave me all the information on Dad's accounts and businesses and told me they were mine.

This man could be any one of dozens of friends—or enemies—he and Dom made over the years, and I might be able to help Marcel's contacts narrow down their search if I can get him to let anything important slip.

"I detected a hint of an accent in your voice." I raise a brow at him. "Italian?"

He grins again. "And here I thought I'd done such a good job of losing it over the years. It makes it easier to blend in."

My hand stills next to the drawer pull. I could take out the gun and point it at him, but he isn't likely to respond to that type of threat. It's better to be direct and show him I won't back down. "I don't like playing these games, Damon. I think it's time we lay all our cards on the table, like you suggested. Tell me who you are and what your end game is with the Hawkes. Tell me what all of this is about. I'm now tied to you in business, but I don't like people spying on me...or surprises."

Like falling for Kennedy Hawke.

That woman has complicated my life more than I ever knew possible. She's torn through my resolve, twisted my plans, and made me rethink everything.

All of that in only a few weeks.

"I don't like surprises, either, Cass, yet my life has been full of them. Some that have left irreparable scars, and others that have brought me tremendous wealth—that I've now shared with *you*." His eyes go almost black. "Did I misplace that trust, Cassius? You hid your relationship with Kennedy Hawke from me when I thought you wanted the Hawkes gone as much as I do."

Gone.

"Is that your goal? To kill off all the Hawkes?"

He issues a low, deep, sinister chuckle. "What joy would that bring? Far too easy and far too quick. I have a much longer game and one that's much, much more fun."

23

TWO WEEKS LATER

KENNEDY

The sun finally breaks through the heavy layer of clouds that has hung over the city all morning, dropping a drizzle here and there and sometimes downpours that send water rushing through the streets.

I should see it as a good sign.

It's finally shining down on us on such a big day, a literal ray of light beaming on The Hawke Hotel lot like God's bestowing his blessing on everything about to happen today.

But staring out the limo window at the people gathering on the damp ground, waiting for the festivities to start, it's hard not to think of all the things that could go wrong.

Despite two weeks of meticulous planning, bringing in added security forces, and triple-checking everything, it's impossible not to feel that same unease that crept up right before all hell broke loose at the Daily Grind.

Isaac drums his fingers on the leather seat beside me in the back of the limo. "We'll have to go out there at some point."

I turn my head away from the heavily tinted window toward him and give a tight smile. "I know." I glance at my watch. "We'll start in a few minutes."

He leans across me to take a peek out my window, something he probably couldn't have done a week ago, but just like me, his injuries are healing. He's moving a lot better with a lot less pain. Well enough that he felt like he could be here today, even though I'm quite confident that Jack tried to talk him out of coming.

After assessing the people mingling on the site, he releases a little sigh and leans back into his seat. "Much smaller crowd than I imagined."

I offer a little sardonic laugh. "Can you blame people for not wanting to come? The last event we had ended with gunfire and me, you, and Uncle Stone on the goddamn sidewalk, bleeding, with Roselli dead right next to us. I wouldn't want to be here, either, if I were them. Frankly, I'm surprised *anyone* but family came."

Instead of the almost thousand people we originally anticipated for the groundbreaking, only two or three hundred mingle around under the large white tents set up as shelter from the rain. They wait for the ceremony, when Dad and Uncle Gabe, who are already out there schmoozing, will pick up their shovels and break ground on the project that's been such a long time coming, but I can't miss the way people look around nervously.

At the dozens of armed guards around the perimeter.

Up on the rooftops of various buildings surrounding the lot where snipers wait at the ready.

Even at each other, as if they might be looking at someone who could be a threat.

All the things designed to keep us safe during this ceremony are only putting everyone on edge.

My knee starts bouncing, and Isaac leans forward slightly to catch my eyeline.

"Ken? Are you sure you're okay?"

It's the same question everyone's been asking me for weeks —the one I've answered with "I'm fine" so many times that it's become a reflex. But looking at Isaac, knowing what he's gone through since the shooting, all the pain and anger and uncertainty, I can't lie to him.

I scrunch my skirt in my hand tightly and force a smile at him. "I'm as all right as I'm going to be."

His dark brows draw low over Caribbean-blue eyes. "You haven't left your parents' house in two weeks, other than to go to the office and Nana's for dinner."

I raise a brow at him. "Where else would I go?"

He shrugs. "I don't know. Out to live your life?"

What life?

This whole fiasco has only served to prove what I already knew years ago—I have none.

I work. I sleep. I box. I fuck. I do it all over again.

There has never been room in my days for anything else, and I never wanted it. It seems even more important now to double down and recommit myself to ensuring Hawke Enterprises has the future Dad, Gabe, and everyone else have fought so hard for and lost so much to secure.

Besides, with the way bullets seem to fly around us, just waltzing around as if there isn't somebody out there trying to put holes into a Hawke would be absurd. Especially when we still don't know who the fuck it is.

Of course, it could be Cass.

He's proven himself over and over again to be an excellent liar—in the courtroom and bedroom. A master manipulator like him could convince anyone of anything.

But deep down in my gut, every time I remember the look

on his face when he asked if I really believed he could ever hurt me, I know he couldn't have.

Which leaves only one other option...

The continued frustration we all share over our inability to identify Damon has only grown over the last few weeks. Even with the bits and pieces of information we cobbled together from what Cass said to me and what Allie and Angie could remember from speaking with Damon at the café during the months preceding the fire, all we've managed to determine is that he's likely Italian.

Real big fucking help.

Even Cutter and Valentina Marconi's contacts over there haven't been able to shed any light on who he might be, and Cutter's hacker friend, Preacher, has scoured endlessly, coming up empty. Whoever Damon is, he's a ghost, and he went to a lot of trouble to stay that way.

It makes the groundbreaking and what we plan to do today even more essential. We're putting ourselves directly in the public eye, with the press broadcasting everything live.

We haven't all been out in the open like this together since the shooting, and if anything is going to draw out the mysterious Damon, it will be an opportunity like this.

We're sitting ducks...

"We have everything ready, Ken." Isaac pats my hand. "It's safe."

I shake my head. "Nothing's ever going to be safe again."

"You really believe that?"

Shrugging, I continue to watch the people milling about, getting more anxious by the minute. "How can I not? When I let that man into my life..."

Of everyone, Isaac has the most reason to hate me for what I did. He ended up with three holes in him, and his father is still in a coma because of it. But, despite his initial anger, Isaac has never once blamed me, and even now, he grabs my hand and squeezes it.

"We all make decisions that have unintended consequences, Kennedy. Do you think, when I hooked up with Jack back in Chicago after I graduated, that I could have thought in a million years that she was Valentina and Cutter's daughter or that we would have a daughter ourselves and that they would end up here in New Orleans and bring the mob after them?" He laughs and then releases my hand to rub at his stubbled jaw. "Life just throws twists and turns, and we have to roll with them."

"You call what happened a twisty turn?" I glance over at him. "I call it an assassination attempt."

His eyes darken. "It definitely was, but we're ready to act. We're ready to take a stand against Cass, Falco, and Damon." He glances at his watch. "And it's time to go."

I inhale a deep breath, readying myself, then push open the door so we can step out. Immediately, two members of the new security personnel are at my side, with two more at Isaac's as he climbs out of the car.

The door slamming closed behind me makes me flinch, and I squeeze my eyes closed and take a deep breath.

We're prepared for anything.

No one's getting hurt today.

All we're doing is taking a stand.

I keep telling myself that as I walk through the crowd toward where the rest of the family has already gathered, Isaac at my side.

He leans in. "You're okay. You can do this."

I can.

I *should* be able to, but I can't help my eyes from darting over every single face in the crowd, searching for one in particular—the one I never want to see again, yet that has haunted my dreams and every waking moment since we parted.

Cass hasn't tried to contact me, not even once.

It's what I asked for, what I wanted, but this hollow sense of dread still occupies my chest for what might be coming for him...and for me.

Falco is going down, and that means taking him down with it. I hate that for Charlotte, for what all of this could eventually do to her, but at least I know I did what I could to keep him from ending up in the bayou in pieces. And that's all he'll ever get from me besides hatred.

Speaking up on his behalf, arguing for his life when the people I love most would have so easily ended it, tore me apart in ways I didn't even know were possible.

The pain from getting hit with that bullet is nothing compared to the agony I've felt since I fled from his house that day. That kind of betrayal creates a wound that never heals.

Each step I take through the crowd toward the front where the rest of the family waits tenses my shoulders even more. Only a dull ache remains in my injured arm, no longer confined to the sling, but it seems to throb heavier now—a thump, thump, thump strumming through my body as I force my feet to advance.

We make it to the front of the crowd, and Mom and Dad offer me smiles that don't quite reach their eyes.

Dad motions me over to him. "You ready for this, sweetheart?"

I force a smile and nod. "Yep."

That's why I've been hiding out in the limo with Isaac for forty-five minutes while everyone else was out here.

Being exposed, out in public like this, for the first time since the shooting, ratchets up my anxiety, and my hands tremble.

Bishop shifts over next to me and loops her arm through mine. Whether she sees how freaked out I am or just senses it, she's right here to support me, like she always is. And knowing she's strapped with at least two weapons and could also kill anyone with her bare hands helps tamp down some of the rising panic.

I mouth "Thank you" to her, and she grins as Dad moves toward where Uncle Gabe waits with the microphone in hand.

Gabe taps it, the noise making a few people cringe. "If I can have everyone's attention."

The chatter fades away as Gabe waits for everyone to move closer and prepare for the ceremony.

"First of all, the rest of the Hawkes and I want to thank all of you for coming today to what is a monumental event that's been a long time coming." He motions back toward the lot, where four massive excavators wait to start the actual work once the ceremony is done. "The Hawke Hotel will be here in less than a year, the most luxurious and custom boutique hotel not only in New Orleans but along the entire Gulf Coast. And it took a lot for us to get to where we are today." His eyes dart over to Isaac and me. "Not all of us could be here…"

He doesn't say the reason why, but everyone—including the guests in attendance—knows he's referring to Stone and Nora. The press coverage of the shooting and Stone's condition continues despite there being little change. So many people in this city love and respect him, and his absence today is felt by all.

Gabe looks at Isaac and Coen and nods. "They're here with us in spirit, and I'd like to pass the microphone over to Savage Hawke, my best friend and business partner for almost forty years."

Dad accepts the mic, scanning the crowd with a tight smile. "We've been waiting for this day for a long time, but it doesn't come without complications."

Our guests grow a little restless with his words, and he glances over at me and Isaac.

"As many of you know, the Hawkes were attacked less than a month ago, and we've been facing attacks from another enemy for a lot longer than that."

He uses his free hand to point down the street, and all eyes dart that way quickly before returning to him.

"Falco Enterprises has tried to compete with us in every business we own in this city, and they have failed. Failed to crush us. Failed to shake us. Failed in every endeavor. And the fact that they want to put up a hotel just down the street from us only means that they'll fail at that as well." Dad releases a humorless laugh. "They say imitation is the sincerest form of flattery. Well, I have news for Falco. They will not be able to imitate this. The Hawke Hotel will be beyond anyone's wildest dreams. It's one I've had for a long time, one my family shares, and we're committed to ensuring everything goes smoothly." He looks directly into the cameras from the local media outlets pointed right at him. "And that means, anyone who gets in our way won't be around to do it again."

The threat hangs in the air.

A few people shift uncomfortably, but it's as direct a statement as he can make to Cass and Damon.

We've already set things in motion, with Isaac filing fifty-two different lawsuits, injunctions, and complaints over the last two weeks against Falco Enterprises with every court, permitting agency, or law enforcement he can to try to get them shut down.

Now that we know it's Cass and we aren't fighting blindly anymore, the strategy to take out Falco has changed to full-on shock and awe. And when it comes to the shooting, if we find out he *was* behind it or even knew it was a possibility, even I won't be able to protect him from what's coming.

～

CASS

I SHOULD HAVE ANTICIPATED the threat Savage just made; I've been waiting for it for weeks. Then, the tsunami of legal filings started appearing.

Isaac is coming after Falco at one hundred and ten percent, and it won't just be in the courtroom. They're going to do everything they can to end this, to end *me*, unless I can convince them that Damon is the real threat here.

And he is.

Any paltry, lingering doubts disappeared the moment I saw what the paper tucked inside my suit coat pocket holds—the information we've all been looking for.

Who he is.

Which explains why he's here.

Why every single thing that's occurred in the last several months has happened.

And why it's been so damn hard and took weeks for Marcel's contacts to finally come back with anything on the photos.

Everything makes sense now, seen through the lens of knowing the enemy.

It's clear now who the *real* enemy is.

At first, I spent the last few weeks looking over my shoulder, wondering if the Hawkes were going to do what Kennedy kept threatening, have me killed and dumped in the bayou, and worrying what would happen to Charlotte.

But then it hit me; it was undeniable.

Kennedy would never do that to Charlotte. No matter what she said in anger on her way out of my life, she could never take mine and leave my little girl without me.

She isn't the enemy. She never was.

It's Damon—the man who said Charlotte's name as a threat.

It isn't the Hawkes.

They may have killed Dad. Gabe might have been the one who pulled that final trigger, but Dad put himself in the line of fire just like I did with Charlotte.

If I end up at the bottom of the bayou, my head in an alligator's mouth, it will be as much my fault as it was my father's that he found himself in the sights of Gabe Anderson's sniper rifle all those years ago.

Gabe was protecting Kennedy's mom, and if he hadn't, she wouldn't even be here. That thought has rattled around my brain and hammered against my skull so many times over the last two weeks that I've barely been able to think of anything else.

How *wrong* I've been about everything.

The Hawkes have to know the truth, and there wasn't any way I was getting within a hundred feet of them with all the security they've had around them. Plus, with Marcel watching Kennedy, it became clear she wasn't going anywhere besides her parents' house, work, and her grandmother's for Sunday dinner, and I certainly wasn't going to be able to get to her at any of those places.

But waiting here at the back of the crowd, hidden by the umbrella I brought to shield me from the drizzle, it's the closest I've been to her in weeks, yet it feels like we're thousands of miles apart.

She stands next to her dad in a pinstripe pencil skirt and fitted white blouse that shows off all her curves. My hands itch to run over them, to touch every inch of her. To feel her undulate under me and writhe from the pleasure I can give her. But it's impossible not to notice the way her body trembles.

Kennedy's fucking terrified, and it's all my fault.

I brought this on them, on *her*, by agreeing to partner with Damon. If I hadn't, none of this would've ever happened.

Actually, it probably *would* have, but it never would have

looked like I intentionally partnered with the devil himself to physically harm them. What she once accused me of has become true without me even knowing it. I sold my soul to beat the Hawkes, and now, I'm paying the price.

Not only have I lost any chance at Kennedy ever trusting me again, but I've placed myself in a position I never wanted to be —where I might leave Charlotte in the same place I was at her age.

Alone.

Terrified.

I refuse to allow that to happen, even if it means coming here today and risking the Hawkes' wrath to try to tell them the dark truth.

Savage leans over and whispers something to Kennedy, who jerks back slightly like she doesn't understand what's happening. Gabe approaches and holds out a shovel. Her eyes widen as she looks between her dad and her uncle and shakes her head.

What are they doing?

Gabe says something to her, and she finally accepts the shovel from him and turns to look at the rest of her family, who all nod. Isaac accepts a shovel from Gabe as well, and the two of them approach the designated spot for the groundbreaking.

Holy shit, they're passing the torch.

Savage takes up the mic again. "Gabe and I thought it was fitting that my daughter, Kennedy, and our nephew, Isaac, be the ones to physically break this ground. The Hawke Hotel is our future, and so are they." He issues a little chuckle. "Gabe and I aren't going anywhere anytime soon, but more and more, we're relying on them to take us forward into the unknown ahead, to guide the business and the family into another generation of success."

Even from here, I can see how her father's words affect Kennedy. She tries to wipe away tears quickly and forces a smile, but the hand holding the shovel begins to tremble.

All that weight still sits on her shoulders.

And she no longer thinks she can bear it.

My heart aches for the woman who was never supposed to get anywhere near it. She fought me every step of the way, insisted she hated me, but I never truly *felt* that until that last look she gave me before she climbed into the SUV outside the house.

In those two seconds, I knew it was all over.

I was a goner for Kennedy Hawke.

Now I watch her and Isaac dig their shovels into the ground and flip over the first soil for the start of the foundation of The Hawke Hotel, the thing I've been fighting so hard against for so long. And I'm actually *happy* for her. That she didn't let what she undoubtedly saw as my betrayal prevent this from happening. I just wish I could believe this is really what she wants, all this responsibility, the job being her whole life.

The crowd erupts and cheers and claps, and Savage returns to the mic. "Thank you everyone. It's about to get very loud here with all the machinery getting to work, but we have an afterparty with cocktails and tremendous food prepared by one of our best chefs over at The Hawke Nest. Please feel free to join us there immediately to celebrate."

The people around me begin to disperse, but I stand my ground, not daring to approach the Hawkes with the number of armed personnel surrounding them and the property.

I'm only going to have *one* chance at this, and even then, I may not make it far enough to say what I need to without receiving a bullet between my eyes.

But I have no choice.

I have to try.

A path opens leading toward the front, like the sea parting and showing me the way to salvation. At this point, that means throwing myself on the Hawkes' mercy.

As more people move out of the way, Kennedy becomes

visible again, and my eyes lock with hers. Even from here, I can see her breath catch, and I slowly make my way toward her, both hands wrapped around the umbrella so anyone can see I'm unarmed.

It doesn't take more than two seconds for one of the security guards to see me.

The burly man with the stern scowl approaches immediately, hand on his weapon. "I'm going to have to ask you to stop, sir." He examines me closely. "I suggest you leave the property at once."

He either knows who I am or at least suspects it. Undoubtedly, the Hawkes have provided my photograph and told everyone to watch for me.

Kennedy had to know I would come.

She had to know I would try to see her, try to talk to her.

That I couldn't just let her walk away.

But she has no idea how important it is that she listens to me now.

I slowly lower the umbrella and rest the end in the dirt, then hold up my hands. "I'm going to reach into my inner coat pocket."

The guard narrows his eyes. "Don't do that, sir."

He pulls his weapon but keeps it in front of him, not pointing it at me yet.

I grab the front panel of my coat and open it so he can see the papers sticking out, then grab them with two fingers and hold them up. "It's important the Hawkes see this information immediately."

That's especially true because Damon has remained aloof and suspiciously absent the last several weeks since our last in-person meeting. Aside from checking in via phone to get updates on the permits and advanced timeline, he hasn't shown his face again.

Given his threat to me and parting words about his plans

for the Hawkes, his disappearance can't mean anything good is coming—for any of us.

As one of the Hawkes' security men stares me down, blocking my way to them, apparently unmoved by my production of a random piece of paper, the air around us seems to still.

I sense rather than hear someone approaching me from behind. A man steps around me and motions for the security guard to step out of the path, sliding in front of me to block my advance toward the Hawkes.

Cutter Jackson...

Gnarly scars climbing up his neck and over his face, partially hidden by the aviator sunglasses over his eyes, make it impossible for this to be anyone else. This is a man who likes to kill and is very good at it, and right now, he has his sights set on me.

"You have a lot of fucking balls showing up here, Whitaker."

"Mr. Jackson"—I incline my head toward him and hold up the piece of paper—"I assure you, I have good reason."

One of his blondish brows rises over his glasses. "Because you have a death wish?"

I shake my head and open the paper so he can see it. "No, because I'm trying to prevent any more violence."

Cutter leans in slightly toward the paper, but with his eyes covered, it's impossible to see what he's focusing on. A moment later, his head snaps up, his lips pressing into a firm line and his jaw tightening. "Where the hell did you get this?"

I shake my head. "I won't reveal my sources, but trust me, this is real. And it explains everything."

He glances over his shoulder toward the Hawkes, and I finally see Kennedy frozen in place, her wide blue eyes locked on mine. Unlike during the time we spent together, she's completely unreadable.

Too many things have happened since the last time I

touched her. Too many things said since the last time we spoke. But there's still a longing there, one I share.

"Please let me show her."

Cutter turns back to me and pulls his gun, then raises it and points it straight at my temple. "I'm going with you, and if you try anything, I pull this trigger before you even know it's coming."

24

KENNEDY

The moment his eyes land on me, heat rushes through my entire body, that same warmth I always feel every time he looks at me—from that very first night at the fundraiser from behind that mask until the day I fled from him.

I scan the parting crowd and finally find him. Those beautiful green eyes bore into me, and my heart stops. His slow, torturous approach reminds me of just how dangerous all this is. The man, who only a few weeks ago was caring for me as if he couldn't bear the thought of anything or anyone hurting me, was, at the same time, capable of betraying me so completely.

He could do it again now.

Keep reminding yourself of that.

If I don't, I'll be tempted to run to him and throw myself in his arms just to feel his touch again somewhere besides my dreams. Because they're never enough.

They never could be.

Cass was right when he said no one will ever be able to compare to what he does to me. I'll never *feel* as much as I do

522

with that man. I'll never *crave* as much as I do him, more and more each minute we spend apart. I'll never *regret* as much as I do letting him into my life and my heart.

Everything seems to move in slow motion, like I'm watching a movie unfold in front of me.

I vaguely hear Gabe telling someone to "get them out of here," then his hand curls around my arm. "Come on, Kennedy. You need to leave."

When I don't react, he tightens his grip slightly, and his words finally register, breaking the strange stranglehold Cass' gaze has on me.

"What?" I shake my head and scan around me, only to find everyone except Dad and Isaac being ushered to the cars by Saint, Bishop, and some of the other security personnel. "No, I'm not leaving."

I knew it was coming—the flight of the Hawkes from imminent danger.

It was always the plan—to get everyone *away* and *safe* if there was any sign of Cass or Damon, if our threat worked to draw them out and to us. We were supposed to leave it to Dad, Gabe, Cutter, Saint, Bishop, and the men they paid, but now that I've seen Cass, there's no way I'm letting them drag me away. It seems Isaac feels the same way as he stands his ground, too.

Gabe gets his "don't fuck with me" look. "Don't do this, Kennedy. You shouldn't be here. It isn't safe."

"I'm not going anywhere." I look back at Cass, who still makes his way through the lingering crowd. "He won't hurt me."

Bishop returns from the vehicles to stand beside me, and she pushes Gabe's hand from my arm and wraps hers around my shoulder. "Let her stay. I've got her."

Gabe looks ready to argue, his jaw tensing the closer Cass comes.

Dad moves up next to us, his hard blue eyes locked on the man who destroyed me and brought all this pain to the family. "Let her stay. She knows him better than anyone."

In this family, Savage Hawke always has the final word, and Gabe knows better than to argue with him, especially when it comes to his own daughter. I don't agree with his statement, though.

I *don't* know Cass.

Not really.

All I know is who he wanted me to see.

And now that he's here, that picture of him inextricably mixes with the other—of the man who could spend years plotting his revenge. Who could attack our businesses at every opportunity. Who could try to *ruin* us while he was also ruining my will.

One of the security guards finally spots Cass and moves to block his approach. I can't hear what's being said from this distance, but Cass reaches for something in his coat pocket.

I tense. My mind flashes back to that day when the only warning I had was the squeal of tires before pain and the sharp crack of gunfire became my entire world. If Cass pulls a weapon, he'll be dead in two seconds.

All the breath rushes from my lungs before I can scream for him to stop, but he removes a single sheet of paper and holds it out for the guard to see and says something that makes the other man stiffen slightly.

Cutter approaches them from his concealed spot to the side of the main gathering area, where he's been watching everything unfold and trying to spot the mysterious Damon if he dares to show his face.

Jack's father places himself between Cass and us, and Cass opens the paper and shows it to Cutter. Almost immediately, Cutter tenses, then glances toward us, but those damn shades he hides behind make it impossible to read the man.

What the fuck is going on?

This wasn't part of the plan.

We anticipated something else completely.

A threat.

An attack.

But this is Cass, alone, with a single sheet of fucking paper that seems to have rattled the unrattlable Cutter Jackson.

He turns back and says something to Cass, pulling his gun and pointing it directly at Cass's head.

"No!" I jerk out of Bishop's hold, lunging forward to try to prevent the unthinkable without even considering the consequences.

My heel catches in the dirt, and Gabe lashes an arm out and wraps it around my waist, pulling me back before I can go any farther.

Goddamn these fucking heels!

And to think I once bragged about what I'm capable of in them when every time I'm around Cassius Whitaker, things just go wrong. This stumble allowed Gabe to catch me, might prevent me from getting to Cass and stopping Cutter's hand.

Gabe whispers in my ear, "What the hell are you doing, trying to get yourself killed?"

I wish I had a fucking answer for that, but as soon as I saw Cutter point the gun at him, I saw my entire world falling apart again.

In one quick twitch of Cutter's finger, I saw Charlotte alone in that big house. I saw her growing up without her loving, protective father. I saw me going every day of my life without ever experiencing being in his arms again. I saw myself losing everything, and all of it steals my breath.

Cutter glances in our direction, keeping the gun trained on Cass. He seems to consider the situation for a moment, then motions for Cass to approach us.

Each tentative step brings Cass closer to me, but it doesn't move him any farther away from the barrel of Cutter's gun.

The man who organized all the security for the event quickly scans the various snipers surrounding the lot, ensuring they're still in place and ready if need be.

Cass' gaze never leaves mine as he approaches, like he, too, is afraid to look away in case he can never find my eyes with his again. He stops a few feet in front of me, rightfully sensing that no one is going to allow him to move any closer.

Cutter inclines his head toward Cass. "He has something we all need to see."

I can't see anything right now but the pain and apology darkening Cass' green eyes. When I left him, it felt so fake, like he was saying it to placate me and to try to apologize-away all that he had done when he really wasn't sorry about any of it. But he looks different now. Almost defeated.

Whatever has happened to him in the last few weeks has broken him.

Dad raises a brow, his skepticism written all over his scowl and the hard set of his broad shoulders. "Well?"

Cass steps forward and extends his trembling hand. The paper in it shakes as he holds it out to Dad without ever taking his eyes off me. "I told Kennedy I had a private investigator trying to hunt down what we could on Damon, and we finally got him."

I glance over at Dad as he stares down at the paper. His jaw hardens, and his gaze darts to Isaac, then back to me.

"What is it?"

Isaac comes to stand beside him and rips the paper from his hands. The color that had just started to return to his face after the trauma his body endured drains away again as he stares at whatever is written on that page. He shakes his head. "No, it's impossible."

Gabe releases me to go over and snatch the paper. He examines it carefully, his eyes hardening. "It's not possible."

Cutter keeps his gun trained on Cass while glancing toward Gabe. "I would've said the same thing after the time I spent in Calabria. But with some of the resurrecting acts I've seen over the years, it shouldn't surprise me that this one would come back from the dead."

Saint steps forward and grabs the page. "Who?"

My body trembles so badly, I'm afraid my legs will go out from under me, but Bishop wraps her strong arm around me again, when all I really want is the touch of the man who's only a few feet from me but feels light years away. "Will somebody tell me what the fuck is going on?"

Cass swallows thickly, his gaze darting over everyone who's looked at the paper when no one answers. "Damon's real name is Damiano Satriano."

"Satriano?" Of course, the name means something to everyone here. "The asshole who wanted to marry Jack?"

Cutter nods. "Their family has had full control of the Calabria region for fifty years, and before that, they shared it with three other families going back generations. Valentina's father dealt with them before she took over—"

Dad holds up a hand to stop him. "But I thought the Satrianos were gone, that you took out his home and headquarters and decimated his men after they threatened Giacomina and Viviana. You said there wasn't anyone left."

That's what we all believed—that anyone who *might* have somehow survived the slaughter was in the wind, no longer a threat. An attack like the one Cutter arranged sends a pretty clear message—that we're not to be fucked with. And it's been months since Isaac killed Leonardo Satriano without anything obviously connected to the family happening.

Cutter's jaw tics. "I did. This isn't one of his men who took his name to try to step up. This is his older brother, the one he supposedly killed to take the position as the head of the family in the first place."

My head spins, all the information making me dizzy. None of this makes any sense, but I can't tell if my brain is just a jumbled mess from seeing Cass again or due to the anxiety that's been crippling me the entire time I've been here.

Cass turns to Cutter, despite the other man having a gun trained on him. "I suspected he was connected and detected the hint of an Italian accent, just like my father. I had my investigator take photos of him, and he sent them to some European contacts. They ran him through facial rec. At first, they didn't find anything...because they weren't going far enough back. Those photos on that page are from almost forty years ago. But it's *him*. And it would explain everything."

It would...

Isaac was the one who pulled the trigger to kill his brother.

Damon started showing up as a customer at Hawke's Daily Grind not even a month later. I never paid close enough attention to the silver-haired man who always sat out on the patio, but it would make sense he was doing reconnaissance on us in a public space where it wouldn't draw any questions.

He made The Grind a target.

That's why it burned.

And the shooting at the reopening was likely targeting Roselli *and* us.

All these puzzle pieces we've been trying—and failing—to get to click together now finally do.

Saint passes the page to Bishop, and I snatch it from her hand and stare down at old, grainy photos of a handsome, young, dark-haired man. I couldn't possibly have made the connection, couldn't have looked at these and known they were the man I walked past at least a dozen times on my way to grab coffee and say hi.

I look away from the pictures to Gabe, Isaac, Dad, Cutter,

and finally Cass. "So what? He's here to kill all of us to get revenge?"

Cass shakes his head, his entire demeanor darkening to match the sky above us. "No. It's so much worse than that."

~

CASS

KNOWING how shaken Kennedy already is, having to say these words to her feels like someone stomping on the already-shattered pieces of my heart and grinding them into dust. "He said killing you all would be too easy, that there wouldn't be any fun in it. He said it's a game. He made it sound like a chess match, that he had pieces he was moving around."

All the Hawkes watch me intently, their faces alternating between anger and the same terror I felt that day I walked into my office and found Kennedy holding the photo.

At that moment, I knew I had lost her, that there was no coming back from it. And now, the Hawkes truly know what they're up against, and it means things are only going to get more dangerous for the family that has already suffered so much.

Gabe crumples up the paper with Damon's picture on it. "What kind of game?"

I shake my head. "That's just it. I don't know. He wouldn't tell me. The last time we met was two weeks ago." I dart my gaze to Kennedy. "He said he knew about Kennedy and me, and he knows about Charlotte."

Savage nods slowly. "Your daughter."

Even saying her name in front of these people that I've gone to such lengths to protect her from for so many years makes acid crawl up the back of my throat. "Yes, my daughter. I've had her with a private nanny and in private schools under a different name. I've done everything I can since she was born to keep anyone from finding her, to keep all of *you* from finding her. I've had security on her and my house twenty-four-seven since you all showed up and pointed your guns at me."

The glare Savage gives me could burn through solid concrete, and his hands curl into fists. "As if we'd ever hurt a child..."

I want to call out the audacity of his anger and say he *did* hurt me by taking my father, by sending my mother into such a wild spiral that she OD'd after Dad's death. That he hurt *me* by forcing me to be with that wretched woman who called herself my grandmother. That he hurt me more than he could ever know.

But the Hawkes aren't the enemies anymore.

I have to keep reminding myself of that. After so many years of diligent work and a sole focus, forcing my brain to flip that switch off isn't as easy as I had imagined it to be.

When I was with Kennedy, when we were in our heated moments, I didn't see her as a Hawke. If I had, nothing ever would have happened. I compartmentalized the parts of my life, tried to justify what I was doing for Falco in the same breath I was kissing her.

It was *always* going to be a losing proposition.

And while I may still harbor hatred for the Hawkes for what they did, for what it did to my life, if I hang on to it any longer, it's going to destroy Charlotte's.

I swallow through the lump in my throat, staring at Kennedy's father when he knows what I've done to his daughter. "She's my entire life and I'm hers. I have to protect her. That's why I'm here, why I brought this to you—"

Gabe, Saint, and Cutter, who have been consistently scanning the area, suddenly stiffen, something in the air shifting in a way that makes goosebumps break out over my entire body.

A dark SUV approaches from down the road—one I'm all-too familiar with.

Damon.

There isn't any time for anyone to act, for anyone to try to flee. The SUV pulls to a stop at the curb, and the back door opens. Immediately, a dozen weapons point toward the silver-haired man stepping from the back, but rather than seeming concerned, he advances toward us slowly with a grin on his lips, his security standing back by the SUV, as if he's unconcerned that we'll light him up the way the Hawkes should.

"Well, well, well, it looks like I missed the party." His eyes meet mine. "Cass, surprised to see you here. Was I right about your weakness for Ms. Hawke?"

I clench my jaw and my fists at my sides, ready to lunge at the man who threatened not only Kennedy but Charlotte.

His disappearance and reappearance now aren't by chance. Nothing this man does is unplanned. This was designed to create the biggest impact—and doing it on the biggest day in Hawke Enterprises' history, in this place, certainly does that.

Cutter steps toward him, gun aimed directly at his chest. "We know who you are, Damiano."

Damon's smile only grows, and he looks over at me, raising a brow. "You finally figured it out. Did you?"

I nod slowly. "I did."

He raises his hands and offers a slight shrug. "It was only a matter of time before someone did."

Cutter growls. "And now that we have, it's time to take out the garbage."

Damiano shakes his head. "Uh-uh-uh, let's not act too hastily here. Any one of you pulls the trigger and I'm gone, but what about the rest of my organization?"

Everyone freezes, and his grin grows.

"Did you think I've been sitting around, twiddling my thumbs for the last forty years since my brother tried to kill me?" He issues a low, dark chuckle that matches the feeling settling over the group. "No, *amici miei.* As I once explained to Cass, I have a lot of friends, friends in very high places, places that make New Orleans, Louisiana, look like a teeny, tiny dot on the map in comparison."

To prove his point, he motions up to one of the snipers perched on a rooftop, and the barrel of his rifle shifts from Damon's direction right toward Savage.

"If anything happens to me, if I so much as get a fucking papercut, it will unleash a wrath upon you that you could never have contemplated."

There it is.

The real Damiano.

No more dancing around with pretty words and vague threats. He's made his stand, and he's shown his power.

I immediately cut my gaze to Kennedy, who has watched all this unfold with Bishop's arm around her, shaking like a leaf. In a split second, she brushes off her cousin's hold, squares her shoulders, and stalks forward across the uneven ground in her fuck-me heels. Pure rage overtakes her features that were so full of fear only moments ago as she moves to stand in front of her father—square in the path of that sniper's bullet if he pulls the trigger. "Fuck you, Damiano!"

"Kennedy!" My heart stops, and I lurch forward, wrapping my arms around her to try to move her out of the line of fire. "What the hell are you doing?"

She shoves at my chest, trying to break free of my hold. "Protecting my dad! Let me go!"

Never!

As incredible as it is to see her relentless fire return, this isn't the time or place I want to see it, and Damiano is the not the man to focus it on.

Damiano's sinister chuckle floats through the air, and I glance over my shoulder at him. "The pussy is always what does us in, isn't it? Here, I thought we would make excellent partners, Cassius. It's the reason I approached you in the first place. If I had known you had such a penchant for pretty blondes, I might've had a rethink on that plan."

Kennedy stills in my arms, the inherent danger of fighting me and him finally getting through to her. She stares at me with so many emotions swimming in her blue eyes that I could spend a lifetime trying to unravel them.

Gabe issues a low growl, his hand flexing next to his weapon, though he doesn't dare draw it with the sniper's rifle aimed at us. "What do you *want*?"

One of Damiano's silver brows rises. "Everything. Everything my brother stole from me. Everything he built after. Everything I was born to have. My brother had the right idea, going after Cutter and Valentina's beautiful daughter, Giacomina. An alliance between our families would've been magnificent, but since she's no longer available"—he glances to Isaac, who looks ready to beat him to death with his bare hands—"I'm going to have to pursue other avenues to reach my ultimate goals."

Isaac sneers at him. "That's why you took out Roselli... because you want New Orleans."

He grins. "Am I that transparent?" Laughing lightly, he sweeps out his hands. "Who wouldn't want such a beautiful city?" His hard gaze cuts over to Cutter. "Cutter here decimated my brother's remaining businesses in Calabria. It only made sense for me to set up shop elsewhere."

Savage glowers at the man. "Why are you here? Just to issue more threats?"

Damiano shakes his head and smiles. "I don't issue threats. I make promises. My brother may have betrayed me; he may have tried to have me killed, but he failed because my people are always loyal to me. I knew of his treachery well in advance and arranged it so that when they did examine the dental records of the individual killed in the blast, they'd match my own."

He flashes another grin, and only now do I notice how perfect his teeth are. Too perfect. The man pulled out his own teeth to fake his death all those years ago.

What does that say about what else he's capable of?

Kennedy nudges my chest this time, and I shift slightly, still keeping myself between her and a potential bullet but giving her a better view of Damiano.

He scans everyone carefully, from Saint to Gabe, across Savage, Kennedy, and me, to Isaac and Bishop, and finally Cutter. "I came today to issue my congratulations on the groundbreaking"—he slowly begins to back away toward his waiting vehicle—"and to say I'll be seeing you around."

A single shot rings out, breaking the silence, and I throw myself over Kennedy, knocking her down to the ground and covering her the best I can as I scan the area, trying to figure out where it came from.

The man with the rifle trained on us tumbles from his rooftop perch and slams into the ground below, and Cutter motions for me to get up off Kennedy.

"The threat has been neutralized." He looks toward another sniper across the street and nods at him. "My friend, Mouth..."

Kennedy pushes at me slightly, and I shift my weight off her and get to my feet, holding out my hand to help her up. The moment she's standing, I drag her against me, burying my face against her neck.

Instead of pushing me away, she clings to me as hard as I do her. "What the hell does that mean, that he'll see us around?"

"I don't know, *Cherie*, but I don't like it one fucking bit."

No one does.

Any one of them would've emptied their magazine into him if it weren't for his earlier warning and the threat above us.

The ominous words he just spoke hang heavy in the air.

Kennedy grasps the front of my shirt, clinging to me, and she pulls her head back and shakes me, looking up at me and searching my eyes as if I have some sort of knowledge they don't. "You know him better than we do. What does it *mean*?"

Maybe I do know.

Because Damiano was right about one thing—we *would* have made great partners. We shared a similar goal and our hatred for the Hawkes. But there's one difference that he didn't see—I am *not* my father.

I could never pull the trigger. I could never put a bullet in any of these people. I could never take someone's life the way Dad did. But it didn't mean I wasn't going to try to hurt them another way.

Watching his SUV pull away from the curb, I'm confident I know what he's planning. "He's going to torture you."

Everyone's heads snap back toward me.

Savage eyes me suspiciously. "What do you mean?"

I give him a sad smile and rub at the back of my neck. "He's going to do the same thing that I did. He's going to break you down, piece by piece, bit by bit. He wants you to always be watching your back, to never know when it's coming. The arson at the Daily Grind was only the first step. That was moving his pawn. There will be more."

An icy chill settles over the group as we all exchange looks and try to figure out where to go from here. And I can't help but notice the way everyone watches me, like they're waiting for more.

This is why I came today, my chance to try to make things right. This is where I beg for the Hawkes' mercy and pray they aren't as vengeful as the man who just left the lot.

I run my hands over Kennedy's back, needing to feel her, to ensure she's real and still in my arms while I make this ask. "I've spent the last few weeks thinking about this, about what a mistake I made. I can't have this fall back on my daughter."

Kennedy's eyes soften as she looks at me.

"You know what they say. The enemy of my enemy is my friend." I raise a brow, looking to her father, then to Gabe—the heads of the family, the men who facilitated the death of my father all those years ago. "I want this conflict between us to stop."

Savage gives me a hard look. "And we're supposed to all of a sudden trust you?"

"Yes." Kennedy's single word sounds like a cannon going off in my ears. She looks at her father and her uncles, then at Isaac and Bishop before her gaze falls back on me, a tear trickling down her cheek. "I've seen him with Charlotte. He would never knowingly do anything to hurt her or put her in harm's way, and that includes getting involved with someone who so callously walks around threatening and killing people." She glances back at her dad. "He didn't know about Damon. He may have set out to hurt us, but not like this. We can trust him. We need his help. We need everyone on our side." She turns her head to look at me again. "I need him."

Those three simple words send a jolt through me that almost makes me collapse to my knees in front of the woman. "Do you mean it?"

She nods, and I tug her against me tightly, burying my face against her neck and inhaling her scent that I've missed so much, never wanting to let her go again.

I fucked this up in so many ways.

I've done so much to hurt her.

And now, it's time to figure out a way to fix it.

25

CASS

Charlotte climbs into bed, pulling the covers up over her as I kneel beside her. She stares up at me with her big green eyes, filled with so many questions I've been avoiding answering since I came home with Kennedy a few hours ago. "How long is Kennedy staying?"

Thank God.

That one isn't so bad.

I smile at her and brush her hair back off her forehead. "I don't know, *Bebelle*. I hope a really long time."

She grins at me and nods. "Me, too. I'm glad she isn't mad at you anymore."

Laughing, I shake my head. "I think Kennedy is still plenty mad at me, sweetheart."

Her brow furrows. "But she came back."

Over the last two weeks, I've had to field endless questions about why Kennedy never stopped over to say hi after she went home. Eventually, saying I didn't know wasn't good enough, and I had to tell Charlotte that I had fucked up and done something to upset Kennedy. That was something she could under-stand, but she has yet to fully grasp the intricacies of apologies and forgiveness.

I nod slowly as I think about everything that happened today and the anger Kennedy still had for me, even as I approached her across that lot. "Yeah, she did come back, but you can care about someone and still be mad at them for the way they act and things they do. Haven't you been mad at Daddy before for certain things?"

"Yeah, like when you beat me at Monopoly."

"But you still love me, right?"

She nods. "Do you love Kennedy?"

Fuck.

My hand stills on her forehead.

I haven't had the balls to ask myself that question, mostly because I was too afraid of my own answer. But after seeing her jump in front of her father today, the sheer terror that raced through me at the thought that anything could happen to her —again—I know the answer. "I do, *Bebelle*."

"Does she love you, too?"

My chest tightens at her question, and I lean in to kiss her on the forehead and try to end the conversation before it completely goes off the rails.

"She does." Kennedy's voice from the open door makes me stiffen.

I turn slowly to find her leaning against the jamb in one of my T-shirts and a pair of shorts that show off every inch of her long legs.

Holy shit.

How much of that did she hear?

Clearly enough to hear my confession of love to Charlotte, but I definitely never expected her to reciprocate. Not with everything I've done. I thought she would make me suffer, never say the words or wait until I had been saying them to her for so long that her silence became painful.

But maybe there's been enough suffering—for all of us.

Turning back to Charlotte, I flip off her bedside lamp. "Goodnight."

"Goodnight, Daddy." She waves at Kennedy. "Goodnight, Kennedy."

Kennedy smiles at her and waves back. "Goodnight, kiddo."

She pushes off the doorframe as I approach her and gives me a knowing grin. I urge her out into the hallway with a hand at her waist and tug the door closed behind us. As soon as it clicks into place, I immediately pull her into my arms and back her against the wall next to the door.

"Did you mean it?"

Her grin only grows. "Mean what?"

I issue a low growl and pin her tighter, my growing cock caught between us. "Did you mean it when you said you loved me?"

She tries to fight the smile, but the corners of her perfect lips twitch.

This woman who holds my heart in her hands is enjoying toying with it far too much.

I dip my head closer. "What? You're going to say it once and then torture me by withholding the words forever?"

She loops her arms around my neck. "That might not be a bad idea."

"It is a terrible fucking idea." I press my lips to hers, relishing the feel of having her back in my arms again, back in my house, back in my life, where she belongs. Because somehow, over the past month, she's become an integral part of it.

I don't know how or why fate would throw such a twist like this at me, would make me fall in love with the one woman I never should have touched. But now that it's happened, there's no escaping it. There's no denying that I can never walk away from Kennedy Hawke.

Not for all the money or power in the world. Not for revenge. Not for anything, except maybe Charlotte. But Kennedy would never put me in a position to have to make that choice.

It's just one of the many things I love about her.

I tear my mouth away from hers and lift her to wrap her legs around my waist. She grinds her cunt against my cock, the heat searing me through the thin fabric of her shorts and even my pants.

Everything this woman does is pure fire. There's no denying it. I'm a cliché—a moth drawn to her, sucked in by the heat and beauty. But I wouldn't want to be anywhere else.

I walk us back toward my room, devouring her mouth, unable to give or take enough, and she matches my eagerness, her lips moving over mine until we're both breathless.

But when I set her on her feet next to the bed, she presses her hands against my chest, stopping me from moving farther. "What?"

I drag my head back and search her gaze.

She raises a blond brow. "You don't think it's that easy, do you?"

"That what's that easy?"

"That I'm just suddenly back and we can go on like nothing ever happened?"

I flutter my lips over her forehead and press them to her skin. "Of course not, *Cherie*. I know I fucked up. I fucked up worse than anyone has ever fucked up in their entire life, probably."

She chuckles softly, the sound so beautiful coming from her when there's been so much anguish lately. "I can agree with that assessment, Counselor."

It's probably an understatement.

I take her face between my palms and tilt it up to me, forcing her to look into my eyes and hear me when I say this. "I've known since the first time I saw you that I wanted you, Kennedy. That I wanted this, and I never thought I could have it. Not in the long term. I couldn't have *this* and my revenge. But now...I don't have to choose."

Kennedy shakes her head. "No, you don't."

"We're a united front, right?"

She presses her forehead to my chest and releases a heavy sigh. "We are."

"Do you think your family feels the same way?"

They did let me walk away from the confrontation today with my life and with her, though I think that was more because they knew fighting her wouldn't get them anywhere, anyway. But it's a far cry from accepting me into the family, accepting that I'm a part of Kennedy's life in the long term.

"I'll talk to them."

"You really think talking is going to solve anything?"

She shakes her head and lifts it from my chest. "I don't know because I don't know what's coming for us."

The suddenly somber mood settles over us, but I refuse to let this night go to shit with fears of tomorrow. "Whatever happens, whatever that fucker Damiano is planning, we're going to face it together, and I'll protect you always, the same way I do Charlotte. I'll never promise you anything I can't deliver and will never lie to you."

"I believe you."

"Do you believe me when I say I love you?"

She stares up at me through her thick lashes and nods. "I do because I love you, too."

They're the most beautiful words I've ever heard, and I crash my mouth to hers again. She tightens her hold on my neck and groans against my lips, shifting her hips to press against my cock.

The worries of tomorrow are forgotten on a wave of lust. We both crave this moment to reconnect, to have what we did for that brief period in time, what we both want again so badly.

Maybe it is possible to have second chances in life because I just found one with Kennedy, even though I've done absolutely nothing to deserve it.

I lower her onto the bed, and she shifts back until her head lands on the pillow, looking as beautiful as ever—in the place she *swore* she would never be.

Where she *belongs*.

After all the fighting, all the angry words tossed at me, all the betrayal and pain, it's time for us to have something else.

I crawl across the mattress and lower myself over her, pressing my length between her spread legs.

She moans and tangles her fingers through my hair. "But you did break one promise to me already."

"Yeah? What's that?"

"That first night, you said the time would come when you would destroy me..." She grins. "But you haven't yet."

The challenge in her words releases a carnal hunger, a primal drive in me that makes me growl and smash my mouth against hers.

She has no idea what she's asking for.

KENNEDY

THE CHANGE in him is instant, his eyes, switching from the pale green to a dark emerald, sharp enough to cut me. Maybe it wasn't my best choice of words, but after everything that's happened, I want to feel alive the way only he can make me. And I don't want him to handle me with kid gloves just because we almost died today.

The exact opposite.

This is what I want—him, totally and completely unleashed.

He devours my mouth so hard that it sucks all the air from my lungs. Then he tears his lips away and reaches down to rip off the shorts that cover my thighs.

The sound of the fabric ripping fills the room.

I should probably be pissed about it because I love them and hated that I left them here when I fled without my bag, but all it does is make moisture pool between my legs where I'm already aching for him.

His fingertips brush against my sensitive skin as he pulls away the ruined material. I try to press my thighs together against the throb, but he shoves his hand between them, clutching my pussy and keeping me from moving.

"That was a bad idea, Kennedy. I hope you're ready."

Fuck, why is that so hot?

He grinds his palm against my clit, sending a jolt of pleasure through me, and my hips buck up against it, seeking more. Then his hand is gone and gripping my hip to flip me over onto my stomach.

Cass uses his knees to spread my legs wide, exposing me completely to him. A shudder rolls through me as he pushes my shirt up and drags kisses down my spine until he gets to my ass.

"Do you want me to you fuck you here, Kennedy?"

Fuck.

I squeeze my eyes closed, pressing my face against the pillow, and nod.

His low rumble of approval rolls through my body. "Good, because I want to take your ass more than I want just about anything right now."

Jesus Christ.

How can this man be like this in bed and so gentle with me and his daughter when we need it?

My mind has such a hard time wrapping around the dichotomy every time we're together. It's the same thing that allowed him to be Falco while he was also trying to destroy the family.

But that's over now.

The sound of his zipper lowering and him shucking off his pants hits my ears a moment before the press of his warm body along the back of mine. His hard cock nudges against my cunt, and I squeeze my legs, pinning it between my thighs.

He groans and brushes his lips to my ear. "Don't worry, *Cherie*. I'm going to fuck you there, too."

Good God.

I shift under him, needing something to happen to release this tension. "Please, Cass, I need..."

Cass presses a gentle kiss to my cheek so tenderly that it's almost painful. "I know what you need, *Cherie*."

He's right.

He always has.

From that first day we met, the first time he ever touched me, he's always given me exactly what I need, and I know he will now, too.

He shifts back, and the head of his cock nudges inside my slick core. Strong hands grip my hips and drag them back and up, spreading me wider and exposing me even farther. He drives into me in one hard thrust that sends me rocking forward, gripping the comforter for purchase.

"Fuck." The word falls from my lips, and the next slam of his hips wrenches my breath from my throat. I drop my cheek back to the pillow. "Fuck, fuck, fuck!"

It's so hard, so deep. He fills me so completely that the tears start to stream down my face before I can stop them. He keeps driving into me, his hands tightening at my hips, and I clench around him, forcing the head of his cock to drag against that exact spot that I love so much.

He issues a low growl and lowers his head, reaching to grip my chin and force my face back slightly to take my mouth in a mind-bending kiss while his hips continue to slam against my ass. "Do you want to come like this?"

I nod against the pillow, but his dark chuckle sends a rush of trepidation through me.

"I don't think so, Cherie. That isn't what you need."

"Yes, it is." I open my eyes and look back at him. "Please..."

He shakes his head, his lips brushing back and forth against my cheek with the movement. "No, trust me, *Cherie*."

I do.

Even though he's given me so many reasons not to, I do trust him, and with each thrust, he drives himself deeper inside me, cements himself even further into my heart.

I cling to the comforter, allowing him to manipulate my body and move me where and how he wants me as he continues to pound into my core. My whole body starts to shake, my orgasm so close, that low burn starting deep in my belly.

He can sense it, too, and he jerks his cock free.

I almost cry out at the loss, but then he reaches into the bedside table and pulls out a bottle of lube, spreading the cool liquid across my asshole.

"Shit!" I jerk at the sensation, but then he's right there, kissing me again and gliding his fingers inside my cunt where his cock just was.

"Fucking hell are you wet, Kennedy...I probably didn't even need lube for this, but I would never hurt you. You know that."

I give a sharp nod as the head of his cock presses against my tight entrance. Instinctively, I squeeze my ass cheeks together, trying to stop the intrusion.

"Shh. Relax for me, *Cherie*. Take a deep breath and let it out slowly."

Instead of fighting him like I naturally want to, I do as I'm told, sucking in the air scented with that slight ocean smell that always lingers around him, then letting it out slowly as I sink deeper into the mattress.

The head of his cock slips past the tight opening.

"Fuck."

That word falling from his lips ignites an inferno inside me, as does the strange feeling of him spreading me there. He shifts his fingers inside my cunt and drags them along the wall, and when he gets to where his cock is, it makes my whole body twitch.

He slowly eases himself in farther, then drags back a little so that he can push even deeper. A few more slow, cautious movements like that, and he's finally settled fully inside me.

I've never experienced anything so strange and so glorious as having my ass filled by his cock, with his fingers jammed inside my cunt. He starts a slow rhythm, dragging his fingers inside me, his thumb slipping up over my clit while his cock moves in and out of my ass.

I buck against him, and he hushes me again as he moves inside me. Heat spreads through every part of me, a searing rush that builds and builds until it feels like I might explode and literally light the bed on fire.

"Almost there, *Cherie*. You need to relax and let go."

Instinctively, I fight his command, clenching around him in both places, and I open my eyes to find him gritting his teeth, the pure blaze of lust burning across his gaze as he stares down at me.

"Always wanting a fight, aren't you, Kennedy?"

I shake my head and grin at him. "Not always."

He leans down and kisses me again, stilling his hips. "No,

not always, *Cherie*. And never again like what happened when you left me."

It's a promise I know he'll keep, for mine and for Charlotte's sake.

Cass resumes his mind-bending ministrations until my entire body is trembling so badly beneath him that the entire bed shakes. And then it hits me, the orgasm to end all orgasms. A conflagration that ignites my entire body and sets me rocketing off into the stars that flash against my closed lids.

He doesn't even beg me to look at him this time.

I couldn't, even if I tried.

He just keeps pounding into me. "Fuck, *Cherie*. Feeling your cunt tighten on my fingers as you come and your ass tightening on my cock—" His words trail off as he comes on a roar, emptying himself inside me and collapsing on top of my prone body with his glorious weight and heat pressing me down into the mattress.

I never thought I could feel so complete, that anything other than work and ensuring the Hawke empire grows and maintains its strength could ever be so important...

But this moment has changed everything.

I do love Cassius Whitaker, the man I probably should still despise, and I always will. Even if sometimes I hate how easily he broke me.

EPILOGUE

THREE MONTHS LATER

CASS

Staring out at the progress being made on The Hawke Hotel, I can't fight the smile that pulls at my lips. Things are finally starting to take shape, visual evidence of everything overcome to get to this point. It feels like such a long time coming, but for Kennedy, it's been even longer—and a much harder road.

To think, only a handful of months ago, I was actively trying to *stop* this by any means necessary.

Kennedy loops her arm through mine and rests her head on my shoulder. "What do you think?"

I glance down at her and raise a brow. "About what?"

Rolling her eyes, she smacks my arm. "About the suggestion I just made, about the landscaping around the pool."

I wrack my brain, trying to think of anything she might have said about it, but the last few moments are a complete blank except for what was happening in my own head. I didn't even hear her say anything. "I'm sorry, I didn't hear you."

She glowers at me, but a smile dances in her eyes. "We've

only been together for three months, and you already have selective hearing syndrome."

"Ha fucking ha."

A slow grin curls her lips. "You are taking after your daughter now."

It's my turn to scowl at her for her observation that Charlotte seems to have things going in one ear and out the other lately whenever I speak to her. "She listens to *you*."

Kennedy tips her head back, laughing. "She likes me more."

"Yeah, yeah."

She offers a slight shrug. "What? It's true, she does."

I nod slowly. "That'll change; just you wait. Once you have to punish her for something, she's going to start seeing you in a whole different light."

For the last five years, I've been raising her alone, having to be the sole disciplinarian, which means she very often sees me as the bad guy for doing things necessary to protect her—from others *and* her own choices.

Kennedy's mouth drops open. "I've *punished* her before."

I bark out a laugh that carries across the lot and draws the attention of a few of the construction workers who are closest to us. They glance over and offer me a strange look as I turn to face Kennedy and pull her against me playfully. "You do *not* punish her."

She pulls back from me and props her hands on her hips, drawing my gaze to how incredible she looks in that skirt and black fuck-me pumps. "Yes, I do."

I shake my head, imagining all the things I want her to do to me while she's wearing them, then force myself to meet her gaze again. "Telling her she has to wait an hour to watch TV is *not* punishment. Taking away the TV completely for a week would be."

Her pink lips twist into a scowl. "That seems a bit harsh."

"Five-year-olds sometimes need a bit of harsh. There have

to be limits. If there aren't, they'll take things so far that they'll get lost."

A very somber look overtakes her face, replacing the light, happy way she's appeared all day while we've been examining the progress on both hotels. "I don't want to overstep with her. I'm not her..."

She trails off, but she doesn't have to say it for me to know where she was going with that or why she feels so uneasy all of a sudden.

I tug her against me, squeezing her tightly and thinking about everything that's happened over the last three months: Kennedy moving in with us, the new alliance between Falco Enterprises and Hawke Enterprises, the tension between me and the rest of her family that is starting to slowly—very, very, very slowly ease—and watching how she's been with Charlotte, how happy she makes my daughter and my daughter seems to make her.

"You *are* her mother now."

Kennedy pulls her head back, and tears shimmer in her eyes. "No, I'm not."

"Yes, you are. You are in every way that matters." I wipe away the droplets streaking her cheeks. "You're there with her every day to help make her breakfast, to help her with homework—"

"Her homework is just drawing pictures and learning the alphabet."

I chuckle. "So it's not rocket science. That doesn't matter. You still help her, right?"

She sniffles slightly. "Yeah."

"And you read to her at night, and you kick her ass at Monopoly, and you tuck her in, and you bandage her booboos and comfort her when she's crying, and you do everything a mother would do. So, you *are*, whether she calls you that or not."

Her lip trembles, like the thought of Charlotte thinking of her that way is too much for her to handle. "I don't know if I can—"

She sucks back a sob, and I brush another tear from the corner of her eye.

"You're already doing it. Me saying that word doesn't change anything."

Her head bobs. "It does. It's a lot of responsibility."

For a split second, panic seizes my chest—that she really can't handle being someone's mother, that this little family we've created over the last few months has all been some dream that's going to vanish as quickly as I got it. "You don't want it?"

She smacks my chest, her eyes wide and filled with concern. "Of course, I do. I love being with you two."

I do, too.

Even if we constantly have to have security and be looking over our shoulders because we never know when Damiano might appear again with another sinister plot, things have been good. Really good. It's the kind of life and family I'd always imagined I would have, but that seemed to slip through my fingers.

That's what makes me nervous about what's coming.

How easily it could disappear.

I swallow through the sudden dryness in my throat. "Let's make it official, then."

She narrows her eyes at me. "What do you mean?"

I motion behind her toward the lot where my hotel is going up—without the financial help of Damiano Satriano. The one I originally planned, smaller but still incredible, that will no longer compete with the Hawke Hotel but will be part of the same hotel group, working together to build an entire new district for nightlife completely within our control.

"We're already locked together in business, right?"

Kennedy nods.

"And you've been living with me for three months."

She pulls her bottom lip between her teeth, watching me anxiously.

Just do it, Cass.

"We should get married, and you should adopt Charlotte."

Her lips part on her barked laugh, and she shakes her head. "Is this supposed to be a fucking proposal?"

Chuckling, I brush my lips over hers. "Sort of. I kind of suck at it, huh?"

"You would think, with it being your second time, you would know better."

I scowl at her. "Let's not bring up my ex-wife, please. She's been out of my life for a fucking long time. Good riddance."

She offers me an apologetic look. "Sorry. Bad choice of words and timing to bring her up."

"Yeah. So...you can make it up to me by saying yes."

"You really want to get married again?" Her brow furrows. "The first time didn't go so well."

I sigh as I watch the two hotels going up, the sounds of construction rumbling through the air. Something new is starting despite all the uncertainty. Only months ago, in this exact spot, Satriano came and issued his threat. It's one all of us are incredibly aware of, like it's a ticking time bomb that could go off at any second.

"I don't want to waste any time we have together." I turn my gaze back to her. "And I know this is it for me. *You* are it for me. The two of us, Falco and Hawke."

She grins at me. "Falco does mean hawk."

"I know"—I shrug—"so maybe it was always meant to be."

Amusement dances in her eyes. "Maybe it was."

"Is that a yes?"

I raise a brow at her, and her lips twitch into a smile.

"I guess it is."

It isn't the most enthusiastic *yes* I've ever heard, but when it comes to Kennedy, fighting me has become a true art form. This is just another way for her to maintain a bit of control and to toy with me in a way she knows will get me worked up, just so I'll take it out on her later.

Kennedy's brow furrows. "Are you sure Charlotte will be okay with this...us getting married and me adopting her?"

The concern and fear in her question shatters me. She cares so damn much.

"She's going to be ecstatic. I promise."

I press a kiss to her lips, slow and sweet, trying to relay to her all the things I really fucking suck at saying with words. How much she means to me. How continually sorry I am for everything I put her through. How thankful I am that she gave me a second chance and that she loves me and Charlotte as much as we do her.

A shadow falls on us and pulls me back from her, and I glance up, freezing instantly at the familiar bird circling overhead. "Holy shit."

"What?" She glances up, and her eyes widen slightly. "Is that a—"

I nod. "Yeah, that's a hawk."

Her gaze cuts to mine. "Kind of weird timing, isn't it?"

"It's more than weird timing. Hawks don't normally come into the city like this. We have them out in the country, in the bayou, yeah, but there's no reason for them to be this far into New Orleans."

She watches it spiral above us in lazy circles. "That is strange."

"What's really weird is...I've seen that bird before."

Kennedy gives me an incredulous look. "You can't *possibly* know that."

"I do. Before we even met..." I stare down at her as the breeze blows a strand of hair into her face. Pushing it behind her ear, I let my fingers linger against her smooth, warm skin. "I was meeting with Marcel at Café Du Monde. I had to go get beignets for Charlotte. I promised I would before I went to court that morning, and I was sitting there at that table, thinking about the fire at The Grind, trying to figure out who could have been behind it, and *that* bird circled overhead."

She shakes her head. "There's no way it's the same bird."

"Sure looks like it."

Her eyes dart back up to it. "Fate then?"

I shrug. "At the time, I thought it was an omen. And I don't know if I believe in fate..."

"Cass..."—she says my name so softly, it's barely a whisper —"our lives have been crossed since before I was even born. Our families at war for thirty-plus years."

"Not anymore and never again. I promise." I drop a kiss on her temple. "You think your dad is ever going to be on board with that?"

She laughs and drops her forehead against my chest, squeezing me tightly. "They'll warm up to you, I promise."

I run my hand up and down her back. "Sometimes it doesn't feel like that."

"Well, you have Nana's vote, and that's really all that matters."

Chuckling, I bury my face in her hair. "Your grandmother is quite a character."

"I know. And when we tell her we're getting married, she'll tell everybody to stop giving you such a hard fucking time and cold shoulder, and no one argues with my nana."

"I hope not. It could make for a really awkward wedding to have the father of the bride trying to kill the groom."

Kennedy laughs and tips her head back, the most light, carefree sound when there's still so much uncertainty and tension hanging around us. Her phone rings in her purse, and she pulls back from me and takes it out, glancing down at it. "It's Allie; I should take this."

"Okay."

She steps away from me, and I wander over toward the foundation and the beginnings of the floors rising into the bright sky.

It's strong, sturdy.

It has to be in the sandy, silty soil here.

But what the Hawkes have designed, what I'm helping them build here, is going to be rock solid and stand the test of time, just like Kennedy and I are.

~

KENNEDY

I STEP AWAY FROM CASS, keeping my eyes on the hawk circling above us as I answer the call. "Hey, Al. What's up?"

"Uh, hey, are you busy?"

The slight hesitation in her voice makes my smile falter, and I drag my gaze from the bird out to the construction site, watching a crane lift a giant beam into place.

"I'm actually down at the site with Cass. We just came to check on a few things."

"Oh…"

"Why? What's wrong?"

Immediately, "concerned cousin" mode kicks in.

Over the last few months, Allie has become increasingly quiet, almost secretive, which is so unlike her. The more her belly grows, the worse it seems to become, and even though she has a few more weeks before she's due, instead of being excited about the arrival of the baby, she seems more *afraid* of it.

"Tell me what's wrong, Al."

She releases a heavy sigh. "Well, um, it's about the baby's father..."

I stop in my tracks.

The baby's father?

As far as I know, she's never discussed who stuck that bun in her oven with anyone, not even Angelina or Jude. All of us have done what we can to try to pry the information out of her during her pregnancy, but she just keeps telling us he doesn't want to be involved, so it's a non-issue.

I have had my suspicions for a long time, which I used to get her to leave me alone with Cass in the first place all those months ago, but I've never flat-out asked her. I don't want to drive a wedge between us and have her feel like I'm judging her or she can't come to me for something.

But whatever is going on now seems to have really shaken her.

I walk back over to the car and lean against it. "What about the baby's father?"

"I don't know. Maybe this isn't a good idea."

The tension in her voice makes my heart ache for her. She's been going through this, for all intents and purposes, alone. Though you're never truly alone when you're a Hawke, and she's had all of us hovering over her entire pregnancy, she isn't letting anyone in. Not really. She's keeping all of us at arm's length.

"Al, don't shut me out. Tell me what's wrong. Have you talked to Angelina or Jude about it?"

"No. I can't."

"Why not?" My suspicion grows in the back of my head.

"Look, I know everybody has been wondering who the father of the baby is, and I know who you think it is, but you're wrong."

For some reason, that makes me release a sigh of relief. If the father had been who I thought the father was, it would've created a firestorm worse than when Angie and Jude got together.

I kick a rock with my pointed toe. "Are you going to tell me who it is?"

"No." Her response comes clipped and leaves no room for argument. "I just want to get your advice on how to handle something."

"Okay, shoot."

Even though I'd love to know who the father is to try to explain her strange behavior, her talking to me is better than her keeping whatever she has bottled up inside secret until it eventually breaks her.

I've been there, battling with what I was doing with Cass and hiding it from everyone. It wasn't comfortable or easy, and I hate to see her going through the same thing.

"Well, I haven't seen him for a long time, since before I was really showing."

"Okay..."

"But I ran into him the other day unexpectedly."

"And? Come on, Al. Get to the point here. You've got me on pins and needles."

She mutters something unintelligible to herself. "And he saw my belly."

"Holy shit. Did he not know you were pregnant?"

Her heavy sigh fills the line as an answer to my question.

"Allie, you didn't *tell* him?"

A tiny sob slips through the line, sending a pang of guilt straight to my chest for how accusatory that sounded. "No, I couldn't. If you knew everything, you would understand why."

The hawk swoops down from the sky and grabs something from the site, soaring back up into the vast expanse of blue as I try to make sense of what she just said. "But you told everyone he knew and didn't want to be involved."

"Because that's what I assumed would happen. He isn't

exactly the 'settling down and have kids' type of guy, nor is he the type of guy I would want to raise a child with." She sucks in a sharp breath, trying to control her crying. "There's stuff you don't know. Stuff you don't understand."

"Then tell me. Explain it."

"I-I'm scared."

The way her voice shakes with the words, my heart aches to pull her into my arms and hold her and tell her it will all be okay. But I don't know that it will. Not when I have no idea what's actually happening.

"Why, Al?"

She sobs again, an anguished sound that slices at my chest. "Because now he knows I'm pregnant, and he suspects it's his."

"Suspects?"

"Well, we weren't exactly exclusive when we were together. I wasn't seeing anyone else, but I know he was. I could see it in his eyes when he looked at me that he was wondering, but he didn't come out and ask."

"Then why are you so worried?"

A long silence lingers through the line, and I watch Cass walk over and speak to the site foreman, pointing at the area that will eventually have the pool and spa.

"What if he wants to try to take the baby from me?"

I bark out a totally inappropriate laugh and slap my hand over my mouth. "Shit, I'm sorry, Allie. That isn't funny. It's just so absurd. Do you really think Isaac would let someone take your baby? Do you think any of us would?"

"I know you would try to stop it, but—"

"But what? Honey, I can't help you if you don't tell me everything, if you don't let me know what's really happening."

She sniffles and fights another sob. "The father of the baby, he could be...trouble."

A chill slides down my spine. "What kind of trouble?"

"The kind we really don't want with everything else that's going on."

Squeezing my eyes closed, I pinch the bridge of my nose. "Jesus, Allie, who did you get yourself involved with?"

"I didn't know who he was." She sobs again, the sound filled with so much fear and anguish I can practically feel it. "I *swear*."

"Holy shit." I think back to when she first announced her pregnancy and what was happening at that time. "I swear to God, if you tell me the father of the baby is Damon, I'll—"

"No, no. God no. God no. No. It's not him."

I release a heavy, relieved sigh. "Oh, thank God. You had me going there for a second. I was about to lose my shit. That's all we would need—a mafia Don, literally blood-tied to the family."

She sucks in a sharp breath.

"Allie?"

The phone jostles. "Shit, I have to go."

"Al, what is it?"

"Sorry, I'm at the cafe. I'm working today. Someone just walked in, and I have to go."

She ends the call, and I stare down at the phone.

What the fuck was that?

Cass approaches, his brow furrowed. "What's wrong? You're staring at your phone like you just got awful news."

I glance up at him. "I think I might have."

"What is it?"

Instantly, that cold sense of dread I've felt so much over the last several months that I should be used to it settles over me, and I clench my phone in my hand. "I'm not sure, but it sounds like Allie's in trouble."

"In trouble, how?" Cass' eyes widen. "Did she go into labor?"

I shake my head. "No, but it does involve the baby."

He comes and leans against the car with me. "What did she say?"

A lot and yet nothing, really.

I probably shouldn't reveal anything she just told me in confidence, but Cass and I are technically engaged now, so it's not like she can't expect me to reveal things in the marital bed —or standing in front of the marital property as it might be. "She said the father of the baby didn't know she was pregnant."

Cass winces. "So, she lied to everyone when she said he didn't want to be involved?"

"Yeah, but she ran into him, and he knows and suspects it's his."

"What did he say to her?"

I shake my head. "I'm not sure. She said he didn't flat out ask, but she's worried that he might try to take the baby."

"Why the hell would he do that?"

Shrugging, I stare at my phone, as if it might hold some of the answers. "I don't know. She didn't get a chance to explain anything and still won't tell me who the fuck it is."

"Then I think it's time that we have a little sit down with her and Isaac, don't you?"

I nod. If anyone can protect that baby from its father, it's our legal pit bull—one of them. "Or I could go talk to Uncle Stone."

Cass raises a brow. "Do you think he's up for it?"

I offer a slight shrug. "I don't know. I mean, he seems to be getting some of his energy back, even though they barely let him out of that hospital bed more than a couple of minutes a day. It might give him something to occupy his mind with rather than everything going on with him."

It's a miracle he survived it all or that he woke after a two-month coma, but the damage the bullets did and the loss of oxygen to his brain during the moments he coded on the table have left him struggling to regain what he once had.

Cass shrugs. "It's not a bad idea. Why don't we go to the hospital right now?"

"Let's swing by the café. I want to make sure Allie's okay. If she can come with us, that'll be even better."

"Okay."

I slip my phone into my purse and turn toward him, pressing my hands against his chest. "You know, underneath all this aggressive, asshole exterior, you're actually a really decent guy."

He barks out a laugh and presses a kiss to my lips. "Well, I guess that's good, since you're marrying me."

"I *am* marrying you."

I haven't had a chance to really process it yet, but the idea of walking down the aisle and saying "I do" to this man just feels so right after everything that has gone wrong.

And so fucking much has gone wrong.

This will be something for the Hawkes to look forward to— a big, white New Orleans wedding.

∾

ALESSANDRA

HE WALKS into the Daily Grind, looking every bit as handsome as he did the day he put this baby in me, and walks up to the counter, his laser focus on me. "We need to talk about that baby."

∾

I HOPE you enjoyed *Relentless Hawke*. Delve further into the Hawke Family world with Allie and Pope's forbidden second chance romance, in *Reckless Hawke*!

Get your copy: books2read.com/ RecklessHawke

To stay up to date on news, sales, and releases from Gwyn, join her newsletter here: www.gwynmcnamee.com/ newsletter

ACKNOWLEDGMENTS

Whew. This story was incredible to write, and I am so thankful to my amazing team of angels who help me get it ready for you! A huge thanks to Renee, Patricia, Stephie, and Caoimhe, you are all incredible and I couldn't do it without you!

ABOUT THE AUTHOR

Gwyn McNamee is an attorney, writer, wife, and mother (to one human baby and two fur babies). Originally from the Midwest, Gwyn relocated to her husband's home town of Las Vegas in 2015 and is enjoying her respite from the cold and snow. Gwyn has been writing down her crazy stories and ideas for years and finally decided to share them with the world. She loves to write stories with a bit of suspense and action mingled with romance and heat.

When she isn't either writing or voraciously devouring any books she can get her hands on, Gwyn is busy adding to her tattoo collection, golfing, and stirring up trouble with her perfect mix of sweetness and sarcasm (usually while wearing heels).

Gwyn loves to hear from her readers. Here is where you can find her:

Website: http://www.gwynmcnamee.com/

Facebook: https://www.facebook.com/AuthorGwynMcNamee/

FB Reader Group: https://www.facebook.com/groups/1667380963540655/

Newsletter: www.gwynmcnamee.com/newsletter

Twitter: https://twitter.com/GwynMcNamee

Instagram: https://www.instagram.com/gwynmcnamee

Bookbub: https://www.bookbub.com/authors/gwynmcnamee

Tiktok: https://www.tiktok.com/@authorgwynmcnamee

OTHER WORKS BY GWYN MCNAMEE

Billionaires of New Orleans:

The Hawke Family Series

Savage Collision (The Hawke Family - Book One)

He's everything she didn't know she wanted. She's everything he thought he could never have.

The last thing I expect when I walk into The Hawkeye Club is to fall head over heels in lust. It's supposed to be a rescue mission. I have to get my baby sister off the pole, into some clothes, and out of the grasp of the pussy peddler who somehow manipulated her into stripping. But the moment I see Savage Hawke and verbally spar with him, my ability to remain rational flies out the window and my libido takes center stage. I've never wanted a relationship—my time is better spent focusing on taking down the scum running this city—but what I want and what I need are apparently two different things.

Danika Eriksson storms into my office in her high heels and on her high horse. Her holier-than-thou attitude and accusations should offend me, but instead, I can't get her out of my head or my heart. Her incomparable drive, take-no prisoners attitude, and blatant honesty captivate me and hold me prisoner. I should steer clear, but my self-preservation instinct is apparently dead—which is exactly what our relationship will be once she knows everything. It's only a matter of time.

The truth doesn't always set you free. Sometimes, it just royally screws you.

AVAILABLE AT ALL RETAILERS:

books2read.com/SavageCollision

Tortured Skye (The Hawke Family - Book Two)

She's always been off-limits. He's always just out of reach.

Falling in love with Gabe Anderson was as easy as breathing. Fighting my feelings for my brother's best friend was agonizingly hard. I never imagined giving in to my desire for him would cause such a destructive ripple effect. That kiss was my grasp at a lifeline— something, anything to hold me steady in my crumbling life. Now, I have to suffer with the fallout while trying to convince him it's all worth the consequences.

Guilt overwhelms me—over what I've done, the lives I've taken, and more than anything, over my feelings for Skye Hawke. Craving my best friend's little sister is insanely self-destructive. It never should have happened, but since the moment she kissed me, I haven't been able to get her out of my mind. If I take what I want, I risk losing everything. If I don't, I'll lose her and a piece of myself. The raging storm threatening to rain down on the city is nothing compared to the one that will come from my decision.

Love can be torture, but sometimes, love is the only thing that can save you.

AVAILABLE AT ALL RETAILERS:

Books2read.com/Tortured-Skye

Stone Sober (The Hawke Family - Book Three)

She's innocent and sweet. He's dark and depraved.

Stone Hawke is precisely the kind of man women are warned about— handsome, intelligent, arrogant, and intricately entangled with some dangerous people. I should stay away, but he manages to strip my soul bare with just a look and dominates my thoughts. Bad decisions are in my past. My life is (mostly) on track, even if it is no longer the one to medical school. I can't allow myself to cave to the fierce pull and ardent attraction I feel toward the youngest Hawke.

Nora Eriksson is off-limits, and not just because she's my brother's employee and sister-in-law. Despite the fact she's stripping at The Hawkeye Club, she has an innocent and pure heart. Normally, the only thing that appeals to me about innocence is the opportunity to taint it. But not when it comes to Nora. I can't expose her to the filth permeating my life. There are too many things I can't control, things completely out of my hands. She doesn't deserve any of it, but the power she holds over me is stronger than any addiction.

The hardest battles we fight are often with ourselves, but only through defeating our own demons can we find true peace.

AVAILABLE AT ALL RETAILERS:

books2read.com/StoneSober

Building Storm (The Hawke Family - Book Four)

She hasn't been living. He's looking for a way to forget it all.

My life went up in flames. All I'm left with is my daughter and ashes. The simple act of breathing is so excruciating, there are days I wish I could stop altogether. So I have no business being at the party, and I definitely shouldn't be in the arms of the handsome stranger. When his lips meet mine, he breathes life into me for the first time since the day the inferno disintegrated my world. But loving again isn't in the cards, and there are even greater dangers to face than trying to keep Landon McCabe out of my heart.

Running is my only option. I have to get away from Chicago and the betrayal that shattered my world. I need a new life-one without attachments. The vibrancy of New Orleans convinces me it's possible to start over. Yet in all the excitement of a new city, it's Storm Hawke's dark, sad beauty that draws me in. She isn't looking for love, and we both need a hot, sweaty release without feelings getting involved. But even the best laid plans fail, and life can leave you burned.

Love can build, and love can destroy. But in the end, love is what raises you from the ashes.

AVAILABLE AT ALL RETAILERS:

books2read.com/BuildingStorm

Tainted Saint (The Hawke Family - Book Five)

He's searching for absolution. She wants her happily ever after.

Solomon Clarke goes by Saint, though he's anything but. After lusting for him from afar, the masquerade party affords me the anonymity to pursue that attraction without worrying about the fall-out of hooking-up with the bouncer from the Hawkeye Club. From the second he lays his eyes and hands on me, I'm helpless to resist him. Even burying myself in a dangerous investigation can't erase the memory of our combustible connection and one night together. The only problem... he has no idea who I am.

Caroline Brooks thinks I don't see her watching me, the way her eyes rake over me with appreciation. But I've noticed, and the party is the perfect opportunity to unleash the desire I've kept reined in for so damn long. It also sets off a series of events no one sees coming. Events that leave those I love hurting because of my failures. While the guilt eats away at my soul, Caroline continues to weigh on my heart. That woman may be the death of me, but oh, what a way to go.

Life isn't always clean, and sometimes, it takes a saint to do the dirty work.

AVAILABLE AT ALL RETAILERS:

books2read.com/TaintedSaint

Steele Resolve (The Hawke Family - Book Six)

For one man, power is king. For the other, loyalty reigns.

Mob boss Luca "Steele" Abello isn't just dangerous—he's lethal. A master manipulator, liar, and user, no one should trust a word that comes out of his mouth. Yet, I can't get him out of my head. The time we spent together before I knew his true identity is seared into my brain. His touch. His voice. They haunt my every waking hour and occupy my dreams. So does my guilt. I'm literally sleeping with the enemy and betraying the only family I've ever had. When I come clean, it will be the end of me.

Byron Harris is a distraction I can't afford. I never should have let it go beyond that first night, but I couldn't stay away. Even when I learned who he was, when the *only* option was to end things, I kept going back, risking his life and mine to continue our indiscretion. The truth of what I am could get us both killed, but being with the man who's such an integral part of the Hawke family is even more terrifying. The only people I've ever cared about are on opposing sides, and I'm the rift that could end their friendship forever.

Love is a battlefield isn't just a saying. For some, it's a reality.

AVAILABLE AT ALL RETAILERS:

books2read.com/SteeleResolve

You can find information on the rest of Gwyn's books on her website:

www.gwynmcnamee.com

www.ingramcontent.com/pod-product-compliance
Lightning Source LLC
Chambersburg PA
CBHW071939030726
47501CB00014B/1923